THE
Untameable
GREEKS

MAYA BLAKE

THE
Untameable
GREEKS

MILLS & BOON

THE UNTAMEABLE GREEKS © 2023 by Harlequin Books S.A.

The publisher acknowledges the copyright holders of the individual works as follows:
WHAT THE GREEK'S MONEY CAN'T BUY
© 2014 by Maya Blake   First Published 2014
Philippine Copyright 2014   Fourth Australian Paperback Edition 2023
Australian Copyright 2014   ISBN 978 1 867 29828 1
New Zealand Copyright 2014

WHAT THE GREEK CAN'T RESIST
© 2014 by Maya Blake   First Published 2014
Philippine Copyright 2014   Fourth Australian Paperback Edition 2023
Australian Copyright 2014   ISBN 978 1 867 29828 1
New Zealand Copyright 2014

WHAT THE GREEK WANTS MOST
© 2014 by Maya Blake   First Published 2014
Philippine Copyright 2014   Fourth Australian Paperback Edition 2023
Australian Copyright 2014   ISBN 978 1 867 29828 1
New Zealand Copyright 2014

Published by
Harlequin Mills & Boon
An imprint of Harlequin Enterprises (Australia) Pty Limited
(ABN 47 001 180 918), a subsidiary of HarperCollins
Publishers Australia Pty Limited
(ABN 36 009 913 517)
Level 19, 201 Elizabeth Street
SYDNEY NSW 2000 AUSTRALIA

MIX
Paper | Supporting
responsible forestry
FSC® C001695

Printed and bound in Australia by McPherson's Printing Group

CONTENTS

All about the author...
Maya Blake

MAYA BLAKE fell in love with the world of the alpha male and the strong, aspirational heroine when she borrowed her sister's Harlequin® books at age thirteen. Shortly thereafter the dream to plot a happy ending for her own characters was born. Writing for Harlequin® is a dream come true. Maya lives in South East England with her husband and two kids. Reading is an absolute passion, but when she isn't lost in a book she likes to swim, cycle, travel and Tweet!

You can get in touch with her via email at mayablake@ymail.com, or on Twitter, @mayablake.

What The Greek's Money Can't Buy

CHAPTER ONE

'COME ON, PUT your back into it! Why am I not surprised that you're slacking as usual while I'm doing all the work?'

Sakis Pantelides reefed the oars through the slightly choppy water, loving the exhilaration and adrenaline that burned in his back and shoulders. 'Stop complaining, old man. It's not my fault if you're feeling your age.' He smiled when he heard his brother's hiss of annoyance.

In truth, Ari was only two-and-a-half years older, but Sakis knew it annoyed him when he taunted him with their age difference, but of course he never passed up the chance to niggle where he could.

'Don't worry, Theo will be around to bail you out next time we row. That way you won't have to *strain* yourself so much,' Sakis said.

'Theo would be more concerned about showing off his bulging muscles to the female coxes than he would to serious rowing,' Ari responded dryly. 'How he ever managed to stop showing off long enough to win five world championships, I'll never know.'

Sakis heaved his oars and noted with satisfaction that he hadn't lost the innate rhythm despite several months away from the favourite sport that had at one time been his sole passion. Thinking about his younger brother, he couldn't help but smile. 'Yeah, he always *was* more into his looks and the ladies than anything else.'

He rowed in perfect sync with his brother, their movements barely rippling through the water as they passed the halfway point of the lake used by the exclusive rowing club a few miles outside of London. Sakis's smile widened as a sense of peace stole over him.

It'd been a while since he'd come here; since he'd found time to connect with his brothers like this. The punishing schedules it took to manage the three branches of Pantelides Inc meant the brothers hadn't got together in way too long. That they had even been in the same time zone had been a miracle. Of course, it hadn't stayed that way for long. Theo had cancelled at the last minute and was right this moment winging his way to Rio on a Pantelides jet to deal with a crisis for the global conglomerate.

Or maybe Theo had cancelled for another reason altogether.

His playboy brother wasn't above flying thousands of miles for a one-hour dinner date with a beautiful woman. 'If I find out he blew us off for a piece of skirt, I'll confiscate his plane for a month.'

Ari snorted. 'You can try. But I think you're asking for a swift death if you attempt to come between Theo and a woman. Speaking of women, I see yours has finally managed to surgically remove herself from her laptop...'

He didn't break his rhythm despite the jolt of electricity that zapped through him. His gaze focused past his brother's shoulder to where Ari's attention was fixed.

He nearly missed his next stroke. Only the inbuilt discipline that had seen him win one more championship than his brothers' five apiece stopped him from losing his rhythm.

'Let's get one thing straight—she's *not* my woman.'

Brianna Moneypenny, his executive assistant, stood next to his car. That in itself was a surprise, since she preferred to stay glued to his in-limo computer, one finger firmly on the pulse of his company any time he had to step away.

But what triggered the bolt of astonishment in him more

was the not-quite-masked expression on her face. Brianna's countenance since the day she'd become his ultra-efficient assistant eighteen months ago had never once wavered from cool, icy professionalism.

Today she looked…

'Don't tell me she's succumbed to the Sakis Pantelides syndrome?' Ari's dry tone held equal parts amusement and resignation.

Sakis frowned, unease stirring in his belly and mingling with the emotions he refused to acknowledge when it came to his executive assistant. He'd learned the hard way that exposing emotion, especially for the wrong person, could leave scars that never really healed and took monumental effort to keep buried. As for mixing business with pleasure—that had been a near lethal cocktail he'd sampled once. Never again. 'Shut up, Ari.'

'I'm concerned, brother. She's almost ready to jump into the water. Or jump your bones, more like. Please tell me you haven't lost your mind and slept with her?'

Sakis's gaze flitted over to Moneypenny, trying to pinpoint what was wrong from across the distance between them. 'I'm not sure what's more disturbing—your unhealthy interest in my sex life or the fact that you can keep rowing straight while practising the Spanish Inquisition,' he murmured absently.

As for getting physical with Moneypenny, if his libido chose the most inappropriate times—like now—to remind him he was a red-blooded male, it was a situation he intended to keep ignoring, like he had been the last eighteen months. He'd wasted too much valuable time in this lifetime ridding himself of clinging women.

He strained the oars through the water, suddenly wanting the session to be over. Through the strokes, he kept his gaze fixed on Moneypenny, her rigid stance setting off alarm bells inside his head.

'So, there's nothing between you two?' Ari pushed.

Something in his brother's voice made his hackles rise. With one last push, he felt the bottom of the scull hit the slope of the wooden jetty.

'If you're thinking of trying to poach her, Ari, forget it. She's the best executive assistant I've ever had and anyone who threatens that will lose a body part; two body parts for family members.'

'Cool your jets, bro. I wasn't thinking of that sort of poaching. Besides, hearing you gush over her like that tells me you're already far gone.'

Sakis's irritation grew, wishing his brother would get off the subject.

'Just because I recognise talent doesn't mean I've lost my mind. Besides, tell me, does *your* assistant know her Windsor knot from her double-cross knot?'

Ari's brows shot up as he stepped onto the pier and grabbed his oars. 'My assistant is a man. And the fact that you hired yours based on her tie-knotting abilities only confirms you're more screwed than I thought.'

'There's nothing delusional about the fact that she has more brains in her pinkie than the total sum of my previous assistants, and she's a Rottweiler when it comes to managing my business life. That's all I need.'

'Are you sure that's all? Because I detect a distinct…*reverence* in your tone there.'

Sakis froze, then grimaced when he realised Ari was messing with him. 'Keep it up. I owe you a scar for the one you planted on me with your carelessness.' He touched the arrow-shaped scar just above his right brow, a present from Ari's oar when they had first started rowing together in their teens.

'Someone had to bring you down a notch or three for thinking you were the better-looking brother.' Ari grinned, and Sakis was reminded of the carefree brother Ari had been before tragedy had struck and sunk its merciless claws into him.

Then Ari's gaze slid beyond Sakis's shoulder. 'Your Rottweiler's prowling for you. She looks ready to bare her teeth.'

Sakis dropped his oars next to the overturned scull and glanced over, to find Brianna had moved closer. She now stood at the top of the pier, her arms folded and her gaze trained on him.

His alarm intensified. There was a look on her face he'd never seen before. Plus she held a towel in one hand, which suggested she was expecting him not to take his usual shower at the clubhouse.

Sakis frowned. 'Something's up. I need to go.'

'Did she communicate that to you subliminally or are you two so attuned to each other you can tell just by looking at her?' Ari enquired in an amused tone.

'Seriously, Ari, cork it.' His scowl deepened as he noted Brianna's pinched look. Again acting out of the ordinary, she started towards him.

Moneypenny knew never to disturb him during his time with his brothers. She was great like that. She knew her place in his life and had never once overstepped the mark. He started to walk away from the waterfront.

'Hey, don't worry about me. I'll make sure the equipment is returned to the boathouse. And I'll have all those drinks we ordered by myself too,' Ari stated drolly.

Sakis ignored him. When he reached speaking distance, he stopped. 'What's wrong?' he demanded.

For the very first time since she'd turned up for an interview at Pantelides Towers at five o'clock in the morning, Sakis saw her hesitate. The hair on his nape rose to attention. 'Spit it out, Moneypenny.'

The tightening of her mouth was infinitesimal but he spotted it. Another first. He couldn't remember ever witnessing an outward sign of distress. Silently, she held out his towel.

He snatched it from her, more to hurry her response than a need to wipe his sweat-drenched body.

'Mr Pantelides, we have a situation.'

His jaw tightened. 'What situation?'

'One of your tankers, the Pantelides Six, has run aground off Point Noire.'

Ice cascaded down his back despite the midsummer sun blazing down on him. Sakis forced a swallow. 'When did this happen?'

'I got a call via the head office from a crew member five minutes ago.'

She licked her lips and his apprehension grew.

'There's something else?'

'Yes. The captain and two crew members are missing and…'

'And what?'

Her pinched look intensified. 'The tanker hit an outcropping of rocks. Crude oil is spilling into the South Atlantic at an estimated rate of sixty barrels per minute.'

Brianna would never forget what happened next after her announcement. Outwardly, Sakis Pantelides remained the calm, ruthlessly controlled oil tycoon she'd worked alongside for the past eighteen months. But she would've failed in her task to make herself indispensable to him if she hadn't learned to read between the lines of the enigma that was Sakis Pantelides. The set of his strong jaw and the way his hands tightened around the snow-white towel told her how badly the news had affected him.

Over his shoulder, Brianna saw Arion Pantelides pause in his task. Her eyes connected with his. Something in her face must have given her away because before she'd taken another breath the oldest Pantelides brother was striding towards them. He was just as imposing as his younger brother, just as formidable. But, where Sakis's gaze was sharp with laser-like focus and almost lethal intelligence, Arion's held a wealth of dark torment and soul-deep weariness.

Brianna's gaze swung back to her boss, and she wasn't even slightly surprised to see the solid mask of power and ruthless efficiency back in place.

'Do we know what caused the accident?' he fired out.

She shook her head. 'The captain isn't responding to his mobile phone. We haven't been able to establish contact with vessel since the initial call. The Congolese coast guard are on their way. I've asked them to contact me as soon as they're on site.' She fell into step beside him as his long strides headed for the car. 'I've got our emergency crew on standby. They're ready to fly out once you give the word.'

Arion Pantelides caught up with them as they neared the limousine.

He put a halting hand on his brother's shoulder. 'Talk to me, Sakis.'

In clipped tones, Sakis filled him in on what had happened. Arion's gaze swung to her. 'Do we have the names of the missing crew members?'

'I've emailed the complete crew manifest to both your phones and Theo's. I've also attached a list of the relevant ministers we need to deal with in the government to ensure we don't ruffle any feathers, and I've scheduled calls with all of them.'

A look flickered in his eyes before his gaze connected with his brother's. When Sakis's brow rose a fraction, Arion gave a small smile.

'Go. I'll deal with as much as I can from here. We'll talk in one hour.' Arion clasped his brother's shoulder in reassurance before he strode off.

Sakis turned to her. 'I'll need to speak to the President.'

Brianna nodded. 'I've got his chief of staff on hold. He'll put you through when you're ready.'

Her gaze dropped to his chest and immediately shifted away. She stepped back to move away from the potent scent of sweat and man that radiated off his deep olive skin. 'You need to change. I'll get you some fresh clothes.'

As she headed towards the boot of the car, she heard the slide of his rowing suit zip. She didn't turn because she'd seen it all before. At least that was what she told herself. She hadn't seen Sakis Pantelides totally naked, of course. But hers was a twenty-four-seven job. And, when you worked as close as she did with a suave, self-assured, powerful tycoon who saw you as nothing but a super-efficient, sexless automaton, you were bound to be exposed to all aspects of his nature. And his various states of undress.

The first time Sakis Pantelides had undressed in front of her, Brianna had taken it in her stride, just as she'd brutally trained herself to take most things in her stride.

To feel, to trust, to give emotion an inch, was to invite disaster.

So she'd learned to harden her heart. It had been that…or sink beneath the weight of crushing despair.

And she refused to sink…

She straightened from the boot with a pristine blue shirt and a charcoal-grey Armani suit in one hand and the perfectly knotted double Oxford tie Sakis favoured in the other. She kept her gaze trained on the sun-dappled lake beyond his shoulder as she handed the items over and went to retrieve his socks and hand-made leather shoes.

She didn't need to see his strong neck and shoulders, honed perfectly from his years of professional, championship-winning rowing, or his deep, ripped chest with silky hairs that arrowed down to his neat, trim waist and disappeared beneath the band of his boxers. She most certainly didn't need to see the powerful thighs that looked as if they could crush an unwary opponent, or pin a willing female to an unyielding wall…in the right circumstances. And she especially didn't need to see the black cotton boxer briefs that made a poor effort to contain his—

A loud beep signalling an incoming call from the limo's phone startled her into dropping his socks. She hastily picked them up and slid into the car. From the corner of her eye, she saw Sakis step into his trousers. Silently, she held out the remaining items and picked up the phone.

'Pantelides Shipping,' she said into the receiver as she picked up her electronic tablet. She listened calmly to the voice at the other end of the line, tapping away at her keyboard as she added to the ever-growing to-do list.

By the time Sakis slid next to her, and slammed the door, impeccably dressed, she was on her fifth item. She paused long enough to secure her seat belt before resuming her typing.

'The only answer I have for you right now is no comment. Sorry, no can do.' Sakis stiffened beside her. 'Absolutely not. No news outlet will be getting exclusives. Pantelides Shipping will issue one press release within the hour. It will be posted on our company's website and affiliated media and social network links with the relevant contact details. If you have any questions after that, contact our press office.'

'Tabloid or mainstream media?' Sakis asked the moment she hung up.

'Fleet Street. They want to verify what they've heard.' The phone rang again. Seeing the number of another tabloid, she ignored it. Sakis had more pressing phone calls to make. She passed him the headset connected to the call she'd put on hold for the last ten minutes.

The tightening of his jaw was almost imperceptible before complete control slid back into place. His fingers brushed hers as he took the device from her. The unnerving voltage that came from touching Sakis made her heartbeat momentarily fluctuate but that was yet another thing she took in her stride.

His deep voice brimmed with authority and bone-deep assuredness. It held the barest hint of his Greek heritage but Brianna knew he spoke his mother tongue with the same stunning fluency and efficiency with which he ran the crude-oil brokerage arm of Pantelides Shipping, his family's multi-billion-dollar conglomerate.

'Mr President, please allow me to express my deepest regret at the situation we find ourselves in. Of course, my company takes full responsibility for this incident and will make every effort to ensure minimal ecological and economic distress. Yes, I have a fifty-man expert salvage and investigation crew on its way. They'll assess what needs to be done... Yes, I agree. I'll be there at the site within the next twelve hours.'

Brianna's fingers flew over her tablet as she absorbed the conversation and planned accordingly. By the time Sakis concluded the call, she had his private jet and necessary flight crew on standby.

They both stopped as the sleek phone rang again.

'Would you like me to get it?' Brianna asked.

Sakis shook his head. 'No. I'm the head of the company. The buck stops with me.' His gaze snagged hers with a compelling look that held hers captive. 'This is going to get worse before it gets better. Are you up to the task, Miss Moneypenny?'

Brianna forced herself to breathe, even as the tingle in her shoulder reminded her of the solemn vow she'd taken in a dark, cold room two years ago.

I refuse to sink.

She swallowed and firmed her spine. 'Yes, I'm up to the task, Mr Pantelides.'

Dark-green eyes the colour of fresh moss held hers for a moment longer. Then he gave a curt nod and picked up the phone.

'Pantelides,' he clipped out.

For the rest of the journey to Pantelides Towers, Brianna immersed herself in doing what she did best—anticipating her boss's every need and fulfilling it without so much as a whisper-light ruffle.

It was the only way she knew how to function nowadays.

By the time she handed their emergency suitcases to his helicopter pilot and followed Sakis into the lift that would take them to the helipad at the top of Pantelides Towers, they had a firm idea of what lay ahead of them.

There was nothing they could do to stop the crude oil spilling into the South Atlantic—at least not until the salvage team got there and went into action.

But, glancing at him, Brianna knew it wasn't only the disaster that had put the strain on Sakis's face. It was also being hit with the unexpected.

If there was one thing Sakis hated, it was surprises. It was why he always out-thought his opponents by a dozen moves, so he couldn't be surprised. Having gained a little insight into his past from working with him, Brianna wasn't surprised.

The devastating bombshell Sakis's father had dropped on his family when Sakis had been a teen was still fodder for journalists. Of course, she didn't know the full story, but she knew enough to understand why Sakis would hate having his company thrown into the limelight like this.

His phone rang again.

'Mrs Lowell. No, I'm sorry, there's no news.' His voice held the strength and the solid dependable calm needed to reassure the wife of the missing captain. 'Yes, he's still missing, but please be assured, I'll personally call you as soon as I have any information. You have my word.'

A pulse jumped in his temple as he hung up. 'How long before the search and rescue team are at the site?'

She checked her watch. 'Ninety minutes.'

'Hire another crew. Three teams working in eight-hour shifts are better than two working in twelve-hour shifts. I don't want anything missed because they're exhausted. And they're to work around the clock until the missing crew are found. Make it happen, Moneypenny.'

'Yes, of course.'

The lift doors opened. Brianna nearly stumbled when his hand settled in the small of her back to guide her out.

In all her time working for him, he'd never touched her in

any way. Forcing herself not to react, she glanced at him. His face was set, his brows clamped in fierce concentration as he guided her swiftly towards the waiting helicopter. A few feet away, his hand dropped. He waited for the pilot to help her up into her seat before he slid in beside her.

Before the aircraft was airborne, Sakis was on the phone again, this time to Theo. The urgent exchange in Greek went right over Brianna's head but it didn't stop her secret fascination with the mellifluous language or the man who spoke it.

His glance slid to her and she realised she'd been unashamedly staring.

She snapped her attention back to the tablet in her hand and activated it.

There'd been nothing personal in Sakis's touch or his look. Not that she'd expected there to be. In all ways and in all things, Sakis Pantelides was extremely professional.

She expected nothing less from him. And that was just the way she wished it.

Her lesson had been well and truly learned in that department, in the harshest possible way, barring death—not that she hadn't come close once or twice. And all because she'd allowed herself to *feel*, to dare to connect with another human being after the hell she'd suffered with her mother.

She was in no danger of forgetting; if she did, she had the tattoo on her shoulder to remind her.

Sakis pressed the 'end' button on yet another phone call and leaned back against the club seat's headrest.

Across from him, the tap-tap of the keyboard filled the silence as his assistant worked away at the ever-growing list of tasks he'd been throwing at her since they'd taken off four hours ago.

Turning his head, he glanced at her. As usual her face was expressionless save the occasional crease at the corner of her eyes as she squinted at the screen. Her brow remained smooth and untroubled as her fingers flew over the keyboard.

Her sleek blonde hair was in the same pristine, precise knot it had been when she'd arrived at work at six o'clock this morning. Without conscious thought, his gaze traced over her, again feeling that immediate zing to his senses.

Her dress suit was impeccable—a black-and-white combination that looked a bit severe but suited her perfectly. In her lobes, pearl earrings gleamed, small and unassuming.

His gaze slid down her neck, past slim shoulders and over the rest of her body, examining her in a way he rarely permitted himself to. The sight of the gentle curve of her breasts, her flat stomach and her long, shapely legs made his hands flex on his armrests as the zing turned stronger.

Moneypenny was fit, if a little on the slim side. Despite his slave-driving schedule, not once in the last year and a half had she turned up late for work or called in sick. He knew she stayed in the executive apartment in Pantelides Towers more and more lately rather than return to… He frowned. To wherever it was she called home.

Again he thanked whatever deity had sent her his way.

After his hellish experience with his last executive assistant, Giselle, he'd seriously contemplated commissioning a robot to handle his day-to-day life. When he'd read Brianna's flawless CV, he'd convinced himself she was too good to be true. He'd only reconsidered her after all the other candidates, after purporting to have almost identical supernatural abilities, had turned up at the interviews with not-so-hidden agendas—ones that involved getting into his bed at the earliest opportunity.

Brianna Moneypenny's file had listed talents that made him wonder why another competitor hadn't snapped her up. No one that good would've been jobless, even in the current economic climate. He'd asked her as much.

Her reply had been simple: 'You're the best at what you do. I want to work for the best.'

His hackles had risen at that response, but there had been no guile, no coquettish lowering of her lashes or strategic crossing of her legs. If anything, she'd looked defiant.

Thinking back now, he realised that was the first time he'd felt it—that tug on his senses that accompanied the electrifying sensation when he looked into her eyes.

Of course, he dismissed the feeling whenever it arose. Feelings had no place in his life or his business.

What he'd wanted was an efficient assistant who could rise to any challenge he set her. Moneypenny had risen to each challenge and continued to surprise him on a regular basis, a rare thing in a man of his position.

His gaze finally reached her feet and, with a sharp dart of astonishment, he noted the tiny tattoo on the inside of her left ankle. The star-shaped design, its circumference no larger than his thumb, was inked in black and blue and stood out against her pale skin.

Although he was staring straight at it, the mark was so out of sync with the rest of her no-nonsense persona, he wondered if he was hallucinating.

No, it was definitely a tattoo, right there, etched into her flawless skin.

Intrigued, he returned his gaze to the busy fingers tapping away. As if sensing his scrutiny, her fingers slowed and her head started to lift and turn towards him.

Sakis glanced down at his watch. 'We'll be landing in three hours. Let's take a break now and regroup in half an hour.'

Despite the loud whirr of her laptop shutting down, he noticed her attention didn't stray far from the device. Her attention never wavered from her work—a fact that should've pleased him.

'I've ordered lunch to be served in five minutes. I can hold it off for a few more minutes if you would like to look over the bios of the people we need to speak to when we land?' Her gaze met his, her blue eyes cool and unwavering.

His gaze dropped again to her ankle. As he watched, she slowly re-crossed her legs, obscuring the tattoo from his gaze.

'Mr Pantelides?' came the cool query.

Sakis inhaled slowly, willed his wavering control to slide back into place. By the time his gaze reconnected with hers, his interest in her tattoo had receded to the back of his mind.

Receded, but not been obliterated.

'Have lunch served in ten. I'll go take a quick shower.' He rose and headed for the larger of the two bedrooms at the rear of his plane.

At the door, he glanced back over his shoulder. Brianna Moneypenny was reaching for the attendant intercom with one hand while reopening her laptop with the other.

Super-efficient and ultra-professional. His executive assistant was everything she'd said on the tin, just like he'd explained to Ari.

But it suddenly occurred to Sakis that, in the eighteen months she'd worked for him, he'd never bothered looking *inside* the tin.

CHAPTER TWO

'I NEED TO get to the site asap once we land,' Sakis said in between bites of his chef-made gourmet beef burger.

Brianna curbed her pang of envy as she forked her plain, low-fat, crouton-free salad *niçoise* into her mouth and shook her head. 'The environment minister wants a meeting first. I tried to postpone it but he was insistent. I think he wants a photo op, this being an election year and all. I told him it'd have to be a brief meeting.'

His jaw tightened on his bite, his eyes narrowing with displeasure. Brianna didn't have to wonder why.

Sakis Pantelides detested any form of media attention with an almost unholy hatred, courtesy of the public devastation and humiliation Alexandrou Pantelides had visited on his family two decades ago. The Pantelides' downfall had been played out in full media glare.

'I have a helicopter on standby to take you straight to the site when you're done.'

'Make sure his people know my definition of *brief.* Do we know what the media presence is at the site?' he asked after swallowing another mouthful.

Her gaze darted to his. Green eyes watched her like a hawk. 'All the major global networks are present. We also have a couple of EPA ships in the area monitoring things.'

He gave a grim nod. 'There's not much we can do about the Environmental Protection Agency's presence, but make sure security know that they can't be allowed to interfere in the salvage and clean-up process. Rescuing the wildlife and keeping pollution to a minimum is another top priority.'

'I know. And…I had an idea.' Her plan was risky, in that it could attract more media attention than Sakis would agree to, but if she managed to pull it off it would reap enormous benefits and buy back some goodwill for Pantelides Shipping. It would also cement her invaluable status in Sakis's eyes and she could finally be rid of the sinking, rock-hard feeling in her stomach when she woke in a cold sweat many nights.

Some might find it shallow but Brianna placed job security above everything else. After everything she'd been through as a child—naively trusting that the only parent she had would put her well-being ahead of the clamour of the next drug fix— keeping her job and her small Docklands apartment meant everything to her. The terror of not knowing where her next meal would come from or when her temporary home would be taken from her still haunted her. And after her foolish de- cision to risk giving her trust, and the steep price she'd paid for it, she'd vowed never to be that helpless again.

'Moneypenny, I'm listening,' Sakis said briskly, and she realised he was waiting for her to speak.

Gathering her fracturing thoughts, she took a deep breath.

'I was thinking we can use the media and social network sites to our advantage. A few environmental blogs have started up, and they're comparing what's happening with the other oil conglomerate incident a few years ago. We need to nip that in the bud before it gets out of hand.'

Sakis frowned. 'It isn't even remotely the same thing. For one thing, this is a surface spill, not a deep sea pipeline breach.'

'But…'

His expression turned icy. 'I'd also like to keep the media out of this as much as possible. Things tend to get twisted around when the media becomes involved.'

'I believe this is the ideal time to bring them round to our side. I know a few journalists who are above-board. Perhaps, if we can work exclusively with them, we can get a great result. We've admitted the error is ours, so there's nothing to cover up. But not everyone has time to fact-check and the public making assumptions could be detrimental to us. We need to keep the line of communication wide open so people know everything that's going on at every stage.'

'What do you propose?' Sakis pushed his plate away.

She followed suit and fired up her laptop. Keying in the address, she called up the page she'd been working on. 'I've started a blog with a corresponding social networking accounts.' She turned the screen towards him and held her breath.

He glanced down at it. '"Save Point Noire"?'

She nodded.

'What is the point of that, exactly?'

'It's an invitation for anyone who wants to volunteer—either physically at the site or online with expertise.'

Sakis started to shake his head and her heart took a dive. 'Pantelides Shipping is responsible for this. We'll clean up our own mess.'

'Yes, but shutting ourselves off can also cause us a huge negative backlash. Look—' she indicated the numbers on the screen '—we're trending worldwide. People want to get involved.'

'Won't they see it as soliciting free help?'

'Not if we give them something in return.'

His gaze scoured her face, intense and focused, and Brianna felt a tiny burst of heat in her belly. Feverishly, she pushed it away.

'And what would that something be?' he asked.

Nerves suddenly attacked her stomach. 'I haven't thought that far ahead. But I'm sure I can come up with something before the day's out.'

He kept staring at her for so long, her insides churned

harder. Reaching for his glass, he took a long sip of water, his gaze still locked on her.

'Just when I think you're out of tricks, you surprise me all over again, Miss Moneypenny.' The slow, almost lazy murmur didn't throw her. What threw her was the keen speculation in his eyes.

Brianna held his gaze even though she yearned to look away. Speculation led to curiosity. Curiosity was something she didn't want to attract from her boss, or anyone for that matter. Her past needed to stay firmly, irretrievably buried.

'I'm not sure I know what you mean, Mr Pantelides.'

He glanced down at the laptop. 'Your plan is ingenious but, while I commend you for its inception, I'm also aware that keeping track of all the information flowing in will be a monumental task. How do you propose to do that?'

'If you give me the go-ahead, I can brief a small team back at the head office to take over. Any relevant information or genuine volunteer will be put through to me and I can take it from there.'

The decisive shake of his head made her want to clench her fist in disappointment. 'I need you with me once we get on site. I can't have you running off to check your emails every few minutes.'

'I can ask for three-hourly email updates.' When his gaze remained sceptical, she rushed on. 'You said so yourself—it's a great idea. At least let me have a go at trying to execute it. We need the flow of information now more than ever and getting the public on our side can't hurt. What do we have to lose?'

After a minute, he nodded. 'Four-hourly updates. But we make cleaning up the spill our top priority.'

'Of course.' She reached for the laptop but he leaned forward, took it from her and set it down beside his plate.

'Leave that for now. You haven't finished your meal.'

Surprised, she glanced down at her half-finished plate. 'Um...I sort of had.'

He pushed her plate towards her. 'You'll need your strength for what's ahead. Eat.'

Her gaze slid to his own unfinished meal as she picked up her fork. 'What about you?'

'My stamina is much more robust than yours—no offence.'

'None taken at all.' Her voice emerged a little stiffer than she intended.

Sakis quirked one eyebrow. 'Your response is at variance with your tone, Miss Moneypenny. I'm sure some die-hard feminist would accuse me of being sexist, but you really need it more than I do. You barely eat enough as it is.'

She gripped her fork harder. 'I wasn't aware my diet was under scrutiny.'

'It's hard to miss that you watch what you eat with almost military precision. If it wasn't absurd, I'd think you were rationing yourself.' His eyes were narrowed in that unnervingly probing way.

Her pulse skittered in alarm at the observation. 'Maybe I am.'

His lips tightened. 'Well, going without food for the sake of vanity is dangerous. You're risking your health, and thereby your ability to function properly. It's your duty to ensure you're in the right shape so you can fulfil your duties.'

The vehemence in his tone made her alarm escalate. 'Why do I get the feeling we're talking about more than my abandoned salad?'

He didn't answer immediately. His lowered lids and closed expression told her the memory wasn't a pleasant one.

He settled back in his seat, outwardly calm. But Brianna saw the hand still wrapped around his water glass wasn't quite so steady. 'Watching someone wilfully waste away despite being surrounded by abundance isn't exactly a forgettable experience.'

Her grip went slack. 'I'm sorry…I didn't mean to dredge up bad memories for you. Who do you…?'

He shook his head once and indicated her plate. 'It doesn't matter. Don't let your food go to waste, Moneypenny.'

Brianna glanced down at the remnants of her meal, trying to reconcile the outwardly confident man sitting across from her with the man whose hands trembled at a deeply disturbing memory. Not that she'd even been foolish enough to think Sakis Pantelides was one-faceted.

She recalled that one moment during her interview when he'd looked up from her file, his green eyes granite-hard and merciless.

'If you are to survive this job, I'd strongly urge you to take one piece of advice, Miss Moneypenny. Don't fall in love with me.'

Her response had been quick, painful memory making her tongue acid-sharp. 'With respect, Mr Pantelides, I'm here for the salary. The benefits package isn't too bad either, but most of all I'm here for the top-notch experience. To my knowledge, love never has and never will pay the bills.'

What she'd wanted to add then was that she'd been there, done her time and had the tattoo to prove it.

What she wanted tell him now was that she'd endured far, far worse than a hungry stomach. That she'd known the complete desolation of coming a poor second to her mother's love for drugs. She'd slept rougher than any child deserved to and had fought every day to survive in a concrete jungle, surrounded by the drug-addled bullies with vicious fists.

She held her tongue because to speak would be to reveal far more than she could ever afford to reveal.

Curiosity gnawed at her but she refused to probe further. Probing would invite reciprocity. Her past was under lock and key, tucked behind a titanium vault and sealed in concrete. And that was exactly where she intended to keep it.

In silence, she finished her meal and looked up with relief as the attendant arrived to clear away their plates.

When the phone rang, she pounced on it, grabbing the familiarity that came with work in an effort to banish the brief moments of unguarded intimacy.

'The captain of the coast guard is on the line for you.'

Sakis's gaze swept over her face, a speculative gleam in his eyes that slowly disappeared as he took the phone.

With an inward sigh of relief, Brianna reached for her laptop and fired it up.

Sakis's first glimpse of the troubled tanker made his gut clench hard. He tapped the helicopter pilot on the shoulder.

'Circle the vessel, would you? I want to assess the damage from the air before we land.'

The pilot obliged. Sakis's jaw tightened as he grasped the full impact of the damage of the tanker bearing the black and gold Pantelides colours.

He signalled for the pilot to land and alighted the moment the chopper touched down. A group of scandal-hungry journalists stood behind the cordoned-off area. From painful experience, Moneypenny's suggestion to bring them on-side rankled, but Sakis didn't dismiss the fact that in this instance she was right.

Ignoring them for now, he strode to where the crew waited, dressed in yellow, high-visibility jumpsuits.

'What's the situation?' he asked.

The head of the salvage crew—a thickset, middle-aged man with greying hair—stepped forward. 'We've managed to get inside the tanker and assessed the damage with the investigation team—we have three breached compartments. The other compartments haven't been affected but, the longer the vessel stays askew, the more likely we are to have another breach. We're working as fast as we can to set up the pumps to drain the compartment and the spillage.'

'How long will it take?'

'Thirty-six to forty-eight hours. Once the last of the crew get here, we'll work around the clock.'

Sakis nodded and turned to see Brianna emerge from the hastily set-up tents on the far side of the beach. For a moment he couldn't reconcile the woman heading towards him with his usual impeccably dressed assistant. Not that she had a hair out of place, of course. But she'd changed into cargo pants and a white T-shirt which was neatly tucked in and belted tight, emphasising her trim waist. Her shining hair made even more vivid by the fierce African sun was still caught in an immaculate knot, but on her feet she wore weathered combat boots.

For the second time today, Sakis felt the attraction he'd ruthlessly battened down strain at the leash.

Ignoring it, he turned his attention to the man next to him. 'It'll be nightfall in three hours. How many boats do you have conducting the search?'

'We have four boats, including the two you provided. Your helicopter is also assisting with the search.' The captain wiped a trickle of sweat off his face. 'But what worries me is the possibility of pirates.'

His gut clenched. 'You think they've been kidnapped?'

The captain nodded. 'We can't rule it out.'

Brianna's eyes widened, then she extracted her mini-tablet from her thigh pocket, her fingers flying over the keypad.

One corner of her lower lip was caught between her teeth as she pressed buttons. A small spike of heat broke through the tight anxiety in his gut. Without giving it the tiniest room, Sakis smashed down on it. *Hard.*

'What is it, Moneypenny?' he asked briskly after he'd dismissed the captain.

Her brow creased but she didn't look up. 'I'm sorry, I should've anticipated the pirates angle…'

He caught her chin with his forefinger and gently forced her head up. When her gaze connected with his, he saw the trace of distress in her eyes.

'That's what the investigators are here for. Besides, you've had a lot to deal with in the last several hours. What I need is the list of journalists you promised. Can you handle that?'

Her nod made her skin slide against his finger. Soft. Silky. Smooth.

Stási!

He stepped back abruptly and pushed the aberration from his mind.

Turning, he moved towards the shoreline, conscious that she'd fallen into step beside him. From the air, he'd guestimated that the oil had spread about half a mile along the shore. As he surveyed the frantic activity up and down the once pristine shoreline, regret bit deep.

Whatever had triggered this accident, the blame for the now-blackened, polluted water lay with him, just as he was responsible for the missing crew members. Whatever it took, he would make this right.

The captain of the salvage crew brought the small boat near and Sakis went towards it. When Brianna moved towards him, he shook his head.

'No, stay here. This could be dangerous.'

She frowned. 'If you're going aboard the tanker, you'll need someone to jot down the details and take pictures of the damage.'

'I merely want to see the damage from the inside myself. I'm leaving everything else in the hands of the investigators. And, if I need to, I'm sure I can handle taking a few pictures. What I'm not sure of is the situation inside the vessel and I won't risk you getting injured under any circumstances.' He held out his hand for the camera slung around her neck.

She looked ready to argue with him. Beneath her T-shirt, her chest rose and fell as she exhaled and Sakis forced himself not to glance down as another spike of erotic heat lanced his groin.

Theos…

The unsettling feeling made him snap his fingers, an irritatingly frantic need to step away from her charging into him.

'If you're sure,' she started.

'I'm sure.'

By the time she freed herself from the camera strap and handed it over, her face had settled once more into its customary serene professionalism.

Her fingers brushed his as he took the camera and Sakis registered a single instance of softness before the contact was disconnected.

Taking a deep breath, he started to walk away.

'Wait!'

He turned back. 'What is it, Moneypenny?' His tone was harsh but couldn't stop the disturbing edginess creeping over him.

She held out a large yellow jumpsuit. 'You can't get on the boat without wearing this. The health and safety guidelines require it.'

Despite the grim situation, Sakis wanted to laugh at her implacable expression as she held him to account.

'Then by all means…if the guidelines require it.'

He took the plastic garment, shook it out and stepped into it under her watchful eye. He glanced at her as he zipped the jumpsuit and once again saw her lower lip caught between her teeth.

With more force than was necessary, he shoved the small digital camera into the waterproof pocket and trudged through the oil-slicked water.

An hour later, the words of his lead investigator made his heart sink.

'I retired from piloting tankers like these ten years ago, and even then the navigation systems were state-of-the-art. Your vessel has the best one I've ever seen. There's no way this was systems failure. Too many fail-safes in place for the vessel to veer this far off course.'

Sakis gave a grim nod and pulled his phone from his pocket. 'Moneypenny, get me the head of security. I want to know everything about Morgan Lowell... Yes, the captain of my tanker. And prepare a press release. Unfortunately, the investigators are almost certain this was pilot error.'

Brianna perused the electronic page for typos. Once she was satisfied, she approached where Sakis stood with the environment minister. His yellow jumpsuit was unzipped to the waist, displaying the dark-green T-shirt that moulded his lean, sleekly muscular torso. She'd never thought she'd find the sight of a man slipping on a hideous yellow jumpsuit so...hot and unsettling.

He turned, and she held her breath as his gaze swept over her. The crackle of electricity she'd felt earlier when their fingers had touched returned.

Abruptly she pushed it away. They were caught in a severely fraught set of circumstances. What she was experiencing was just residual adrenaline that came with these unfortunate events.

'Is it ready?' he asked.

She nodded and passed the press release over, along with the list of names he'd requested. He skimmed the words then passed the tablet back to her. Brianna knew he'd memorised every single word.

'I'll go and prep the media.'

She headed for the group of journalists poised behind the white cordon. As she walked, she practised the breathing exercises she'd mastered long before she'd come to work for Sakis Pantelides.

By the time she reached the group, she'd calmed her roiling emotions.

'Good evening, ladies and gentlemen. This is how it's going to work. Mr Pantelides will give his statement. Then he'll invite questions—one from each of you.' She held out a hand at the immediate protests. 'I'm sure you'll understand that it'll take hours for every question you've jotted down to be answered and frankly we don't have time for that. Right now the priority is the salvage operation. So, one question each.' Control settled over her as her steely gaze held the group's and received their cooperation.

Yes, that was more like it. Not for her the searing, jittery feelings of the last few hours, ever since she'd looked up on the plane and caught Sakis's gaze on her ankle tattoo; since he'd touched her on the beach, told her not to worry that she'd missed the pirates angle. Those few minutes had been intensely...*rattling.*

The momentary heat she'd seen in his eyes had thrown her off-balance. At the start of her employment she'd taken pains to hide the tattoo but, after realising Sakis took no notice of what she wore or anything about her, she'd relaxed. The sensation of his eyes on her tattoo had smashed a fist through her tight control.

It had taken hours to restore it but, now she had, she was determined not to lose it again.

There was too much at stake.

Feeling utterly composed, she glanced over to where Sakis waited at the assembled podium. At his nod, she signalled security to let the media through.

She stood next to the podium and tried not to let his deep voice affect her as he started speaking. His authority and confidence as he outlined the plans for the salvage mission and the search for the missing crew belied the tension in his body. From her position, she could see the rigid outline of his washboard stomach and the braced tension in his legs. Even though his hands remained loose at his sides, his shoulders barely moved as he spoke.

A camera flashed nearby and she saw his tiniest flinch.

'What's going to happen to the remaining oil on board?' a reporter asked.

His gaze swung to where the minister stood. 'For their very generous assistance, we're donating the contents on board the distressed vessel to the coast guard and army. The minister has kindly offered to co-ordinate the distribution.'

'So you're just going to give away oil worth millions of dollars, out of the goodness of your heart? Are you trying to bribe your way out of your company's responsibilities, Mr Pantelides?'

Brianna's breath stalled but Sakis barely blinked at the caustic remark from a particularly vile tabloid reporter. That he didn't visibly react was a testament to his unshakeable control.

'On the contrary, as I said at the start, my company assumes one hundred per cent liability for this incident and are working with the government in making reparations. No price is too high to pay for ensuring that the clean-up process is speedy and causes minimum damage to the sea life. This means the remaining crude oil has to be removed as quickly as possible and the vessel secured and towed away. Rather than transfer it to another Pantelides tanker, a process that'll take time, I've decided to donate it to the government. I'm sure you'll agree it makes perfect sense.' His tone remained even but the tic in his jaw belied his simmering anger. 'Next question.'

'Can you confirm what caused the accident? According to your sources, this is one of your newest tankers, equipped with state-of-the-art navigation systems, so what went wrong?'

'That is a question for our investigators to answer once they'd finished their work.'

'What does your gut feeling say?'

'I choose to rely on hard facts when stakes are this high, not gut feelings,' Sakis responded, his tone clipped.

'You haven't made a secret of your dislike for the media. Are you going to use that to try and stop the media from re-porting on this accident, Mr Pantelides?'

'You wouldn't be here if I felt that way. In fact—' he

stopped and flicked a glance at Brianna before facing the crowd, but not before she caught a glimpse of the banked unease in his eyes '—I've hand-picked five journalists who will be given exclusive access to the salvage process.'

He read out the names. While the chosen few preened, the rest of the media erupted with shouted questions.

One in particular filtered through. 'If your father were alive and in your place, how would he react to this incident? Would he try and buy his way out of it, like he did with everything else?'

The distressed sound slipped from Brianna's throat before she could stop it. Silence fell over the gathered group as the words froze in the air. Beneath the podium, out of sight of the media's glare, Sakis's hands clenched into white-knuckled fists.

The urge to protect him surged out of nowhere and swept over her in an overwhelming wave. Her heart lurched, bringing with it a light-headedness that made her sway where she stood. Sakis's quick sideways glance told her he'd noticed.

Facing the media, he inhaled slowly. 'You have to go to the afterlife to ask my father that question. I do not speak for the dead.'

He stepped from the podium and stood directly in front of her. The breadth of his broad shoulders blocked out the sun.

'What's wrong?' he demanded in a fierce whisper.

'N…nothing. Everything is fine…. Going according to plan.' She fought to maintain her steady breathing even as she flailed inside. Needing desperately to claw back her control, she searched blindly for the solid reassurance of her mini-tablet.

Sakis plucked it out of her hands, his piercing gaze unwavering as it remained trained on her. '*According to plan* would be these damned vultures finding another carcass to pick on and leaving us to get on with the work that needs to be done.' From his tone, there was no sign that the last question had had a lasting effect on him, but this close she saw his pinched lips and the ruthlessly suppressed pain in his eyes. Another wave of protectiveness rushed over her.

Purpose. That was what she needed. Purpose and focus.

Swallowing hard, she held out her hand for her tablet. 'I'll take care of it. You've chosen the journalists you want to cover the salvage operation. There's no need for the rest to hang around.'

He didn't relinquish it. 'Are you sure you're all right? You look pale. I hope you're not succumbing to the heat. Have you had anything to eat since we got here?'

'I'm fine, Mr Pantelides.' He kept staring at her, dark brows clamped in a frown. 'I assure you, there's nothing wrong.' She deliberately made her voice crisp. 'The sooner I get rid of the media, the sooner we can get on with things.'

He finally let her take the tablet from him. Hardly daring to breathe, Brianna stepped back and away from the imposing man in front of her.

No. No. No...

The negative sound reverberated through her skull as she walked away. There was no way she was developing feelings for her boss.

Even if Sakis didn't fire her the moment she betrayed even the slightest non-professional emotion, she had no intention of letting herself down like that ever again.

The tattoo on her ankle throbbed.

The larger one on her shoulder burned with the fierce reminder.

She'd spent two years in jail for her serious error in judgement after funnelling her need to be loved towards the wrong guy.

Making the same mistake again was not an option.

CHAPTER THREE

SAKIS WATCHED BRIANNA walk away; her back was held so rigid her upper half barely moved. His frown deepened. Something was wrong. Granted, this was the first crisis they'd been thrown into together, but her conduct up till now had been beyond exemplary.

Right up until she'd reacted strongly to the journalist's question. A question he himself had not anticipated. He should've known that somehow his father would be dredged up like this. Should've known that, even from beyond the grave, the parent who'd held his family in such low, deplorable regard would not remain buried. He stomped on the pain riding just beneath his chest, the way he always did when he thought of his father. He refused to let the past haunt him. It no longer had any power over him.

After what his father had done to his family, to his mother especially, he deserved to be forgotten totally and utterly.

Unfortunately, at times like these, when the media thought they could get a whiff of scandal, they pounced. And this time, there was no escaping their rabid focus…

The deafening sound of the industrial-size vacuum starting up drew his attention from Brianna, reminding him that he had more important things to deal with than his hitherto unruffled personal assistant's off behaviour, and the unwanted memories of a ghost.

He zipped his jumpsuit back up and strode over to the black, slick shoreline. Half a mile away, giant oil-absorbing booms floated around the perimeter of the contaminated water to catch the spreading spill. Closer to shore, right in the middle of where the oil poured out, ecologically safe chemicals pumped from huge sprays to dissolve as much of the slick as possible.

It's not enough. It would never be enough because this shouldn't have happened in the first place.

His phone rang and he recognised Theo's number on his screen.

'What's happening, brother? Talk to me,' Theo said.

Sakis summarised the situation as quickly as he could, leaving out nothing, even though he was very aware that the mention of kidnap would raise painful, unwanted memories for Theo.

'Anything I can do from here?' his brother asked. The only hint of his disturbance at being reminded of his own kidnap when he was eighteen was the slight ring of steel in his voice when he asked the question. 'I can put you in touch with the right people if you want. I made it my business to find out who the right contacts are in a situation like this.' His analytical brain wouldn't have made him cope with his ordeal otherwise.

That was Theo through and through. He went after a problem until he had every imaginable scenario broken down, then he went after the solution with single-minded determination—which was why he fulfilled his role as trouble-shooter for Pantelides Inc so perfectly.

'We've got it in hand. But perhaps you could cause an outrageous scandal where you are, distract these damned paparazzi from messing with my salvage operation.'

'Hmm, I suppose I could skydive naked from the top of *Cristo Redentor*,' Theo offered.

For the first time in what felt like days, Sakis's lips cracked in a smile. 'You love Rio too much to get yourself barred from the city for ever for blasphemy.' His gaze flicked to where Brianna stood alone, having dispersed the last of the journalists. She was back on her tablet, her fingers busy on the glass keyboard.

Satisfaction oozed through him. Whatever had fractured his PA's normal efficiency, she had it back again.

'Everything's in hand,' he repeated, probably more to reassure himself that he had his emotions under control.

'Great to hear. Keep me in the loop, *ne*?'

Sakis signed off and jumped into the nearest boat carrying a crew of six and the vacuum, and signalled to the pilot to head out.

For the next three hours, while sunlight prevailed, he worked with the crew to pump as much sludge of out the water as possible. From another boat nearby, the journalists to whom he'd granted access filmed the process. Some even asked intelligent questions that didn't make his teeth grind.

Floodlights arrived, mounted on tripods on more boats, and he carried on working.

It was nearing midnight when, alerted to the arrival of the refresh crew, he straightened from where he'd been managing the pump. And froze.

'What the hell?'

The salvage-crew captain glanced up sharply. 'Excuse me, sir?'

But Sakis's gaze was on the boat about twenty yards to his left, where Brianna held the nozzle of a chemical spray aimed at the slick, a distressed look on her face as she swung her arm back and forth over the water.

The first of the changeover crew was approaching on a motor-powered dinghy. Sakis hopped into the small vessel and directed it to where Brianna worked.

Seeing him approach on a direct course, she changed the angle of her nozzle to avoid spraying him, her face hurriedly set in its usual calm expression. It was almost as if the bleakness he'd glimpsed moments ago had been a mirage.

'Mr Pantelides, did you need something?'

For some reason, the sound of his father's name on her lips aggravated him. For several hours he'd managed not to think about his father. He wanted to keep it that way. 'Put that hose down and get in.'

She turned the spray off, eyes widening. 'Excuse me?'

'Get in here. *Now.*'

'I…I don't understand,' she said. Her voice had lost a little of the sharpness and she looked genuinely puzzled as she stared down at him.

He saw the long streak of oil across her cheek. Her once white T-shirt had now turned grimy and slick and her khaki cargo pants had suffered the same fate.

But not a single hair was out of place.

The dichotomy of dirt, flawless efficiency and the bleakness he'd glimpsed a moment ago intrigued him beyond definition. The intrigue escalated his irritation. 'It's almost midnight. You should've left here hours ago.' He manoeuvred the dinghy until it bumped the boat, directly below where she stood on the starboard side.

From that angle, he couldn't miss the landscape of her upper body—more specifically, the perfect shape of her breasts or the sleek line of her jaw and neck as she glanced down at him.

'Oh. Well…I'm here to work, Mr Pantelides. Why should I have left?'

'Because you're not part of the salvage team, and even they work in six-hour shifts. Besides this—' he waved at the nozzle in her hand '—is not part of your job description.'

'I'm aware of what my job description is. But, if we're being pedantic, you're not part of the crew either. And yet here you are.'

Sakis felt a shake of surprise. In all her time with him, she'd never raised her voice or shown signs of feminine ire. But in the last few minutes, he'd seen intense emotion ream over her face and through her voice. Right now, Sakis had the distinct feeling she was extremely displeased with his directive. A small spurt of masochistic pleasure fizzed through him at the thought that he'd unruffled the unflappable Miss Moneypenny.

'I'm the boss. I have the luxury of doing whatever the hell I want,' he said softly, his gaze raking her face, secretly eager for further animated reaction.

What he got was unexpected. Her shoulders slumped and she shrugged. 'Of course. But, just in case you're worried about the corporate risks, I signed a waiver before coming aboard. So you'll suffer no liability if anything happens to me.'

Irritation returned, bit deeper. 'I don't give a damn about personal liability or corporate risks. What I do give a damn about is your ability to function properly tomorrow if you don't get enough sleep. You've been up for over eighteen hours. So, unless you have super powers I'm not aware of, put that hose down and get down here.' He held out a hand, unwilling to examine this almost clawing need to take care of her.

She didn't put the hose down. Instead she handed it over to a salvage crew member. Finally, she faced Sakis.

'Fine. You win.' Again he saw the tiniest mutinous set to her lips and wondered why that little action pleased him so much.

He was tired; he *must* be hallucinating. He certainly wasn't thinking straight if the thought of getting under his executive assistant's skin held so much of his interest.

She swung long, slim legs over the side of the boat and dropped into the dinghy. The movement made the vessel sway. She swayed with it, and threw out a hand to steady herself as Sakis turned.

Her torso bumped his arm and her hand landed on his shoulder as she tried to find her feet. His arm snagged her waist, encountered firm, warm muscle beneath his fingers.

Heat punched through his chest and arrowed straight for his groin.

'*Stasi!*'

'I…I'm sorry,' she stammered, pulling away with a skittishness very unlike her.

'No harm done,' he murmured. But Sakis wasn't so hot on that reassurance. Harm was being done to his insides. Heat continued to ravage him, firing sensations he sure as hell didn't want fired up. And especially not with his PA.

A quick glance showed she'd retreated to the farthest part of the small dinghy with her arms crossed primly around her middle and her face averted from his. He tried not to let his gaze drop to her plump breasts…but, *Theos*, it was hard not to notice their tempting fullness.

With a muttered curse, his hand tightened on the rudder of the dinghy and steered it towards shore.

This time she didn't refuse his offer of help when they stepped into the shallow water. After making sure the vessel was secure, he followed her onto the floodlit beach.

When he neared, he caught another glimpse of distress on her face.

'What's wrong? Why were you on the salvage boat? And, before you trot out "nothing", I'd advise you not to insult my intelligence.'

He saw her hesitate, then shove her hands into her pockets. This time, he couldn't stop himself from staring at her chest. Thankfully, she didn't notice because her gaze wasn't on him.

'I was talking to the some of the locals earlier. This cove was a special place for them, a sanctuary. I…I felt bad about what's happened.'

Guilt lanced through him. But, more than that, the rare glimpse into Brianna Moneypenny's human side intrigued him more than ever. 'I'll make sure it's returned to them as pristine as it once was.'

Her gaze flew up and connected with his, surprise and pleasure reflected in her eyes. 'That's good. It's not nice when your sanctuary is ripped away from you.' The pain accompanying those words made him frown. Before he could probe deeper, she stepped back. 'Anyway, I assured them you would make it right.'

'Thank you.'

She started to walk towards the fleet of four-wheelers a short distance away. Their driver stood next to the first one.

'I reserved a suite for you at the Noire. Your case was taken there a few hours ago and your laptop and phones are in the jeep. I'll see you in the morning, Mr Pantelides,' she tagged on.

Sakis froze. '*You'll see me in the morning?* Aren't you coming with me?'

'No,' she said.

'Why not?'

'Because I'm not staying at the hotel.'

'Where exactly are you staying?'

She indicated the double row of yellow tents set up further up on the beach, away from the bustle of the clean-up work.

'I've secured a tent and put my stuff in there.'

'What's wrong with staying at the same hotel I'm staying in?'

'Nothing, except they didn't have any more rooms. The suite I reserved for you was the last one. The other hotels are too far away to make the commute efficient.'

Sakis shook his head. 'You've been on your feet all day with barely a break— Don't argue with me, Moneypenny,' He raised a hand when she started to speak. 'You're not sleeping in a flimsy tent on the beach with machines blasting away all around you. Go and get your things.'

'I assure you, it's more than adequate.'

'No. You say I have a suite?'

'Yes.'

'Then there is no reason why we can't share it.'

'I would rather not, Mr Pantelides.'

The outright refusal shocked and annoyed him in equal measures. Also another first from Brianna Moneypenny was the fact that she wasn't quite meeting his gaze. 'Why would you *rather not*?'

She hesitated.

'Look at me, Moneypenny,' he commanded.

Blue eyes… No, they weren't quite blue. They were a shade of aquamarine, wide, lushly lashed and beautiful…and they met his in frank challenge. 'Your room is a single suite with one double bed. It's not suitable for two, um, professionals, and I'd rather not have to share my personal space.'

Sakis thought of the countless women who would jump at the chance to share 'personal space' with him.

He thought of all the women who would kill to share a double bed with him.

Then he thought of why he was here, in this place: with *his* oil contaminating a once incredibly beautiful beach; *his* crew missing; and the tabloid press just waiting for him to slip up, to show them that the apple hadn't fallen far from the tree.

The sick feeling that he'd forced down but never quite suppressed enough threatened to rise again. It was the same mingled despair and anger he'd felt when Theo had been taken. The same sense of helplessness when he'd been unable to do anything to stop his mother fading away before his eyes, her pain raw and wrenching after what his father and the media had done to her.

'I don't give a damn about your personal space. What I do give a damn about is your ability to fire on all cylinders. We discussed this—you being up to standing by me in this situation we find ourselves in. You assured me you were up to the task. And yet, for the last ten minutes, you've shown a certain…mutiny that makes me wonder whether you're equipped to handle what's coming.'

Her outrage made her breathing erratic. 'I don't think that's a fair observation, sir. I've done everything you've asked of me, and I'm more than capable of handling whatever comes. Just because I disagree with you on one small issue doesn't make me mutinous. I'm thinking about you.'

'Then prove it. Stop arguing with me and get in the jeep.'

She opened her mouth; closed it again. When she looked

at him, her eyes held a hint of fire he'd seen more than once today. The fire *he'd* tried—and failed—to bank fired up deep in his groin.

'I'll go and get my things,' she said.

'No need.' He exchanged glances with the driver and the young man headed towards the row of tents. Sakis leaned against the jeep's hood. 'You can fill me in on the results of your social media campaign while we wait.'

He saw how eagerly she snatched at her tablet and suppressed another bout of irritation. Whatever was causing this abnormal behaviour, he needed to nip it in the bud pretty darned quick. The crisis on his hands needed all his attention.

'I've found six individuals who I think will be useful to us. One's a professor of marine biology based in Guinea Bissau. Another, a husband and wife team who are experts in wildlife rescue. They specialise in disaster rescue such as this. The other three have no specialities but they have a huge social media following and are known for volunteering on humanitarian missions. I'm having all six vetted by our security team. If they pass the security test, I'll arrange for them to be flown over tomorrow.'

'I'm still not convinced bringing even more focus on this crisis is the best way to go, Moneypenny.' His insides tightened as he thought of his mother. 'Sometimes you don't see the harm until it's too late.' He thought of her devastation and misery, the incessant sobbing, and finally the substitution of food with alcohol when it'd hit home that the husband she'd thought was a god amongst men, the man she'd thought was true to her and only her, had had a string of affairs with mistresses around the globe, some of whom had dated back to before he'd put his wedding ring on her finger.

The year he'd turned fifteen had been the bleakest year of his life. It was the year he'd had every child's basest fear confirmed—that his father did not love him, did not love anyone or anything but himself. It was also the start of Sakis's hatred of the media, who'd not only exposed his worst fears but trumpeted it to the world.

Ari had withstood the invasion of their lives with his usual unflappable demeanour, although Sakis had a feeling his brother had been just as devastated, if not more so, than he had been. Theo, thirteen at that time, with fresh teenage hormones battering him, had gone off the rails. To this day, their mother had never found out how many times Theo had run away from home because Ari, seventeen going on seventy, had found him every single time and brought him back.

In all that chaos, Sakis had watched his mother deteriorate before his eyes, culminating in her seeking a solution so horrific, he still shuddered at the memory.

He pushed the events of decades past out of his mind and focused on the woman in front of him, who watched him with barely veiled curiosity.

Silently, he held her gaze until hers fell away. That he immediately wished it back made him suppress a frustrated growl.

'The journalists we hand-picked know this could be the opportunity of a lifetime for them as long as they play ball. I'll make sure they portray an open and honest account of what we're doing to remedy the situation, while infusing the appropriate rhetoric to protect the company's reputation.'

A smile tugged at his mouth. 'You should've been a diplomat, Moneypenny.'

Her shoulder lifted in a shrug that drew his attention to where it had no business being, specifically the pulse beating beneath her flawless skin.

'We all have something we desire more than anything. Wasting the opportunity when it presents itself is plain foolishness.'

The temptation to look inside the tin was too much to pass up. 'And what is it *you* want?'

Her startled gaze flew to his. 'Excuse me?'

'What do you want more than anything?'

She shook her head and looked away, a hint of desperation in the movement. He saw her relieved expression as his driver approached, her small carry-all in his hand.

Striding forward, she took the case from the surprised driver and stowed it in the boot. Then she opened the back door and got in.

Sakis took his time to walk to the other door. He ignored her nervous glance and waited until they were both buckled in and the jeep was moving along the dusty road running alongside the beach. The moment she relaxed, he pounced. 'Well?'

'Well what?'

'I'm waiting for an answer.'

'About what I want?' she asked.

Her stall tactics didn't go unnoticed. 'Yes,' he pressed.

'I…want the chance to prove that I can do a good job and be recognised for it.'

He exhaled impatiently. 'You already do an exemplary job, and you're highly paid and highly valued for it.'

He battled the disappointment rising inside. He'd wanted *personal*. From the assistant he'd warned against getting personal. So what? Finding out a little bit about what went on behind that professional façade didn't mean either of them risked losing their highly functional relationship. Besides, Moneypenny knew of his liaisons; she arranged the lunches, dinners and the odd, discreet parting gift.

The balance needed adjusting, just a little. 'Do you have a boyfriend?'

Her head whipped round, perfect eyebrows arching. 'I beg your pardon?'

'It's a very simple question, Moneypenny. One that demands a simple yes or no answer.'

'I know it is, but I fail to see how that's *relevant* within the realms of our working relationship.'

He noted the agitated cadence of her breathing and hid a

smile. 'I believe it's company policy to have a yearly appraisal. You've been working for me for almost eighteen months and you're yet to have your first appraisal.'

'HR gave me my appraisal six months ago. They sent you the results, I believe.'

'Probably, but I haven't read it yet.'

'So you want to do your own evaluation…*now*?'

He shrugged, a little irritated with himself now that he was pushing the subject. But, now the question was out there, it niggled and, yes, he wanted to know if Brianna Moneypenny had urges just like the rest of the human race. She wasn't a robot. She'd felt warm and most definitely feminine when her body had brushed against his on the boat. Her comment about restoring the beach for the local inhabitants had also uncovered a hitherto hidden soft side he hadn't expected.

Moneypenny was human. And compassionate. And he was curious about her.

He shifted to ease the sudden restless throb in his body. 'Call it a mini-appraisal. I just want to know if anything on your CV has changed since you joined me. You listed your marital status as single when I employed you. I merely want to know if that's changed in any significant way.'

'So you want to know, purely from a professional point of view, whether I'm sleeping with anyone or not?' Her tone dripped cynicism. 'Do you want to know which brand of underwear I prefer and what I like for breakfast as well?

Sakis felt no shame. *Redressing the balance.* Plus he needed something to take his mind off what had been a hellish day… if only for a moment. 'Yes to my first question; the other two are optional.'

Brianna's chin lifted. 'In that case, since it's for *purely professional* purposes, no, I don't have a lover, my underwear is my own business and I have an unhealthy weakness for pancakes. Are you satisfied?'

The thrill of gratification that arrowed through him made his pulse race dangerously. Disturbingly.

He glanced at the tight coil of golden hair that gleamed as they passed under bright streetlights, at her pert nose and generously wide and full mouth; the dimple that winked in her cheek when she pursed her lips in irritation, like she was doing now...

The thrill escalated, rushing through his blood.

Theos...

He rubbed at his tired eyes with the heels of his palms. What the hell was wrong with him? Strong coffee; that was what he needed. Or a stiff drink to knock everything back into perspective.

Because there was no way in hell he planned on following through with this insane attraction to Moneypenny. No damned way...

The streets were deserted as they approached the leafy centre of Pointe Noire. Their hotel was pleasant enough with a sweeping circular driveway that ended in front of the white three-storey, shutter-windowed pre-colonial building.

The manager waited in the foyer to greet them personally, although his gaze widened when it lit on Brianna.

'Welcome to the Noire, Monsieur Pantelides. Your suite is ready, although I was told you would be the sole occupant?'

'You were misinformed.'

'Ah, well, my apologies for the lack of more prestigious suites but the rooms were all booked up the moment the crash...er...the moment the unfortunate event happened.' He couldn't quite keep the gloating pride from his voice.

As the manager called the lift and they entered the small space, he sensed Brianna's tension mount. The moment they were let into the suite, he understood why.

The 'suite' label had clearly been a lofty idea in someone's deluded mind. The room was only marginally larger than a double room with the sleeping area separated from the double sofa by a TV and drinks unit.

He only half-listened as the manager expounded on the many features of the room. His attention was caught on Brianna, who stood staring at the bed as if it was her mortal enemy, her shoulders stiff and her face even stiffer. Had their whole reason for being here not so dire, he'd have been amused.

He dismissed the manager. He'd barely left when a knock came at the door.

Brianna jumped.

'Relax, it's only our bags,' he reassured her with a frown.

'Oh, yes, of course.'

The porters entered and Sakis made sure they left just as quickly.

Silence reigned, thick and heavy, permeating the air with a sexual atmosphere he recognised but was determined to ignore. It had no business here.

And yet, it refused to be stemmed.

He watched as she came towards him and reached for the bag the porter had left beside him.

'You take the shower first,' he said. The image that slammed into his mind sent a dark tremor through him but he forced himself to breathe through it.

She straightened and her gaze darted to the bathroom door in the so-called suite. 'If you're sure.'

'Yes, I'm sure.' Then, unable to stop himself, even while every sense screamed at him to step away, he reached out and rubbed the smudge on her cheek.

Her breath caught on a strangled gasp, sending another punch of heat through him. His senses screamed harder, but his fingers stayed put, stroking her soft, warm skin.

'You have an oil streak right there.' He rubbed again.

With a sharply drawn breath, she moved away, but her eyes stayed on him, and in their depths Sakis saw the clear evidence of lust…and another emotion he'd never seen in a woman's eyes when it came to him: fear.

What the hell?

Before he could question her, she swung away. 'I…I'll try not to take too long.'

With quick strides, she disappeared into the bathroom and slammed the door, leaving him standing there staring at the door with a growing erection and an ever-rising pulse rate that made him certain he risked serious health problems if he didn't get it under control.

Thee mou… Of all the times and places—and sheer idiocy, bearing in mind the recipient—it seemed his libido had taken this moment to run rampant and to focus its attention on the one person he should absolutely not focus on.

Crisis heightened the senses and made men and women succumb to inappropriate urges, leading to serious errors of judgment that later came back to bite them in the ass.

Whatever was happening here, he needed to kill it with a swift, merciless death. And he certainly needed not to think of Moneypenny behind that door, removing her clothes, stepping naked, beneath the warm shower…

Moving the drinks cabinet, he poured himself a shot of whiskey. As he downed it, his gaze strayed to the bathroom door.

Nothing was going to happen. He refused to let it.

As if hammering home the point, he heard the distinct sound of the lock sliding home.

And poured himself another drink.

Brianna sagged against the door, unable to catch her breath. The bag slid uselessly from her fingers and she didn't need to look down to see evidence of her body's reaction to Sakis Pantelides. She could feel every inch of her skin tightening, burning, reacting to his touch as if he was still rubbing her cheek.

No. No. No!

Anger lent her strength, enough to tug her boots off and fling them away with distressed disgust. Her oil-smudged cargo pants went the same way, followed by her once white T-shirt. About to reach for the bra clasp, she glanced up and caught the reflection of her tattoo in the wide bathroom mirror.

Sucking in a deep breath, she stepped forward, clutched the sink and struggled to regulate her breathing.

She stared hard at the tattoo on her shoulder. *I refuse to sink.* It was the mantra she'd recited second by second in her darkest days. And one she'd tapped from whenever she needed strength or self-belief…anything to get her through a tough day. It was a reminder of what she'd survived as a child and as an adult. A reminder that depending on anyone for her happiness or wellbeing was asking to be devastated. She'd made that mistake once and look where she'd ended up.

The tattoo was a reminder never to forget. To keep swimming. Never to sink.

And yet it was exactly what she was doing; sinking into Sakis's eyes, into the miasma of erotic sensations that had reduced her control to nothing. Sensation that had grown with each look, each careless touch, and was now threatening to choke all common sense out of her.

Her hand settled over her heart as if she could stem its chaotic beating. Then she slowly traced it down, past the scar on her hip to the top of her panties and the heat pooling just below.

The urge to touch herself was strong, almost supernatural. The urge to have stronger, more powerful hands touch her *there* was even more visceral.

Gritting her teeth, she traced her fingers back up to the scar. Slowly, strength and purpose returned.

Between the tattoo and the scar, she had vivid reminders of why she could never let her guard down again, never trust another human being again. She intended to cling to them with everything she had. Because the purpose she'd seen in Sakis's eyes had scared her.

A determined Sakis was a formidable Sakis.

She would need all the strength she could muster. Because she had a feeling this crisis was far from over; that Sakis would demand more from her than he ever had.

She whirled from the sink and entered the shower. By the time she'd washed the grime off her body, a semblance of calm had returned.

She dried herself and dressed quickly in a T-shirt and the short leggings she used for the gym that—thank God—she'd had the forethought to pack. If she'd been alone, the T-shirt would've sufficed but there was no way she was going out there, sharing a room with Sakis Pantelides, with a thigh-skimming T-shirt and bare legs.

The fiery sensation she'd managed to bank threatened to rise again. Quickly, she brushed her teeth, pulled her hair into its no-nonsense bun and left the bathroom.

Sakis stood outside on the tiny balcony that served the room, a drink in his hand, staring out into the sultry, humid night. His other hand was braced on the iron railing.

She paused and stared as he turned his head. His commanding profile caught and held her attention. His full lower lip was now drawn in a tight line as he stared into the contents of his glass. A wave of bleakness passed over his face and she wondered if he was replaying the journalist's question about his father.

Sakis didn't often display emotion, but she'd seen the way he'd reacted to that personal question. And his answer had been a revelation in itself. He bore no loving memories of his father but he certainly bore scars from his father's legacy.

Unbidden, the earlier wave of protectiveness resurged.

He lifted his glass and swallowed half its contents. Mesmerised, she watched his throat as he swallowed, then her gaze moved to his well-defined chest as he heaved in a huge breath.

Move! But she couldn't heed the silent command pounding

in her brain. Her feet refused to move. She was still immobilised when he swung towards the room.

He stilled, dark-green eyes zeroing in on her in that fiercely focused, extremely unnerving way.

After several seconds, his gaze travelled over her, head to bare toes, and back again. Slowly, without taking his gaze off her, he downed the rest of his drink. His tongue glided out to lick a drop from his lower lip.

The inferno stormed through her, ravaging her senses with merciless force.

No. Hell, no! This could *not* be happening.

Her fingers tightened around her bag until pain shot up her arms. With brutal force, she wrenched her gaze away, walked towards the sofa and dropped her bag beside it.

'I'm done with the bathroom. It's all yours.' She cringed at the quiver in her voice, a telling barometer of her inner turmoil. Her tablet lay where she'd left it on the table. Itching for something to do with her dangerously restless hands, she grabbed it.

He came towards her and passed within touching distance to set his glass down on the cabinet. Brianna decided breathing could wait until he was out of scenting range.

'Thanks.' He grabbed his bag and walked to the door. 'And Moneypenny?'

The need to breathe became dangerously imperative but not yet; a few more seconds, until she didn't have to breathe the same air as him. 'Yes?' she managed.

'It's time to clock off.'

The tightness in her chest grew. 'I just wanted to—'

'Turn that tablet off and put it away. That's an order.'

It was either argue with him, or breathe. The need for oxygen won out. She placed the tablet back on the table and stuffed her hands under her thighs.

Satisfaction gleamed in his eyes as he opened the bathroom door. 'Good.' His gaze darted to the bed. 'You take the bed,

I'll take the sofa,' he said. Then he entered the bathroom and shut the door behind him.

Brianna sucked in a long, sustaining breath, trying desperately to ignore the traces of Sakis's scent that lingered in the air. She eyed the bed, then the sofa.

The logic was irrefutable. She pulled out and made up the sofa bed in record time. And she made damned sure she was in it and turned away from the bathroom door by the time she heard the shower go off.

The consequences of giving lust any room was much too great to contemplate. Because giving in to her emotions, trusting it would turn to more—perhaps even the love she'd been blindingly desperate for—was what had landed her in prison.

Being in prison had nearly killed her.

Brianna had no intention of failing. No intention of sinking again.

CHAPTER FOUR

She woke to the smell of strong coffee and an empty room. Relief punched through her as she tossed the light sheet aside and rose from the sofa bed. A quick glance at the ruffled bed showed evidence of Sakis's presence but, apart from that, every last trace of him had been wiped from the room, including his bag.

Before she could investigate further, her tablet pinged with an incoming message.

Grasping it, she tried to get into the zone—business as usual. Just the way she wanted her life to run. Turning the tablet on, she went through the messages as she poured her coffee.

Two of them were from Sakis, who'd taken up residence in the conference room downstairs. Several of them were from people interested in joining the salvage process or blogging about it. But there was still no word about the missing crew.

After answering Sakis's message to join him downstairs as soon as she was ready, she tackled the most important emails, took a quick shower and dressed in a clean pair of khaki combat trousers and a cream T-shirt.

By the time she'd tied her hair into its usual French knot, the events of last night had been consigned a 'temporary aberration' status. Thankfully, she'd been asleep by the time he emerged from the bathroom and, even though she'd woken once and heard his light, even breathing, she'd managed to go back to sleep with no trouble.

Which meant she really didn't have to fear that the rhythm of their relationship had changed.

It hadn't. After this crisis was over, they would return to London and everything would go back to machine-smooth efficiency.

She shrugged on her dark-green jacket, grabbed her case and went downstairs to find Sakis on the phone in the conference room.

He indicated the extensive breakfast tray; she'd just bitten into a piece of honeyed toast when he hung up.

'The salvage crew have contained the leak in the last compartment and the transport tanker for the undamaged oil will arrive in the next few hours.'

'So the damaged tanker can be moved in the next few days?'

He nodded. 'After the International Maritime Investigation Board has completed its investigation it will be tugged back to the ship-building facility in Piraeus. And, now we have a full salvage team in place, there's no need for any remaining crew to stay. They can go home.'

Brianna nodded and brushed crumbs off her fingers. 'I'll arrange it.'

Even though she powered up her tablet ready to action his request, she felt the heat of his gaze on her face.

'You do my bidding without question when it comes to matters of the boardroom. And yet you blatantly disobeyed me last night,' he said in a low voice.

She paused mid-swallow and looked up. Arresting green eyes caught and locked onto hers. 'I'm sorry?'

He twirled a pen in his hand. 'I asked you to take the bed last night. You didn't.'

She forced herself to swallow and tried to look away. She really tried. But it seemed as if he'd charged the very air with a magnetic field that held her captive. 'I didn't think your jump-when-I-say edict extended beyond the boardroom to the bedroom, Mr Pantelides.'

Too late, she realised the indelicacy of her words. His eyes gleamed with lazy green fire. But she wasn't fooled for a second that it was harmless.

'It doesn't. When it comes to the bedroom, I like control, but I'm not averse to relinquishing it…on occasion.'

Noting that she was in serious danger of going up in flames at the torrid images that cascaded through her mind, she tried to move on. 'Logic dictated that since I'm smaller in stature the sofa would be more suited to me. I didn't see the need for chivalry to get in the way of a good night's sleep for either of us.'

One brow shot up. 'Chivalry? You think I did it out of *chivalry*?' His amusement was unmistakeable.

A damning tide of heat swept up her face. But she couldn't look away from those mesmerising eyes. 'Well, I'm sure you had your own reasons… But I thought…' She huffed. 'It doesn't really matter now, does it?'

'I suggested it because it wouldn't have been a hardship for me.'

'I'm sure it wouldn't, but you don't have a monopoly on pain and discomfort, Mr Pantelides.'

He stiffened. 'Excuse me?'

'I just meant…whatever the circumstances of your past, at least you had a mother who loved you, so it couldn't have been all bad.' She couldn't stem the vein of bitterness from bleeding into her voice, nor could she fail to realise she'd strayed dangerously far from an innocuous subject. But short of blurting out her own past this was the only way she could stop the slippery slope towards believing Sakis cared about her wellbeing.

She'd suffered a childhood hopelessly devoid of love and comfort, and the threat of a life of drugs had been an ever-present reality. Sleeping on a sofa bed was heaven in comparison.

His narrowed eyes speared into her. 'Don't mistake guilt for love, Moneypenny. I've learned over the years that this so-called love is a convenient blanket that's thrown over most feelings.'

She sucked in a breath. 'You don't think that your mother loves you?'

His jaw tightened. 'A weak love is worse than no love. When it crumbles under the weight of adversity it might as well not be present.'

Brianna's fingers tightened around her tablet as shock roiled through her. For the second time in two days, she was glimpsing a whole new facet of Sakis Pantelides.

This was a man who had hidden, painful depths that she'd barely glimpsed in all the time she'd worked for him.

'What adversity?'

He shrugged. 'My mother believed the man she *loved* could do no wrong. When the reality hit her, she chose to give up and leave her children to fend for themselves.' Casually, he flipped his pen in his hand. 'I've been taking care of myself for a very long time, Moneypenny.'

She believed him. She'd always known he possessed a hardened core of steel beneath that urbane façade, but now she knew how it'd been honed, she felt that wave of sympathy and connection again.

Ruthlessly, she tried to reel back the unravelling happening inside her.

'Thanks for sharing that with me. But the sofa was really no hardship for me either and, as long as we're both rested, that should be the end of the subject, surely?'

His eyes remained inscrutable. 'Indeed. I know when to pick my battles, Moneypenny, and I will let this one go.'

The notion that there would be other heated battles between them disturbed her in an altogether too excited way. Before she could respond, he carried on.

'You'll also be happy to know there won't be any need for me to crowd your personal space any longer. Another room has become available. I've taken it.'

Expecting strong relief, she floundered when all she felt was a hard bite of disappointment.

'Great. That's good to know.'

Her tablet pinged a message. Grateful beyond words, she jumped on it.

After breakfast they returned to the site, suited up, and joined the clean-up process. Towards mid-afternoon, she was working alongside Sakis when she felt him tense.

The pithy Greek curse he uttered didn't need translating. 'What the hell are they doing here?'

Her heart sank when she saw the TV crew. 'This is one wave we're just going to have to ride. Nothing I can do to send them away, but I may be able to get them to play nice. You just have to trust me.' The moment the words left her lips, she froze.

So did he. Trust was an issue they both had problems with. She had no business asking for his when she hid a past that could end their relationship in a heartbeat.

But slowly, the look in his eyes changed from hard-edged displeasure to appreciative gleaming. '*Efkharisto*. I have no idea what I'd do without you, Moneypenny,' he said in a low, rumbling voice.

Her heart lurched, then hammered with a force that made her fear for the integrity of her internal organs. 'That's good, because I've devised this cunning plan to make sure that you don't have to.'

A corner of his mouth rose and fell in a swift smile. His gaze dropped to her lips, then rose to recapture hers. 'When Ari threatened to poach you, I nearly knocked him out with my oar,' he said, his voice rumbling in that gravel-rough pitch that made the muscles in her stomach flutter and tighten.

'I wouldn't have gone.' Not in a million years. She loved working with Sakis, even if the last two days had sent her on a knuckle-rattling emotional rollercoaster.

'Good. You belong to me and I have no intention of letting you go. I'll personally annihilate anyone who tries to take you away from me.'

Her pulse raced faster. *Work. He's talking about your professional relationship. Not making a statement of personal intent.* Brianna forced that reminder on her erratic senses and tried to breathe normally. When her belly continued to roil, she sucked in air through her mouth.

Sakis made a small, hoarse sound in his throat. Heat arched between them, making her skin tingle and the flesh between her legs ache with desperate need.

Hastily she took a step back. 'I...I'll go and speak to the TV crew.'

She turned and fled. And with every step she prayed desperately for her equilibrium to return.

The TV crew refused to leave but agreed not to interview any member of the crew. For that she had to be content.

Sakis's meeting with the maritime disaster investigators went smoothly because he had already admitted liability and agreed to make reparations, and he barely blinked at the mind-bogglingly heavy fine they imposed on Pantelides Inc.

But his behaviour with her was anything but smooth. Throughout the meeting, Sakis would turn to her for her opinion, touch her arm to draw her attention to something he needed written down or shoot her a question. Fear coursed through her as she realised that the almost staid, rigidly professional team they'd been seventy-two hours ago had all but disappeared.

By the time the meeting concluded, she knew she was in trouble.

Sakis pushed a frustrated hand through his hair and paced the conference room, anger beating beneath his skin. The investigators had just confirmed the accident was human error.

Striding to his desk, he threw himself in the chair.

'Has Morgan Lowell's file arrived yet?' he asked Brianna.

She came towards him and he tried not to let his gaze drop to the sway of her hips. All damned day, he'd found himself checking her out. He'd even stopped asking himself what the hell was wrong with him because he knew.

Lust.

Untrammelled, bloody, lust. From the easily controlled attraction he'd felt when he'd first met her, it now threatened to drown him with every single breath he took in her presence.

She held out the information he'd asked for and he tried not to stare at the delicate bones of her wrist.

'What do we know about him?' he asked briskly.

'He's married; no children; his wife lives with his parents. As far as we can tell, he's the sole provider for his family. And he's been with the company the last four years. He came straight from the navy, where he was a commander.'

'I know all of that.' He flicked past the personal details to the work history and paused, a tingle of unease whispering down his spine. 'It says here he's refused to take leave in the last three years. And he's been married…just over three years. Why would a newly wedded man not want to be with his wife?'

'Perhaps he had something to prove, or something to hide,' came the stark, terse response.

Surprised, he glanced up. Unease slid through her blue eyes before she lowered them. He continued to stare, and right before his eyes his normally serenely professional PA became increasingly…flustered. The intrigue that had dogged him since seeing that damned tattoo on her ankle rose even higher.

He sat back in his chair. 'Interesting observation, Moneypenny. What makes you say that?'

She bit her lip and blood roared through his veins. 'I…didn't mean anything by it. Certainly nothing based on solid fact.'

'But you said it anyway. Instinctive or not, you suspect there's something else going on here, no?'

She shrugged. 'It was just a general comment, gleaned from observing natural human behaviour. Most people fall into one of those two categories. It could be that Captain Lowell falls into both.' She firmed her lips as if she wanted to prevent any more words from spilling out.

'What do you mean?' he asked. Impatience grew when she just shook her head. 'Come on, you have a theory. Let's hear it.'

'I just think the fact that both Lowell and his two deputies are missing is highly questionable. I can't think why all three would be away from the bridge and not respond when the alarm was raised.'

Ice slammed into his chest. 'The investigators think it was human error but you think it was deliberate?' Reactivating the tablet, he flicked through the rest of Morgan Lowell's work history but nothing in there threw up any red flags.

On paper, his missing captain was an extremely competent leader with solid credentials who'd piloted the Pantelides tanker efficiently for the last four years.

On paper.

Sakis knew first-hand that 'on paper' meant nothing when it came right down to it.

On paper Alexandrou Pantelides, his father, had been an honourable, hard-working and generous father to those who hadn't known better. Only Sakis, his brothers and mother had known it was a façade he presented to the world. It was only when a scorned lover had tipped off a hungry journalist who'd chosen to dig a little deeper that the truth had emerged. A truth that had unearthed a rotten trough full of discarded mistresses and shady business dealings that had overnight heaped humiliation and devastation on the innocent.

On paper Giselle had seemed an efficient, healthily ambitious executive assistant, until Sakis's rejection of her one late-night advance had unearthed a spiteful, cold-blooded, psychopathic nature that had threatened to destabilise his company's very foundation.

'On paper' meant nothing if he couldn't look into Lowell's eyes, ask what had happened and get a satisfactory answer.

'We need to find him, Moneypenny,' he bit out, bitterness replacing the ice in his chest. 'There's too much at stake here to leave this unresolved for much longer.' For one thing, the media would spin itself out of control if word of this got out. 'Contact the head of security. Tell them to dig deeper into Lowell's background.'

Sakis looked up in time to see Brianna pale a little. 'Is something wrong?' he asked.

Her mouth showed the tiniest hint of a twist. 'No.'

His gaze dropped to hands that would normally be flying over her tablet as she rushed to do his bidding. They were clasped together, unmoving. 'Something obviously is.'

Darkened eyes met his and he saw rebellion lurking in their depths. 'I don't think it's fair to dig into someone's life just because you have a hunch.'

Her words held brevity that made Sakis frown. 'Did you not suggest minutes ago that Lowell could be hiding something?'

She gave a reluctant nod.

'Then shouldn't we try and find out what that something *is*?'

'I suppose.'

'But?'

'I think he deserves for his life not to be turned inside out on a hunch. And I'm sorry if I gave you the impression that was what I wanted, because it's not.'

A tic throbbed in his temple. Restlessness made him shove away from the desk. His stride carried him to the window and back to the desk next to where she sat, unmoving fingers resting on her tablet.

'Sometimes we have to bear the consequences of unwanted scrutiny for the greater good.' As much as he'd detested the hideous fallout, having his father's true colours exposed had ultimately been to his benefit. He'd learned to look beneath the surface. Always.

She looked at him. 'You're advocating something that you hated having done to you. How did you feel when your family's secrets were exposed to the whole world?'

Shock slammed into him at her sheer audacity. Planting his hands on the desk, he lowered his head until his gaze was level with hers. '*Excuse me?* What the hell do you think you know about my family?' he rasped.

She drew back a touch but her gaze remained unflinching. 'I know what happened with your father when you were a teenager. The Internet makes information impossible to hide. And your reaction to the tabloid hack's question yesterday—'

'There was *no* reaction.'

'I was there. I saw how much you hated it.' Her voice was soft with sympathy.

The idea of being pitied made his fist tighten on the table.

'And you think this should make me bury my head in the sand about Lowell?'

'No, I'm just saying that turning his life inside out doesn't feel right. Since you've been in his shoes—'

'Since I don't know anything more than what his human resources file says, that's a lofty conclusion to draw. And, unlike what you think you know about me and my family, what I find out about Captain Lowell won't find its way to the tabloid press or any social media forum for the world at large to feast over and make caricatures out of. So I say no, there is *nothing* even remotely similar between the two situations.'

She drew in a slow, steady breath. 'If you say so.' Her gaze dropped and she pulled the tablet towards her.

Sakis stayed exactly where he was, the urge to invade her space further an almighty need that stomped through him. In the last twenty-four hours, his PA had acted out of character, challenged him in ways she'd never done before.

The incident with the tent and the sleeping on the sofa bed, he was willing to let go. This latest challenge—breaching the taboo subject of his father—should've made him fire her on the spot. But, as much as he hated to admit it, she was right. The journalist's question *had* shaken him and unearthed volcanic feelings he preferred masked.

In silence, he watched her compose a succinct email to his security chief, stating his exact wishes.

The electronic 'whoosh' of the outgoing email perforated the silence in the conference room. It was as if the very air was holding its breath.

Brianna raised her head after setting the tablet down. 'Is there anything else?'

His gaze traced over her. A tendril of hair had escaped its tight prison and caressed the wild pulse beating in her neck. His fingers tingled with the need to smooth it away and trace the pulse with his fingers; to keep tracing down the length of her sleek neck to the delicate collarbone hidden beneath her T-shirt.

'You disagree with what I'm doing?'

Her full pink lips firmed. That dimple winked again. His groin tightened unbearably.

'Privacy is a right and I detest those who breach it. I know you do too, so I'm struggling with this a little, but I also get why it needs to be done. I also apologise if I stepped out of line but…I trust you when you say you won't let it fall into unscrupulous hands.'

Her last words drilled down and touched a soft place inside him, soothed the ruffled edge of his nerves a little. 'You have my word that whatever we discover about Lowell will be held in strictest confidence.' The knowledge that he was reassuring her, was justifying his behaviour to his assistant, threw him a little, as did the knowledge that he *wanted* her to approve of what he was doing. He pushed the feeling away as she nodded.

The movement slid the silky hair against her nape. The

soft scent of her crushed-lilies shampoo hit his nostrils and his fingers renewed their mad tingling.

'And, Moneypenny?'

She glanced up. This close, her eyes were even more enthralling. His heart raced and his blood rushed south with a need so forceful, he sucked in a shocked breath.

'Yes?' Her lips were parted, the tip of her wet tongue peeking through even teeth.

Sakis struggled to remember what he'd meant to say. 'I don't trust easily but that doesn't mean I don't appreciate people who place their trust in me. In all the time you've worked for me, you've proved yourself trustworthy and someone I can rely on. Your help especially in the past two days has been priceless. Thank you.'

Her eyed widened. God, she was beautiful. How the hell had he never noticed that?

'Of…of course, Mr Pantelides.'

Curiously, she paled a little bit more. Sakis frowned then chalked it down to exhaustion. They'd both been driven by dire circumstances to the pinnacle of their endurance. He needed to let her go to her room instead of crouching over her like some dark lord about to demand a virgin sacrifice.

He grimaced and stepped back, slamming down the need to stay where he was. Tension stretched over every of inch of his skin until he felt taut and uncommonly sensitive. 'I think we find ourselves in a unique enough situation where it's okay for you to call me Sakis.'

She shook her head. 'No.'

His brow shot up. 'Just…*no*?'

'I'm sorry, but I can't.' Edging away from him, she sprang to her feet. 'If that's all you need tonight, I'll say goodnight.'

'Goodnight…Brianna.' Her name sounded like the sweetest temptation on his lips.

She hesitated. 'I would really prefer it if you kept calling me Moneypenny,' she said.

Immediate refusal rose to his lips. Until he remembered he was supposed to be her unimpeachable boss, not a demanding lover who was at this moment repeating her given name over and over in his mind. 'Very well. See you in the morning, Moneypenny.'

He straightened from the table and watched her walk away, her pert bottom tight and deliciously curvy beneath her khaki pants, causing blood to rush hot and fast southward.

He still sported a hard-on that wouldn't die when his phone rang in his suite an hour later. He stopped pacing his small balcony long enough to snag it from the coffee table where he'd dumped it.

'Pantelides.'

The short conversation that ensued made him curse long and fluently for several minutes after he hung up.

CHAPTER FIVE

THE FIRM HAMMERING on her door made Brianna's already racing heart threaten to knock itself into early retirement. Considering the way it'd been racing for the past hour—ever since her wits had deserted her in the conference room—it would've been merciful.

What the hell had she been *thinking*?

Hard knuckles gave the wooden door another impatient workout.

Consciously loosening her tense shoulders, she blew out a reassuring breath and forced composure back into her body. The hastily pulled together bland look was in place when she answered the door.

Sakis stood on the threshold, frowning down at his phone.

'What's wrong?' she asked before she could stop herself. The feeling that passed through her, she recognised as worry, a curiously recurring feeling over the past two days. *Not cool, Brianna.* In fact, a wincingly large percentage of her reactions today had been…off. From the moment he'd stared down at her and told her in that mesmerising voice, 'I don't know what I'd do without you,' her judgement had been skewed.

Watching him pace with mounting frustration all day, wishing there was something she could do, had rammed home the fact that her professional equanimity was still very much in jeopardy.

Now…now he looked as if he'd clawed frustrated fingers

through his hair several times. And the lines bracketing his mouth had deepened. She cleared her throat.

'I mean, is there something you need, Mr Pantelides?'

His gaze flicked over her then returned to her face. 'You haven't changed for bed yet. Good. The pilot is readying the chopper for take-off in fifteen minutes.'

'Take-off?'

His hand tightened around the phone as it signalled another incoming message. 'We're leaving for the airport. I've called an emergency meeting first thing in the morning back in London.'

'We're returning to London? But…why?'

His lips firmed. 'It seems more vultures are circling over our disaster.'

Stunned, she stared at him. The thought that anyone would want to challenge Sakis Pantelides at any time, let alone when he was at his most edgy and dangerous, made her doubt his opponent's sanity. 'Media or corporate?'

His smile was deadly. 'Corporate. I'm guessing the usual suspects who chest-thump every now and then will be feeling bolder in light of the slumping share price as a result of the tanker accident.'

She retrieved the bag she'd left at the foot of her bed. 'But the shares have started to recover again after the initial nose-dive. Your statement and the very public admission of liability made it stabilise very quickly. Why would they…?'

'News of a takeover bid would make it plunge again and that's what they're counting on.' His phone pinged again and he growled. 'Especially if two of those companies are announcing their intended merger in the morning.'

He cursed in Greek, using a particular word that made heat rise to her cheeks as she dove into the bathroom for her toiletries bag.

'Which two companies?' she called out as she zipped up

her bag and checked the room to make sure she hadn't left anything important.

Exiting, she saw the lines of fatigue etched into his face and her heart lurched.

'Moorecroft Oil and Landers Petroleum.'

It was only because he'd turned away, his attention once more on this phone, that Sakis didn't see she'd stopped dead in her tracks; that the blood had drained from her face with a swiftness that made her dizzy for a moment.

It couldn't be. No. It had to be pure coincidence that the petroleum company shared the same name with Greg, her ex-boyfriend. Landers was a fairly common name…wasn't it? Besides, Greg's company when she'd been a part of it before he'd struck the deal that had doomed her, had been a gas-brokering company; a company that had since declared bankruptcy. And certainly not one large enough to take on the juggernaut that was Pantelides Shipping.

'I'd like to get out of here this side of— Brianna? What's wrong?'

For goodness' sake, pull yourself together!

Dry-mouthed and heart thumping, Brianna forced herself to breathe. 'Nothing; it's the heat, I think.'

Keen eyes scoured her face and gentled a fraction as he pocketed his phone. 'Not to mention the lack of sleep. My apologies for dragging you off like this. You can sleep on the plane.'

Stepping forward, he held out his hand for her bag. Their fingers touched, lingered. Heat shot through her and she hastily pulled back from the scorching contact. Swallowing, she followed him out and shut the door behind her. 'I'll be fine. And you'll need me to find out everything we can about the two companies.' Not to mention *she* needed to know whether Greg had anything to do with Landers Petroleum.

The thought that he might have started another company,

might be cultivating another patsy the same way he'd culti-vated her, made her stomach lurch sickeningly.

Could she alert Sakis without drawing attention to her-self? Out herself as the needy woman, so desperate for love she hadn't seen the trap set for her until it'd been too late?

Her belly churned with fear and anxiety as they left the hotel and rode the short helicopter journey to the private han-gar at Agostinho Neto airport.

Dear God. She could lose everything.

The thought sent a shudder so strong, she stumbled over her own feet a few steps from the airplane.

Sakis caught her arm and steadied her. Then his fingers dropped to encircle her wrist, keeping a firm hold on her as he mounted the steps into the plane.

She swallowed down the wholly different trepidation that stemmed from having Sakis's hand on her. She tried to pull away, but he held on until they stood before the guest-cabin bedroom opposite the plane's master suite. He opened the door and set her bag down just inside it, then led her back to the seating area.

At Sakis's signal, the pilot shut the door.

'Buckle up. Right after we take off, we're going to bed.'

Her mouth dropped open as her pulse shot sky- high. *'I beg your pardon?'* she squeaked. Her whole body throbbed and she couldn't glance away from his disturbingly direct gaze.

His grim smile held a wealth of masculine arrogance as he shoved a frustrated hand through his hair. Taking his seat op-posite her, he set his phone—which had thankfully stopped pinging—on a nearby table. 'A…poor choice of words, Mon-eypenny. What I mean is, it's the middle of the night in Lon-don. Not much we can do from here.'

'I can still pull up as much information as I can on the companies…'

He shook his head. 'I already have people working on that. You need to get some sleep. I need you sharp and—'

'You need to stop treating me like some fragile flower and let me do my job!'

Moss-green eyes narrowed. 'Excuse me?'

Anger lent her voice desperation and she leaned forward, hands planted on the table separating them. The fact that this close she could almost touch the stubble layering his hard, chiselled jaw and see the darker, mesmerising flecks in his irises sparked another tingle of awareness through her. But the remotest possibility that Greg could be lurking in the periphery of her life, ready to expose her, made her stand her ground.

She'd gone through too much, sacrificing everything she had to prevent her debilitating weakness from being exposed. She no longer needed love. She'd learned that she could live without it. What she couldn't live with was having her previous sins exposed to Sakis Pantelides.

'You seem to think I need a full night's sleep or a warm bed to function properly, but that couldn't be farther from the truth.' Warning bells rang in her head, telling her seriously to apply brakes on her runaway mouth. But she couldn't help herself. 'I've slept in places where I had to keep one eye open or risk losing more than just the clothes on my back. So please don't treat me like some pampered princess who needs her beauty sleep or she'll go to pieces.'

His eyes narrowed, followed almost instantly by a keen speculation that screamed what was coming next. 'When did you sleep rough?' His voice was low, husky, full of unabashed curiosity.

Alarm bells shrieked harder, in tandem with the jet engines powering for take-off. Sharp memories rose, images of drug dens and foul-smelling narcotics bringing nausea she fought to keep down. 'It doesn't matter.'

He leaned forward on his elbows and stared her down. 'Yes, it does. Answer me.'

'It was a very long time ago, Mr Pantelides.'

'Sakis,' he commanded in that low, deep tone that sent a shiver through her.

Again she shook her head. 'Let's just say my childhood wasn't as rosy as the average child's, but I pulled through.'

'You were an orphan?' he probed.

'No, I wasn't, but I might as well have been.' Because her junkie mother had been no use to herself, never mind the child she'd given birth to. The remembered pain bruised her insides and unshed tears burned the backs of her eyes. She blinked rapidly to stop them falling but a furtive glance showed Sakis had noticed the crack in her composure.

The plane lifted off the ground and shot into the starlit sky.

Sakis's gaze remained on her for long minutes. 'Do you want to talk about it?' he asked gently.

Brianna's heart hammered harder. 'No.' She'd already said too much, revealed far more than was wise. Deliberately unclenching her fists, she prayed he would let the matter rest.

The jet started to level out. Snatching his phone from the table, Sakis nodded and unbuckled his seatbelt. 'Regardless of your protests, you need to sleep.' He held out his hand to her. The look on his face told her nothing but her acquiescence would please him.

Immensely relieved that he wasn't probing into her past any longer, she thought it wise to stifle further protest. Unbuckling her seatbelt, she placed her hand in his and stood. 'If I do, then so do you.'

His smile was unexpected. And breath-stealing. Heat churned within her belly, sending an arrow of need straight between her thighs.

'We've dovetailed right back to the very point I was trying to make. I have every intention of getting some sleep. Even super-humans like me deserve some down time.'

A smile tugged at her lips. 'That's a relief. You were beginning to show us mere mortals up.'

His smile turned into an outright laugh, his face transforming into such a spectacular vision of gorgeousness that her breath caught. Then her whole body threatened to spontaneously combust when his hand settled at her waist. With a firm nudge, he guided her back down the aisle.

'No one in their right mind would call you a mere mortal, Moneypenny. You've proved beyond any doubt that you're the real thing—an exceptionally gifted individual with a core of integrity that most ambitious people lose by the time they reach your age.'

At the door to her cabin, she turned to face him, her heart hammering hard enough to make her head hurt a little. 'I think what you've done since the tanker crashed shows you're willing to go above and beyond what most people would do in the same circumstances. *That* is integrity.'

His gaze dropped to her lips, lingered there in a way that turned her body furnace hot. 'Hmm, is this the start of an exclusive mutual admiration society?'

The breath she'd never quite managed to recapture fractured even further. When his eyes dropped lower, her nipples tightened, stung into life by green fire that lurked in those depths. Reaching behind her, she grasped the doorknob, desperate for something to cling to.

'I'm just trying to point out that I'm nothing special, Mr Pantelides. I just try to be very good at my job.'

His gaze recaptured hers. 'I beg to differ. I think you're very special.' He stepped closer and his scent filled her nostrils. 'It's also obvious no one has told you that enough.' The hand that still rested at her waist slid away to cover the hand she'd gripped on the door. Using the pressure of hers, he turned the knob. 'When this is all over, I'll make a point to show you just how special you are.'

The door gave way behind her and she swayed backward, barely managing to catch herself before she stumbled. 'You… don't have to. Really, you don't.'

His smile was a touch strained and he braced his hands

on the doorjamb as if forcibly stopping himself from entering the room. 'You say you're not special and yet you refuse even the promise of a reward where most people would be making a list.'

'I work for one of the most forward-thinking men in one of the best organisations in the world. That's reward enough.'

'Careful, there; you're in danger of swelling my ego to unthinkable proportions.'

'Is that a bad thing?' She wasn't sure where the need for banter came from but her breath caught when his sensual lips curved in a dangerously sexy smile.

'At a time when everything around me seems to be falling apart, it could be a lethal thing.' His gaze shot to the bed and his smile slipped a fraction, in proportion to the escalating strain on his face. 'Time for you to hit the sack. *Kalispera*, Brianna,' he murmured softly before, stepping back abruptly, he strode to his own door.

At the click of his door shutting, Brianna stumbled forward and sagged onto the bed, her knees turned to water.

She glanced down at her shaking hands as reality hit her square in the face.

Sakis Pantelides found her attractive. She wasn't naïve enough to mistake the look in his eyes, nor was she going to waste time contemplating the *why*. It was there, like a ticking time bomb between them, one she needed to diffuse before the unthinkable happened.

Brianna could only hope that, once they were back on familiar ground, things would return to normal.

They had to. Because, frankly, she was terrified of what she would let happen if they didn't.

Sakis stood under the cold shower and cursed fluidly. *Theos.* I seemed as if he'd spent the last forty-eight hours cursing in one form or the other. Right now, he cursed the rigid erection that seemed determined to defy the frigid temperature.

He wanted to have sex with Brianna Moneypenny. Wanted to shut off the shower, stride next door, strip the clothes off her body and drive into her with a grinding force that defied rhyme or reason.

He slapped his palm against the soaked tile and cursed some more. Gritting his teeth, his hand dropped to grip his erection. A single stroke made him groan out loud. Another stroke, and his knees threatened to buckle.

With an angry grunt, he dropped his hand and turned the shower off. He was damned if he was going to fondle himself like an over-eager teenager. Things were fraught for sure. That and the fact that he hadn't had sex in months was messing with his mental faculties, making him contemplate paths he would never otherwise have done. For God's sake, sex had no place in his immediate to-do list.

What he needed to do was focus on getting the threat of a takeover annihilated and the situation at Pointe Noire brought under control.

Once they were back on familiar ground, things would return to normal.

He ruthlessly silenced the voice that mocked him not to be so sure…

Three hours later, Brianna sat wide awake in her luxurious cabin bed, staring through a porthole at the pitch-black night that rested on a bed of white clouds. She'd left her tablet in one of the two briefcases she'd seen the stewardess stow in Sakis's cabin. Short of knocking on his door and asking for it, she had nothing to do but sit here, her thoughts jumbling into a mass of anxiety at what awaited her in London.

She had no doubt Sakis would trounce the takeover bid into smithereens—he was too skilled a businessman not to have anticipated such a move. And he was too calculating not to have the answers at his fingertips.

All the same, Greg had proved, much to her shock and disbelief, that he was just as ruthless—and without a single ounce of integrity—and she shuddered at the chaos he could bring to Sakis should he be given the opportunity.

Her shoulder tingled as her tattoo burned. Raising her hand, she slid her fingers under her light T-shirt and touched the slightly raised words etched into her skin.

Greg had succeeded in taking away her livelihood once; had come terrifyingly close to destroying her soul.

There was no way she could rest until she made sure he wasn't a threat to Sakis and to her. Not that he had any reason to seek her out. No, she was the gullible scapegoat he'd led to the slaughter—then walked away from scot-free. The last thing he'd expect was for her to have risen from the ashes of the fire he'd thrown her in.

That was how she wanted things to stay. Once upon a time, she'd harboured feelings of revenge and retribution; how could she not, when she'd been stuck in an six-by-eight dark space, racked alternatively with fear and deep bitterness? But those feelings had burned themselves out.

Now she just wanted to be Brianna Moneypenny, executive assistant to Sakis Pantelides, the most dynamically sexy, astoundingly intelligent man she knew.

A man she'd come disastrously close to kissing more than once in the last forty-eight hours…

No. Her fingers pressed down harder over the tattoo, letting the pain of each word restore her equilibrium.

Nothing had changed.

Nothing *could* change.

The board members were gathered in the large, grey mosaic-tiled conference room on the fiftieth floor of Pantelides Towers, the iconic, futuristically designed building poised on the edge of the River Thames.

Sakis strode in at seven o'clock sharp. He nodded to the

men around the table and the three executives video-conferencing in on three wide screens.

Brianna's heart thumped as she followed him in. She had no idea if the information-gathering Sakis had implemented before they'd boarded the plane had yielded any results. He didn't know either—she'd asked him. Only the files currently placed in front of each executive held the answer as to whether Greg Landers was in part behind this hostile takeover bid.

Seeing a spare copy on the stationery table off to one side of the boardroom, Brianna moved towards it.

'I won't need you for this meeting. Return to the office. I'll come and find you when I'm done.'

Shock ricocheted through her. She barely managed to keep it from showing on her face. 'Are you sure? I can—'

His jaw tensed. 'I think we've already established that you're invaluable to me. Please don't overplay your hand, Moneypenny. Otherwise alarm bells will start ringing.'

The tight grit behind his words took her aback. It was the same tone he'd used since he'd emerged from his cabin an hour before they'd landed. His whole façade was icily aloof and the potent sexual charge that had surrounded them a few short hours before, the fire in his eyes as he'd looked at her outside her cabin on the plane, was nowhere in sight.

She held her breath for the relief that confirmed that things were back to normal, only to experience a painful pang of disconcerting disappointment, immediately followed by a more terrifying notion.

Did Sakis know? Had he somehow found out about her past? She stared at him but his expression gave nothing away, certainly nothing that indicated he knew her deepest, darkest secret.

He didn't know. She'd been much too careful in exorcising her past; had used every last penny she'd owned two years ago to ensure there would be no coming back from what she'd been before.

All the same, it took a huge effort to swallow the lump in her throat. 'I don't… I'm not sure I know what you're talking about. I'm only trying to do—'

'Your job. I know. But right now your job isn't here. I need you to take point on the situation on Point Noire. Make sure the media are kept in line and the investigators update us on developments. I don't want the ball dropped on this. Can you handle that?'

Her gaze slid to the file marked confidential lying so innocuously on the table, fear and trepidation eating away inside her. Then she forced her gaze to meet his. 'Of course.'

The hard glint in his eyes softened a touch. 'Good. I'll see you in a few hours. Or sooner, if anything needs my attention.'

He stepped into the room and the electronic door slid shut behind him. Brianna gasped at the bereft feeling that hollowed out her stomach.

He isn't shutting you out. It's just a delicate situation that needs careful handling.

Nevertheless, as she walked back towards her office and desk situated just outside Sakis's massive office suite, she couldn't help but feel like she'd lost a part of her functioning self.

Ridiculous.

For the next several hours, she threw herself into her work. At two o'clock on the button, her phone rang.

'I haven't had an update in four hours,' came Sakis's terse demand.

'That's because everything's in hand. You have enough on your plate without resorting to micro-management,' she snapped, then bit her lip. She was letting her anxiety get the better of her. 'What I mean is, you have the right people in place to deal with this. Let them do their jobs. It's what you pay them for, after all.'

'Duly noted.' A little bit of the terseness had leached from his voice but the strain still remained. She could barely hold back from asking the question burning on her lips: *is Greg Landers one of those challenging to take over Pantelides Shipping*? 'Update me anyway.'

'The tug boat is on site and preparing to move the tanker away. The salvage crew co-ordinator tells me our marine biologist is providing invaluable advice, so we scored big there.'

'*You* scored big.' His voice had dropped lower, grown more intimate. A fresh tingle washed over her.

'Um…I guess. The social media campaign has garnered almost a million followers and the feedback shows a high percentage support Pantelides Shipping's stance on the salvage and clean-up process. The blogger is doing a superb job, too.'

'Brianna?'

'Yes?'

'I'm glad I took your advice about the media campaign. It's averted a lot of the bad press we could've had with this crash.'

Her normal, professional, politically correct answer faded on her tongue. Heart hammering, she gripped the phone harder and spoke from the heart. 'I care about this company. I didn't want to see its reputation suffer.'

'Why? Why do you care?' His voice had dropped even lower.

'You…you gave me a chance when I thought I would have none. You could've chosen someone else from over a hundred applicants for this job. You chose me. I don't take that lightly.'

'Don't sell yourself short, Brianna. I didn't pick your name out of a box. I picked you because you're special. And you continue to prove to me every day what a valuable asset you are.'

She loved the way he said her name. The realisation sent a pulse of heat rushing through her.

'Thank you, Mr Pantelides.'

'Sakis,' came the rumbled response.

She shook her head in immediate refusal, even though he couldn't see her. 'N…no,' she finally managed.

'I *will* get you to call me Sakis before very long.' His voice held a rough texture that made her tremble.

Closing her eyes, she forced herself to breathe and focus. 'How are things going with the…the board meeting?'

'Most of the key players have been identified. I've fired the warning shot. They can heed it or they can choose to come at me again.' His words held a distinct relish that made her think he almost welcomed the challenge of his authority. Sakis was a man who needed an outlet for his passions, hence the rowing when he could, and the fully equipped gyms in his penthouse and homes all around the world.

He would be just as passionate in the bedroom. She hurriedly pushed the thought away.

'Have we heard anything else?' he asked, his voice turning brisk once more.

She knew he meant the missing crew. 'No, nothing. The search parameters have been widened.' And because she feared what would spill from her lips if she hung on, she said, 'I need to make a few more phone calls; rearrange your schedule…'

He went silent for several seconds, then he sighed. 'If Lowell's wife calls, put her straight through to me.'

'I will.' She hung up quickly before she could ask about what he'd found out. Unwilling even to think of it, she threw herself back to her work.

At six, the executive chef Sakis employed for his senior staff poked his head through her office door and asked if she wanted dinner.

She rolled her shoulders, registered the stiffness in her body and shook her head.

'I'm going to hit the gym first, Tom. Then I'll forage for myself, thanks.'

He nodded and left.

Picking up her phone and tablet, she quickly made her way via the turbo lift to the sixtieth floor, where Sakis's private multi-roomed penthouse suites were located. There were six suites in total, four separate and two inter-connected. Sakis used the largest suite which was linked by a set of double doors to her own suite when she stayed here. From this high, the view across London's night sky was stunning. The Opera House gleamed beneath the iconic London Eye, with the Oxo Tower's famous lights glittering over the South Bank.

She took the shortcut through Sakis's living room, her feet slowing as they usually did when confronted with the visually stunning architectural design of the penthouse.

One side was taken up by a rough sandstone wall dominated by a huge fireplace regulated by a computerised temperature monitor. Directly in front of the fireplace, large slate-coloured, square-shaped sofas were grouped around an enormous stark white rug, which was the only covering on the highly polished marble floors.

Beyond the seating area, on carefully selected pedestals and on the walls were displayed works of art ranging from an exquisite pair of katanas, said to have belonged to a notorious Samurai, to a post-impressionist painting by Rousseau that galleries around the world vied for the opportunity to exhibit.

Moving towards her own suite, her gaze was drawn outside to the gleaming infinity pool that stretched out beyond the gleaming windows. The first time she'd seen it, she'd gasped with awe and thanked her lucky stars that she didn't suffer from vertigo when Sakis had shown her around the large deck where the only protection from the elements was a steel and glass railing.

From this high up, the Thames was a dark ribbon inter-spersed by centuries-old bridges, and from where she stood she could almost make out the Tube station where she caught the train to her flat.

Her flat. Her sanctuary. The place she hadn't been for days. The place she could lose if Sakis ever found out who she really was.

Her spine straightened as she approached the large wooden swivel door that led to her suite.

As long as she had breath in her body she would fight for what she'd salvaged from the embers of her previous life. Greg wouldn't be allowed to win a second time.

Entering the bedroom where Sakis had insisted she kept a fully furnished wardrobe in case he needed to travel with her at short notice, she changed into her pair of three-quarter-length Lycra training shorts and a cropped T-shirt.

She pounded the treadmill for half an hour, until endorphins pumped through her system and sweat poured off her skin. Next she tackled the elliptical trainer.

She was in the middle of stretching before hitting the weights when Sakis walked in.

He stopped at the sight of her. His hair was severely ruffled, the result of running his hands through the short strands several times, and he'd loosened his tie, along with a few buttons. Between the gaping cotton, she saw silky hairs that bisected his deep, chiselled chest.

Their eyes clashed through the mirrors lining two sides of the room, before his gaze left her to slowly traverse over her body.

Brianna froze, very much aware her breath was caught somewhere in her solar plexus. And that her leg was caught behind her, mid-stretch. The hand braced against the mirror trembled as his gaze visibly darkened with a hunger that echoed the sensation spiking up through her pelvis.

'Don't let me interrupt you,' he drawled as he went to the cooler and plucked a bottle of water off the shelf. Leaning against the rung of bars holding the weights, he stared at her as he drank deeply straight from the bottle.

She tried not to let her eyes devour the sensual movement of his throat as he swallowed. With a deep breath that cost her every ounce of self-control she possessed, she lifted and grabbed her other foot behind her, extending her body into a taut stretch, while studiously avoiding his gaze.

She'd never been more aware of the tightness of her gym clothes or the sheen of sweat coating her skin. Thankfully, she'd secured her hair so tight it hadn't escaped its bun…yet.

Sinking low, she extended in a sideways stretch that made her inner thigh muscles scream. Her heartbeat was hammering so loudly in her ears, she was sure she'd imagined Sakis's sharp indrawn breath.

Silence grew around them until she couldn't bear being the sole focus of his gaze. Rising after her last stretch, she contemplated the wisdom of approaching where he stood, right in front of the weights she needed.

Contemplated and abandoned the idea. Instead, she mimicked him and went to the well-stocked fridge for a bottle of water. 'How did the rest of the board meeting go?' she asked to fill the heavy silence.

Sakis tossed the empty bottle in the recycle bin, pulled his tie free, rolled it up and stuffed it in his trouser pocket. 'I had no doubt we would find the relevant weak points. Everyone has skeletons in their closets, Moneypenny. Things they don't want anyone else to discover. Growing up as a Pantelides taught me that.' His voice was pure steel, but she caught the underlying thread of pain beneath it.

She wanted to offer comforting words but the mention of skeletons sliced her with apprehension, tightening her insides so she could barely breathe. 'What sort of skeletons?'

'The usual. In this case, less than stellar financial record-keeping; one or two shady dealings that deserve closer scrutiny.'

'Are…are we talking about Landers Petroleum?' She held her breath.

'No.' He dismissed them with a wave of his hand. 'They're small fry compared to Moorecroft Oil and were probably hitching their wagon to the big boys in hopes of a large payday. For now, I'm more interested in Moorecroft. They're the ones who started this, but they should've cleaned up their own backyard before attempting to sully mine. Tomorrow morning, their CEO, Richard Moorecroft, will be receiving a call from the Financial Conduct Authority. He'll need to answer a few hairy questions.'

She told herself it was too early to hope this was over but she allowed herself a tiny breath of relief. 'And…you think that's the end of it?'

His hand went to the next unopened button and slid it free. 'If they know what's good for them. If they don't and they keep sabre-rattling, things will just get decidedly…dirtier.'

'You mean you'll dig deeper,' she murmured, unable to take her gaze off the hands slowly revealing more and more of his mouth-watering torso. 'What are you doing?' she gasped, her fist tightening around the plastic bottle as another bolt of heat drilled through her belly. It cracked under the force of her fist, echoing loudly through the room.

'Taking a leaf out of your book.' He shrugged out of his shirt, balled it up and threw it into the corner.

'I… But…'

He paused, his hand on his belt. 'Does my body make you uncomfortable, Moneypenny?'

Her tongue threatened to not work. 'You've undressed in front of me many times.'

'That wasn't what I asked you.' The belt slid free.

Arousal roared to life, tightening her nipples into deliciously painful points, weakening her knees, shooting fiery sensation between her legs. 'W…what does it matter? I'm invisible, remember? You've never seen me in the past.'

He came forward, his long legs eating up the short distance between them until he stood in front of her.

'Only because I've trained myself not to look…not to betray the slightest interest. Not since…' He paused, lips pursed. Then, shaking off whatever thought he'd had, he shrugged.

'You're not invisible to me now. I see you. *All* of you.' His gaze slid down, paused and caressed the valley between her breasts, before reaching out to boldly stroke the hard, pointed crests. Her needy gasp made him caress her more intimately, rolling her nipple between his fingers until she had to bite her lip hard to keep from crying out. 'And just like I knew you would be like…a potent wine, promising intoxication even before the first sip.'

Reason tried to surge forth through the miasma of sensation shaking her very foundations. But her body had a mind of its own. It swayed towards him but she managed to stop herself from taking the fatal step.

'I wouldn't really know. I…I don't drink.' Another ruthless stance she'd taken since Greg. That last night before the police had crashed in and carted her away, he'd plied her with vintage champagne and caviar. She'd been so drunk she'd been barely coherent when her life had taken a nosedive into hell.

'My, what a virtuous life you lead, Moneypenny. Do you have any vices *at all*? Apart from your pancakes, that is?'

'None that I wish to divulge,' she responded before she managed to stop herself.

Sakis gave a low, rich laugh that soaked into her senses before fizzing pleasure along her nerve endings. 'I find that infinitely intriguing.' His gaze dropped to her mouth in a blatant, heated caress. His lips parted and a slow rush of breath hissed through them. Slowly, almost leisurely, he stepped closer, bringing his body heat within singeing distance.

Move, Brianna!

Her feet finally heeded the frenzied warning fired by her brain but she'd barely taken a step when Sakis reached out. He caught her around the waist and brought her flush against him.

The contact fired through her, so powerful and potent, she lost her footing. One strong hand cupped her chin and raised her head to his merciless gaze. In his eyes, she read dangerous intent that made her stomach hollow with anticipation and feverish need, even as the last functioning brain cells shrieked for her to fight against the dangerous sensations.

'I'm going to kiss you now, Moneypenny,' Sakis breathed. 'It's not wise and it probably won't be safe.'

'Then you shouldn't do it…' She half-pleaded but already wet heat oozed between her thighs.

He gave a half-pained groan. 'I can't seem to stop myself.'

'Mr Pantelides—'

'Sakis. Say it. Say my name.'

She shook her head.

His head dropped another fraction. 'You're doing it again.'

'D-doing what?'

'Refusing to obey me.'

'We're no longer in the office.'

'Which is all the more reason why we should drop formalities. Say my name, Brianna.'

The way he said her name, the soft stresses on the vowels, made her insides clench hard. She tried desperately to fight against the overwhelming sensation. 'No.'

He walked her back until he had her pinned between the gym wall and the solid column of his hot body. The hard muscles of his bare chest were torture against her heavy breasts but it was the firm, unmistakeable imprint of his erection against her belly that made her stop breathing.

'Luckily for you, the need to taste you overwhelms the need to command your obedience.' His lips brushed hers in the fleetest of caresses. 'But I *will* hear you say it before very long.'

Eyelids too heavy to sustain fluttered downwards. Drowsy with lust, she fought to answer him. 'Don't count on it. I have a few rules of my own. This is one of them.'

The very tip of his tongue traced her lower lip, again with the fleetest of touches, and the fiery blaze of need raged through her. 'What's another?'

'Not to get involved with the boss.'

'Hmm, that's one I agree with.'

'Then…what are you *doing*?' she asked plaintively.

'Proving that this isn't more than temporary insanity.' His voice reflected the dazed confusion she felt.

'Won't walking away prove the same thing? As you said, this might not be exactly wise.'

'Or this is nothing but a no-big-deal kiss. It'll only become a big deal if we aren't able to handle what happens afterwards.'

No big deal. Was it really? And would it hurt to experience just a kiss? They were both clothed…well, he was technically only half-clothed…but she could put the brakes on this any time she wanted…couldn't she?

'Afterwards?' she blurted.

'Yes, when we go back to what we are. You'll continue to be the aficionado who runs my business life and I'll be the boss who demands too much of you.'

'Or we could stop this right now. Pretend it never happened?'

A hard gleam entered his eyes. 'Pretence has never been my style. I leave that to people who wish to hide their true colours; who want the world to perceive them as something other than what they are. I detest people like that, Moneypenny.' His mouth dropped another centimetre closer, his hands tightening around her waist as his eyes darkened with hot promise. 'It's why I won't pretend that the thought of kissing you, of being inside you, hasn't been eating me alive these past few days. It's also why I know neither of us will misconstrue this. Because you're above pretence. You're exactly who you say you are. Which is why I appreciate you so much.'

He kissed her then, his mouth devouring hers with a hunger so wild, so ferocious, it melted every single thought from her head.

Which was fortunate. Because otherwise she wouldn't have been able to stop herself from showing her reaction to his stark words; from blurting out that she was not even remotely who he thought she was.

CHAPTER SIX

SAKIS FELT HER moan of desire shudder through her sexy body and groaned in return. *Theos*, he'd been so determined not to be seen by another woman in the work environment in the way that Giselle had portrayed him in court and in the media that he'd deliberately blinded himself to just how sexy, how utterly feminine and incredibly gorgeous, Brianna was. Now he let his reeling senses register her attributes—the hands' span soft but firm curve of her bare waist underneath his fingers; the saucy shape of her bottom and the way the supple globes felt in his hands.

And *Theos*, her mouth! Delicious and silky soft, it was pure torture just imagining it around the hard, stiff part of his anatomy. Sure enough, the image slammed into his brain, firing the mother lode of all sex bombs straight to his groin.

He wanted her with a depth that seriously disturbed him. He wanted her spread underneath him, naked and needy, in endless positions...

She gave a hitched cry as his tongue breached her sweet plump lips and mercilessly plunged in. He was being too rough. His brain fired at him to slow down but he couldn't pull back. He'd had a taste of her but somehow that first taste had demanded a second, a third...

He pressed down harder, demanding more of her. His hips ground into her lower body until he was fully cradled between her thighs but even that wasn't enough. His hands cupped her breasts and another shudder raked through her as his fingers tweaked her nipples. Blood roared through his ears at the thought of tasting them, of suckling them, tugging on them with his teeth.

When her hands finally rose to clutch his bare shoulders, when her nails dug into his skin, the rush of lust was so potent he feared he'd pass out there and then.

What the hell was happening here?

He'd never been this swept away by lust, even when he'd been in the clutches of his hormones as a young adult. Sex was great. He was a healthy, virile male who was rich and powerful enough to command the best female attention whether he wanted it or not. When he wanted it, he went all in for the enjoyment of it.

But never had he experienced this urgency, this slightly crazed need that threatened to take him out at the knees.

And they hadn't even left first base yet!

Brianna opened her mouth wider to accommodate his rough demand. One hand left his shoulder and plunged into his hair, scraping his scalp as her fingers tightened.

He welcomed the mild pain with a glee that seriously worried him.

He'd never gone for kinky but with every scrape of her fingers his erection grew harder, more painful. God, he was so turned on, he couldn't see straight.

Which was why it took a full minute to realise the fingers in his hair were pulling him back, not egging him on; that the hand on his shoulder was pushing him away with more than a little desperation.

'No!' The force of his kiss smothered the word but it finally penetrated his lust-engorged senses.

With a shocked groan, he lifted his head and staggered back.

Brianna stared up at him, her ragged breath rushing through lips swollen with the force of his kisses. But it was the expression in her turquoise eyes that froze his insides. Besides the shock mingled with arousal, the apprehension was back again.

Self-loathing ripped through him like a tornado. He might not have understood why she'd been terrified the first time, but this time he knew the blame lay squarely with him. He'd fallen on her like a horny barbarian.

He clenched his fists and took another step back. His chest rose and fell like a felon in the heat of pursuit and he dimly registered that he hadn't bothered to breathe since he'd first tasted her.

'I...think this has gone far enough,' she said, her eyes darkening as they fell to his chest and skittered away.

Sakis wanted to refute that, to growl that it hadn't gone far enough. But he would be speaking from the depths of whatever insanity gripped him.

Insanity...

Was that what he'd scornfully professed he wanted to test?

Well, now he knew. His gaze dropped to her mouth again and fresh need slammed into him.

Damn it...He *knew*, and yet he wanted more. Of course, 'more' was out of the question. Brianna held far more value to him as his assistant than she would as his lover.

Potential lovers were a dime a dozen. He only had to scroll through his diary...

The thought of doing just that for the sake of slaking the lust-monkey riding him made his mouth curl with distaste. He wasn't his father, taking and discarding women with barely a thought between incidents, not caring about who bore the brunt of his actions.

Sucking in another breath, he forced a nod.

'*Ne*, you're right.' He licked his lower lip, tasted her again and nearly groaned. He clawed a hand through his hair and fought to regain the control that had been all but non-existent since he walked into the gym, fully intent on a mind-clearing workout, only to find her contorted in a highly suggestive stretch that had fried his brain cells. 'Let's chalk it down to the pressure of the past seventy-two hours.'

A look passed through her eyes before her lids lowered. 'Is this how you normally deal with a crisis?'

He gave another tight smile, whirled away and came face to face with his image.

Theos, no wonder she was frightened.

He looked like a crazed animal, a monster with wild eyes burning with stark hunger and a raging hard-on. He kept his back to her then forced himself to answer evenly.

'No, I normally fly down to the lake and take a scull out on the water. Or I come here to the gym and use the rowing machine. Physical labour helps me work things through.' Unfortunately, the physical he had in mind now involved Brianna beneath him, her thighs spread out in response to his hard, demanding thrusts.

'Um…okay. I guess I was in your way, then. Shall I…let you get on with it?' The slight question in her tone demanded reassurance.

Sakis had none to give. He remained exactly where he was, his back to her as he willed his body under control.

'Mr Pantelides?'

He winced at the rigid formality in those two words. Gritting his teeth, he turned to face her. 'Don't worry, Moneypenny. Nothing's changed. You tasted sweet enough but this was nothing to lose my head over. Our little experiment is over. The board is reconvening at eight. I'll see you in the office at seven-thirty.'

A gym workout was now out of the question. Brianna's scent lingered in the air and threatened to mess with his mind.

'Okay. I'll see you in the morning, then. Goodnight, Mr—'

'*Kali nichta*, Moneypenny.' He cut her off before she could trot out his title again.

Sakis scooped up his shirt, thought about putting it back

on and discarded the idea. Since he couldn't stay here, a two-— no, make that three-—mile swim in his pool was the next best option.

He was still staring at his shirt when she walked past him smelling of crushed lilies, rampant sex and sweat. God, what a combination. Against his will, his gaze tracked her sleek form. The taut, bare skin of her waist taunted him, as did the tight curve of her ass as she swayed her way out. With each sexy stride, the fire sweeping through his groin threatened to rage out of control.

It took a full minute after she'd left to realise he was still standing in the middle of the gym, clutching his shirt, gazing at the space where she'd been. With his fist tightening around the creased cotton, Sakis forced himself to admit that things indeed were about to get way worse before they got better.

And not just with his company.

'You tasted sweet enough but this was nothing to lose my head over...' Brianna forced herself to dwell on the relief rather than the sharp hurt burrowing inside her. The dangerous theory had been tested, the fire had been breached and they'd come out unscathed.

Are you sure? Brianna kicked off her leotard with more force than was necessary. 'Yes, I'm sure,' she said out loud. 'One-hundred per cent sure,' she added for good measure.

Her top followed and she strode into the lavish cream-and-gold decorated bathroom. Turning on the shower, she stepped beneath the spray. Hot rivulets coursed over her face, over the mouth Sakis had devoured less than five minutes ago, and a fresh wave of desire rushed over her.

'No!' Her hands shook as she reached for the shower gel and spread it over her body. This wasn't happening. *But it was... It had...*

She'd let Sakis kiss her, had fallen into his hands like a ripe peach at harvest. She'd chosen to test the waters and had almost drowned in the process.

Because that kiss had rocked her to the depths of her soul. He'd kissed her like she was the last tangible thing in his universe, like he wanted to devour her. Aside from the pleasure of it, she'd felt his need as keenly as the need she'd fought so hard to suppress.

She didn't want to *need*. For as long as she could remember, needing had only brought her disaster. As a child, her needs had come last for a mother who was only interested in her next drug fix. As a grown woman, she'd let her need for affection blind her into believing Greg's lies.

Nothing would make her return to that dark, *needful* place.

Her fingers drifted once again to her tattoo.

Whatever it was Sakis needed, he could find it elsewhere.

Sakis was already in the office when she arrived just before seven. He was on the phone but cool, green eyes skated over her as she entered. Replaying the pep talk she'd given herself before she'd come downstairs, she indicated his half-finished espresso cup and he nodded. The gaze that met hers as she stepped forward to pick up his cup was all ruthless business. There was no hint of the gritty, desire-ravaged man from the gym last night.

Sakis Pantelides, suave CEO and master of his world, was back in residence.

Brianna forced herself to emulate his expression as she walked out on decidedly shaky legs towards the state-of-the-art coffee machine in the little alcove just behind her office. Setting the cup beneath the stainless silver spouts, she pressed the button.

Last night's lurid dreams, which had kept her tossing and turning in heated agitation, needed to be swept under the carpet of professionalism where they belonged. It was obvious

Sakis had consigned the gym incident to 'done and forgotten'. She needed to do the same or risk—

'Is the machine delivering something other than coffee this morning? The daily horoscope, perhaps?' he drawled.

She whirled around. Sakis stood directly behind her, his powerful and overwhelming physique shrinking the space to even smaller proportions. 'I…sorry?'

His gaze flicked to the freshly made espresso and back to her face. 'The coffee is ready and yet you're staring at the machine as if you're expecting a crystal ball to materialise alongside the beverage.'

'Of course I wasn't. I was just…' She stopped, then with pursed lips picked up his cup and handed it to him. 'I wasn't that long, Mr Pantelides.'

His lips pursed at the use of his name but, now they were back in the work environment and back to being *professional*, he couldn't exactly object.

Expecting him to move, her heartbeat escalated when he stayed put, blocking her escape back to her office. 'Was there something else?'

His gaze dropped to her lips as he took a sip of his espresso. 'Did you sleep well?'

Unwanted flames licked at the muscles clenching in her belly. She wanted to tell him that how she slept was none of his business. But she figured answering him would make him get out of her way faster. 'I did. Thank you for asking.'

She waited. He didn't move. 'I didn't,' he rasped. 'Last night was the worst night's sleep I've had in a very long time.'

'Oh… Um…' She started to lick her lips, thought better of it and blew out a short breath instead. Seriously, she had to find a way to douse these supremely inconvenient flames that leapt inside her whenever he was near. 'It's been a stressful few days. It was bound to affect you in some way sooner or later.'

One corner of his mouth lifted. '*Ne*, I'm sure you're right.' Once again his gaze dragged over her mouth. The tingling of her lips almost made her rub her fingers over them, to do something to make it stop.

She clamped her hands round her middle instead. 'Was there something else you needed?'

He threw back the rest of the hot espresso and placed the cup on the counter. Several seconds passed in silence then he heaved a sigh. 'I'm…sorry if I frightened you last night. I didn't mean to get so carried away.'

Brianna's breath caught. 'I wasn't… You didn't…' She stopped speaking, her senses clamouring a warning as he stepped closer.

'Then why did you look so scared? Has someone hurt you in the past?'

She meant to say no, to diffuse the highly inquisitive gleam in his eyes before it got out of hand. But… 'Haven't we all been hurt at some point by someone we trusted? Someone we thought loved us?' Her stark answer hung in the air between them.

He paled a little, the lines bracketing his mouth deepening. 'I hope I didn't remind you of this person.'

'Not any more than I reminded you of your father.'

Her breath caught in her chest as anguish etched into his face. Until two days ago, she'd only known him to display the utmost control when it came to matters of business. Except this wasn't business. This was intensely private and intensely painful. Witnessing his raw pain made the ice surrounding her heart crack. Before she knew it, her hands were loosening and she was reaching for his arm. She stopped herself just in time. 'Sorry, I didn't mean to bring that up.'

His smile was grim as his fingers clawed through his hair. 'Unfortunately, memories once resurrected aren't easy to dismiss, no matter how inconvenient the timing.'

'Is there ever a convenient time to dredge up past hurt?' Pain ripped through her question.

He heard it and froze. Green eyes speared hers in a look

so intense her heart stuttered. 'Who hurt you, Brianna?' he asked again softly.

Feeling herself floundering, she sagged against the counter for support. 'I…this isn't really a topic for the office.'

'*Who*?' he insisted.

'You had problems with your father. Mine was with my mother.' Her voice sounded reedy, fraught with the anguish raking through her.

His smile held no mirth. 'Look at us: a pair of hopeless cases with mummy and daddy issues. Think what a field day psychologists would have with us.'

Not once in the past eighteen months had she believed she had anything in common with Sakis. But hearing his words brought a curious balm to her pain.

'Maybe we should ask for a group discount?' She attempted her own smile.

His eyes darkened then the pain slowly faded, to be replaced by another look, one she was becoming intimately familiar with. 'Was there a reason you came looking for me?' she asked a third time.

Sakis's jaw tightened. 'The investigators have confirmed there's a connection between the crash and the takeover.'

'Really?'

He nodded. 'It's highly suspect that a day after my tanker crashes Moorecroft Oil and Landers Petroleum make a bid for my company.' He turned and headed back into his office. 'Their timing was a little too precise for it to be opportunistic.'

She entered his office in time to see him snatch up his phone. 'Sheldon.' He addressed his head of security. 'I need you to dig deeper into Moorecroft Oil and Landers Petroleum.'

At the mention of Landers, Brianna froze. Thankfully, her ringing phone gave her the perfect excuse to return to her desk.

When Sakis emerged, she'd found some semblance of control, enough to accompany him into the board meeting without giving the state of her agitation away.

The conference call to Richard Moorecroft descended into chaos less than five minutes after Sakis had him on the line.

'How dare you accuse me of such a preposterous thing, Pantelides? You think I would stoop so low as to sabotage your vessel in order to achieve my ends?'

'You haven't achieved anything except draw attention to your own devious dealings.' A note of disdain coated Sakis's voice. 'Did you really think I'd roll over like a puppy because of one mishap?'

'You underestimate the might of Moorecroft. I'm a giant in the industry—'

'The fact that you feel the need to point that out impresses me even less.'

A huff of rage came over the conference line. 'This isn't over, Pantelides. You can count on it.'

'You're right, this isn't over. As we speak, I'm digging up any connection between what happened to my tanker and your company.'

'You won't find any!' The bravado in Moorecroft's voice was tinged with a shadowy nervousness that made Sakis's eyes gleam.

'Pray that I don't. Because, if I do, you can rest assured that I *will* come after you. And I won't be satisfied until I rip your precious company to little pieces and feed them to my pet piranhas.' The menace in his voice made ice crawl over Brianna's skin. 'And any accomplices will not be spared either.'

He stabbed the 'end' button and glanced around the other members of his board. 'I'll apprise you of any news if the investigation reaps any information.'

Sakis turned to where Brianna sat three seats to his left. He'd deliberately placed her out of his eyeline so she wouldn't prove a distraction. Not that he hadn't noticed her tapping away all during the conference. Now that he'd let himself experience the power of his attraction for her, he noticed everything about her. From the way her sleek, navy designer skirt hugged her bottom, to the arch of her feet when she walked into his presence.

At the most inappropriate times he'd caught himself wondering how long her hair was, whether it would feel soft and silky. Many times during his sleepless night, he'd pictured himself kissing her again, imagining the many ways he'd explore her lips again given another chance.

Only now, he noticed a little bit more. Like the vulnerability she tried to hide beneath the brusque exterior. Whatever her mother had done to her still had the power to wound her. His chest tightened with the need to go to her, brush his knuckles down her cheek and reassure her that he would take care of her…

Theos!

With gritted teeth, he tried to pull himself back under control. There would be no reassuring, just as there would be no repeat of last night's events. What happened in his gym last night couldn't be allowed to happen again.

Absolutely, without a shadow of a doubt.

So why was he walking towards her, letting his gaze devour the exposed line of her neck as she bent over her tablet? Why was he imagining himself lifting her up from that chair, sliding that tight skirt up—did she favour garter belts or thigh-high stockings?—and bending her over his boardroom table?

Stasi.

He was losing it and it wasn't even nine o'clock in the morning! With a curt command, he dismissed his board members.

He waited until the room cleared before he murmured her name.

She lifted her head and stared straight at him. Deep turquoise eyes met his and Sakis wasn't sure whether the interest it held was personal or professional. That he couldn't even read her properly any more, sent a fizz of annoyance through him.

'So, what happens now? I didn't think you'd let Moorecroft know we were investigating his connection with the tanker.'

Stopping a mere foot from her, he shrugged. 'I called his bluff and it paid off. I wasn't sure until I heard it in his voice. He's involved.'

'Then why not go after him?'

'He knows he's cornered. Between the FCA investigation and my own, he'll either come clean or he'll try to do whatever he can to cover his tracks. Either way, his time is fast running out. I'll give him a few hours to decide which way he wants to go.'

'And if he reveals a connection?'

Sakis heard the tremble in her voice and wondered at it.

'Then I'll make sure he pays to the fullest extent.' His father had got away with shady business deals for a long time before he'd been brought to justice. The same newspapers that had uncovered his treachery had uncovered the many families and employees his father had duped out of their rightful rewards.

Once his father had been put behind bars and Ari had been old enough to take over the reins of the company, the first thing he'd done was make sure the affected families were recompensed.

Letting anyone get away with fraud and duplicity would never happen.

He glanced down into the face of the woman whose body had invaded his dreams last night. She'd paled considerably, her eyes wide and haunted. His frown deepened.

'What's wrong?'

She surged to her feet and started gathering her things. 'Nothing.'

'Wait.' He placed a halting hand on her waist and immediately felt her tense. Another stream of irritation rushed upward.

'Y-yes?' Her voice wasn't quite steady and her head was bent, hiding her expression.

'Brianna, what's the hell is going on?'

'Why should there be anything wrong? I'm merely returning to my office to get on with the rest of the day.' Her words emerged in a rush.

Something was definitely wrong; something he'd said. He replayed his last words in his head, then his lips pursed.

'You think my views are too harsh?'

Her mouth tightened but she still avoided eye contact. 'What does it matter what I think?'

'Tell me, what would you do?' His hand curved firmly around her waist. When she moved, he felt the warm softness beneath his fingers. He wanted to pull her closer, glide his hand upward and cup her breast the way he had last night. It took every single ounce of willpower for him to hold himself still.

'I…I would listen to them, find out the motive behind their actions first, before I throw them to the wolves.'

'Greed is greed. Betrayal is betrayal. The reason for it ceases to matter once the act is done.'

Her soft lips pursed. Her nostrils flared and Sakis caught a sense of anger bubbling beneath her skin. 'If you truly believe that, then I don't see the point of you asking me.'

'Under what circumstances would you forgive such an action?'

She gave a small shrug. The movement drew his attention to her breast. Sakis swallowed and cursed the heat flaring through his groin. 'If the act was done to protect someone you cared about. Or perhaps it was done without the perpetrator knowing he was committing an act of betrayal.'

Sakis's lips twisted. 'My father's betrayal was an active undertaking. So is Moorecroft's.'

Her eyes clashed with his then she glanced away. 'You can't assign your father's sins to every situation in your life, Mr Pantelides.'

This was getting personal again. But he couldn't seem to stop himself from spilling the jagged pain in his chest. 'My father actively cheated and bribed his way through his business dealings for decades. He betrayed his family over and over, letting us think he was one thing when he was in fact another. Even after he was found out, he was remorseless. Even jail didn't change him. He went to his grave unrepentant.' He sucked in a breath and forcibly steered his thoughts away from the bitterness of his past. 'You're deluding yourself if you think there's such as a thing as blind, harmless betrayal.'

A shaft of pain and sympathy flitted through her eyes, just like it had back at Point Noire. She even started to move towards him before she visibly stopped herself.

Sakis felt curiously bereft that she succeeded.

'I'm sorry for what happened to you. I...I have emails to catch up on so, if you don't mind, I'll get back to the office.'

'No.'

She stared at him in surprise. 'No?'

He glanced at his watch. 'You haven't had breakfast yet, have you?'

'No, but I was going to order some fruit and cereal from the kitchen.'

'Forget that. We're going out.'

'I don't see why—'

'I do. We've both been cooped up in here since yesterday. Some fresh air and a proper meal will do us some good. Come.' He started to walk out and felt a hint of satisfaction when after several seconds he heard her footsteps behind him.

Sakis took her to a café on a quiet street in Cheapside. The manager greeted him with a smile and offered them a red high-backed booth set back from the doorway. One look at the menu and her eyes flew to collide with Sakis's.

He was regarding her with a seriously sexy smile on his face.

'All they serve here are pancakes,' she blurted.

'I know, which is why I brought you here. Time to indulge that *weakness* of yours.' The way he stressed the word made a spike of heat shoot through her.

'But…why?' Frantically, she scrambled to gather her rapidly unravelling control. Far from being back on the professional footing she'd thought, the morning was turning into one huge, personal landmine. One she wasn't sure she would survive.

'Because it's perfect ammunition.' Again he smiled and her heart lurched.

'You see my weakness for pancakes as *ammunition*?' She felt her lips twitch and allowed herself a small smile. Just then, a waiter walked past with a steaming heap of blueberry pancakes dripping in honey. She barely managed to stifle her groan, but Sakis heard it.

A dark, hungry look entered his eyes that made her stomach muscles clench hard. 'I'm not so sure whether to be pleased or irritated that I've uncovered this piece of information about you, Brianna. On the one hand, it could be the perfect weapon to get you to do whatever I want.'

'I already do whatever you want.' The loaded answer made heat crawl up her neck. His keen gaze followed it then scoured her face before locking on hers.

'Do you? I distinctly recall a few times when you've refused to do my bidding.'

'I wouldn't have lasted two minutes if I'd pandered to you in any shape or form.'

'No, you wouldn't have. I told Ari you were my Rottweiler.' She gave a shocked gasp. 'You compared me to a dog?'

He grimaced and had the grace to look uncomfortable. 'It was a metaphor but, in hindsight, I should've used a more… flattering description.' He beckoned the waiter who'd been hovering a booth away.

Her curiosity got the better of her. 'How would you describe me?'

He didn't answer immediately. Instead he gave the waiter their order—coffee and two helpings of blueberry pancakes.

Brianna stopped the waiter with a hand on his arm. 'Can I have a side-helping of blueberries, please? And a bowl of honey? Oh, and some icing sugar and fresh cream…and two wedges of lemon…and some butter…' She stopped when she saw Sakis's eyebrow quirk in deep amusement. She dropped her arm and this time was unable to stop her blush from suffusing her face as their waiter walked away. 'Sorry, I didn't mean to sound like a complete glutton.'

'Don't apologise for your desires. Indulging every now and then is completely human.'

'Until I have to pay for it with hours in the gym. Then I'll hate every single mouthful I'm about to take.'

Immediately her mind homed in on what had happened between them last night. From the way his green eyes darkened, he was remembering too. God, what was wrong with her? Or maybe that was the wrong question. She knew what was wrong. Despite cautioning herself against it, she was attracted to Sakis with a fierce compulsion that defied reason. She accepted that now. What she needed was a cure for this insanity before it raged out of control.

'If you regret the act before it's happened, you take away the enjoyment of it.'

'So you're saying I should just ignore what will come afterwards and just live in the moment?'

His gaze dropped to her lips, the heat of it almost a caress that made her want to moan. 'Exactly.' He breathed the word then said nothing else.

Silence grew between them, the only sound the distant clatter of plates and cutlery from other diners.

She could only stand it for a few minutes until she felt as if she'd combust from the sizzling tension in the air. Forcefully, she cleared her throat and searched for a neutral subject, one that would defuse the stressful atmosphere. 'You were going to tell me what your description of me would be.' *Oh, nice one, Brianna.*

He sat back in his seat, extended his arm along the back of

the booth. Her eyes fell on rippling muscle beneath his shirt and she barely managed to swallow.

'Perhaps now is not the time, or the place.'

Leave it, Brianna...leave it. 'Oh, is it that bad?'

'No, it's that *good*.'

She breathed deeply and opted for silence. When their food arrived, she pounced on it, feeding her culinary appetite the way she couldn't let herself feed on the dark, carnal promise in Sakis's eyes.

She looked up several minutes later to find him watching her with an expression of mingled shock and amusement.

'Sorry, it's your fault. Now you've unleashed my innermost craving, there's no stopping me.' She took another sinful bite and barely managed to stop her eyes rolling in pleasure.

'On the contrary, seeing you eat something other than a salad and with such...relish is a pleasurable experience in itself.'

'Don't worry; I'm not going to re-enact a *When Harry Met Sally* moment.'

A puzzled frown marred his forehead. 'A what?'

She laughed. 'You've never seen that clip where the actress simulates an orgasm in a restaurant?'

He swallowed. 'No, I haven't. But I prefer my orgasmic experiences not to be simulated. When it comes to orgasms, only the real thing will do. Do you not agree?'

Dear Lord, was she really having breakfast with her boss, discussing orgasms? 'I wasn't... This was...' She stopped, silently willing her racing pulse to quieten. 'I was merely making conversation. I don't have an opinion on orgasms one way or another.'

His low laugh caressed her senses like soft butterfly wings. '*Everyone* has an opinion on orgasms, Brianna. Some of us may have stronger opinions than others, but we all have them.'

She was not going to think about Sakis and orgasms together. *She was not.* 'Um…okay; point taken. But I'd rather not discuss it any longer, if that's okay with you?'

He finished the last of his pancakes and picked up his black coffee. 'Certainly. But some subjects have a habit of lingering until they're dealt with.'

'And other subjects deserve more attention than others. What was your other point?'

'Sorry?'

'Before the subject went…sideways you said "on the one hand". I was wondering what the other was.'

It was a purely diversionary tactic, but she wanted—no, needed—to get off the subject that was making desire dredge through her pelvis like a pervasive drug, threatening to fool her into thinking she could taste the forbidden and come out whole.

There would be no coming out whole once she gave in to the hunger that burned within her, that burned relentlessly in Sakis's eyes. Wanting—or, God forbid, *needing*—a man like Sakis would destroy her eventually. Their conversation in the boardroom had reiterated the fact that he was emotionally scarred from what his father had done to him. He would never allow himself to trust anyone, never mind reaching the point of *needing* another human being to the extent she suspected she would crave if she didn't control her feelings.

'On the other hand, I'm glad I know this weakness. Because I have a feeling you don't give yourself permission enough to enjoy the simple things in life.'

Her heart hammered with something suspiciously like elation. 'And you…you want to give me that?'

'I want to give you that. I want to indulge you like you've never been indulged before.'

Simple words. But oh, so dangerous to her current state of mind.

'Why?' she blurted before she could stop herself.

Her question seemed to surprise him. His lashes swept

down and veiled his eyes. 'For starters, I'm hoping to be re-warded with one of those rare smiles of yours.' He looked back up and his expression stopped her breath. There was a solemn kinship, a gentleness in their depths, that made her heart flip. 'And because I had my brothers while I dealt with my daddy issues. But you, as far as I know, are an only child, correct?'

Emotion clogged her throat. 'Correct,' she croaked, bat-tling the threat of tears.

That weird connection tightened, latched and embedded deeply, frightening but soothing at the same time. 'Let's call this therapy, then.' He glanced down at her plate where one last square of honey-soaked pancake was poised on her fork. 'Are you finished?'

She hadn't but the thought of putting that last morsel in her mouth while he watched with those all-seeing eyes was too much to bear. 'Yes, I'm done. And thank you…for this, I mean. And for…' She stumbled to a halt, alien feelings rush-ing through her at dizzying speed.

He nodded, stood and held out his hand. 'It was my plea-sure, *agapita*.'

By the time they returned to the office, Brianna knew some-thing had fundamentally changed between them. She didn't even bother to figure out a way back to equanimity; she couldn't. Curiously, she didn't feel as devastated at losing that particular battle.

It helped that they were barely in the door when Sakis threw out a list of things he wanted her to do but, despite the breakneck speed of dealing with his demands, they were soon both plugged into events at Point Noire, especially the clean-up process and the still missing Pantelides Six crewmembers.

After speaking to Morgan Lowell's wife Perla for the fifth time at six o'clock, Sakis threw his pen on his desk and ran both hands over his stubbled jaw.

'Are you okay?'

Tired eyes trained on her with breath-stopping intensity.

'I need to get out of here,' he rasped as he strode to the door and shrugged into his designer overcoat.

She swallowed and nodded. 'Do you want me to book a restaurant table for you? Or call a friend to…um…' She stopped, purely because the thought of arranging a date for Sakis with one of the many women who graced his electronic diary stuck in her gut like a sharp knife.

'I'm not in the mood to listen to inane conversation about the latest Hollywood gossip or who is screwing whom in my circle of friends.'

His response pleased her way more than it should have. 'Okay, what can I do?'

His eyes gleamed for a moment, before he looked away and headed towards the door. 'Nothing.' He stopped with a hand on the door. 'I'm meeting Ari for a drink. And you're logging off for the night. Is that clear, Moneypenny?'

She nodded slowly and watched him walk out, hollowness in her stomach that made her hate herself. She wanted to be with him. She wanted to be the one who wiped away that look of weariness she'd seen in his eyes. And all through today, every time he'd called her 'Moneypenny', she'd wanted to beg him to call her 'Brianna'. Because she loved the way he said her name.

She glanced down at the fingers resting on her keyboard and wasn't surprised to see them trembling. Her whole being trembled with the depth of the feelings that had been coursing through her all day. Frankly, it scared the hell out of her.

Hurriedly, she shut down the computer and gathered her tablet, phone and handbag. She'd just slid her chair neatly into the space beneath her desk when the phone rang. Thinking it was Sakis—because who else would ring her at seven-thirty on a work night?—she pounced on the handset.

'Hello?'

'May I speak to Anna Simpson?'

A spear of ice pinned her in place as her lips parted on a soundless gasp. A full minute passed. Her lungs burned until she managed to force herself back from the brink of unconsciousness. 'Excuse me, I…I think you've got the wrong number.'

The ugly laugh at the end of the line shook her to the very soul. 'We both know I don't have the wrong number, don't we, sweetheart?

She didn't respond—couldn't—because the phone had fallen from her nerveless fingers.

Another full minute passed. 'Hello?' came the impatient echoing voice. 'Anna?'

Numbness spreading through her, she picked up the phone. 'I told you there…there's no one by that name working here.'

But it was too late. She recognised the taunting, reedy voice at the end of the line. It was a voice she'd been dreading hearing again since her return from Point Noire.

'I can play along if you prefer, Anna. Hell, I'll even call you by your new name, *Brianna Moneypenny*. But we both know to me you'll always be Anna, don't we?' mocked Greg Landers.

CHAPTER SEVEN

'WHAT DO YOU want, Greg?' Brianna snapped into her mobile phone as she threw her bag on the tiny sofa in her small living room.

'What? No hello, no pleasantries? Never mind. I'm glad you were sensible enough to return my call. Although, I don't get why you didn't want to speak to me at your office. I made sure Pantelides wasn't there before I called.'

Shock made her grip the edge of the seat. 'You're having him watched?'

'No, I'm having *you* watched. You're the one I'm interested in.'

'Me?'

'Yes. For now, at least. Tell me, why the name change?'

Bitterness rose in a sweltering tide, bringing a sickening haze that made the furnishings of her small flat blur. 'Why the hell do you think? You destroyed my life, Greg. After you lied and swore under oath in court that I embezzled funds from your company, when we both know that it was you who set up that Cayman Islands account in my name. Do you think after what you put me through anyone would've hired me once they knew I'd been to prison for embezzlement?'

'Tsk-tsk, let's not blow things out of proportion, shall we? You served well under half of the four-year prison term. If it's any consolation, I only expected you to get a slap on the wrist.'

'It's *not* a consolation!'

'Besides,' he continued as if she hadn't interrupted, 'I hear those prisons are just a step down from glorified holiday camps.'

The scar on her hip—the result of a shiv, courtesy of an inmate whose attention she wouldn't return—burned at the careless dismissal of what had been a horrific period of her life. 'It's a shame you decided not to try it out for yourself, then, instead of turning coward and letting someone else take the blame for your greed. Now, are you going to tell me what this call is about or shall I hang up?'

'Hang up and I'll make sure your salacious past is the first thing Pantelides reads about when he steps into that ivory tower of his tomorrow morning.'

Brianna's hand tightened around the phone at the ruthless tone. 'How did you find me, anyway?' Not that it mattered now. But she'd used every last penny to erase her past, to make sure every trace of Anna Simpson was wiped clean as soon as she'd attained her freedom.

'I didn't. *You* found *me*, through the wonderful medium of TV. Imagine my surprise when I tuned in, like every environmentally conscious individual out there who's horrified about the Pantelides oil spillage, to find you right behind the main man himself. It took me a few minutes to recognise you, though. I much prefer you blonde to the brunette you used to be. Which is the real thing?'

'I fail to see…' She stopped because the Greg she'd known, the man she'd once foolishly thought herself in love with, hadn't changed. He believed himself a witty and clever conversationalist and was never one to get to the point until he was ready. It was one of the things—many things, she realised now—that had irritated her about him. 'Blonde is my natural colour.'

Greg sighed. 'Such a shame you chose to wear that dull brown when I knew you. Maybe I'd have thought twice before taking the route I took.'

'No, you wouldn't have. Your slimy nature makes you interested in taking care of number one. Are you going to tell me what you want any time soon?'

'You're distressed so I'll let that insult slide. But be careful now or I'll forget my manners. Now, what do I want? It's very simple: I want Pantelides Shipping. And you're going to help me get it.'

You're out of your mind was the first of many outraged responses that rushed into her head. She managed to stop herself before they spilled out. Slowly, she sank onto her sofa, the only piece of furniture in her living room aside from a lone coffee table, as her mind raced.

'And why would I do that?'

'To protect your dirty little secret, of course.'

She licked her lips as fear threatened to swamp any semblance of clear thinking. 'What makes you think my boss doesn't already know?'

'Don't take me for a fool, Anna.'

'My name is Brianna.' The woman Greg thought he knew no longer existed.

'If you want to keep calling yourself that, you'll give me what I want. And don't bother telling me Pantelides knows about your past. He's scrupulous when it comes to any hint of scandal. You're the last person he'd employ if he knew your past was as shady as his father's.'

This time her gasp was audible. It echoed around the room in tones of pain, shock and anger. 'You know about his father?'

'I do my homework, sweetheart. And if he'd bothered to do his he'd have discovered who you really were. But I'm glad he didn't, because now you're in the perfect position to help me.'

The vice tightened harder around her chest. 'What exactly is it you want me to do?'

'I need information. As much as you can get your hands on. Specifically, which of the board members hold the largest shares, aside from Pantelides. And which of the other members will be amenable to selling what shares they have.'

'You know this will never work, don't you? Sakis—Mr Pantelides—will crush you if you come within a whisper of his company.'

'God, you haven't gone and done it again, have you, Anna?' came the soft taunt.

Brianna shivered. 'Done what?'

'Offered that foolish little heart of yours on a silver platter to another boss?' he murmured in a pitying voice.

'I don't know what you're talking about.' But deep down there was no hiding from the truth. Her feelings for Sakis had morphed from purely professional to something else. Something she was vehemently unwilling to examine right now, when she needed all her wits about her to defend herself against what her grimy ex was intent on pulling her into.

'You have four days, Anna. I'll be in touch and I expect you to have the information I need.'

Her mouth went dry. Her heart hammered with sick fear and loathing and the unmistakeable, sinking feeling of inevitability. 'And if I don't?'

'Then your boss will wake up to a most tantalising double-page spread of his treasured assistant in the tabloid press on Saturday morning. I'm pretty sure with very little effort I can get Pantelides Shipping to start trending again on all social media.'

Her belly quivered and she clenched her muscles hard. 'Why are you doing this? Haven't you done enough? Aren't the millions you squirrelled away enough?'

'Every Joe Bloggs knows how to make a million these days. No, sweetheart, my ambitions are set much higher than that. I'd hoped my association with Moorecroft would see me there but the fool folded at the first sign of adversity. Fortunately, I have you now.'

'I haven't agreed to anything.'

'But you will. You covet your position almost as much as I covet the prospect of acquiring Pantelides Shipping. Make no mistake, I will have it.'

'Greg—'

'I'll be in touch on Friday. Don't disappoint me, Anna.'

He hung up before she could appeal to his better nature. Who was she kidding? Greg had no better nature. He was a vulture who ruthlessly fed on the weak.

The discovery that he'd engineered her to take the fall for his failing company over three years ago had rocked her to the core. When he'd pleasantly asked her to act as his co-director, she'd thought nothing of it, especially when he'd brought in a legal expert to explain things to her. Of course, it'd turned out the so-called legal expert had been in on the scheme to bleed his company dry before declaring bankruptcy and leaving her to take the fall.

She'd had time to dwell on her stupidity and gullibility in the maximum-security prison the judge had sentenced her to, to set an example.

Brianna staggered up from the sofa, swaying on shaky legs as her mind spun with the impossibility of her situation.

The very idea of betraying Sakis made her stomach turn over in revulsion.

He would never forgive her if she brought his company under unpalatable scrutiny so soon after his tanker's crash and having the memory of his father resurrected.

She could resign with immediate effect. But what would stop Greg from spewing his vitriol purely out of spite?

Telling Sakis the truth was out of the question.

Betrayal is betrayal. The reason for it ceases to matter once the act is done.

Casting her gaze around the almost empty room, another shiver raked through her.

Run!

The stark reality of her harsh childhood had made it impossible for her to fully imbed herself in any one place, even this place she called her sanctuary. At least, if she had to run, she could be out of here in less than half an hour.

She pressed her lips together as a spike of rebellion clayed her feet. Why should she run? She'd done nothing wrong. Her only folly had been to delude herself into thinking Greg cared for her. But she'd paid the price for it.

No more. *No more!*

Throwing down the mobile phone, she went into her equally sparsely furnished bedroom. The bed lay on wooden slats on the floor. Aside from a super-sized *papier-mâché* cat she'd bought at a Sunday market months ago, only a tall, broad-leafed ficus plant graced the room. Her only indulgence was the luxury cashmere throw and the fluffy pillows on the bed. Even the built-in wardrobe held only the collection of designer suits Sakis had insisted she used her expense account for when she'd joined Pantelides Shipping. Her own clothes consisted of a few pairs of jeans and tops, one set of jogging bottoms and jumper and two pairs of trainers.

Those would be easy to pack.

No; she refused to think like a fugitive. She had nothing to be ashamed of.

With shaky fingers, she undressed and entered the *en suite* bathroom, suddenly eager to wash away the grime of her conversation with Greg. But his threat lingered in the air, in the water. No matter how much she scrubbed, she felt tainted by the thought that she had even contemplated betrayal to save her own skin.

The pounding at her door finally registered over the hammering of her heart and the rush of the shower. Twisting the tap shut, she heard the faint sound of her mobile just before another round of hammering made her lunge for her dressing down. With a quick sluice of a towel over her body, she went to her door and peered through the peephole.

The massive frame of Sakis looming through the distorted

glass quickly eroded the relief that Greg hadn't found his way to her flat.

It seemed the two people responsible for the angst in her life were determined to breach her sanctuary at all costs today.

Pulse skittering out of control, Brianna cracked open the door. 'I...I didn't know you knew where I lived.' She looked into his clenched-jawed face and her words died on her lips. 'Why are you here?'

'I came here because...' He stopped, then clawed a hand through his hair. 'Hell, I'm not exactly sure why I came here. But I know I didn't want to be at the penthouse by myself.' He raked his hand through his hair again. The weariness she'd glimpsed on his face earlier seemed amplified a hundred-fold. The soft place inside her chest that had been expanding since their pancake episode this morning widened even further and she found herself stepping back.

'I... Would you like to come in?'

Lips pursed, he nodded. Standing to one side in the narrow hallway, she held her breath as he entered her sanctuary.

Immediately, he dwarfed the space. She shut the door and entered the living room to find him pacing the space in short, jerky strides.

'Can I get you a drink?' She hadn't touched the bottle of scotch that had come with her Christmas hamper last year. Now she was grateful for it as she produced the bottle and Sakis nodded.

She took out a glass, poured a healthy measure and passed it to him.

'Aren't you having one?' Despite his question, his gaze was focused on the amber liquid in his hand.

'I don't really...' She stopped. After what she'd been through already tonight, what she sensed was coming, perhaps a small drink wouldn't hurt. She poured a single shot for herself, took a sip and nearly choked as the liquid burned a fiery path through her chest.

With a grim smile, Sakis tossed his own drink back in one unflinching gulp. He set his glass down on the coffee table and faced her.

'Why did you leave?'

The reason for returning home blazed at the back of her mind. Although she'd done nothing wrong, guilt clawed through her nevertheless. She licked her lips then froze when his eyes darkened. 'I haven't been home in a while. I just wanted to touch base.'

'And touching base precluded you from answering your phone?'

She glanced at the phone she'd abandoned on the sofa after her call with Greg. Picking it up, she activated it and saw twelve missed calls on the screen.

'Sorry, I was in the shower.'

His agitated pacing brought him closer. He stopped a couple of feet from her. But the distance meant nothing because she could feel the heat of his body reaching out, caressing her, claiming her. Tendrils of damp hair that had escaped the knot clung to her nape, sending tiny rivulets of water down her back. Supremely conscious that she was naked beneath her gown, she tried to take a step back but her feet were frozen on the carpet.

His gaze traced over her and stopped at the rapid rise and fall of her chest. She watched his fists clench and release as stark hunger transformed his face into a mesmerising mask.

'I'm sorry to have disturbed you,' he rasped, but nothing in his tone or his face showed contrition. Instead, his stare intensified, whipping the air around her until a helpless moan escaped her lips.

Abandoning reason, Brianna stepped closer, bringing her body flush against his. Knowing she risked betraying her very soul, but unable to stop herself, she cupped his jaw. 'You ordered me to stop working. I didn't think you'd need me tonight.'

Her breath caught as his gaze moved hungrily over her lips.

'No, Brianna. Far from it. I need you. More now than I've ever needed you before. You're the only one who makes the world make sense to me.'

'I…I am?'

'*Ne*. I didn't like it when I couldn't reach you.' His head dropped a fraction until his forehead touched hers. 'I can't function without you by my side.'

'I'm here now,' she whispered, her throat clogged with emotions she couldn't give name to. No, scratch that: it was desire, passion and compassion all rolled into one needful and relentless ache. That visceral need to connect with Sakis that she'd never felt with anyone else, not even her own mother. 'Whatever you need, I'm here.'

One hand fisted her damp, precariously knotted hair, pulling it back almost roughly so her face was tilted up and exposed to his. 'Are you?' he enquired roughly.

She gave a shaky nod. 'Yes.'

'Be very sure, *glikia mou*. Because this time I won't be able to stop. If you don't want me to go any further, tell me now.' His eyes searched her urgently, his need clearly displayed in the harsh whistle of breath that escaped his parted lips.

The hard body plastered to hers made thinking near impossible but Brianna knew one thing—this could be her one chance to be with Sakis. After Friday, she'd be out of a job—one she would be sacked from or have to resign from.

From a purely selfish point of view, this could be her last chance to experience the fervid promise of bliss she'd felt in the gym last night—to be bold enough to reach for something she'd once dared to crave.

'Brianna?' His fierce tone held a hint of vulnerability that struck deep.

Sakis needed her. And she…she needed to blank out the heartache the future held.

'Yes, I want you…'

He swallowed the words with the savage demand of his kiss. The hand at her waist lowered to grasp her bottom and he pulled her into stinging contact with his groin, giving a low groan as the force of his erection probed her belly.

For an endless age, he devoured her mouth with a hunger born of desperation. Brianna gave as much as she got, her hunger just as maddeningly urgent. When his tongue curled around hers, she opened her mouth wider to feel even more of it.

Sakis groaned again and walked her back until the back of her legs touched her small sofa. He'd barely pushed her down before he covered her with his immense body. Searing heat engulfed her as they lay plastered from chest to thigh. Raising his head, his gaze scoured her face as if imprinting her features on his memory. When it touched her lips, the urge to lick them overcame her. She passed her tongue over them and watched in secret delight as his eyes darkened dramatically.

'I suspected that underneath those severe business suits you were a seductress, Moneypenny.'

'I'm sure I have no idea what you mean.' She licked her lips again.

His growl was her first warning but she was too far gone to heed it.

Brianna quickly pulled his head down and brushed his lips with hers. She kissed him again and felt her heart leap with joy when he deepened it.

When he suddenly surged off her and stood, Brianna fought not to cry out in disappointment. But he merely shrugged out of his jacket and tie before plucking her off the seat. 'I'm so lucky to have you. But my gratitude does not extend to making love to you on a sofa made for elves.'

'Oh. I guess it is a little on the small side, isn't it?'

'Perhaps not, if you're trying to be inventive. We'll leave it for another time.'

The thrill that went through her escalated when he caught

her up in his arms and took her lips in another searing kiss. 'Which way to the bedroom?'

Brianna pointed and he immediately steered her in that direction. At the door, she hesitated. What would he think when he saw how sparsely decorated her room was? She was scrambling to think of excuses when he pulled her hips into his groin.

'I don't mind doing it standing up if that's what you'd prefer, *glikia mou*. Just say the word,' he breathed against her neck, one hand sneaking up to cup her bare breast where her gown had fallen open. With another groan, he squeezed before teasing the nub between his fingers. 'But say it quickly before I combust from neglect.'

'The…the bedroom is fine.' She opened the door and held her breath. But Sakis was only interested in the bed, not the state of the near-empty room. He propelled her firmly towards it, shucking off his shoes, socks and shirt without letting go completely. With a firm hand he pushed her onto the bed and fell onto his knees behind her.

Pulling her back, he ground his hips into her. 'You have no idea how many times I've imagined you in this position before me.' Urgent hands slid up her dressing gown and he growled with ragged need as he bared her naked bottom to his heated gaze. '*Theos*, no knickers. This is even better than I imagined.' Roughly, he reached for the sleeves of the gown and jerked it off her completely.

Brianna was thankful she wasn't facing him so that she didn't have to explain her tattoo to him just yet, especially since, with the depth of her need, she wasn't sure she wouldn't blurt out the truth behind it. The other thing was her scar. She couldn't hide it for ever but she was grateful she didn't have to explain it right this minute.

Because the sensation of Sakis touching her naked bottom, caressing and decadently moulding it, made her senses melt.

'*Theos*, I love your ass,' he growled with dirty reverence.

Pure feminine delight fizzed through her. 'I can tell,' she responded breathily.

His laugh was low and deep, doing nothing to disguise his hunger. She jerked with surprise and delight when she felt his mouth touch each globe in an open-mouthed kiss before biting lightly on her flesh.

He continued to knead her with his large hands, massaging down to her hips before returning to fondle her with both hands. The eroticism of the act made her breath catch. But it was when he pushed her forward and spread apart her thighs that she stopped breathing.

Sakis blew a hot breath on her parted folds, making her thighs quiver in anticipation of what was to come. When it came, when the tip of his tongue flicked over her most sensitive place, Brianna couldn't stop the cry of pleasure that spilled from her throat. Hands shaking in a monumental effort to keep her from collapsing onto the bed, she clamped her eyes shut and held her breath for another burn of sensation.

Another flick, then several more, then Sakis opened her wider, baring her to his gaze. He muttered something in Greek before he placed the most shocking, open-mouthed kiss on her. He devoured her as if she was his favourite meal. Sensation built upon sensation until Brianna wasn't sure which move pleased her more—his teeth grazing her clitoris or his relentlessly probing tongue inside her.

All she knew was that the majestic peak that promised both exquisite torture and intense pleasure loomed closer. Fire burned behind her closed lids. Her fingers spasmed into a death grip on her sheets. With one long, merciless pull of his mouth on her clitoris, he sent her over the edge.

He gave a long, satisfied groan as he drank her in. For endless minutes, he lapped her with his tongue until her convulsions ceased. Vaguely, she heard him leave the bed and shuck off his trousers. Limp and breathless, she started to sag.

One hand caught her around the waist. 'Stay right there; I'm not finished with you yet.'

Brianna clawed back reason enough to demand huskily, 'Um…condom?'

'Taken care of.' His hand caressed up her stomach to cup one breast before teasing her nipple. She felt the other fumble for the loose knot in her hair. 'You know I've never seen your hair down?'

'Hmm…yes.'

He pulled her up and released the knot, then groaned as his fingers weaved through the heavy blonde tresses that went all the way down her back. '*Theos*, it's a travesty to keep this gorgeous hair tied up day after day. You deserve punishment for that, Moneypenny.'

The sharp tap on her rump sent excitement sizzling along her nerves. She bit her lip when she felt the thick evidence of his desire lying between the crease of her bottom, a relentless reminder that there was another experience to be celebrated.

'You don't think you've tortured me enough?' she asked.

His thumbs flicked over her nipples. 'Not nearly enough, *pethi mou*. Open your legs wider.'

She obeyed because she wanted this more than she wanted her next breath. At the first probe of his erection, she held her breath. He used one hand to hold her still and fed another inch inside her.

Stars burst across her vision. 'Sa—' How could it be that she was bared to him in the most intimate of ways and yet the taste of his name on her lips felt a touch too far?

'Say it,' he commanded.

'I can't…'

He started to withdraw. Her body clenched in fierce denial. 'No!'

'Say my name, Brianna.'

'Sa…Sakis,' she gasped. He pushed back in with a deep groan. 'Oh God.'

'*Again!*'

'S...Sakis!'

'Good girl.' He plunged in until he was fully embedded, then held still. 'Now, tell me how you want this to go. Fast or slow. Either way will be torture for me but I want to please you.'

Brianna wanted to tell him he'd already pleased her, a thousand times more than she'd ever imagined possible.

'Now, *glikia mou*, while my brain still functions...' Pushing her forward, he covered her with his body and trapped her splayed hands under his on the bed.

The first signs of her climax clawed at her. 'Fast, Sakis. I want it fast. And hard.'

'*Theos!*' His response through clenched teeth was a hot breath in her ear. 'Your wish is my command.' With a loud groan, he pulled out and surged back in, then proceeded to set a blistering pace that made her die a little each time her orgasm drew closer.

When he rocked back on his knees, Brianna's chest collapsed onto the bed, her feeble arms unable to sustain the barrage of sensations that rippled through her. Taking one last, gasping breath, she screamed as blissful convulsions seized her. Dimly, she heard Sakis's long, drawn-out growl as his pleasure overtook him. Deep within her, she felt his thickness pump his pleasure over and over until he was spent.

He collapsed sideways onto the bed and took her with him. In the dark room, he tucked her back against his chest, their harsh breaths gradually slowing until only the occasional spasm raked through them.

CHAPTER EIGHT

WHAT FELT LIKE hours later, Sakis pulled her closer and brushed back her hair from her face.

The kiss he planted on her temple was gentle but possessive. 'That was sensational, *glikia mou*.'

'What does that mean?'

He gave a low laugh. 'You have an intelligent mind, Moneypenny. Find out.'

'You like to say my surname quite a lot. In fact, you don't go more than a minute or two when we're talking before going "Moneypenny this" or "Moneypenny that".'

She felt his grin against her neck. 'And this surprises you? I find your surname very intriguing, sexy.'

She fought not to tense at the interest in his tone and responded with forced lightness. 'Sexy?'

He shrugged. 'Before I met you, I'd only ever heard that name in a spy movie.'

'And you think she's sexy?'

'Extremely, and also hugely underestimated.'

'I agree with you there. But she was often overlooked in favour of sexier, in-your-face female leads; she was also the one who never got her guy.'

Sakis drew closer and traced his lips along the line of her shoulder. 'Well, I think we've remedied that tonight. Plus, she had astonishing staying power. Just like you. No one in their right mind would overlook you, Moneypenny, even though you try to hide it with that hypnotic swan-glide.'

She laughed. 'Swan glide?'

'Outwardly, you're serene, so damned efficient, and yet below you're paddling madly. Watching you juggle virtual balls is damned sexy.'

'Damn; and there I thought no one could see the mad paddling underneath.'

'Sometimes, there's just a little ruffle. Like when I misbehave and you itch to put me in my place.'

'So you know you're misbehaving? Acceptance is the first step, I suppose.'

She shivered as he rocked his hips forward in a blatantly masculine move that had her moaning. But then he pulled out of her a second later and flipped her to face him. 'Like all men in my position, I live to push the boundaries. But I get that I need an anchor sometimes. You're my anchor, Brianna.' He spoke with a low but fierce intensity that made tears prickle behind her eyes.

'Sakis…I…'

He kissed her, a slow, luxurious exploration that soon became something else, something more. She wanted to protest when he lifted his head. 'Hold that thought; I need to change condoms. Bathroom?'

She pointed and watched him head towards her tiny bathroom, her eyes glued to his toned, chiselled physique. The thought that she was about to make love with this virile, sexy man again made her tremble so hard, she clutched the pillow.

But, alone, dread began to creep in. She'd gone beyond *what the hell am I doing?* Now she had to deal with *what the hell am I going to do?*

Sakis might not have meant to but tonight he'd revealed just how much he treasured and respected her. How ironic that, just when she could've felt secure in the knowledge that her job was safe, that she didn't need to prove herself as the invaluable asset in Sakis's life, she would have to walk away.

Because there really was no choice. She would never betray Sakis the way he'd been betrayed before. As for Greg, he deserved to burn in hell.

She toyed with confessing but brushed it away. Now she understood just what he'd been through with his father, she couldn't bear for him to look at her and see another fraud, someone who'd failed to reveal the whole truth about her past.

Her only option would be to resign and find herself another job somewhere far away, perhaps in another country even, where neither Greg's vile threats or Sakis's condemnation would touch her.

A deep pool of sadness welled up inside her, bringing with it a sharp pain that made her groan and bury her face in the pillow.

She jumped when a warm hand caressed her back.

'Should I be offended that you were so far away you'd forgotten I exist?'

Composing herself, she turned to face him. *God, he was gorgeous*, even with the shadows of the past few days' stress lurking in his eyes. Perhaps that was what made him even more breath-taking—the fact that, despite being the ruthless entrepreneur feared by most competitors, he still had a caring heart.

Unable to stop herself, she reached for him and glided her hand over his warm, sculpted chest to draw him closer. 'I hadn't forgotten. I always know when you're near, Sakis. Always.'

His eyes darkened as he stretched out beside her and took her mouth in a long, deep kiss. 'I can't believe I waited this long to make you mine.'

The stamp of possessiveness in his voice made her heart jump in thrilling delight even though deep down she knew it was a futile reaction. She would never be truly his because this wouldn't last beyond the week. She pushed the disturbing thoughts away.

'Even though I was sweet enough, but nothing to lose your head over?' She quoted his words back at him and watched a shamefaced look cross his features.

He cursed under his breath. 'I think we both know that was a blatant lie.'

'What was the truth then?'

His lips drifted lazily over hers but she wasn't fooled that it was a casual caress. Against her thigh his re-energised erection pulsed with urgent demand, eliciting an electrifying reaction inside her body.

'The truth was that I wanted nothing more than to throw you on the nearest gym mat and take you until you couldn't speak. What would you have done if I'd said that, instead of the lame excuse I came up with?'

She leaned up and caught his earlobe in a saucy bite. 'I'd have said *bring it on.*'

The tremor that went through him preceded a guttural curse as he surged over her and proceeded to claim her in the most elemental way possible.

Within seconds, he had her on the knife-edge of need, a need so visceral she didn't know whether to beg for mercy or to beg him never to stop.

'S…Sakis…please,' she begged as he roughly tongued one nipple.

'I love the sound of my name on your lips. Say it again,' he murmured against her skin, his gaze rising to capture hers.

She shook her head in silent denial. A fiercely determined light entered his eyes and her heart sank.

He tugged on her engorged nub. 'Say my name, Brianna.'

'Why?' she asked defiantly.

'Because there's something potent and infinitely sexy about you crying out my name in the heat of passion.'

'But it sounds… It feels…'

'Too intimate?' He continued the erotic path between her breasts, his gaze never leaving hers as she nodded. 'It makes it all the more intense, no?'

Firm hands parted her thighs and one thumb lazily stroked her.

'Yes.' She sucked in a jagged breath as arousal spiked her blood with drugging pleasure. Her lids grew heavy and her back arched off the bed as the pressure escalated.

'That's it; lose yourself in it, Brianna…'

The lazy, continental drawl of her name had the right effect. Liquid heat oozed through her, making her limbs grow heavy and weak. *'Oh God.'*

'Wrong deity,' he said on a low laugh. The sound grazed over her, adding another dimension to the emotions bombarding her. Teeth bit her inner thigh; his warm tongue immediately soothed the bite, then proceeded to draw in ever closer circles to where his thumb wrecked mindless chaos.

Pleasure roared through her, eliciting the exact response she knew he wanted.

Sakis. The name echoed through her, over and over, seeking release. *Sakis.*

Her skin tightened as her climax grew closer. His tongue lapped her once, twice.

At the outer reaches of her mind, she heard a tearing sound. Sakis.

His thumb left her clitoris and was replaced immediately by his tongue. Brianna shut her eyes on a long, keening moan that was ripped from the depths of her soul.

Dear Lord, she was going to come like she never had before. She reached out, intending to grip the sheets, and instead encountered hot, muscled flesh.

Her eyes flew open just as he reared above her and plunged, hot, stiff and deep inside her.

'Sakis!'

'Yes! *Theos*, you look so hot like that.'

She repeated his name in a strangled litany as the most forceful orgasm she'd ever had laid her to waste. Through it all he kept up the rhythm, his groans of pleasure prolonging hers, so she milked him with her muscles.

'Brianna, *eros mou.*' He fell onto his elbows and plunged his fingers into her hair, holding her down as he plundered her mouth with his. 'You're incredible,' he breathed against her lips as he surged deeper inside her. 'I can't get enough of you.'

His fingers tightened in her hair as his mouth drifted over her jaw to her neck. His breath grew harsh, his body momentarily losing its steady rhythm as waves of pleasure washed over them.

Gritting his teeth, Sakis forced back control into his body, if only temporarily, because he knew he was fighting a losing battle. But it was a battle he was perfectly willing to surrender.

The warm, sexy body undulating beneath him blew his mind. While half of him declared himself insane for waiting this long to give in to the spellbinding attraction, the other half rejoiced at waiting. It was clear Brianna wouldn't have given in under normal circumstances.

Something had happened today at the café. He didn't know what and couldn't pinpoint it but the simple meal had taken an unexpected turn, had shaken him in a way that had left him reeling.

She'd felt it too; he knew it. Whether it was the reason she'd ended up here, he didn't know, but he intended to grasp this golden opportunity with both hands.

Her inner muscles tightened again and he nearly lost it. The swollen temptation of her roughly kissed mouth parted on a breath and he groaned. Sweet heaven, everything about her blew his mind, but never in a thousand years had he dreamed the sex with her would be this great, this intense.

She breathed his name again, as if now she'd given herself permission to use it she couldn't say it enough. That was okay with him…more than okay. The sound of his name on her lips was a potent aphrodisiac all by itself.

He was leaning down to take those impossibly delectable lips again when he saw it. Buried beneath the cascade of her hair was an elegant scroll across her left collarbone.

She surged blindly up at that moment, impatient for his kiss, and her hair fell away.

'I refuse to sink', the tattoo read. And beside it was a tiny etching of a soaring phoenix.

He already knew she was brave beyond words. The glimpse of her life she'd shared with him had alerted him to a not-so-rosy past, perhaps a harsh childhood. Sakis was struck again by how little he really knew of her. Nevertheless, he knew he didn't need to dig to find out she had a core of integrity that had remained unblemished, despite whatever adversities she'd faced.

The knowledge jolted something deep and alien inside him. Shockingly, he desired her even more. He bucked into her and revelled in her hitched breathing. But he wanted more; felt an unrelenting need to touch her in the way she'd touched him tonight.

'Open your eyes, *pethi mou*,' he demanded hoarsely.

Slowly her lids parted, displaying exquisite turquoise eyes drenched in desire. 'What?'

'I want you to see me, Brianna. Feel what you do to me and know that I appreciate you more than you know.'

Her mouth dropped open in wordless wonder. Unable to help himself, he kissed her again. Then all too soon the climax that had been building inexorably surged with brutal force. He spread her thighs wider and pumped hard and fast inside her.

Her cry of ecstasy echoed his own minutes later as he came in a torrent of dizzying pleasure.

He waited until their breaths had returned to normal before he brushed aside her hair and looked closely at the tattoo. Slowly, he let his finger drift over it, telling himself he'd imagined it, when she stiffened.

'This is interesting…'

The invitation to confess was blatant.

But Brianna couldn't open that can of worms. Not after she'd already opened so much of herself that she was sure Sakis could see straight through her by now. God, how had she imagined that she could just live in this moment, satisfy the clawing need then walk away?

With just a handful of words, Sakis had split her heart wide open.

I want you to see me… You're my anchor, Brianna… I appreciate you more than you know.

'Brianna?' The demand was more powerful.

She scrambled to find a reasonable explanation. 'I got it after I left my…my last job…' She stopped, her heart hammering as she realised that she was highly emotional from their love-making and really shouldn't be talking.

'Most people take a holiday between jobs. But you got a tattoo?' Scarily, his curiosity had deepened. 'And a symbolic one, at that. Did you feel as if you were sinking?' His fingers drifted over the words again, and despite her roiling emotions she shivered with fresh need.

She forced a laugh. 'I guess I'm not most people.' *Stop talking now. Stop. Stop. Stop!* 'And yes, I felt like I was sinking. For a while I lost my way.' God, no…

His fingers touched the phoenix then he brushed it with his mouth. 'But then you triumphed.'

She let out a shaky breath. 'Y-yes.'

'Hmm, we're agreed on one thing—you're not most people. You're exquisitely unique.' His hand drifted down, paused over her breast then trailed lower to touch the scar on her hip. 'And this?'

Her breath caught anew. How had she thought he wouldn't notice? He'd spent an inordinate amount of time exploring every inch of her body, much to her shameless delight. Of course Sakis's astute gaze would've caught the slightly puckered flesh where the sharp, white-hot lance of the inmate's blade had stabbed deep and ruptured her spleen.

'I…I was attacked. It was a mugging.' That at least was the truth. What she couldn't confess was where she'd been when it had happened.

His fingers stilled then he swore hard. 'When?'

'Two years ago.'

He cupped her jaw. 'Was your attacker caught?'

Brianna shut her eyes against the probing of his. 'Yes, they were caught. And there was even some semblance of justice.' If you could call six months' solitary confinement for a prisoner already serving life 'justice'.

That seemed to satisfy Sakis. When she risked a glance at him, the harshness she'd heard in his voice was not evident in his face. 'Good,' he breathed as his fingers resumed its bone-melting caress. 'I'm glad.'

Before she could draw another breath, his head dropped and his lips touched the puckered scar. Her skin heated then burned as his lips, then his tongue moved over her flesh.

She expected him to ask about her ankle tattoo, the one she'd caught him eyeing on the plane. But he seemed to have regained his zealous exploration of her body.

Her breath hitched as his mouth wreaked blissful havoc. Within seconds, her brain ceased to function.

Brianna woke to the sound of movement in her bedroom. Struggling up from an exquisitely saucy dream featuring Sakis, she opened her eyes to find him standing at the foot of her bed, his gaze on her as he secured his cufflinks.

The look on his face immediately gripped her attention. Gone was the lover who'd whispered ardent words of pleasure and worship against her skin last night. In its place was Sakis, billionaire shipping magnate. But, as she watched, she saw the mask slip to reveal the stress he hadn't completely banished.

'I have to go,' he said. 'There's been a development.'

Brianna sat up and pushed her hair from her face. 'What?'

His fingers stilled on his cuff. 'The bodies of two crew-members have been found.'

Shock and grief rocked through her in equal measures. 'When did you find out?'

'Ten minutes ago. They were found two miles away where converging tides had hidden the bodies. The investigators think they drowned.'

She started to throw the covers off, experienced a fierce wave of self-consciousness and talked herself out of it. This wasn't the time. 'Give me ten minutes to shower and I'll come with you. I… We need to see about getting them home.'

He rounded the bed and stopped in front of her. One hand caressed her cheek. 'It's been taken care of. I woke my head of HR. Those men died on my company's watch so they're my responsibility. He's arranging everything, but I'm meeting the families this morning to express my condolences…' He stopped and breathed in deep.

A wave of sadness washed over her. 'It wasn't the outcome any of us wanted. Which two were found?'

'The deputy captain and the first officer.'

'So there's still no sign of Morgan Lowell?'

'No.'

Which meant they still had no answer to what had happened to the tanker. 'I'll do my best to keep it out of the press but there are no guarantees.' She strove for a semblance of professionalism—professionalism which became precarious as his arms banded around her waist and pulled her closer. Desire's inferno raged through her body.

'It's all been handled. Foyle assures me there's a procedure to dealing with this. We can't do anything more.'

'So for now I'm redundant?'

'Never,' he breathed. 'You will never be redundant to me.'

The intensity of his answer sent alarm skittering over her skin. She was in danger of fooling herself again. In danger of believing that Sakis was beginning to want her, to need her the way she'd once dreamed of being needed.

Forcing a laugh, she pulled out of his arms. 'Never say never. Shower time; I'll be out in ten.' She backed away, all the while noting he remained where he stood, his intense eyes on her. 'Um, there's coffee in the kitchen if you want some. I'm afraid I don't have much in the way of food as I wasn't expecting to stop here last night.'

Finally, he nodded. 'Coffee will suffice.'

Brianna held her breath until he left her room, then flew into the bathroom.

Eight minutes later she was slipping on high-heeled designer leopard-print shoes as she pinned her hair up in its usual chignon. With one last look to check her appearance, she tugged the sleeves of her black Prada suit, picked up her large handbag containing her tablet and left the room.

Sakis stood at her tiny living-room window gazing down at the street below. He turned at her entrance and handed her the second cup in his hand just before his phone buzzed. As she sipped her coffee, Brianna couldn't stop staring at the magnificent man who paced her living room.

A man who'd not only taken her body but had found his way into parts of her heart she'd imagined had withered and died.

The thought of walking away from this man for ever gouged her with pain that left her breathless. When he speared her with those mesmerising eyes, she fought hard to stop her feelings from showing.

She would have time to deal with the heartache later. Because, of course, there would be heartache. Her feelings for Sakis had gone way beyond the professional. She'd known that before she'd slept with him last night. This morning, watching him struggle with fresh adversity made those feelings more intense.

So intense she set her coffee cup down before her trembling hands gave her away. 'Do you need anything else before we leave?'

'Yes. Come here.'

She went willingly, unable to resist him. He looked around the room then set the coffee mug on the window sill. 'You'll enlighten me as to why this apartment has barely any furniture in it later, but for now I have a greater need.'

'What?'

He pulled her closer and cupped her face in his large hands. 'I haven't said good morning properly. I may not get the chance once we leave here.' He sealed his mouth over hers in a long, exploratory kiss. When he finally lifted his head, his eyes were the dark green she associated with extreme emotion. 'Good morning, *pethi mou*,' he murmured.

'G-good morning,' she responded in a voice husky with fresh need.

Reluctantly he dropped his hand and stepped back. 'Let's get out of here now or we'll never leave.'

The journey to the office was completed in near silence. Sakis seemed lost in thought, his answers monosyllabic as she tried to slip back into professional mode.

As they entered the underground car park at Pantelides Towers, she couldn't bear it any more. Turning to him, she waited until he faced her. 'If you're wondering how to play this, you need not worry. No one needs to know about what happened last night. I know what happened with Giselle—'

'Is ancient history. What's going on between us is different.'

Her heart lurched then hammered. 'You mean you don't mind if anyone finds out?'

He stiffened. 'I didn't say that.'

The hurt that scythed through her was as unbearable as it was irrational.

When the car stopped she scrambled to get out. Sakis grabbed her arm to stay her and waved the driver away when he approached.

'Wait, that didn't come out right. What I meant was that the last thing I want is for you to be caught in the crosshairs because of my past. It's very easy for the wrong person to put two and two together and come up with fifteen. You don't deserve to suffer for my father's sins.'

She sagged backwards. 'Was he… He wasn't always that bad, was he?' It was unthinkable that they both could've suffered such outwardly different, but inwardly similar and painful upbringings. At least, she hoped not, because her heart ached for the pain in his voice every time he spoke about his father.

She had come to terms, somewhat, with her non-relationship with her mother.

He sucked in a long breath. 'Yes, he was. He was a philanderer and an extortionist who was corrupt to the core and very clever at hiding his true colours. When his deeds were finally uncovered, our lives were turned inside out. Our every word and deed was scrutinised. Several times, our house staff discovered tabloid journalists digging through our garbage in the middle of the night, looking for more dirt.'

Distress for him scythed through her. 'That's horrible.'

'As horrible as that was, I mistakenly thought that was the worst of it.'

She was almost afraid to ask. 'What else did you find?'

'It turned out my father had mistresses stashed all over the globe, not just the secretary who'd grown tired of his philandering ways and empty promises—she was the one who blew the whistle that started the ball rolling, by the way. Once the first mistress crawled out of the woodwork, they were unstoppable. And you know why they all came forward, every single one of them?'

She shook her head despite the dread crawling through her stomach.

'*Money.* With my father's arrest and all our assets frozen, they knew the money that funded their lavish lifestyles would dry up. They had to sell their stories quickly and to the highest bidder before they became yesterday's news—regardless of the fact that their actions would push my mother into attempting to take her own life.'

She gasped. '*God*, I'm so sorry, Sakis.'

Pain was etched deep on his face but he slid his fingers through hers and brought her hand up to his mouth. But, although his touch was gentle, the gleam in his was anything but. 'So you see why I find it hard to trust the motives of others?'

Dry-mouthed, she nodded. 'I do, but it doesn't hurt to occasionally give the benefit of the doubt.' The knowledge that she was silently pleading for herself sent a wave of shame through her.

His gaze raked her face, his own features a harsh stamp of implacability. Then slowly, as she watched, his face relaxed. He reached across and cupped her face, pulled her close and kissed her.

'For you, Brianna, I'm willing to suspend my penchant for expecting the worst, to let go of my bias and cynicism—because, believe me, in this instance I relish the chance to be proved wrong.'

But he wasn't proved wrong.

At three o'clock that afternoon, Richard Moorecroft rang with a full confession for his part in the tanker crash.

CHAPTER NINE

AN HOUR LATER, Sakis was pacing his office when he heard his head of security enter and exchange greetings with Brianna.

'Get in here, both of you!' he bellowed, the anger he was fighting to contain roiling just beneath his skin.

He turned from his desk as they entered. He tried to concentrate on his security chief. But, as if it acted independent of his control, his gaze strayed to Brianna.

She was as contained and self-assured as he'd always known her to be. There was no trace of the woman who'd writhed beneath him last night, screaming her pleasure as he'd taken her to the heights of ecstasy, or the gentle soul who'd listened to him spill his guts about his father in the car, her eyes haunted with pain for him.

He wanted to hate her for her poise and calm but he realised that he admired her for it—something *else* he admired about her. *Theos*, his list of things he admired about Brianna Moneypenny grew by the day. Anyone would think she meant more to him than—

His mind screeched to a halt but his legs were weakening with the force of the unknown emotion that smashed through him. Folding his arms, he gritted his teeth and perched on the edge of his desk.

'What do you have for me?' he demanded from Sheldon.

'As you requested, we dug a little deeper into the financials of First Mate Isaacs and Deputy Captain Green. A deposit of one hundred thousand euros was made into each of their accounts seven days ago.'

Sakis's hands tightened around his biceps as bitterness tightened like a vice around his chest. 'Have we traced the source of the funds?' Even now when he had the evidence, he didn't want to believe his employees were guilty.

Only this morning, he would've believed the worst. But Brianna's caution to give them the benefit of the doubt had settled deep within him. When he'd given her words further thought he'd realised how much he'd let cynicism rule his life. Letting go even a little had felt…liberating. He'd breathed easier for the first time in a very long time.

But now the hard ache was back full force along with memories he couldn't seem to bury easily.

'Moorecroft used about half a dozen shell companies to obfuscate his activities. Without his confession it'd have taken a few more days but knowing where to look helped. It also helped that the crew members did nothing to hide the money they received,' Sheldon said.

'Because they thought they were home free,' Sakis rasped. The confirmation from Moorecroft that he'd paid his crew to deliberately crash his tanker to spark a hostile takeover made a tide of rage rise within him. Sakis could forgive the damage to his vessel—it was insured and he would be more than compensated for it once the investigation was over. But it was the senseless loss of lives he couldn't stomach, along with the fact that the rest of his crew had been put at severe risk.

After his phone call with Moorecroft, with the pain-racked faces of his dead employees' families fresh in his mind, he hadn't hesitated to let his broken adversary know to expect full criminal charges against him.

He'd experienced a twinge when he'd looked up from the phone call and caught Brianna's expression but he'd pushed the feeling away.

Greed had driven another man to put others' lives at risk. There was no way he could forgive that.

'What about Lowell's account?'

'We're trying to access it but it's a bit more complicated.'

Sakis frowned. 'How complicated?'

'His salary was wired to a routing account that went to a Swiss bank account. Those are a little tougher to crack.'

Surprise shot him upright. He turned to Brianna. 'Did we flag that up in his HR details?'

She bit her lip. Heat flared in his groin, followed closely by another guilty twinge for his harsh tone. 'No,' she answered.

Sakis sucked in a deep breath. 'That will be all, Sheldon. Let me know as soon as you have anything new.'

Sheldon nodded and left.

Silence reigned for several minutes. Then Brianna walked forward. 'I'm expecting an "I told you so".'

He settled his attention fully on her in a way he'd been reluctant to do with another person in the room. Even now he feared his features would betray the extent of the alien emotions roaring through him.

Theos, he needed a drink. *Why the hell not?*

'There's no point. It is what it is.'

'Then why are you pouring yourself a drink in the middle of a work day?'

'It's not the middle of the day, it's almost five o'clock.'

'It's five o'clock for most people but for you it's not, since you work till midnight most nights.'

Sakis barely glanced at the fifty-year-old single malt as he lifted it to his lips and drained it. 'If you must know, I'm trying to understand what drives anyone to depths of betrayal such as this with little regard for how it'll hurt their family and people who care about them.'

She started to come towards him and his senses leapt, but at the last moment she veered away and started straightening the papers on his desk. Sakis barely stopped himself from growling his frustration.

'And are you getting any answers from the bottom of your glass?'

He slammed the glass down and strode to where she stood. 'Are you trying to rile me? Because, trust me, you're succeeding.'

'I'm just trying to make you see that you can't blame yourself for the choices other people make. You can either forgive them or...'

'Or?'

For a single moment, her face creased with something similar to the bitterness and despair clawing through him. 'Or you can cut them out of your life, I suppose.'

He frowned. 'Who cut you out of their life, Brianna?'

Stark pain washed over her features before she tried to mask it. 'This isn't about me.'

He took her by the arms. 'It most definitely is. What did she do to you?'

She made a sound that caught and tightened around his heart. The sort of sound a wounded animal made when they were frightened.

'She...she chose drugs over me.' She stopped and sucked in a gulping breath. 'I don't really want to talk about this.'

'You encouraged me to bare my soul to you this morning. I think it's only fair that you do the same.'

'More therapy?' She tried pull away but he held fast.

'Tell me about her. Where is she? Is she still alive?'

A sad little shiver went through her. 'Yes, she's alive. But we're not in touch. We haven't been for a while.'

'Why not?'

She cast a desperate glance around, anywhere but at him. 'Sakis, this isn't right. I'm your... You're my boss.'

'We went way beyond that last night. Answer my question, unless you wish me to demonstrate our revised positions?'

Her lips parted on a tiny gasp that made him want to plunge his tongue between them but he restrained himself. For once, the need to see beneath the surface of Brianna Moneypenny trumped everything else.

'I…I've already told you I didn't grow up in the best of circumstances. Because of her drug habit we…lived on the street from when I was about four until I was ten. Sometimes I went for days without a proper meal.'

Shock slammed through Sakis. For several moments he was unable to reconcile the woman who stood before him, poised and breathtakingly stunning, with the bedraggled, haunted image she portrayed.

'How… Why?' he demanded, cursing silently when he saw her pale face.

Bruised eyes finally met his. 'She couldn't hold down a job for longer than a couple of weeks but she was cunning enough to evade the authorities for the better part of six years. But finally her luck—if you can call it that—ran out. Social Services took me away from her when I was ten. I found her when I turned eighteen.'

Another bolt of shock went through him. 'You *found* her? After what she did to you, you went to look for her?'

Her eyes darkened with pain. When his hands slid down her arms to hers, she gripped him tight. But he knew her mind was firmly in the past.

'She was my mother. Don't get me wrong, I hated her for a long time, but I had to eventually accept the fact that she was also a human being caught in the grip of an addiction that almost ruined her life,' she said.

Sakis saw her raw pain, clenched his jaw and silently cursed the woman who'd done this to her. More than anything, he wanted to obliterate her pain.

Theos, what the hell was happening to him?

Wait… 'Almost?'

She gave a jerky nod. 'She got it together in the end. In the eight years we were apart, she beat her addiction and got her act together. I…can't help but think I was the one who was holding her back.'

His growled curse made her jump. Leaning down, he kissed her hard and fast.

'She never made an effort to kick her habit when I was around. And she would get this look in her eyes whenever she looked at me—like she hated me.'

Sakis wanted to swear again, but he bit his tongue. 'No child should ever be blamed for being born. She had a duty to look after you. She failed. So she got herself better, then what?'

'She remarried and had another child.'

'So, it was a happy ending for her?' He couldn't stop a hint of bitterness from spilling out. He and his brothers hadn't been granted a happy ending. And his mother continued to live a hollow existence, a shadow of the vibrant woman she'd been for the first decade of his life. 'But she cut you from her life?'

'Yes; I suppose she didn't want the reminder,' she answered lightly; a little too breezily.

Sakis knew she was glossing over her pain. Wasn't it the same way he'd glossed over his for years? But something else struck him, made him reel all over again.

She'd had a mother who had done her wrong in the most fundamental of ways—she'd failed to look after her daughter when she was young and helpless and needed her most. And yet, Brianna had gone out of her way to find her after she was grown and on her own two feet.

The depth of compassion behind such forgiveness rocked him to his soul. 'I never forgave my father for what he did to us, and especially what he did to my mother. Hell, sometimes I think he purposefully died of a heart attack in her arms just to twist the knife in further, because she sure as hell almost died mourning him.'

She touched his cheek with fingers that trembled. 'Don't

be too hard on her. She had her heart broken the same way yours was.'

But then he'd had his brothers and the myriad cousins, aunts and uncles who'd rallied round when the going had got tough. Even in his darkest days, there'd always been someone around and, although he'd never been one to reach out, deep down he'd known there was someone around.

Whereas, Brianna had had nobody.

His insides clenched with the same emotion he'd experienced earlier. Like a magnet drawn to her irresistible presence, he pulled her closer.

'You're amazing, do you know that?' he murmured against her hair, satisfied for the moment to just hold her close like this.

'I am?' Her delicate eyelids fluttered as she looked up at him.

'Yes. You have a unique way of holding up a mirror to some of my deeply held beliefs that make me question them.'

She gave a shaky laugh. 'And that's a good thing?'

'Forcing me to examine them is a good thing. Learning to forgive is another…' He felt her stiffen but she felt too good in his arms for him to question her reaction. 'But perhaps I can try to understand the reason why people act the way they do.'

When she tried to pull away, he reluctantly let her place several inches between them.

'I should get back to work.'

Sakis frowned. He didn't want distance. He didn't like the threat of tears in her eyes. But already he could feel her withdrawing.

Belatedly, he remembered where they were.

But so what? They were alone in his inner sanctum. No one would dare breach it without incurring his wrath. Besides, both his door and hers were shut. And all he wanted was a quick kiss. Well…he gave an inner grimace…he wanted way more than that but…

He focused to find her halfway to the door. What the hell...?

In swift strides he reached the door and slammed his hand against the heavy polished steel-and-timber frame, the feeling that he was missing something fundamental eating away at him. She jumped, her wide-eyed gaze swinging to his.

'What's the matter?' he demanded.

'Nothing. I'm just going back to my desk, Mr—'

'Don't you even dare think about calling me that!'

'Okay.' She licked her plump lower lip. 'Sakis...can I go back to my desk?'

His ire grew along with his hard-on. He grasped her waist. 'After what just happened? No way.'

She eyed the closed door with a longing he wanted transferred to him, preferably with single-minded devotion to the granite-hard part of his anatomy. 'Please...'

He tracked back over their conversation and sighed. 'I can't change who I am overnight, Brianna. Forgiveness comes easily to you, but I'm going to need time.'

Her eyes widened even further with alarm. 'I don't want you to change...not unless you want to. I mean, I'm not invested in anything here...with you. Certainly not enough to warrant you going out of your way to make those sorts of reassurances.'

Those words spilling from her lips sent him into the stratosphere. With a snarl born of frustration, anxiety and piercing arousal, he locked the door, caught her around the waist and swung her up in his arms.

'Sakis!'

'Let's just see how invested you are, shall we?'

'Put me down!'

Ignoring her demand, he carried her to the desk she'd straightened so efficiently minutes ago. Setting her on the edge, he slashed one hand across the polished surface, sending the papers flying.

'I seriously hope you don't expect me to clean that up!'

Her colour was hectic, her breath coming out in pants as she glared at him.

Yes, this was what he wanted: her fire, her spirit. He hated the sad, frightened, achingly lonely Brianna. He hated cool, calm and distant Brianna even more, especially after last night. Not after seeing the generous heart and fiery passion that resided beneath the prim exterior.

'If that's what I desire, then you shall do it, no?'

Her chin rose and his senses roared. 'In your dreams. My job description doesn't include cleaning up after you. I'm not your chambermaid.'

He caught her hands and planted them on his chest. 'As of last night, your job description includes doing whatever pleases me in the bedroom.'

Despite her protests, her fingers curled into his chest. He nearly shouted with triumph and relief. 'We're not in the bedroom. Besides, what about what I want?'

His hand fisted in her hair, sought and found the hidden clasp and tugged. Vibrant golden hair spilled over his arm. Using it, he pulled her close until his jaw grazed her soft cheek. 'Call this mutually beneficial therapy. Besides, I'm a quick study, *glikia mou*. I know *exactly* what you want.'

Her breath caught, making him laugh. He pushed her back, using her slight imbalance to swiftly undo the single button of her jacket. It was off before she could take another surprised breath.

'Sakis, for goodness' sake! We're in your office.'

'My *locked* office. And it's the end of the day for everyone else except us.'

'I still think…'

He kissed her, the temptation too much to resist. That it effectively shut her up was a great bonus, as was her fractured moan that vibrated through him.

He made easy work of the zipper of her dress and slid it off with minimal protest. He didn't notice what she wore beneath until he spread her backwards across his desk. A strangled choke made its way up his throat as he froze.

'*Theos*, tell me you haven't been wearing lingerie like these since you started working for me?'

A provocative smile dispelled the nervous apprehension on her face. 'Fine. I won't.'

She stretched under his gaze, arching her back in a sinuous move that made him think of a sleek cat. Over the top of the bustier bra that connected the garter to the top of her sheer stockings, the plump slopes of her breasts taunted him. His mouth watered and his fingers itched to touch with a need so strong he staggered forward. Roughly he pulled one cup down and circled a rosy nipple with his tongue.

Her ragged cry of delight was music to his ears, because the knowledge that he wasn't in this insane feeling alone soothed a stunned and confused part of him.

He rolled the nub in his mouth and tugged with his teeth while he frantically undressed. Naked, he straightened and glanced down at her, spread across his desk like a decadent offering. Struck dumb, he just stared at her stunning perfection.

'You're about to tell me you've imagined me spread out like this across your desk, aren't you?' she asked huskily.

Surprisingly, this particular scenario had never once crossed his mind. 'No, and it's a good thing too. I don't think I'd ever have got any work done if I had a picture such as this in my mind,' he rasped, his voice thick and alien. 'I've imagined you elsewhere though—in my shower, across the back seat of my car, in my lift...'

A shiver went through her. 'Your lift?'

'*Ne*. In my mind, my private lift has seen a lot of action featuring you in very many compromising ways. But *this* beats even my most fevered imaginings.'

He continued to stare at the vision before him. He must have stared for too long because she started to squirm. With one hand he held her down. With the other, he pulled down the skimpiest thong ever created and slid his hands between her thighs. Her wet heat coated his fingers and in that moment Sakis believed he'd never been so turned on. The next moment, he realised he was wrong.

Brianna laid her hand on his thigh and that simple action sent his heart rate soaring out of control. Then her hand moved upward…and her searching fingers boldly settled over his hard length.

'*Theos!*'

'Wrong deity,' she responded saucily.

His laugh scraped his throat as she gripped him hard. From root to tip, she caressed him, over and over, until he was sure he'd lost his hold on reality. His altered state was why he didn't read her intention when she moistened her lip and wriggled down his desk. Before he could admonish her for not staying put, she boldly took him in her perfect mouth.

'Brianna!' He slammed a hand on the desk to steady himself against the deep shudder powering through him. The sight of him in her mouth nearly unmanned him. His breath hissed out as he fought not to gush his climax like a hormonal teenager right then and there. He groaned deep and long as her tongue swirled over him and her hand pumped, teased, threatened to blow his mind to smithereens. '*Yes!* Just like that!'

He suffered the sweet torture until the tell-tale tightening forced him to pull back. When she clung and made a sound of protest, Sakis seriously considered giving in, but no…

The chance to take her again, stamp his possession on her, was paramount. He needed to obliterate that distance he'd sensed her trying to put between them. The reason for it was irrelevant. The need was too strong to question.

He trailed hot kisses down her body, making her squirm anew for him. The seconds it took to locate and put on the condom felt like decades. But at last he parted her thighs and positioned himself at her entrance. She lifted her head and looked at him, her expression one of rapt hunger that almost equalled his own.

'Are you invested in this?' he rasped.

A glimmer of alarm skittered through her eyes. 'Sakis…'

'Are you? Because I am, Brianna.'

Her mouth parted on a shocked exhalation. 'Please, Sakis, don't say that.'

'Why not?'

'Because you don't mean it.'

'Yes, I do. I fought it for as long as I could, but in the end it was no use. I want you. I want this. Do you want it too?'

Her breath shivered out of her. 'Y-yes. I want this.'

He plunged into her, perhaps a little more roughly than he'd intended, but his need was too great. Watching her breasts bounce with each thrust, Sakis wondered if a heart had ever burst from too much excitement, too much need.

Because, even as he took her to the brink, he realised it wasn't enough. He'd never get enough of Brianna. But this… *Theos*, this was a brilliant start. Later he would pause to examine his feelings a little bit more, reassure himself exactly what he was dealing with and how best to handle the strange feelings inside him. Because something *was* happening to him. Something he couldn't define.

As his brain melted from pleasure overload, he let his hands drift upward in a slow caress. His fingers grazed her scar and a feeling of primitive rage rose through him at the person who'd done this to her. If he hadn't received Brianna's reassurance that justice had been done, he'd have hunted the culprit down and torn him apart with his bare hands.

Overwhelming protectiveness—another alien feeling he had to grapple with. Gripping her nape, he forced her up to receive his kiss as he surged one last time inside her, felt her spasm around him and let go.

The rush was the best yet. With a groan that stemmed from

his soul, he shut his eyes and gave in to it. It was a long time before reality descended on him again.

Brianna's arms tightened around Sakis as their breaths returned to normal, fear clutching her heart.

She'd spilled her guts to him about her mother. He'd been outraged on her behalf. He'd shown her sympathy that had touched her soul and made her realise that, while she'd forgiven her mother for an addiction she hadn't been able to conquer, it was the pain of her abandonment when she was clean that hurt the most.

But Sakis had readily admitted forgiveness was a rare commodity to *him*.

She tried to tell herself it didn't matter. Come Friday, when her time ran out, she would be out of here. Greg had taken to sending her hourly reminders of her deadline. To stop Sakis from getting suspicious, she'd put her phone on silent and zipped it out of sight in her jacket pocket.

But her imminent departure wasn't the reason she'd given Sakis a glimpse into her past.

It was because she'd desperately wanted him to see her— not the ruthlessly efficient personal assistant but *her*, Brianna Moneypenny, the person who'd started life as Anna Simpson, daughter of a crackhead, and then had taken her grandmother's maiden name and forged a new identity for herself.

She'd bared herself to Sakis, and now she felt more vulnerable than ever.

His stance on betrayal remained rigid. If he ever found out about her past, he would never forgive her for bringing her soiled reputation to his company.

'I can hear you thinking,' he said, his voice a husky muffle against her neck.

'I've just had sex with you on your desk. That merits a little bit of thinking time, don't you think?'

'Perhaps. But, since it's going to be a familiar feature in our relationship, I suggest you get used to it.'

He heard her sudden intake of breath. Rearing up, he rested on his elbows and speared her with a probing look. One she couldn't meet for long before she settled her gaze on the pulse beating in his neck. 'The word "relationship" frightens you?'

She willed her pulse to slow, forcing the hope that had no business fluttering in her chest to die a swift death. There could be no future between them. None.

'Not the word, no, but I think this is going a little too…fast. We only started sleeping together last night.'

'After eighteen months of holding back. I think asking for restraint right now is asking for the impossible. I'll need several weeks at least to take the edge off.'

She looked into intense green eyes. 'You warned me at my interview, conducted across this very desk, not to even dream of getting involved with you.'

He had the grace to look shamefaced, but even that look held a lethal charm that doomed her. 'It was so soon after Giselle; I was still angry. Everyone I'd interviewed reminded me of her. You were the first one who didn't. When I found myself getting attracted to you, I fought it with everything I had because I didn't want that nasty business repeating itself.'

Unable to resist, she slid her fingers through his thick hair. 'She really did a number on you, didn't she?'

His smile was wry. 'I'm not beyond admitting I was blinded to her true nature until it was much too late.'

'Wow, I'm not sure whether to be pleased or disappointed that you're fallible.'

He straightened and picked her up from his desk as if she weighed nothing. 'I never claimed to be perfect, except when it comes to winning rowing championships. Then I'm unequalled,' he boasted as he started to stride across the office.

'Modesty is such a rare and beautiful thing, Sakis.'

His deep, unfettered laugh made her heart swell with pleasure. 'Yes, so is the ability to state things as they are.'

'No one will accuse you of being a wallflower. Wait, where are you taking me?'

'Upstairs, to get you therapeutically wet and soapy in my shower.'

'I think you're taking this therapy thing a bit far. Sakis, put me down. Our clothes!' She wriggled until he let her slide down his body to stand upright.

'Leave them.' He keyed in the code for his turbo lift.

'Absolutely not. No way am I letting the cleaner find my knickers and stuff all over your office floor!' She ran back and started gathering them. 'And don't just stand there, pick up your own damn clothes.'

With a husky laugh, Sakis followed and picked up his discarded clothes. Then, because she really couldn't stand to leave them, she gathered the strewn papers and placed them back on the desk. When his mocking laugh deepened, she rounded on him.

'Next time, you pick them up yourself.'

He caught her to him and smacked her lightly on the bottom. When she yelped, he kissed her. 'That's for disobeying me again. But I like that you admit there'll be a next time.'

She looked up and her gaze caught his. For the first time, she glimpsed a vulnerability she'd never seen before in his eyes. As if he hadn't been sure she would let anything like what had happened occur between them again.

Desolation caught at her heart. She would pay a steep price for letting this thing continue but the need to be with him in every way until she left was too strong. Going closer, she raised herself on tiptoe and kissed along his jaw.

'There'll be a next time only if I get to go on top.'

Sakis jerked awake to the sound of a phone buzzing. Beside him Brianna was out cold, worn out from the relentless demands he'd made of her body. The same lethargy swirled through him, making him toy with the idea of ignoring the phone.

The buzzing increased.

Rubbing the sleep from his eyes, he started to reach for his phone, but realised the ringing was from Brianna's.

Getting off the bed, he hunted through their discarded clothes until he located the phone in her jacket pocket.

Palming it, Sakis hesitated again. Relief coursed through him when it stopped ringing. But, almost immediately, it started to buzz again. With an impatient sigh, he pressed the button.

'Anna?' A man's impatient voice, one he didn't recognise. Not that he had first-hand knowledge of the men who called Brianna, of course… A spike of intense dislike filled him at the thought of anyone who'd been given the permission to call her…*Anna*?

Sakis frowned. 'You've got the wrong number. This is *Bri-anna's* phone. Who is this?'

And why the hell are you calling at three a.m.?

Silence greeted his demand. A moment later, the line went dead.

Sakis pulled the phone away and searched for the number. It was blocked.

Dropping her jacket, he went back to bed and set the phone down on the bedside table. He tucked his arms beneath his head, unable to stem the unease that spiralled through his gut.

He had no grounds to suspect anything other than a wrongly dialled number. It could be pure coincidence that another man had called his lover demanding to speak to *Anna*.

And yet, Sakis was still awake two hours later, unable to shake the mild dread. When the phone pinged with an incoming message, he snatched it up before it could wake her.

With a sinking feeling in the pit of his stomach, he slid his thumb across the interactive surface. Again the number was blocked but the words on the screen iced his spine:

Just a friendly reminder that you have three days to get me what I need. G.

CHAPTER TEN

IT'S NOTHING. YOU'RE blowing things out of proportion.

Sakis repeated the words over and over as he pulled the handles of the rowing machine in his gym just after six o'clock. Right this moment he'd have loved to be doing the real thing but this wasn't the time to jump in his car and drive to his rowing club, no matter how powerful the temptation.

He smothered the voice that suggested he was running away from the truth.

What truth?

He didn't know what the text on Brianna's phone meant. Sure, the easiest thing would've been to wake her up and demand an answer. Instead, he'd got up, returned the phone to her jacket pocket and high-tailed it to the gym.

He yanked on the row bars and welcomed the burn of pain between his shoulders and the sweat that poured off his skin. He tried to ignore the question hammering through his brain but the truth of his actions was as clear as the scowl he could see in his reflection in the gym's mirrors.

Are you invested in this? When he'd blurted those words out last night, he'd been stunned by the need to hear her answer in the affirmative. Because in that moment he'd realised just how truly invested he was in having Brianna in his life and not just as his personal assistant. Even now, with suspicion warring with his new-found intentions to trust more and judge less, the thought of not having her around made a red haze cloud his senses.

You have three days to get me what I need...

Was it a professional request? Who would be making such a demand of her professionally?

If it was a personal one...

He emitted the deep growl that had been growing in his chest as jealousy spiked through his gut.

At that moment, Brianna walked into the gym and froze. In the mirror, their eyes meshed. The look on his face was fierce and unwelcoming—he knew that. He wasn't surprised when her eyes widened and she hesitated.

'I can come back later if I'm disturbing you.'

With one last, vicious yank on the row bar, he let it go, watched it clatter against the spinning wheel and stood and advanced towards her.

The sight of her in skin-clinging, midriff-baring Lycra made adrenaline and arousal spike higher. The thought of making another of his myriad sexual fantasies come true pounded through his blood and groin with a ferocity that made him grit his teeth. He barely managed to catch himself from lunging for her, and veered towards the row of treadmills.

'Disturb me. I was in danger of letting my imagination get the better of me.' He gave a smile he knew fell far short of the mark and busied himself with programming the treadmill next to his. When he was done, he waved her over.

'Thirty minutes okay?' he asked.

He caught the look of wariness on her face as she nodded and approached the machine.

About to set his own programme, he glanced over and was pretty sure he burst a blood vessel when she bent over to stretch.

'Theos!' His hiss brought her head up and she slowly straightened.

Her gaze travelled down his chest and dropped to the loose

shorts that did nothing to hide the power of her effect of him. When her mouth dropped open, he let out a strained laugh. 'Now you see the power you have over me.'

She stepped onto the treadmill and pressed start. 'You don't sound too happy about it.'

'I like being in control, *agapita*. And you're detonating mine with that tight body of yours.'

He watched the blush creep up from her neck to stain her cheeks. 'It's not exactly a walk in the park for me either, if that helps you?'

Sakis fought to reconcile the blushing, sexually innocent woman in front of him with one who could be capable of duplicity.

Don't judge before you know the facts...

Brianna's words flashed through his churning mind. With a deep breath, he started his own machine and began jogging alongside her.

One minute, one full minute, was how long he lasted before he gave in to the urge to glance over at her. The sight of her breasts bouncing beneath her clinging tank top made him groan. Only his ingrained discipline from his professional rowing days stopped him from losing his footing.

But he didn't glance away. He stared his fill. And then he stared some more as his body moved to the spinning treadmill entirely independent of his frenzied thoughts.

She tried to ignore him. But after stumbling a fourth time, she used the handlebars to raise herself and planted her feet on the stationary part of the machine.

'Sakis, please stop doing that. I can't concentrate.'

He blew out a breath and slammed his hand on the stop button. 'Then let's both end this before one of us does themselves an injury.' He reached over and did the same to her machine. 'If you want a workout, I can think of a much better one.'

'*Sakis!*'

'I can't think why I let you call me Mr Pantelides for the

last eighteen months, when the sound of my name on your lips makes me harder than I've ever been in my life.'

The gurgling sound she made was somewhere between outrage and reproach as he swung her into his arms, but her arms curved around his neck all the same.

'Should I even ask where you're taking me?'

'I'd love nothing better than to bend you over the handlebars of that treadmill, but I don't have a condom down here, and I can't risk one of my executives walking in on us. My steam room will have to suffice this time.'

He made short work of getting her into his shower to sluice off their sweat before he pushed her into the smoky interior of his private steam room.

He ruthlessly ignored the mocking voice that suggested he was hiding behind sex instead of confronting her about the text.

But, as he pulled her astride him and plunged deep inside her, Sakis knew he would have to confront her sooner rather than later. He refused to allow suspicion to eat away at him. He'd found a precious peace of mind in her arms this past couple of days and he refused to let distrust and shadows of the past erode it.

Her arms tightened round him as her climax gathered.

'Oh God, Sakis. It feels so good,' she sobbed against his neck.

His own control cracked wider. 'Yes, *agapita*. It would be a shame if something came along and ruined it.' His hand slid into her hair and brought her head up so he could look into her eyes. 'Wouldn't it?' He pushed higher insider her, possessing her completely.

Her lips parted in a pre-climactic gasp as her muscles gripped him tight. 'Yes.'

'Good. Then let's keep that from happening, yes?'

The touch of confusion that clouded her eyes was washed

away a second later with the onset of ecstatic wonder that transformed her face from stunning to exquisitely beautiful.

He groaned deep as her convulsions triggered his own release, making him loosen his possessive hold on her. Her head fell back onto his shoulder and it was all he could do to hang on as he was plunged into the longest climax of his life.

He walked them back into the shower as spasms continued to seize her frame.

In silence, he washed her, then himself, all the while aware of the puzzled glances she sent his way.

They made it as far as his bedroom before she rounded on him.

'Is this tense silent treatment part of your morning-after ritual or is there something going on here I should know about?'

He damned his suspicious nature and his inability to shake his gut's warning. His gaze swung past the temptation of her wet, towel-clad body to the bedside table and he tensed further when he saw her phone.

She'd seen the message.

'Sakis?'

He met her troubled blue gaze. 'I start negotiations on the China oil deal this morning and they're not the best customers to deal with at the best of times. In light of what's happened, I want nothing to impede this deal.'

Her brow cleared. 'Oh. Well, I don't see anything that will hinder your negotiations.'

His chest lightened at the reassurance then immediately tightened at the thought that the message had been personal, from a man who viewed himself in a position to make demands from the woman Sakis had claimed as his lover. It struck home again just how little he really knew Brianna Moneypenny. Or was it *Anna*?

Sucking in a deep breath, he went to his drawer and pulled out a pair of boxers. 'Are you sure? The last thing we need are skeletons popping out of closets right now. I think my company's had enough of those to last a millennium.'

Her pause lasted a few seconds, but it felt like years to him. 'I'm sure.'

He turned. 'Good.'

When he saw her catch her lower lip between her teeth, his pulse spiked. *Theos*, how could he crave her again after the many times he'd taken her last night and the intense orgasm he'd experienced with her barely fifteen minutes ago? He mentally shook his head, turned away and carried on dressing. If he gave in to his need, they'd never leave this room.

He heard the towel slide from her body and his fingers clenched around his socks.

'So...this is about the Chinese deal and has nothing to do with...with what's happened between us?'

He shoved his leg into his trousers with more force than was necessary. 'I made my feeling clear on that score, *agapita*. You haven't forgotten already, have you?'

'No, I haven't.'

Was that a tremble in her voice? Every instinct screamed at him to ask her about the text.

Private or not, if Brianna was hiding something should he not confront her about it now rather than later?

Heartbeat accelerating wildly, he shrugged on his shirt and faced her.

'Great. Then do you mind telling me what that text on your phone is all about?'

He knows!

It took every single ounce of control Brianna could summon not to let out the cry of anguish that ripped through her chest.

'The text?' She hated the breathless prevarication but she needed to buy herself more time.

'Your phone rang in the middle of the night. Someone asked for Anna then hung up. Then the text came. Care to explain?'

No, no, no, she wasn't ready. She'd woken up this morning and had lain in the bed knowing without a shadow of a doubt that she'd fallen for Sakis. And also that she needed to come clean and throw herself at his mercy. But she hadn't planned to do it now. Not when Sakis had so much on his plate. She'd planned to type up her resignation then hand it to him with a confession about her past in the hope that he would choose forgiveness over condemnation for her lie about who she really was.

'Brianna?' Sakis's voice was as cold as his expression.

Despair washed over her. 'It's a friend... He wants a favour from me.'

He frowned. 'A *favour*. And he calls you at three in the morning? What sort of favour?'

'Help with his...his work.'

His frown intensified. 'So it wasn't a personal call?'

That she could answer without flinching at the half-truth. 'No.'

Her breath caught as he stalked to where she stood. The sight of him, standing so close with his shirt loose and his ridged chest within touchable distance, made heat spike through her.

'He's not from a competitor, is he? He's not trying to poach you?'

'He's not trying to poach me, no.'

His hand tugged her chin up until her face was exposed to his scrutiny. Whatever he saw there must have satisfied him because after a minute he nodded. Tugging her to him, he grabbed the towel she barely held together and whisked it from her body. He sealed her mouth with his and then proceeded to explore her exposed body with demanding hands. Just when she thought she would expire from need, he set her free.

'That's good to know because otherwise I'd have hunted this man down and torn him limb to limb, as I promised. Now, go and get dressed. And wear one of those no-nonsense suits.

It'll kill me to imagine what's underneath it but at least outwardly it'll keep me from jumping you every time you walk into my office.'

A ragged gasp left her at the reprieve she'd been granted and the cowardly way she'd grasped it. In a way, it was a testament to just how pressured Sakis was that he hadn't probed deeper.

Or it could be that he's beginning to trust you?

Anguish made her feet slow as she collected her clothes from last night and went into her suite. She'd been granted a reprieve, yes, but had she rendered her eventual confession worthless by not admitting the truth now? Because surely, once she told Sakis just who'd texted her, he'd damn her for ever?

She loved him. Everything about Sakis made her heart beat faster and her soul ache with regret that they hadn't met in another time…a time before she'd been forced to hide her past and unknowingly compromise her future.

Her phone buzzed as she stepped into the grey-and- black platform heels that matched her grey Versace suit.

She knew who it was before she pressed 'answer'.

'I need more time,' she blurted before he'd finished speaking.

Silence. 'You haven't been found out, have you?' Greg demanded.

Brianna sank down onto the hard seat of the dressing stool in her suite's walk-in closet. 'No, but you calling and texting me at three a.m. doesn't help.'

'If you haven't been found out then what's the problem?' he fired back.

'I just… There's a lot of attention on me right now. I need to make sure I do things properly or this will end badly… for both of us.' Her skin burned with each lie. And any minute she suspected the heavens to crack open and lightning to strike her down.

He gave an irritated sigh. 'I have to go out of town unexpectedly. I could be a few days, maybe a week. You have until I get back to get me the information I need. If you don't have it on my return, it's game over.' His tone vibrated with dark menace. 'Word of warning—don't test me, Anna.'

The name scoured across her senses, making her flinch. She was no longer Anna Simpson. Deciding to change her name had been a step in reinventing herself but it wasn't until she'd seen herself through Sakis's eyes that she'd felt truly reborn.

He'd called her amazing yesterday. And throughout the night he'd shown her a powerful ecstasy beyond the physical, made more wonderful because of her feelings for him.

The thought of living without him, of walking away, sent a poker-hot lance of pain through her heart. She was still silently mourning losing Sakis when she walked into the dining room.

The sight of the assorted platters of pancakes, waffles, chocolate and strawberry syrup and endless more condiments made tears prickle her eyes.

Sakis sauntered towards her, one eyebrow raised. 'We made love long and hard last night, and not once did you cry. I'm trying very hard not to let my ego be dented by the fact that it's the sight of pancakes for breakfast that makes you cry and not our lovemaking.'

'I… It's not… No one's ever done anything like this for me,' she finally blurted.

His expression morphed from teasing to compassionate in a heartbeat. 'It's the least of what you deserve, *glikia mou.*' Cupping her face, he sealed his mouth over hers.

Tell him. Tell him now.

But how could she tell him about Greg without it all coming out wrong? And how could she confess her love without it sounding like a tool with which to beg his forgiveness?

She'd been gifted extra time with him. And she selfishly,

desperately, wanted that time. Maybe she could use it to show him how much he meant to her.

Action, not words.

Clutching his nape, she deepened the kiss until he groaned and reluctantly pulled away.

'For kisses like that, you can have pancakes every day. And, before you mention calories, I assure you the workout you'll get in my bed will ensure calories are never an issue.'

He laughed at the flames creeping into her face, helped her into her seat and forked blueberry pancakes onto her plate.

Sunlight slanted through the windows on a bright London morning, throwing his stunning looks into sharp relief.

His grin as he watched her eat made her heart lift and tighten at the same time. When the look turned smouldering, her belly clenched hard with need.

His buzzing phone ripped through the sensual atmosphere. Sighing, he answered and let the world intrude. Taking the lift down—after a strategic pause, when he kissed her sense-less and threatened to take her where she stood if she didn't stop casting him glances from under her lashes—their day swung into full flow.

When at six o'clock he bellowed her name, she entered his office, tablet fired up and ready. His tense expression made her freeze.

'We've tracked him down to Thailand.'

'Captain Lowell?'

He nodded.

'So he's alive?'

'As of yesterday, yes. Although the authorities think there may be someone else besides my security people after him.' His face settled into grimmer lines.

It couldn't be Greg…could it? Nervously, she licked her lips. 'What do you need me to do?' she asked.

'Nothing for the moment. I'm waiting for the lawyers to apprise me of the full situation, then I'll take it from there.'

'What about the party you wanted me to organise for the crew? Do you want me to cancel it?' She'd been liaising with event organisers all day for the company party Sakis intended to host in Greece.

'No. The party goes ahead. The crew and the volunteers deserve it for the hard work they've put in. I'm not prepared to let one man derail the well-being of my other employees.'

'What about Lowell's wife? Are you going to tell her you've found him?'

A look of distress crossed his face and she knew he was remembering his own mother's situation when the press and gossip-mongers had torn her life apart. 'I don't like keeping her in the dark, but I don't want to cause her pain by revealing half-facts. I'll contact her when we know the full details.'

She nodded and started to return to her desk. 'I'll carry on with arrangements to fly the crew to Greece, then.'

'Wait,' he commanded. He strode to where she stood and kissed her, quick and hard. 'When this is all over, I'm taking you to my Swiss chalet. We'll lock the door behind us and gorge on each other for a week. If one week proves unsatisfactory, we'll take another, and another, until we're too sated to move. Then and only then will we let the world back in. Agreed?'

Her heart skipped several beats. By the time this was over, she'd be gone. But she nodded anyway and hurried back to her desk.

Sinking into her chair, she clenched her shaking hands into fists and fought to stop the unrelenting waves of pain and despair that threatened to drown her.

Eventually, she managed to place a thin veil over her emotions, enough to function for the rest of the day.

The news that Lowell had been arrested and was refusing to cooperate threw the rest of the night into disarray. At one a.m., Sakis stopped pacing long enough to pull her up from the seat on the other side of the sofa where she was busy putting together the itinerary for the next day.

'Go to bed, *agapita*.'

Unable to stop herself, she swayed towards his hard warmth. 'Alone?'

His lips trailed over her cheek to the corner of her mouth. 'I'll join you as soon as I have the latest update from the lawyers.'

By the time he joined her an hour later, Brianna was almost delirious with need. As he took her on another sheet-burning journey of bliss, she knew without a doubt that, no matter where she went, her heart would always belong to Sakis Pantelides.

CHAPTER ELEVEN

SAKIS'S PRIVATE GREEK home was a sun-baked slice of bliss that rose from stunning turquoise waters west of the Ionian Islands. Traditionally built and whitewashed in true Greek style, the large villa nevertheless boasted extensive modern designs: the swimming pool had been designed around the villa and traversed under the indoor-to-outdoor living room, reflecting Sakis's love of water.

On her first night here two days ago, Brianna had walked out of her bedroom to find herself faced with an immense mobile hot-tub on her terrace, in which had resided a smug, gloriously naked Sakis with two crystal glasses and vintage champagne chilling on ice next to his elbow. But, if there was one thing she loved about Sakis's island retreat, it was the peace and tranquillity.

Although on this particular Sunday, with teeming bodies enjoying the unfettered generosity of their host, the island paradise was more island rave.

Brianna stood away from the crowd, absently keeping an eye on a couple of employees who were bent on getting hammered as quickly as possible.

Her phone buzzed in her hand and her heart contracted.

Need update, pronto. G.

Greg's texts had got increasingly frequent and terse in the

last day. Although she'd managed to fob him off with non-answers, she was fast running out of time. From experience, she knew his patience would only hold out for so long.

She fired back an inadequate *'Soon'*, a cold shiver coursing through her veins despite the fierce summer sun.

She'd greedily grasped the chance to spend some more time with Sakis. But, like sand through an hourglass, it had inevitably run out.

Looking over to where the man who'd taken over one-hundred per cent of her waking thoughts stood with his two brothers, her insides twisted.

The three brothers were gorgeous in their own rights. But, to her, Sakis stood head and shoulders above Ari and Theo.

It had nothing to do with the way his lips curved when he smiled, or the way a lock of hair fell over his forehead when he nodded to something Theo was saying to him…

No, there was a presence about him, an aura of strength and self-containment, that struck a deep place inside her. And the fierce protectiveness he'd displayed towards those loyal to him made her heart ache.

How would it have felt to be loved and cherished by a man such as him? Tears prickled her eyes at the thought that she'd never find out; never know how it would feel to be loved just once by somebody worth giving her own love to.

Her phone buzzed again.

How soon?????? Answer me now!

In a fit of anger and torment, she turned it off and dashed blindly towards the steps that led to the beach. Tears blurred her vision but she forged ahead, cursing fate for handing her what she most wanted with one hand and ruthlessly taking it away with the other.

Of course, the beach was occupied with more Pantelides Inc. employees. She plastered on a smile and answered greetings, but continued to walk until the sound of partying and music was far behind her.

Locating a rough, flat rock, she sank down and let the tears she'd held back flow. By the time she was wrung dry, her decision had solidified in her chest.

'So, how's your wonder woman doing?'

Sakis barely managed to stop his teeth from gnashing loudly at Ari's dry query.

'If you don't want me to put a dent in that already messed up face of yours, I suggest you watch your mouth.' He cursed the rough intensity of his tone the moment he spoke.

Sure enough, both Ari's and Theo's eyebrows shot up. A second later, Theo chuckled and nudged their oldest brother. 'The last time he reacted so violently about a girl was when I suggested I bring a lollipop to Iyana when we were kids. I barely managed to avoid being flattened when he tried to run me down with his bike. You better watch out, Ari.'

'Shut the hell up, Theo.' Sakis's mood darkened further as his brothers laughed some more at his expense.

He downed more champagne and raised his head in time to catch Ari's narrow-eyed stare. Staring back defiantly, he watched Ari's mouth drop open.

'Damn it, you've done it, haven't you? You've slept with her. *Theos*, don't you have any brains in that head of yours?'

Theo let out another rich chuckle. 'Depends on which head you're talking about, bro.'

Sakis released the growl that'd been lurking in his chest for what felt like days. 'I'm warning you both, stay the hell out of my personal life.'

'Or what?' Theo countered. 'I recall you taking delight in causing havoc in mine more than a few times. You sent flowers to that crazy woman you knew I was trying as hard as hell to cut out of my life. And remember that time you stole my phone and used it to sex-text the wrestler brother of that model I was dating? I couldn't return to my apartment for a week because he'd camped outside my building. Payback's a bitch, bro, and I'm only getting started.'

He swallowed the searing response because he knew that what was eating at him wasn't his brothers' ribbing.

It was Brianna. And the secret text messages she was still receiving.

She believed he didn't notice her apprehension every time her phone pinged.

Hell, she'd left his bed at five a.m. this morning. When he'd demanded she come back to bed, she'd waved him away with some excuse about making sure everything was in hand for the party.

Five a.m.! Yeah, shocking. Wasn't that the same time you interviewed her for her job?

He smothered the mocking voice and stared into the golden bubbles. This had gone on long enough. He'd swallowed her explanation without probing too deeply. Tonight, after the party, he'd find out what the hell was making her so jumpy. And then he'd fix it. He wanted her undivided attention on him and he sure as hell didn't want her leaving him in bed at the crack of dawn to go do…whatever the hell…

'You're giving us the silent treatment? Really? Wow, you must have it bad!' Theo mocked.

'Sweet mother of— So what if I have a thing for her, hmm?' he demanded wildly.

'Some of us would wonder how many times you had to be burned before you learned your lesson,' Ari said, his gaze and his words holding a steady warning that made Sakis's heart slide to his toes.

'She's not like that, Ari. I…trust her.' It was true. Somehow she'd wormed her way in and embedded herself deep in a place he'd thought dead after his father's betrayal. And, *Theos*, it felt…right. It felt good. He didn't feel so desolate, so bitter any more. And he planned to hang on to it.

'Are you sure?' Ari probed.

Righteous anger rose on Brianna's behalf but he stopped himself from venting it. His brothers were only looking out for him.

He wanted to tell them they didn't need to. But a tiny niggling stopped him. What if they did...?

Brushing the thought away, he turned towards Theo, readying himself for more ribbing.

But his brother's face had turned serious. 'Are the investigators close to wrapping up the Lowell issue?' Theo asked.

The other source of his frustration made his nape tighten. 'Not yet. They think there's a third party at play. Lowell may have been double-dealing both Moorecroft and someone else, someone who's keeping him from talking. They've found a paper trail. They should have a name for me in the next twenty-four hours.'

He heard a drunken shout and looked over to see one of his junior executives falling over a pretty blonde. Realising he hadn't spotted Brianna for a while, he frowned. This was the sort of function where she excelled with her organisational skills.

And yet she was nowhere in sight.

'She went that way, towards the beach,' Ari supplied softly.

Sakis looked at his brother and Ari shrugged, an almost resigned understanding in his eyes.

Were his feelings really so obvious? Who cared? Brianna had breached every single barrier he'd put in place around his heart. He craved her when she wasn't around, and he couldn't have enough of her when she was.

Some might call what he was feeling *love*; he preferred to call it... He searched for a suitable description and came up empty. Whatever it was, he'd decided to risk embracing it, see where it took him.

But before that he needed to get to the bottom of what was bothering her.

The junior executive let out another drunken guffaw. The pretty blonde looked ready to burst into tears. Just then a crash came from the other side of the tent.

'Ari, you go take care of Mr Smooth over there. I'll go check out the other thing?' Theo offered.

Nodding gratefully, Sakis discarded his champagne glass and headed towards his other guests. His heart sank when Ari fell into step beside him.

'Are you sure about what you're doing?' he asked.

'I've never been surer.' His answer held a steady certainty that shifted some hitherto unknown weight from his chest. He wanted Brianna in his life.

Permanently.

'Then I wish you well, brother.' Deep emotion and gratitude shifted through him when Ari clasped his shoulder. Before he could swallow the lump in his throat and respond, Ari was moving towards the crowd. Within seconds, the junior executive had been banished to the water fountain to sober up and the blonde was blushing under Ari's dry-witted charm.

Sakis looked towards the beach just as Brianna reappeared at the top of the steps.

The sight of her made his breath catch. It was the first time he'd seen her in such an outfit. Her dress was made of light cotton in a red-and-gold material and stopped just above her knees. The sleeveless, cinched-in waist and flared design moved with her seductive sway as she re-entered the crowd and smiled at a greeting.

He was striding towards her before he could stop himself, not that he wanted to stop.

Her head swung towards him and Sakis's jaw clenched when he saw the momentary wariness that clouded her eyes before she blinked it away. By the time he reached her, she had her game face on.

'It's almost time for your speech,' she said.

'I wish to hell I hadn't agreed to make one.' He wanted to

take her face in his hands and kiss away whatever was bothering her, office gossip be damned. But she wouldn't welcome that, so he kept his hands to himself.

Soon, he promised himself.

'But you have to. They're expecting it.'

'Right…fine.'

He started to turn away.

'Wait.' She stopped him with a hand on his arm, which she dropped quickly, much to his escalating frustration. 'I…I need to talk to you. Tonight, after the party.'

Real trepidation had darkened her eyes. The unease he'd banked but which had never left him since he'd seen that first text roared to life.

He forced a nod and went to give his speech, then for the next hour he mingled with his employees, the volunteers and salvage crew. But he made sure Brianna was glued to his side. Whatever it was that needed to be aired, he wouldn't let it get in the way of what they had.

He breathed a sigh of relief once the boats arrived to ferry his guests to Argostoli, where the chartered flight waited to take them back to London.

Once the last guest had boarded the boat, he headed towards where Brianna was dismissing the catering staff.

Finally…

The need to touch her made his fingers tingle as he came within a few feet of her. She looked up and her desolate expression made his insides clench hard.

'Brianna? What the hell is it?'

She shook her head and looked around. 'Not here. Can we…can we go inside?'

Breaching the gap between them, he caught her hand and kissed the back of it as he steered her towards the villa. 'Sure, but whatever this is let's make it quick. I've been waiting since the crack of dawn to make love to you again. I'm not sure how much longer I can last.'

Her sideways glance was ragged and pain-filled, and he felt his heart stutter then triple its beat as trepidation ramped up higher.

He passed Theo and Ari in the hallway and barely noticed their exchanged glances.

Entering his study, he shut the door and turned to her. 'What's on your mind?'

For several seconds, she didn't speak. She looked lost, miserable, like the bottom had gone out of her world. His heart swelled with the need to take away her pain.

'Brianna, *pethi mou*, whatever the hell it is, I can't fix it until I know what it is.'

That got her attention. She slowly shook her head. 'That's just it. I don't think you can fix this, Sakis.'

His palms grew cold. Clenching his fists tight, he waited.

'A few years ago, I worked for Greg Landers.'

The name popped like a firework in his brain. 'Landers? The guy who was working with Moorecroft?'

'Yes. But back then he owned a gas brokerage firm.'

'And?' he demanded, because his gut told him there was more. Much, much more. 'He's the one who's been texting you. He's *G*.' He didn't try to frame it as a question. He knew.

She licked her lips and, despite the fear and desperation clawing through his belly, he couldn't stop his body's sexual reaction. 'Yes.'

Sakis breathed in deep, but the control kept unravelling. It took every ounce of strength he had to remain standing. 'Is he your lover?'

She gasped. 'No!' A look very much like shame crossed her face. 'But he was,' she whispered.

He'd never understood jealousy up until now. Never got why it compelled strong emotion in others. In that moment, he understood. All Sakis could see in that moment was *red*, fiery red anger, and white-hot pain. 'Why does he call you "Anna"?'

'Because that's my name. My real name is Anna Simpson. I changed it to Brianna Moneypenny after...after...'

'After what?'

'After I served just under two years in jail for embezzlement and fraud.'

Ice, sharp and deadly, clenched hard around his chest. 'You went to *jail*? For *fraud*?'

Tears brimmed in her eyes as she nodded.

Sakis couldn't breathe. His whole body had gone numb. He'd been betrayed *again*. And this time by a woman he loved. And, yes, he could finally admit that the feeling was love because nothing else came close to describing his emotions.

He tried to move towards her and absently noted that his feet were carrying him in the other direction. Numbness spread until his whole body felt frozen to the core.

'You lied to me,' he rasped around the pain gripping his throat.

Slowly, she nodded. Then she cleared her throat. 'Yes.'

'You colluded with a criminal to defraud and then you wormed your way into my company and my bed to do it all over again. You were helping him to topple my company, risking the livelihood of thousands of people.' His voice shook, his insides raw with agony.

'No! Please listen—I didn't. I'd never do that to you.'

'How long have you and Landers been involved in your little scheme?' he snarled, his senses reeling.

Her arms stretched out towards him, palms open wide in false supplication. 'There's no scheme, Sakis. Please believe me.'

His frozen heart twisted painfully. *'Believe you?* That's a joke, right? How long, Brianna?'

Guilt, raw and glaring, slashed across her whitened features. In that moment, Sakis felt as if he'd been turned to stone then smashed into a million pieces.

'I...I've known about it since that last night at Point Noire.'

'And this abrupt confession? You knew it was only a matter of time before the investigators sniffed you both out, didn't you?'

Brianna couldn't stop the distressed cry that ripped from her throat. 'I wanted to tell you. But I…I didn't want to lose you.'

His devilish laugh sliced through her chest, shredding her already bleeding heart. 'You didn't want to lose me, so you thought you'd do the one thing guaranteed to make that happen? For a woman whose intelligence I once valued, that's shockingly stupid.'

She flinched.

He barely blinked at her pain. 'So, what was the plan? I want to hear it. In detail.'

'Greg wanted information to help him in a new takeover bid: shareholding percentages, personal information about board members to give him an edge.'

His grip on the corner of his desk tightened until his knuckles whitened. 'And you fed him this information? Come clean now because I *will* find out.'

'No! I wouldn't… I'd never…' She stopped and swallowed down the sob that threatened to choke her. 'I know it's too late for me to make you believe me but—'

'What did you expect to receive in return?' he ground out chillingly.

'Nothing! I wanted no part of it. Greg was blackmailing me. He found out I'd changed my name and threatened to expose me.'

'Right; next you'll be telling me you were framed the first time round too.'

'I was!'

'You mean a jury didn't find you guilty and a judge didn't sentence you?' Sakis's numbness was receding and pure rage was taking its place. He welcomed the painful sting in his legs and arms, welcomed the surge of power it brought.

'They did, but Greg had engineered it and made sure I took the fall.'

'How?'

Her tongue darted out to lick her lips. Sakis felt the lash of desire and crushed it dead. 'I signed some papers he asked me to and—'

'Did he force you to?'

'What?'

'You say you signed papers, which I assume implicated you. Did he force you to sign them? Did he stand over you with a gun or threaten you in any way?'

'Um…no, he didn't. He tricked me.'

His disbelieving snort stopped the flow of her words. 'You expect me to believe that the ruthlessly efficient executive assistant who's been in my employ these last eighteen months was the same person who would sign papers without first checking them in triplicate? I assume you were so in love with him, you believed every saintly word that fell from his lips?'

She flinched but remained silent and her hands dropped.

Sakis was glad his rage had ravaged every other emotion otherwise he'd have felt the drowning desolation of that silent confirmation. The woman he loved…loved someone else.

Jerking to his feet, he rounded his desk and called his head of security. Once he'd hung up, he stared down at the papers on his desk, willing his frozen mind to focus. 'Give me your phone.'

She frowned. 'What?'

'Your phone. I know you've got it in your pocket. Hand it over.'

Almost in a daze, she did as he asked. 'What are you going to do with it?'

He threw it in his desk drawer, locked it and pocketed the key. 'As of right now, it's evidence of your duplicity. I'll hand it over to the police when the time is right.'

She sucked in a frightened breath. 'No! Please, Sakis. I can't…I can't go back to prison.'

Despite thinking he was too numb to feel, the torment and horror in her eyes sent a shaft of pain through him.

His gaze dropped to her hip, to the place where her scar resided. 'That's where you sustained that injury, wasn't it? In jail?' he asked, feeling another shot of scalding pain.

'Yes. I was attacked.'

Theos! He turned to face the window so she wouldn't see his eyes clamp shut or the steadying breath he took.

When he heard the knock on his door, relief flooded him. Sheldon entered and Sakis shoved unsteady hands deeper into his pocket and turned around.

'Escort Miss *Moneypenny* off my property. Put her on the same plane returning the other company employees. I want her under twenty-four-hour guard until you hear from me. If she tries to run, you have my permission to physically restrain her and call the police. Is that understood?'

A stunned Sheldon nodded. 'Yes, sir.'

'Sakis, I know you don't believe me, but please be careful. Greg's a slippery bastard.'

He didn't turn around.

'Sakis!' Her desperate plea made him flinch but her betrayal cut too deep.

Nevertheless, he allowed himself one last look. Her face was devoid of colour and her lips trembled uncontrollably. But her eyes, even though they pleaded with him, held a condemnation that made his fists curl in his pockets.

Sakis wasn't sure how long he stood there. It might have been minutes, it might have been hours.

When his door was thrust open, he turned slowly, his body feeling alien and frozen.

'Is everything okay?' Ari asked as he sauntered in, Theo

close behind. There was an almost pitying note in his voice that made Sakis's belly clench hard.

'No, everything is *not* okay.'

'Ah, that's too bad, brother. Because all hell's broken loose.'

CHAPTER TWELVE

BRIANNA DRAGGED HERSELF out of bed and walked to her window, hoping for a miracle but knowing hope was useless.

Sure enough, Sakis's guard dog was in place in the dark SUV, just like he'd been for the last three days. She didn't bother looking out of her kitchen window because she knew there would be another SUV stationed in the back alley behind her building, should she get the notion of flinging herself out of her second-floor apartment window and making a run for it.

Forcing herself to enter her kitchen and turn on the kettle, she sagged against the counter and tried to breathe through the waves of pain that had become her endless reality since she'd been marched from Sakis's Greek office.

She clamped her eyes shut to block out the look on his face after her confession.

You lied to me.

Such simple words, yet with those words her world had fallen apart. Because there was no going back. Sakis would always see her as the woman who'd worked her way into his bed only to betray him, especially when she'd known just how much betrayal and lies had ruined his childhood.

The kettle whistled. About to grab a mug from the cupboard, she heard the heavy slam of a car door, followed almost immediately by another. When several followed, she set the mug down and moved closer to the window.

The sight of a paparazzo clinging to the side of a cherry

picker as it rose to her window was so comical, she almost laughed. When he raised his camera and aimed it towards her, Brianna dived for her kitchen floor. Through the window she'd opened to let in the non-existent summer breeze, she heard him shout her name.

'Do you have a comment on the allegations against you, Miss Simpson?'

Crawling on her belly, she made her way to her hallway just as someone leaned on her doorbell.

The realisation that Sakis had truly thrown her to the wolves sent a lance of pain through her, holding her immobile for a full minute, until her pride kicked in.

She refused to hide away like a criminal. And she refused to be trapped in her own home.

If nothing else, she had a right to defend herself. Gritting her teeth for strength, and ignoring the incessant, maddening trill of her doorbell, she dashed into her room.

Grabbing the first set of clothes that came to hand, she pulled them on. Unfortunately, trainers and her suit didn't go, so she forced her feet into four-inch heels, grabbed her bag and pulled a brush through her hair.

She opened the door and shot past Sakis's shocked guards before they had a chance to stop her.

'Miss Moneypenny, wait!'

She rounded on them as they caught up with her at the top of the stairs. 'Lay a finger on me, and *I'll* be the one calling the police. I'll hit you with assault charges so fast, you'll wonder what century it is.' She felt a bolt of satisfaction when they gingerly stepped back.

She hurried down the stairs, noting that they gave hot pursuit but didn't attempt to restrain her.

The glare of morning sunlight coupled with what seemed like a thousand camera flashes momentarily blinded her.

Questions similar to what the first cherry-picker-riding

pap had flung at her came her way, but she'd been doing her job long enough to know never to answer tabloid questions.

With her sight adjusted, she plunged through the crowd and headed for the high street two hundred yards away. When she heard the soft whirr of an engine beside her, she didn't turn around.

'What the hell do you think you're doing, making yourself paparazzi bait?' came the rough demand as rougher hands grasped her arms.

Brianna's heart lurched. The sight of him, right there in front of her, fried her brain cells with pleasure and pain so strong she couldn't breathe for a few precious seconds.

She'd missed him. *God, she'd missed him.*

Then memories of their last meeting smashed through. Sucking in a painful breath, she pulled herself away. 'Nothing that concerns you any longer, Sakis.'

He caught her elbow. 'Brianna, wait.'

'No. Let me go!' She managed to pry her hand away and walk a few steps before he caught up with her again.

'Didn't my security people warn you about the press headed your way?'

'Why should they have? Wasn't that what you planned?'

The hand he reached out to her shook. Or at least she *thought* she saw it tremble. She was feeling very shaky herself and could've imagined it. 'No, it wasn't. I had nothing to do with this. Brianna, please come with me. We need to talk,' he said urgently.

'Not in this lifetime. You made your feelings about me *abundantly* clear—' She gave a yelp of shock as Sakis pulled her in the limo. 'What the hell—?'

'The paparazzi are increasing by the second. My security won't be able to hold them back for much longer. And I really need to talk to you. *Please,*' he tagged on in a ragged voice.

The mouth she'd opened to blast him with clamped shut again. Glancing closer at him, she noticed the shadows in his eyes and the pinched skin bracketing his lips. Against her better judgement, her heart lurched but she still pulled away until her back was braced against the door. He saw her retreat and his lips firmed.

'You have two minutes, then I'm getting out of this car.'

Before she'd finished speaking, the car was rolling forward. Half a minute later, they were in a school yard three streets away parked in front of a familiar aircraft.

'You landed your helicopter on a school compound in the middle of London?' she asked as he helped her out of the car.

'Technically, this isn't the middle of London, and the school is shut for the holidays. I'll pay whatever fine is levied and, if I have to go jail, well, it'll be worth it.'

'*What* will be worth it?'

He didn't respond, only held the door to the chopper open. With the paparazzi within sniffing distance, it would be only a matter of time before they pounced again.

She got in. Sakis followed her. When he reached over to help her buckle her seatbelt, she shook her head. Having him this close was already shredding her insides. His touch would completely annihilate her.

The journey to Pantelides Towers was conducted in silence. So was the journey in the lift that took them to his penthouse.

'What am I doing here, Sakis?'

He closed his eyes for a second and Brianna remembered how he'd said the sound of his name on her lips made him feel. But that had all been an illusion. Because his unforgiving heart had cast her away from him with the precision of a surgeon wielding a scalpel.

'Where were you going when you left her your apartment?'

'None of your damned business. You can't push me around any more, Sakis. My life is my own—but go ahead, do your worst. I'll fight whatever charges you bring against me. If I lose, so be it. But from here on in, *I* control my destiny.'

She ground to a halt, her breath rushing in and out. Sakis glanced from her face to the phone he'd taken from his pocket.

Belatedly, she realised it was her phone. 'What are you still doing with that? I thought you were going to turn it over to the authorities.' Her voice trembled but she raised her chin and glared at him.

'Not after I saw what was on it.'

'What…what did you see?'

He walked slowly towards her, contrition and desperation in his eyes as he held the screen in front of her face.

'I saw this.' The shaken reverence in his voice sent an electrified current through her. Almost fearing to, she glanced down.

You can go rot in hell, Greg. You once tricked me into taking the fall for something you did. And now you want me to betray the man I love? No chance.

She looked up from the screen, her heart hammering against her ribs. 'So what? You shouldn't believe everything you read. For all you know, I could've sent that text just to throw you off the scent.'

He glanced down at the screen again and stared at the words as if imprinting them on his brain for all time. 'Then why did you warn me about him?'

She shrugged.

'Brianna, Greg confessed that he coerced you into signing the papers he used to divert funds into his offshore account.'

Shock ricocheted through her body. 'He came clean? Why?'

'He's facing charges in three countries for bribing Lowell to crash the tanker. I told him I would delay the Greek charges if he gave me any useful information. He gave up the dates, figures and codes to his Cayman Islands accounts and confessed he tricked you into helping him siphon off the money.'

The handbag she clutched slipped from her fingers. 'So… you believe me?'

Pain washed over his face. 'Wasting time feeling sorry for myself gave Landers time to spill your real identity to the tabloids. But I shouldn't have doubted you in the first place.'

'I don't really care that everyone knows who I was. And, given the overwhelming evidence, you would've been a saint not to doubt me.'

He flung the phone away and stalked to where she stood. He started to reach for her then clasped both hands behind his nape. 'Then I should damn well have applied for sainthood. What he did to you…what *I* did…*Theos*, I'm even surprised you agreed to come here with me.'

'I was heading here anyway,' she confessed.

Surprise flared in his eyes, along with hope. 'You were?'

'Don't flatter yourself, Sakis. I wasn't on my way to beg you for my life back, if that's what you think. I was coming to clear my desk, or ask security to clear it for me if I was still barred from entering these hallowed grounds.'

'You're not barred. You'll *never* be barred, Brianna.'

'You don't have to call me that. You know who I am now.'

The hard shake of his head made a lock of hair fall over his eyes. 'You'll always be Brianna to me. She was the woman I fell in love with. The woman who possesses more strength and integrity in her little finger than anyone else I know. The woman I stupidly discarded before I got the chance to tell her how much I love her and treasure her.'

Her legs finally gave way beneath her. Sakis caught her before she crumpled onto the sofa. They fell back together. His gaze dropped to her mouth that had fallen open with wordless wonder, and he groaned. 'I know what I did was unforgivable but I want to try all the same to make it up—'

'You love me.'

'To you. Name your price. Anything you want, I'll give

it. I've already put steps in place to have your conviction revoked—'

'*You love me?*'

He paused and gave a solemn nod but it was the adoration in his eyes that struck pure, healing happiness into her heart. 'I love you more than I desire my next breath. I need you in my life. I'll do anything, *anything,* to have you back, *agapita.*'

'What does that mean?'

'What does what…? Oh—*agapita*? It means "beloved".'

She pulled back. 'But you started calling me that even before we slept together. It was that day when you took me for pancakes.'

He seemed startled by the remark. Then a smile warmed his stricken face. 'I think my subconscious was telling me how I felt about you.'

She caressed a hand down his rough jaw. 'When did the rest of you catch up?'

'In Greece, after I withstood Ari and Theo's ribbing and I admitted that I didn't want to live without you. I intended to tell you after the party.'

'Tell me again now.'

He repeated it, then pulled back after kissing her senseless, his gaze dark with a vulnerability she'd never seen. 'Can you ever forgive me for what I did?'

His cheeks were warm and vibrant beneath her hands. 'You took steps to find out the truth about what happened to me. You could've walked away and condemned me, but you came back for me. I told you about my past, about my mother, and you didn't judge me or make me feel worthless. I loved you for that. More than I already did before I sent Greg that text.'

The shock on his face made her smile. It was the shock that made her get away with kissing him thoroughly before the alpha male in him took over. When he pulled away from her, she gave a groan of protest.

'Do you have one of those go bags ready for a trip? If you don't, we'll manage, but we need to leave now.'

'I do, but—?'

He was up and striding towards her suite before she could finish the question. He returned, two bags in one hand and the other stretched out to her.

'Where are we going?' Hurriedly, she straightened her clothes and hair.

'I've blocked off my calendar for a month. I believe there's a Swiss chalet waiting for us.'

'You think a month is going to be enough?' Happiness made her saucy, she discovered.

Pulling her close, he kissed her until they were both breathless. 'No chance. But it's a damned good start.'

The fire roared away in the enormous stone hearth as Sakis pulled the luxury throw closer around them and fed her oysters from the shell. Brianna wrinkled her nose at the peculiar taste.

'Don't worry, *agapita*. You get used to it after a while.'

'I don't think I'll ever get used to it; I'm not afraid to admit this is one lost cause to me.'

His eyes darkened. 'I'm glad you didn't condemn me as a lost cause.'

'How could I, when you tell me you fought your own board for me? How hellish was it to keep them from crucifying me?'

'I almost resigned at one point but, when I pointed out that *you* deserved all the credit because you saved the company from another stock market slide, they came round to my way of thinking.'

Her eyes widened. 'I did?'

He nodded. 'Telling me about Greg saved the investigators a lot of time. Once we knew who we were looking for, finding him hiding away in Thailand with Lowell was easy. Didn't you see the arrests on the news?'

'Sakis, I could barely get out of bed to feed myself. Watching the news and risking seeing you was too much.'

He froze and jagged pain slashed his features. '*Theos*, I'm so sorry.'

She kissed him then watched him pile more food on her plate. 'You have enough there to feed two armies. I can't possibly eat all of that.'

'Try. I don't like hearing that you didn't eat because of me. I watched my mother wither away from not eating after what my father did to her.'

Pain for him scoured her heart. 'Oh, Sakis…'

He shook his head. 'Eat, *agapita*, and tell me you forgive me.'

'I'll forgive you anything if you keep calling me that.'

After she ate more than was good for her, he stretched her out on the rug and pulled the sheepskin throw off her. Kissing his way down her body, he repeated the endearment over and over again, until she sobbed with need for him.

In the aftermath of their love-making, he brushed the tears from her eyes and kissed her lids.

'I've made you cry with happiness and there're no pancakes in sight. That, *agapita*, is what I call a result.'

* * * * *

What The Greek Can't Resist

CHAPTER ONE

THE CAR PARK was as quiet as she'd hoped it would be. Inside her trusted Mini's soothing cocoon, Perla Lowell bit the tip of her pen and searched fruitlessly for the right words.

Four lines. Four paltry lines in two hours were all she'd managed to come up with. She swallowed her despair. Three short days from now she'd have to stand up in front of friends and family and make a speech...

And she had no words.

No, scratch that. She had words. But none rang true. Because the truth... No, she couldn't...*wouldn't* subject anyone to the truth. Her whole life for the past three years had been a colossal lie. Was it any wonder her hands shook every time she tried to write? That her heart pounded with self-loathing for the lies she had to perpetuate for the sake of appearances?

But how could she do anything else? How could she repay kindness with humiliation? Because doing or saying anything else other than what was expected would bring devastation that she couldn't live with.

Anger mingled with despair. With a vicious twist she ripped the paper in two. The cathartic sound echoed through the car and spilled out into the night air. As if loosening the stranglehold she'd exercised on her emotions for longer than she cared to remember, the tears she'd been unable to shed so far now pierced through her tightened chest into her throat.

Her fingers gained a life of their own. Two halves of paper became four, then eight. She ripped again and again, until the sheet spilled through her hands in little wisps of illegible confetti. She upended her hands and watched the mess strewn all over the passenger seat. With a jagged groan, she buried her face in her hands, expecting finally, *finally,* to shed a tear.

The tears never came. They remained locked inside, as they had been for the last two weeks, taunting her, punishing her for daring to wish for them when deep down she knew to cry would be shamefully, deeply disingenuous.

Because, deep inside, she felt…relieved. At a time when she should've been devastated, she felt a shameful lightening of being!

Slowly, she dropped her hands and stared through the windscreen. Her vision cleared and she focused on the palatial Georgian structure in front of her.

Despite its recent multi-million-pound revamp, Macdonald Hall had retained its quintessential old English charm, along with its exclusive membership-by-invitation-only Macdonald Club, and the extensive gold standard golf course that lay beyond the imposing façade.

The centuries-old establishment's only nod to the common man was the cocktail bar, which was open to the public from seven until midnight.

Perla sucked in a deep breath and glanced down at the ripped paper. Guilt bit deep as she acknowledged how good it'd felt to let go. Just this once, to not hold herself back, to not watch her every word or smile when she felt like cursing her fate. To be normal…

The feeling wouldn't last, of course. There was still tomorrow to get through and the next day, and the next.

Dark anguish had her reaching for her bag.

She was far enough away from home not to be recognised here. It was, after all, why she'd driven for over an hour to find a quiet spot to compose the hard-to-find words.

Granted, her journey had been futile so far. But she wasn't ready to return home yet; wasn't ready to face the cloying compassionate gestures and well-meaning, concerned but probing looks.

Her gaze refocused on Macdonald Hall.

One drink. Then she'd drive back home and start again tomorrow.

Opening her bag, she searched for the small brush to run it through her hair in an attempt to tame the unruly curls. When her fingers touched the tube of lipstick, she nearly dismissed it.

Scarlet wasn't really her colour, and normally she wouldn't even glance at one that described itself as *Do Me Red*; she only had the sample lipstick because it'd come free with a book purchase. She would never dare to wear anything so bold. So daring. Even on other women, she found the colour too sensual, too *look-at-my-mouth*.

Fingers trembling, she uncapped the tube, angled the rear-view mirror and carefully applied the lipstick. The unexpected result—the wanton, blatantly sultry image that stared back at her—had her rummaging through her bag for a tissue to reverse the damage. When she came up empty, she paused. Her gaze slowly slid back to the mirror.

Her heart hammered.

Was it so bad? Just for tonight, would it be so bad to look, to *feel* like someone else other than Perla Lowell, *complete fraud*? To forget the pain and unrelenting humiliation she'd suffered for the last three years, if only for a few minutes?

Before she could change her mind, she fumbled for the door handle and stepped out of her car into the cool night air. Her party days might be long behind her but

even she knew her simple black sleeveless dress and low
black pumps were appropriate for a cocktail bar on a quiet
Tuesday night.

And if it wasn't, the worst that could happen was she
would be asked to leave. And right now, being thrown out
of an exclusive cocktail bar where no one knew who she
was would be a walk in the park compared to the monumental farce she had to go through.

A smartly dressed concierge greeted her and directed
her through a parquet-floored, oak-panelled hallway to a
set of old-fashioned double doors with the words *Bar* fash-
ioned in burnished gold plate above them.

Another similarly dressed man opened the door and
tipped his cap to her.

Feeling seriously out of her depth, Perla took fleeting
note of the discreetly expensive wood and brocade décor
before her eyes zeroed in on the long, low-slung bar. Seriously intimidating rows of drinks were displayed on a re-
volving carousel and, behind the bar, a bartender twirled
a sterling silver set of cocktail shakers while chatting to a
young couple.

For a split second, Perla considered turning on her heel
and marching straight back out. She forced herself to take
a step and another until she reached the unoccupied end of
the bar. She'd come this far… Sucking in another sustaining breath, she slid onto the stool and placed her handbag
on the counter.

Now what?

'What's a fine girl like you doing in a place like this?'

The cheese-tastic line startled a strained laugh out of
her as she turned towards the voice.

'That's better. For a second there, I thought someone
had died in here and I hadn't been told,' the bartender's
white smile, no doubt tailor-made to drive hormonal girls
wild, widened as his gaze traced her face in blatant ap-

praisal. 'You're the second person to walk in here tonight looking like you're a fully paid-up member of the doom-and-gloom brigade.'

In another lifetime, Perla would've found his boyish, perfectly groomed looks charming. Unfortunately, she existed in *this* lifetime, and she'd learnt to her cost that the outside rarely matched the inside.

She willed her smile in place and folded her hands on top of her purse. 'I...I'd like a drink, please.'

'Sure thing.' He leaned in closer and his eyes dropped to her mouth. 'What's your poison?'

Her gaze darted to the cocktails on display. She had no clue what any of them were. The last time she'd been in a bar like this, the drink in fashion had been Amaretto Sour. She wanted to ask for a Cosmopolitan but wasn't even sure if that was still in vogue these days.

She gritted her teeth again and contemplated walking out. Sheer stubbornness made her stay on the stool. She'd been pushed around enough; endured enough. For far too long she'd allowed someone else to call the shots, to dictate the way she lived her life.

No more. Granted, the scarlet lipstick had been a bad idea—it was clear it drew far too much unwanted attention to her mouth—but Perla refused to let that stand in the way of this one small bolstering move.

Squaring her shoulders, she indicated a dark red drink with lots of sunny umbrellas sticking out of it. 'I'll have that one.'

He followed her gaze and frowned. 'The Pomegranate Martini?'

'Yes. What's wrong with it?' she asked when he continued to frown.

'It's a bit...well, lame.'

Her lips firmed. 'I'll take it anyway.'

'Come on, let me—'

'Give the lady what she wants,' a low, dark drawl sounded behind her right shoulder. The smooth but unmistakable cadence in the masculine voice spelled a foreign accent, possibly Mediterranean, that caused a shiver to dance down Perla's spine.

She froze in her seat, her back stiffening as sensation skittered over her skin.

The bartender visibly paled before nodding quickly and sidling off to prepare her cocktail.

Perla felt his silent presence behind her, a palpable force field that bore down and surrounded her with unmistakable power. Her mind shrieked with danger, but for the life of her she couldn't move. Her hand tightened over the strap of her handbag, her fingers plucking frantically at the beads that decorated the dark satin exterior.

'Turn around,' came the low command.

Her back stiffened some more. Another man who wanted to push her buttons. 'Look, I just want to be left alone—'

'Turn around, if you please,' he instructed again in that low, growly voice.

Not *please* but *if you please*. The slightly old-fashioned turn of phrase piqued her curiosity. Coupled with the dark rumble of his voice, Perla was seriously tempted to do as he asked.

But not enough to give in. She remained facing forward.

'I just saved you from becoming the potential target of a chancer with delusions of swagger. The least you can do is turn around and talk to me.'

Despite her stomach flipping again at the impact of his voice, Perla's lips tightened. 'I didn't want nor need your help…and I don't really want to talk to anyone so…'

She glanced towards the bartender with the intention of cancelling her order. The long drive here…the inspired words she'd hoped to write…the idea of a quick drink… the courage-lending scarlet lipstick—probably *that* most of all—had all been an unmitigated disaster. Again she felt pain tighten her chest and fought to keep her emotions under strict control.

Behind her, the man who thought he was her saviour stood in imposing, stifling silence. She knew he was there because his scent lingered in her nostrils—intriguingly spicy, masculine and raw—and she could hear his firm, steady breathing. Again an alien sensation skittered over her skin. The urge to look over her shoulder scythed through her but she refused the urge. She'd failed herself in so many things. Perla refused to fail at this one thing.

Lifting her hand, she tried to catch the bartender's attention but his gaze was focused behind her…on the man whose presence, even without her knowing who he was or her having seen him, spelled power with a capital *P*.

She watched in stunned silence as the bartender nodded in answer to a silent command, rounded the counter with her drink and headed towards a dark corner of the bar.

Outraged, Perla finally turned to find the man—tall, dark-haired and incredibly broad-shouldered—retreating to the table where her drink had been placed along with another, presumably his.

Pure anger spiked through her. Her heels landed on the polished wood floor and she was marching over to him before she fully registered her intention. 'What the hell do you think you're—?'

He turned to face her and the words dried in Perla's throat.

Gorgeous. Astoundingly. Gorgeous. The description lit up like a neon sign in her head—bright, bold, insistent. And so unbelievably real, Perla could only stare in astonishment. Even as she took in the sheer vitality of his olive skin, the lethal bone structure that made up his striking features and the tinge of grey in his hair and designer stubble—her personal, stupidly debilitating weakness—she knew she should never have turned around; never have followed him.

She should've heeded her instinct and walked straight out.

Dear Lord, hadn't she learned from her mistake? She gave a slight shake of her head and tried to step back. She had no business being here; no business staring at a man the way she was staring at this stranger. If anyone found out...

Move!

Her feet wouldn't comply.

Deep hazel eyes bored into hers, then slowly traced her body from head to toe and back again. Perla found herself holding her breath, her fingers once again working frantically over the beads on her handbag.

The breathtaking stranger's gaze paused at her hair. 'Is that colour real?' he rasped in that knee-weakening, pulse-stroking voice.

'Excuse me?'

'That shade of red. Is it real?' he demanded.

A little bit of her entrancement receded. 'Of course it's real. Why would I dye—?' She stopped as it occurred to her then that he didn't know her and therefore wouldn't know that the last thing she concerned herself with was vanity in the form of artificial hair colour. There was no one to please or pander to and she was too busy surviving to think about frivolous things such as what colour to dye her hair. 'It's real, okay? Now will you explain what you're playing at? That's my drink you've just commandeered.'

'Your manners seemed to have deserted you. I'm merely redressing the situation.' He pulled out a chair. 'Please sit down.'

Lifting an eyebrow, she remained standing.

With a shrug, he remained standing too.

She blew out an irritated breath. 'My manners haven't deserted me. You stepped in and took over a situation I had under control. What did you think, that the bartender would've vaulted over the counter and assaulted me in plain sight of the other customers?' she snapped.

He broke his fascination with her hair and dropped his gaze to capture hers. 'What other customers?' he asked.

'The couple over there—' She broke off as she looked around. The young couple were gone. Aside from a waiter who was clearing a few other tables, only the tall stranger and bartender remained in the bar. As she watched, the waiter walked through a set of swinging doors and disappeared.

She swallowed. 'This is a reputable place. Things like that don't happen here.'

'And what exactly do you base that statistic on? Are you a frequent visitor?'

She flushed. 'No, of course not. And I'm not naïve. I just...I just think—'

'That predators in Savile Row suits are less vicious than those in hoodies?' His smile didn't reach his eyes.

'No, that's not what I meant. I came here for a quiet drink.' Her gaze dropped to the bold and garish-looking cocktail standing next to his dark-coloured spirit.

This was fast getting out of hand, and she needed to think about getting back. Or she would have more explaining to do.

He indicated the chair one more time. 'You can still have it. And you needn't worry about making conversation. We can sit here and not...talk.'

His words piqued her curiosity. Or maybe she just wanted a distraction from the pain and chaos that awaited her the moment she left this place.

She forced herself to look at him—really look past the surface hurt-your-eyes gorgeousness of the man—past the powerful shoulders underneath the impeccable suit and loosened silk tie. His hair was slightly ruffled, as if he'd shoved a hand through it once or twice.

The brackets around his mouth were deeply grooved and when she chanced another look into his eyes, what Perla glimpsed made her heart hammer.

In that instant she knew he wasn't here to prey on unsuspecting or vulnerable women. That wasn't to say women would be safe from the sensual aura and sheer charisma that oozed from him. Far from it.

But for tonight, in this very moment, whoever this man was, the emotions lurking in his eyes weren't of a predatory nature. The pain she saw resonated with her on so deep a level, she found it hard to breathe through it.

His eyes narrowed, as if sensing the direction of her thoughts. He stiffened and his mouth firmed. For a moment she thought he was going to change his mind about his earlier invitation.

Abruptly he moved a step forward, touched the back of the chair. 'Sit down. Please,' he repeated.

Perla sat. In silence, he pushed her drink towards her.

'Thank you,' she murmured.

He inclined his head and raised his glass towards her. 'To not talking.'

She touched her glass to his; a surreal feeling overtook her as she stared at him over the rim of her glass and took a sip of her cocktail. The potent alcohol hit the back of her throat, warming and cooling at the same time. The tartness of the pomegranate burst on her tongue, making her close her eyes in a single moment of pleasure before the strength of his scrutiny propelled her eyelids back open.

Once again, he seemed fascinated with her hair. It took every ounce of self-control she possessed not to fiddle with it. She sucked harder on her straw, partly to finish the drink quicker so she could leave and partly because it gave her something to do other than stare at this hauntingly beautiful man.

They sipped their drinks in silence.

With a very unsettling amount of regret, Perla set her empty glass down.

The stranger followed suit. 'Thank you.'

'For what?'

'For controlling the urge to indulge in idle chit-chat.'

'I told you, that's not what I came here for. If it was, I'd have brought a friend. Or come earlier when I knew there would be more people here. I presume you chose this time for the same reason.'

A shaft of pain flitted over his features but was gone in the next instant. 'You presume correct.'

She shrugged. 'Then there's no need to thank me.'

He stilled, the only movement his gaze as it flew once again to her hair. When it traced down to her mouth, Perla became very much aware of the scarlet lipstick. Before she could stop herself, she licked her tingling lower lip.

His low hiss was an alien sound that sent a fresh wave of goose bumps over her skin. She'd never elicited such a reaction in a man before. Perla wasn't sure whether to be pleased or terrified.

'Are you staying here, at Macdonald Hall?' she asked, in the hope of deflecting the unsettling feeling his hiss had elicited.

The stranger's hand tightened slowly into a fist on the table. 'For tonight and the next few nights, yes.'

She looked from his hand to his face. 'Why do I get the feeling that you don't want to be here?' she asked.

'Because we don't always get to decide our own fate. But I'm obliged to be here for the next few days. It doesn't mean I'm pleased about it.'

She glanced at his empty glass. 'Then I suppose you'll be upgrading to a bottle instead of a glass shortly?'

He shrugged. 'Drinking is one way of making the time pass faster, I suppose.'

Danger crawled across her skin, sparking a flame in her belly, but Perla couldn't move. 'When you're alone in a bar at almost midnight, I don't really see much else to entertain you.' Her voice emerged huskier than she'd ever heard it.

He raised a dark eyebrow. 'But I'm not alone. Not any more. I've saved you, a damsel in distress, and my reward is your company for now.'

'I'm not a damsel in distress. Besides, you don't know me from a blade of grass. I could be one of those predators you described, for all you know, Mr...?'

Her blatant demand for his name went unanswered as he nodded to the bartender and indicated their empty glasses.

'I don't think I should have another drink—'

Hooded hazel eyes trapped hers. 'But we're just getting to know one another. You were telling me about being a ruthless predator.'

'And you wanted to be alone less than ten minutes ago, remember? Besides, what makes you think I want to get to know you?'

His small smile was both self-assured and self-pitying, a curious, intriguing combination. 'I don't. Forgive me for the assumption. If you wish you leave, you may do so.'

Again the courteous words laced with arrogance set her teeth on edge. But Perla found she couldn't look away from the fascinating man, whose extremely powerful aura held a wealth of pain and sadness that drew her...made her hesitate.

She licked her lips and immediately regretted it when his gaze latched onto the movement. 'I don't need your permission but I...I'll stay for another drink.'

He nodded solemnly. '*Efharisto.*' The way his voice and sensual lips formed the word made her stomach perform an annoying little flip.

'What does that mean?'

'Greek, for *thank you*.'

'Oh, you're Greek? I love Greece. I visited Santorini a long time ago for the wedding of a client. I remember thinking at the time it's where I'd like to get married one day. That has got to rank up there as one of the most beautiful places on earth—' Perla drew to a sharp halt as his face tightened suddenly. 'I'm sorry. Mindless chit-chat?'

One corner of his mouth lifted. 'It's not as mindless as I thought it would be. So you love Greece. What else do you love?'

Her gaze dropped to the table, then immediately rose to meet his, almost against her will. 'Is this the part where I say long walks in the rain with that special someone?'

'Only if it's true. Personally, I detest the rain. I prefer wall-to-wall sunshine. And the sea.'

'And the special someone is optional?'

That look she'd caught on his face earlier returned— the cross between ragged pain and guilt—and this time it stayed for several moments before he shrugged.

'If you're lucky enough to have the choice, and to hang onto your good fortune.'

She bit her lip but was stopped from answering as the bartender delivered their order. Again silence ensued as they sipped their drinks. Only this time, when his gaze travelled over her, she boldly watched him back.

The silvery strands that blended into his temples coupled with the designer stubble gave him a seriously gorgeous but distinctly imposing look that sent her heart thudding faster. He looked vaguely familiar. Mentally shrugging, Perla concluded she must have seen him in the newspaper or on TV. His air of importance and easy way he commanded power lent itself to that theory. And, of course, he was here, at Macdonald Hall, one of the most exclusive private sport clubs in the country.

His fingers curled around his glass and she watched him lift his drink to his lips, his gaze staying on hers. Heat rushed through her, filling her up in places she'd begun to think were frozen forever. Perla tried to tell herself it was the alcohol but in an angry rush of rejection she forced herself to face the truth. She was done lying to herself, to glossing over the bare truth in order to lessen her pain.

No more!

She was attracted to this man. To his gorgeous, pain-etched face, the haunted hazel eyes, the strong stubbled jaw she wanted to run her fingers over just to see if it felt as rough as his manly, callused fingers. The mental pictures reeling through her head should've shocked and shamed her. But, for tonight, Perla was determined to suspend shame. And really, when had looking been a crime? And he was as exquisite a specimen as any.

'Be careful, little one. This big, bad wolf has vicious, merciless teeth.'

The softly voiced caution ripped her from her thoughts.

What was she doing?

In a rush, she put down her barely touched drink, stood up and snatched her handbag. 'I…you're right. Caution is usually my middle name so, um…thanks for the drink.' Her tongue felt thick with the lack of knowledge of the proper etiquette. 'And for the company.'

Her breath caught when he stood to tower over her. 'Did you drive here?' he demanded.

'Yes, but I barely touched my second drink and—'

'My driver will deliver you home.'

A mixture of fear and anxiety roiled through her. Imagine the gossip if she returned home in a strange man's car! Granted it was almost midnight but it would only take one sighting for the rumour mill to spin into overdrive. She had enough on her plate to deal with as it was.

'No. That's very kind of you but it's not necessary.'

His striking, very hypnotic eyes narrowed. In that moment, all Perla noticed were his insanely thick eyelashes and the way his mouth turned down when he was displeased. The urge to take that look from his face shocked her into stepping back. When she took another step back, he followed.

'Let me at least walk you to your car.'

'I'm perfectly capable—'

'That wasn't a suggestion.'

'Didn't you warn me about Savile-Row-dressed predators a short while ago?'

That sad, almost haunted smile made another appearance. Those endlessly fascinating fingers delved into his bespoke jacket and emerged with his smartphone. He tapped the three-digit emergency number into it and extended it to her, pointing to the dial button. 'Hit that button if I so much as exhale the wrong way between here and your car. But make no mistake, I'm walking you out of here and seeing you into your car.'

With a shaky hand, she took his phone. His fingers brushed then stilled against hers. Warmth infused her. Without thinking, she rubbed her fingers against his and heard his sharp intake of breath as he fell into step beside her.

The walk to her car took minutes but it felt like the longest walk of her life. Beside her, the tall, dark and dangerous stranger lessened his significantly long stride to match hers. Over and over again, Perla felt the heat of his gaze travel over her. She forced herself not to glance at him. To do so would've wavered her intent, made her give in to the intensely mortifying need that had taken root inside her.

But, with each dreaded step to her car, Perla felt as if she was fighting a losing battle. What had she achieved by coming here? So far, a big fat *nothing*. She hadn't even broached the task she would give everything not to have to deal with. A task she would've given everything not to return to.

Surely it wasn't wrong to make this moment with this perfect stranger last a little longer? She gave an inward sigh.

Who was she kidding? Fate had stuck two fingers up to her over and over. Why should tonight be any different?

She stopped beside her car and turned towards him. With a deep breath, she held out his phone. 'I told you this wasn't necessary. But again, thanks.'

He barely glanced at the gadget. 'You're not out of danger yet.'

She looked up into his face. 'What do you mean?' she asked, her voice a touch too breathless.

He stepped closer, his body heat slamming into her, making her head spin. 'Hang onto it for a little while longer. I don't want to end our conversation, not just yet.'

Perla's pulse rate shot up even higher. 'Why?'

'Because…' He seemed to catch himself just then. A frown creased his brow and he shook his head.

When he stepped back, a spasm of fear that she was losing him made her lean towards him. 'Because…?'

He focused on her. Hazel eyes pinned her to the spot, then rushed to her hair, over her face, her neck, down to her toes before coming back to her face. He muttered something under his breath, something in his native tongue that held no meaning for her.

'Tell me your name.'

Her mouth dried. 'It's…Pearl.' She cringed inwardly at the small fib but, growing up, her unusual name had often been mistaken for the more common *Pearl*. Besides, the anonymity made her feel less exposed.

His hooded gaze dropped to her lips, its message so blatantly sexual, her breath stalled in her chest. 'I have an irresistible urge to kiss you, Pearl. Does that make you want to run?'

The rawness behind the words rocked her to her soul, resonated beside her own turmoil. She watched his eyes slowly grow darker, more tormented. Before she could consciously stop herself, she reached up and cupped his taut cheek.

'No. But it makes me want to know what's wrong,' she said softly.

He made a rough sound under his breath, like a proud but wounded animal. 'Nothing I wish to bore you with tonight.'

'What makes you think I'll be bored? Perhaps I need the distraction as much as you do,' she said in a rush of confession. She swayed closer and stopped herself a mere whisper from him. 'Perhaps I want to give you what you want because it's what I want too?' It felt a little absurd, having this conversation with him. But it also felt…oddly right.

'Be very careful what you wish for, little one,' he breathed.

'Oh, but I have been. Very careful. Too careful at times. I'm tired of being careful.'

His hand reached up to cover hers, pressed her hand harder into his jaw. Underneath her fingers, his stubble bristled against her palm, sparking an electric current that transmitted up her arm and suffused her whole body.

'Don't offer temptation you won't be able to deliver on,' he warned.

'Are you challenging me?'

'I'm offering a word of caution. I don't wish to frighten you so perhaps you should leave now,' he grated out. 'Or stay, if you're brave enough. I accept that the choice is yours. But decide quickly.'

Contrary to his words, his fingers caught and imprisoned a thick strand of her hair, his movement almost reflexive as he passed the tresses through his fingers repeatedly.

Caught in a sensation so alien and yet so right, Perla closed that last tiny gap between them. Strong hands immediately caught her to him. She collided with over six feet of lean muscle that knocked the air out of her lungs.

Before she could draw breath, his lips settled over hers. Every thought flew out of her head as she became lost in pure, electric sensation. He kissed her as if she was life-giving oxygen, as if he needed her to survive. That knowledge more than anything caught a fragile spot inside her; shook it free and allowed her to enjoy this, to become a part of this small healing process that they both needed.

With a groan, she pressed herself closer until she could feel his heartbeat against her breasts, the ridged chest muscles crushing her softer ones. Both his hands encompassed her waist and lifted her up onto the bonnet of her car. Then he plunged both fingers into her hair, angled her face up to his and proceeded to dive deeper into their kiss.

Only the need for air finally separated them.

Perla's breaths puffed out into the cool night and threatened to cease altogether when she saw the smear of scarlet on his lips.

Reaching up, she touched his mouth. He made a sound of mingled pain and pleasure and she almost lost her mind.

'I…I…' She wasn't sure exactly what she wanted to say. Only that she needed to make sense of what was happening to her. 'Is that enough?' From the depths of her soul came a yearning for him to say no.

When he shook his head, her heart soared.

'No, it's not. The taste of you is intoxicating. I want to drown in you.' He captured her face in his hands and kissed her some more, murmuring phrases in Greek she had no hope of understanding. When he released her, he was breathing hard. Pulling her close, he rested his forehead against hers. '*Theos*…this is madness, but I can't let you go. Not yet.' He pulled back and tilted her face to his, his hazel eyes swirling with the same potent need that twisted inside her. 'Stay with me tonight, Pearl.'

Her decision was instant; so frighteningly committed that she forced herself to remain silent when she wanted to blurt it out. Her fingers moved again over his soft, sensual lips. He captured them and kissed her knuckle. It occurred to her that she held his phone in her other hand. One small movement of her thumb and this would be over— decision made.

Or she could give the answer she wanted, no, *needed* to give. Take back a small piece of herself before she had to face the world again.

'I don't even know your name,' she ventured.

'My name is Arion. If it pleases you, you can call me Ari.'

She shook her head. 'It pleases me to call you Arion.'

She loved the way her lips curled around his name. So much so, she said it again. 'Arion...'

His eyes darkened. 'You like my name?' he rasped.

'I *love* your name. I've never heard it before... Arion.' She couldn't resist the temptation to try it out one more time.

He caught her up to him and banded one arm around her waist. His laser-like gaze scoured her face as if he was trying to read her innermost thoughts. 'The way you say my name... You are dangerous, Pearl *mou*.'

Laughter, long suppressed under the pain of just *existing*, scratched from her throat. 'Wow...I'm *dangerous*? That's a first.'

'What have other men called you?'

The question sobered her up. Familiar humiliation threatened to crawl over her but she determinedly pushed it away. Tonight was *her* night, *her* choice. She refused to let thoughts of past failures intrude.

'What do you think they've called me?'

'Breathtaking. Stunning. A beauty Aphrodite herself would be jealous of,' he breathed against her neck as his lips caressed her skin. 'Your hair is incredible, the colour of a Greek sunset.'

Perla's breath hitched in her lungs. Unbidden, tears sprang into her eyes. Blinking wildly before he spotted them, she forced herself not to be drawn in by the seductive words.

'Am I close?' He lifted his head and rubbed his stubble—as rough as she'd imagined it would be—against her cheek.

Liquid heat melted her insides.

'Not even a little. But don't let that stop you.'

'Beautiful Pearl, I want to see your hair spread over my pillow. I want to bury myself in it, strangle myself with it.' The hoarse litany made her draw back and stare at him. Once again, his face was stamped in pain. But, alongside it, desire, strong and unmistakable, burned right into her soul. 'Does that frighten you?'

'I want to say no, but I am a little frightened, yes. I've never done this before but I want to. Very much.' So badly she couldn't think straight. The need to forget, just for a short while, what faced her in the next few days, was so strong she couldn't breathe for the need of it. 'Right now, I'm so desperate for you I don't know how long I can stand it.'

'Then stay. I will give you everything you desire.' About to kiss her again, he suddenly froze. 'Unless you're not free to be with me?'

'What do you mean?'

'Is there a lover or a husband?' came the tight, throaty demand.

The arrow of guilt that lanced through her made her freeze too.

This is your night. Yours! Tomorrow will come soon enough.

'I'm free to be with you, Arion. I'll stay with you tonight if you want me to.'

His suite was *probably* the last word in luxury; the fixtures and fittings ones she'd *probably* have ogled if she'd had a chance to take even a single note.

But with Arion's mouth on hers, his fingers in her hair and his body pressed close and hot against hers, Perla didn't notice one single thing about the third-floor suite, except that the *RS* button he'd pressed in the lift stood for Royal Suite.

She did notice the large red velvet sofa he laid her down on the minute they entered his suite's pitch-sized living room. Although the memory of it disappeared once he'd shrugged off his jacket and tie and freed his shirt from his trousers.

His chest once he unbuttoned his shirt instantly made her mouth dry, then flood with longing as she stared at hard contours and smooth bronzed muscles. Hairless and divine, his stunning beauty made need she'd never known pulse through her.

But that was a fraction of what she felt when he dropped his trousers and stepped out of his cotton boxers. His erection stood strong and proud...and big.

Just then, the enormity of what she was doing hit her between the eyes.

She was about to lose her virginity to a complete stranger.

CHAPTER TWO

A DEEP SHUDDER ripped through Perla and she barely stopped her teeth from chattering like a wooden marionette in a child's hand.

The sound she made as Arion, the man she had no knowledge of a mere hour ago, came towards her made him pause and frown.

'Are you cold?' he asked.

She was anything but. She shook her head, forcing a laugh. 'No. I'm a little nervous. I haven't—' She stopped. What was the use of telling him of her inexperience? Whether she pleased or disappointed him, she'd never set eyes on this gorgeous man again. They were using each other to forget their pain, to hold the darkness at bay. This wasn't the time to spill innermost secrets. It was the time to forget they existed. 'It's nothing.'

He nodded as if he understood. Then he took a single step forward, and angled himself over her. 'I'll make it good. I promise,' he vowed, and she forgot everything else.

The kiss was hotter, deeper than the one he'd delivered at the car. This time his tongue probed her mouth with a sensual force that spoke of his need. Fists clamped in her hair, he went even deeper, his groan of satisfaction echoing her own as her fingers sought and found firm, heated, *naked* shoulders.

His skin felt like pure heaven. Velvety smooth and oh

so gloriously luxuriant, she explored him from shoulder to back, then lower. When she moulded her hands over his bare bottom, then dug her nails into his taut flesh, he wrenched his lips from hers with a tortured groan. His breath came out in pants as he stared down at her, eyes dark with lust.

'Promise me you'll do that when I'm deep inside you.'

Heat drenched her from head to toe. From somewhere she summoned the strength to speak. 'I promise.'

He licked the corner of her mouth in a move so simple and yet so powerfully erotic, she felt as if her insides would combust. She gave a heartfelt groan when he pushed himself off her. 'For that to happen, *glikia mou*, you need to be as naked as I am.'

Perla stared down at herself, stunned that the power of his lust hadn't melted the clothes off her. When he grabbed her arms and pulled her up, she went willingly. The slide of her zip was loud and intrusive in the silent room. Unwanted thoughts once again threatened to ruin the moment. *What the hell are you doing? Leave. Leave now!*

As if he could tell, he quickened his movements. Within seconds, he was bending over her once more, his mouth trailing down her neck, washing away her doubt, re-igniting the flames that had merely been banked.

'Tell me how you like it, Pearl *mou*,' he rasped against the valley between her breasts. 'Tell me your favourite position and I'll do it to you.'

Panic momentarily seized her. She searched her mind for terms she'd heard of. 'Doggie style,' she blurted, then cringed as her face flamed.

Thank God he didn't notice. For some strange reason, he seemed as fascinated with her breasts as he'd been with her hair. Moulding them in his hands, he licked first one hardened nipple, then the other, then pulled them simultaneously into his mouth. At her deep groan, he smiled.

'That is one of my favourite positions too,' he said. His teeth grazed over her nipples, then he trailed kisses lower… lower, until she realised his destination.

He ignored the staying hand she put on his shoulder.

'No…'

'*Yes!*' With a hot look from darkened eyes, he parted her thighs.

She held her breath but, at the first sweep of his tongue, she exhaled as pleasure she'd never known rushed over her. Before she could react to that first wave, he began a series of flicks that made stars dance before her eyes. Expertly, he pleasured her, relentless in his need to make her lose control. Buffeted by sensations she'd never experienced, Perla fought both the urge to withdraw from that wicked tongue and press her hips closer. Her head thrashed on the cushion as an unfamiliar sensation pushed her towards a blissful peak.

'Arion! Oh, God… Oh!' She let out a scream as her climax broke over her. Jerking uncontrollably, she sobbed as pleasure washed over her and sucked her under. When he gathered her in his arms and pulled her into his body, Perla sobbed harder.

Through it all he murmured soft words of praise and comfort, a balm her soul desperately needed. An eternity later, he started to pull away. Her protesting mutter was met with another kiss.

'Patience, *pethi mou*, now the real fun begins,' he said with dark promise.

Slowly, Perla rubbed the tears from her eyes.

Opening her eyes, she found him kneeling on the sofa, sliding on a condom. The sight of him, large and powerful and ready, sent another pulse of lust through her.

When he probed her entrance, Perla felt a moment's twinge, a shaky feeling of disconnect. It faded away the moment he pressed himself deeper. At her body's further resistance, he paused with a groan.

'You're not ready. I'm sorry, I was a little impatient.'

She slid her hands through his hair and barely resisted raising her head to kiss him. 'I want you.'

He gave another groan and kissed her. 'You're not ready and I don't want to hurt you.'

Mistaking his meaning, Perla spread her thighs wider and ventured her hips closer. 'I'm ready now.'

Arion raised his head, a slightly puzzled look crossing his face. 'Pearl—'

'Please, don't keep us waiting.' Emboldened by his groan, she pressed even closer. He slid in another delicious inch.

The discomfort grew as he pushed in but the rush, the pleasure that followed behind it was so much worth the momentary pain. Perla's breath fractured as she sighed in bliss. Arion's grip tightened in her hair with the full surge of his body.

'*Theos!* You're so tight. So gorgeous.' The warmth of his breath washed over her neck a second before his lips found and captured hers. His tongue slid into her mouth, its movement as bold and as raw as his full, relentless thrusts.

Bliss washed over her so completely, Perla had no idea where sensation started and ended. Clamping her legs around his waist, she took him fully into her body. Pleasure crested in giant waves over her. But, just as she prepared to give herself over to it, he pulled out of her. Rising to his feet, he tugged her off the sofa and onto the floor.

'On your knees,' he commanded. 'It's time to give you what you want.'

Her heart hammering with excitement, Perla complied.

He came up behind her, bent her over the seat and entered her from behind.

'Oh, my God!' The cry was ripped from her soul, pleasure so profound radiating from inside her she thought she'd pass out.

Arion's fingers slid through her hair over and over as he thrust inside her. Perla had never thought of her hair as an erogenous area. In fact, up till that moment, she'd never thought pleasure like this was possible.

Dear heaven, how wrong she'd been. She screamed as he pounded into her, his hoarse voice reciting her name over and over. Once again the precipice approached, the stars beckoning with a radiance she knew would touch her for ever. Behind her, Arion slid back and rested on his knees. Firm hands urged her back, all the while continuing the relentless pace that stalled her breath.

'Ride me,' he encouraged, his deep voice raw and urgent.

Spreading her legs wider, Perla eased herself back, the change in pace escalating her pleasure even higher. Hands gripping the sofa to steady herself, she rode herself to ecstasy. Her breath choked on a scream as her orgasm hit her. One hand clamped around her middle, Arion eased another hand over her belly to tease her clitoris, prolonging her climax. The wave seemed endless; he continued to thrust inside her despite her pleas for mercy. Just when she thought she'd expire from pleasure, she heard his deep groan. He buried his face in her hair, his thrusts growing uneven as pleasure spasms gripped him.

Several minutes later, he planted kisses on her neck and shoulder, one hand still gripped on her waist. 'I can't decide whether you're an angel or a witch, sent to torment me or bring me heaven.'

Her breath caught on a soft blissful sigh. 'Can I be both?'

'With hair like that, you can be anything you want.'

She managed to lift her head to glance over her shoulder at him. 'You have a freaky fascination with my hair.'

'A fascination which includes seeing it spread over my pillow.' He pulled out of her with a dark groan, scooped her into his arms and headed down a short hallway.

Once again she barely registered her surroundings. But, even while he secured another condom, Arion's gaze held her captive, the look he sent her exciting her in ways she'd never have dreamt was possible. When he took command of her body once more, Perla gave herself over into his arms, a willing slave for the pleasures in store…

She woke with a start, then fought to regulate her breathing so as not to wake the sleeping man beside her.

A sneak peek at the bedside clock showed it was half past two in the morning.

Perla glanced at Arion—goodness, she didn't even know his surname. Well, he didn't know her real name, which was a blessing in disguise, she supposed. Not that their paths would cross again in a million years.

Her gaze devoured his sleeping form. God, he was truly spectacular, and the pleasures he'd shown her would remain unforgettable. Watching the steady rise and fall of his massive chest, she felt her nipples peak again as excitement crawled over her.

She bit her lip and forced herself to get up. She dressed in silence, holding her breath every time he moved. The small part of her that hoped he would wake and stop her leaving was ruthlessly squashed.

They could never be more than ships passing in the night. She carried too much baggage and, from what she'd glimpsed in his eyes, he carried a shipload of his own baggage. All the same, her fingers slowed on her zip. Maybe it didn't have to be this way, maybe she could…

Stay? Dear Lord, what was she thinking?

Doing anything of that sort was totally out of the question. She had *no* choice but to leave.

If for no other reason than the fact that between now and Friday morning when she had to stand before a congregation and speak, she had her dead husband's eulogy to write.

CHAPTER THREE

THE SMALL CHAPEL was packed to the rafters. Outside, a clutch of news vans and reporters were stationed, poised and ready for the opportunity to snap any picture that would feed the media frenzy of the notoriety behind this funeral.

So far, Perla hadn't found the courage to turn around to see just how many people had wedged themselves into the tiny chapel. The one glance as people had filed in had been enough to terrify her. But she hadn't missed the trio of limousines that had crawled past and parked ominously on the chapel lawn.

Morgan's bosses. Probably Sakis Pantelides and various executives from Pantelides Shipping Inc. The letter announcing their attendance had arrived yesterday.

She supposed she should be thankful they were bothering to attend, considering the nefarious circumstances leading to Morgan's death. A small, bitter part of her wished they hadn't bothered. Their presence here would, no doubt, keep up the media frenzy, and she also couldn't dismiss the fact that she'd had to keep demanding information from Pantelides Inc. before she'd been given very brief details of what had happened to her husband.

Granted, Sakis Pantelides had been gentle and infinitely considerate when he'd broken the horrific news to her but the fact remained that Morgan Lowell, the man she'd married, and whose secret she'd kept—*still kept*—had died under suspicious circumstances in a foreign country after trying to get away with defrauding his employer. Pantelides Inc. had kept a lid on the fact to protect itself from adverse publicity.

What no one realised was that *this* was yet another morsel of unwanted truth she had to keep to herself; another detail she couldn't share with Morgan's parents, who had idolised their son and remained devastated by his death. She'd been forced to gloss over the truth for their sake. Again...

She clenched her hands and forced herself to focus. She had more important things to think about now, like how she could stand up and speak of her husband when another man's face, the fevered recollection of another man's hands and the thrust of his hard body repeatedly flashed through her brain.

Dear God, what had she done? What had she been thinking?

Although guilt clawed through her belly, the shame she expected to feel remained way below an acceptable level. In fact she barely felt anything except the forceful presence of her one-night lover, deep inside her, surrounding her, pulsing around her like a live electric current with every breath she took.

She'd taken three showers this morning, all in the vain hope of washing herself free of his scent. But it was as if he'd invaded her thoughts as well as her pores. Behind her, whispered voices surged higher and she heard shuffling as the congregation made way for new arrivals.

Perla's breath stalled as she caught the familiar scent again. She bit her lip and closed her eyes. *God, please give me strength because I'm seriously losing it here.*

When her elderly neighbour and only friend Mrs Clinton's hand covered hers, she gratefully clutched it. The discerning woman had wisely put herself between Perla and

Morgan's parents but she felt their heartbreak with every fibre of her being.

For their sake, for the kindness and open warmth they'd shown her, she had to keep it together. They were the reason she'd borne this humiliation for so long. Morgan had known that. Had banked on it, in fact, and used it as the perfect blackmail tool when she'd threatened to leave him—

'Not long before it starts. Don't worry, dear; in less than an hour, it'll be over. I went through the same thing with my Harry,' she whispered. 'Everyone means well, but they don't know the best they can do in times like these is to leave you alone, do they?'

Perla attempted a response and only managed a garbled croak. Mrs Clinton patted her hand again reassuringly. With relief, she heard the organ starting up. As she stood, Perla caught the scent again, and quickly locked her knees as she swayed.

She glanced to the side and saw a tall, imposing man with a thin scar above his right eye standing next to a striking blonde.

Sakis Pantelides, the man who'd phoned two weeks ago with news of her husband's death. His condolences had been genuine enough but after her discovery of just what Morgan had done to his company, Perla wasn't so sure his attendance here was an offer of support.

Her gaze shifted to the proprietorial arm he kept around the woman, his fiancée, Brianna Moneypenny, and she felt a twinge of shame-laced jealousy.

He caught her gaze and he gave a short nod in greeting before returning his attention to the front.

She faced forward again, but the unsettling feeling that had gripped her nape escalated. The feeling grew as the ceremony progressed. By the time the priest announced the eulogy reading, Perla's stomach churned with sick nerves. She pushed it away. Whatever emotional turmoil she was experiencing had nothing to do with the Pantelides family and everything to do with what she'd done on Tuesday night. And those memories had no place here in this chapel, today.

No matter what Morgan had put her through, she had to do this without breaking down. She had to endure this for his parents' sake.

They'd offered her the only home she'd ever known, and the warmth she'd only ever dreamed about as a child.

Another pat from Mrs Clinton gave her the strength to keep upright. She thought she heard a sharp intake of breath behind her but Perla didn't turn around. She needed every ounce of focus to stride past the coffin holding her dead husband...the husband who, while he'd been alive, had taken great pleasure in humiliating her; the husband who even in death...seemed to be mocking her.

She got to the lectern and unfolded the piece of paper. Nerves gripped her and, although she knew it was rude, she couldn't look up from the sheet. She had a feeling she would lose her nerve if her gaze strayed from the paper in her hand.

Clearing her throat, she moved closer to the microphone.

'I met Morgan at the uni bar on my first day on campus. I was the wide-eyed, clueless outsider who had no clue what went into a half-fat, double-shot pumpkin spice latte—except maybe the pumpkin—and he was the second-year city dude every girl wanted to date. Even though he didn't ask me out until I was in my last year, I think I fell in love with him at first sight...'

Perla carried on reading, refusing to dwell on how overwhelmingly wrong she'd been about the man she'd married; how utterly gullible she must have been to have had the wool pulled over her eyes so effectively until it was too late.

But now was not the time to think of past mistakes. She read on, saying the *right* thing, *honouring* the man who right from the very beginning of their marriage had had no intention of honouring *her*.

'…I'll always remember Morgan with a pint in his hand and a twinkle in his eye, telling rude jokes in the uni bar. *That* was the man I fell in love with and he'll always remain in my heart.'

Unshed tears clogged her throat again. Swallowing, she folded the sheet and finally gathered the courage to look up.

'Thank you all for coming—'

She choked to a halt as her gaze clashed with a pair of sinful, painfully familiar hazel eyes.

No.

Oh, God, no…

Her knees gave way. Frantically, she clutched at the lectern. She felt her hand begin to slip. Someone shouted and moved towards her. Unable to breathe or halt her crumpling legs, she cried out. Several people rushed towards her. Hands grabbed her before she fell, righted her, helped her down from the dais.

And, through it all, Arion Pantelides stared at her from where he stood next to the man she'd guessed was Sakis Pantelides, icy condemnation blazing from his eyes and washing over her until her whole body went numb.

Ari tried to breathe past the vice squeezing his chest, past the thick anger and acrid bitterness lashing his insides. The pain that rose alongside it, he refused to acknowledge.

Why would he feel pain? He had no one to blame but himself. After all life had thrown at him, he'd dared to believe he could reach out and seek goodness when there was none to be had. Only disappointment. Only heartache. Only disgust.

But still the anger came, thick and fast and strong, as he stared at Pearl…no, *Perla* Lowell, the woman who'd lied about her name and slithered into his bed while her husband's body was barely cold.

Disgust roiled through him. Even now, the memory of what they'd done to each other made fiery desire pool in his groin. Gritting his teeth, he forced his fists to unclench as he stamped down on the emotion.

He'd let himself down, spectacularly and utterly. On the most sacred of days, when he should've been honouring his past, he'd allowed himself to succumb to temptation.

Temptation with absolutely the wrong woman.

One who'd turned out to be as duplicitous and as sullied as the husband she was burying.

'Do you know what's going on with her?' His younger brother, Sakis, slid a glance at him.

Ari kept his gaze fixed ahead, jaw clenched tight. 'It's her husband's funeral. I'd have thought it was obvious she's *drowning in grief.*' How bitter those words tasted in his mouth. Because he knew they were the last emotion Perla Lowell was feeling. A woman who could do what she'd done with him forty-eight hours before putting her dead husband in the ground?

No, grief didn't even get a look-in.

Whereas he... *Theos.*

His gut clenched hard at the merciless lash of memories. He'd gorged himself on her, greedy in his need to forget, to blank the pain that had eviscerated him with each heartbeat.

Turning away from the spectacle playing out on the altar, he followed the trickle of guests who'd started to leave the chapel.

'Are you sure that's all?' Sakis demanded. 'I could've sworn she totally freaked out only when she saw you.'

Ari rounded on him as they exited into dappled sunshine. 'What the hell are you talking about?'

'I don't know, brother, but she seemed to be fixated on you. I thought maybe you knew her.'

'I've never been to this backwater until today, and I only came because *you* insisted you couldn't make it. What are you doing here, anyway?'

'It was my fault. I insisted.' Brianna, his beautiful soon-to-be sister-in-law spoke up. 'I thought, as Lowell's former employer, Sakis should be here. We tried to call you to let you know but your phone was off and the staff at Macdonald Hall said you'd checked out yesterday.'

His jaw clenched harder at the reminder.

He'd been running a fool's errand, desperately trying to track down the woman who'd run out on him in the middle of the night. A day and a half, he'd driven up and down the damned countryside, searching for the Mini whose red paint was a poor match for the vibrant hair colour of the woman who'd made him lose his mind and forget his pain for a few blissful hours.

Theos! How could he not have seen that it was all an illusion? They said sex made fools of men. They'd said nothing about the deadly blade of memory and the consequences of a desperate search for oblivion.

Bringing his mind into focus, he lowered his gaze away from his brother's blatant curiosity.

'We've paid our respects, now can we get the hell out of here?' he rasped.

Sakis nodded at a few guests before he answered him. 'Why, what's the hurry?'

'I have a seven o'clock meeting first thing in the morning, then I fly out to Miami.'

Sakis frowned. 'It's only two o'clock in the afternoon, Ari.'

His body didn't know that because he'd been up all day and all night, searching…chasing a dream that didn't exist.

He was losing it. He needed to get out of there before he marched back into that tiny chapel and roared his fury at that red-headed witch inside.

'I *know* what time it is. If you want to stay, feel free. I'll send the chopper back to Macdonald Hall for you two.' He couldn't get out of here fast enough, although every single bone in his body wanted to confront the duplicitous widow and give her a hefty piece of his mind.

With a nod at his brother and Brianna, he cut his way through the gawping crowd, uncaring that his face was set in a formidable scowl.

From the corner of his eye, he saw a flash of red hair heading his way. Although anger rose up within him, it took a monumental effort not to turn his head and see if it was Perla.

Clenching his fist, he stalked faster towards his limo, the need to be gone a fierce, urgent demand.

'Arion, wait!' Her husky voice was almost lost in the cacophony of the funeral spectacle. And it *was* a spectacle. Morgan Lowell's starring role in his own death via a drug overdose had ensured the media would make a meal of his funeral, even with the scant facts they knew.

Ari froze with one hand on the car door. Slowly, he sucked in a deep breath and turned to face her.

The widow in black. How very apt.

The widow whose bright, fiery red hair shone in the daylight with an unholy, tempting light, the same way it had gleamed temptingly across his pillow three nights ago.

Against his will, his body stirred. Blood pounded through his veins, momentarily deafening him with the roar of arousal. Before he could stop himself, his gaze raked over her.

Although her dress was funeral black, demure, almost plain to the point of drab, he wasn't fooled. He knew what lay beneath, the hot curves and the treacherous thighs, the delight he would uncover should he...

No. Never in a thousand years would he bring himself to touch her. They'd come together in a moment he'd thought was sacred, monumentally divine. Instead, it'd turned out to be a tawdry roll in the hay for her.

'Hello…Arion. I'm guessing your surname is Pantelides.' Green eyes searched his with wariness.

'And I now know your full name is *Perla* Lowell. So tell me, what role are you playing here now? Because we both know the grieving widow routine is just a front, don't we? Perhaps you're silently amused because you have saucy underwear underneath that staid black?'

She gasped, an expression that looked shockingly like deep hurt flashing across her face.

Theos, how utterly convincing she was. But not convincing enough to make him forget he'd nearly lost his mind hanging on for dear life as she rode him with merciless enthusiasm a little over forty-eight hours ago.

'How dare you?' She finally found her voice, even though it shook with her words.

'Very easily. I was the guy you were screwing when you should've been home mourning your husband. Now what the hell do you want?'

Her complexion had paled but then her skin was translucent thanks to her colouring. And yes, his words had been cruel, deliberately so. But she'd sullied his own memory of what the date had meant to him for ever.

And *that* he found hard to forgive.

'I was going to apologise for the…um…small deception. And to thank you for your discretion. But I see I needn't have bothered. You're nothing but a vile, bitter man, one who sees nothing wrong in bringing further pain and anguish on an already difficult day. So if you were truly on your way out of here, I guess the only thing I have to say is *good riddance*.'

Ari hardened his heart against the words. She was in the wrong here, not him. She was clearly deluded if she thought he had something to be ashamed of. Turning, he yanked the back door open.

Before he slid in, he glanced at her one last time. 'Have fun revelling in your role of grieving widow. But when the crowd is gone and you think of reprising your *other* role, be sure to stay away from Macdonald Hall. Before the hour's out, I intend to supply the management with your name and ensure you're never allowed to set foot in there again.'

Fugue state.

Perla was sure that perfectly described her condition as she drifted through the wake, shaking hands, accepting condolences and agreeing that yes, Morgan had been a lovely man and a generous husband. On occasion, she even smiled at a distant uncle or great-aunt's fond anecdote.

The part of her that had reeled at Ari Pantelides's scathing condemnation an hour ago had long been suppressed under a blanket of fierce denial with Do Not Disturb signs hammered all over it.

At the time, she'd barely been able to contain the belief that he thought her some kind of scarlet woman or a trollop who frequented bars in the hope of landing a hot body for the night.

She audibly choked at the thought.

Mrs Clinton, who'd faithfully stuck by her side once they'd returned to the house she'd shared with Morgan and now shared with his parents, gave her a firm rub on the back. 'You're almost there, dear girl. Give it another half hour and I'll start dropping heavy hints that you should be left alone. Enough is enough.'

She glanced at the old dear's face. Perla had never confided the true state of her marriage with Mrs Clinton, or anyone for that matter. The very thought of it made humiliation rise like a tide inside her.

But she'd long suspected that the older woman somehow

knew. Seeing the sympathy in her old rheumy eyes, Perla felt tears well up in hers.

Suddenly, as if the bough had broken, she couldn't stop the tide of hot, gulping tears that rose from deep inside.

'Oh, my dear.' Warm arms hugged her, providing the solace she'd been so cruelly denied throughout her marriage. The solace she'd imagined she'd found in a luxury penthouse suite three days ago, but had turned out to be another cruel illusion.

'I'm sorry, I shouldn't…I didn't mean to…'

'Nonsense! You have every right to do whatever you want on a day like this. Propriety be damned.'

Hysterical laughter bubbled up from her throat but she quickly smothered it. When a glass containing a caramel-coloured liquid that smelled suspiciously like brandy appeared in front of her, she glanced up.

The exquisitely beautiful woman who'd introduced herself as Brianna Moneypenny, soon-to-be Brianna Pantelides, held out the drink, sympathy shining from her expertly made-up eyes.

Perla wiped her own eyes, acutely conscious that she was messing up the make-up she'd carefully applied to hide the shadows under her eyes.

'Thank you.'

'No need to thank me. I've helped myself to a shot too. This is the third funeral Sakis and I have attended in the last month. My emotions are beyond shredded.' She sat down next to Perla, gracefully crossed her legs and offered a kind smile. 'It's nothing compared to what you must be feeling, of course, and if there's anything we can do, please don't hesitate to ask.'

'I…thank you. And please extend my thanks to your fiancé and…and the other Mr Pantelides for taking the time to come…' Perla's voice drifted off, simply because she couldn't think straight when her mind churned with thoughts of Arion Pantelides and the accusations he'd thrown at her. And even though she'd seen him get into his car, she couldn't stop her gaze from scouring the room, almost afraid to find out if he'd returned to tear a few more strips off her.

'Arion has left but I'll let him know,' Brianna said. A quick glance at her showed a sharp intellect that made Perla hope against hope that the other woman wasn't putting two with two and coming up with the perfect answer.

As it was, Perla felt as if she had the dreaded letter *A* branded on her forehead.

'Of course. I appreciate that he must be busy.' She didn't add that, in the light of what Morgan had done, they were the last people she'd expected to attend his funeral. Instead, she took a hasty sip of the brandy for much needed fortitude, and nearly choked when liquid fire burned down her throat.

'Well, he is. But he volunteered to come down here when he thought Sakis couldn't make it. And yet he seemed to have a bee in his bonnet about something. To be honest, it's the first time I've seen him that ruffled.' The speculation in her voice made Perla wish she'd worn her hair down to hide the colour rising in her face. 'It was quite a sight to behold.'

'Um, well…whatever it is, I hope he resolves it soon.'

'Hmm, so do I—'

'Brianna.' Sakis Pantelides chose that moment to approach them and offer his own condolences. Perla fought to find the appropriate response despite the nerves tearing through her stomach.

Then she watched as he turned to his fiancée, his face transforming with a very visible devotion that made Perla's heart lurch with jealousy and pain.

She'd long ago harboured hopes that someone would look at her like that. She'd foolishly believed that someone would be Morgan. Instead, he'd married her and black-mailed her into deceit and humiliation.

As an orphan, tossed from foster home to foster home all her childhood, she'd learned to mask the raw pain and despair of being the odd child that nobody wanted. But the hollow feeling in her belly had never gone away.

Meeting Morgan and suddenly finding herself the sole focus of his charm and wit had tricked her naïve self into believing she'd finally found someone who loved and cared for her, not out of duty, or because the state was paying them to do so, but because she was worth loving.

He'd roughly pulled the wool from her eyes within days of their wedding. But, even then, she'd foolishly believed she could salvage something from the only steady relationship she'd ever known. But weeks had dragged into months and months into years and by the time she'd accepted that she'd once again been cast aside, like a broken toy no one wanted to play with, it'd been too late to leave.

Her shaky breath drew glances from Sakis and Brianna but she couldn't look them in the face. She'd revealed so much already. She feared opening her mouth would be catastrophic, especially as she could feel Sakis Pantelides's keen gaze boring into her.

God, please don't let him guess what I did with his brother.

'I think it's time we left Mrs Lowell in peace, Sakis,' Brianna murmured.

Sakis nodded. 'My lawyers will be in touch with the paperwork regarding your husband's employment entitlements. But if you need anything in the meantime, please do not hesitate to get in touch.'

She glanced at him and immediately glanced away when his gaze narrowed.

He can't know!

Panic clawed at her. Surely Arion hadn't told him?

From the corner of her eye she saw Morgan's parents heading towards them. Clearing her throat, she fought the panic and pasted a suitable smile on her face.

No matter what had gone on between Morgan and her, Terry and Sarah Lowell had welcomed her into their hearts. She couldn't repay them with betrayal.

'I appreciate it, Mr Pantelides. Have a safe journey back to London.'

She turned away, grateful for the distraction that Morgan's wheelchair-bound mother brought to stop her wondering just what Sakis Pantelides knew about her carnal activities with his brother.

And she certainly couldn't think about Arion Pantelides and the heat that rushed under her skin every time she relived what had happened in his hotel room three days ago.

What had happened between them was now firmly in the past. Never to be repeated. What she needed to concentrate on now was picking up the shattered pieces and commencing the uphill battle that was the rest of her life.

CHAPTER FOUR

Three months later.

PERLA LOOKED UP for the umpteenth time as the Pantelides Inc. reception phone rang. The superbly groomed receptionist answered in dulcet tones and sliced another cool look at Perla before turning away.

Her teeth gritted and for a second she fought the urge to march over to the desk and demand she call upstairs again and get her the meeting she'd come here for.

Instead, she smoothed her hand down the black pencil skirt she'd spent her dwindling funds on and forced herself to remain seated. She'd turned up with no prior appointment, but only because her phone calls and emails had gone unanswered. And, truth be told, she'd only been waiting an hour and a half.

But being in the architecturally imposing building that bore the Pantelides name made her nerves jangle with each heartbeat, despite chastising herself that the likelihood that Arion Pantelides was in residence was negligible.

As the head of Pantelides Luxe, the branch of the conglomerate that ran its luxury hotels and casinos around the world—yes, she'd researched him in a moment of madness—Arion Pantelides spent very little time in England. And even if he were here, she'd asked for an appointment with the head of HR in Sakis's absence, not his brother.

So, really, there was no need for her to feel as if she were playing dare in an electric lightning storm.

Nevertheless, when the phone rang again, she held her breath. Expertly waxed eyebrows arched her way and a manicured hand motioned her forward.

Sighing her relief, Perla approached the desk as the receptionist hung up.

With another glance, which was now tinged with heavy speculation, the receptionist slid a visitor's badge along with a short silver key across the sleek glass counter.

'Please wear this at all times. Take the last lift on the right. Turn the key and press the button.'

Perla wanted to ask which floor she needed but she didn't want to look a fool, so she nodded her thanks and walked on shaky feet to the lift.

As it turned out, there was only one button to press. After inserting the key, she stabbed the green button that simply read *AP* and held her breath as the doors slid smoothly shut.

Her trepidation rose along with her meagre breakfast as she was whisked up at warp speed.

She barely had time to swallow the sudden nausea that assailed her before the lift doors were sliding open again. She started to step out, then froze as ice washed over her.

Arion Pantelides stood before her, tall, breathtaking, imposing…and as granite-faced as he'd been on the day she'd buried Morgan.

Perla swallowed. And swallowed again before she could speak. 'I think there's been some sort of misunderstanding. I'm not here to see you. I came to see your brother, my late husband's employer. Or, in his absence, I asked for the head of HR.'

'Sakis isn't here.' He confirmed what she already knew. 'He's on an extended honeymoon.' That voice, deep, husky, tinged with a haunting quality that she'd found intriguing since their first meeting, feathered along her nerves, sending her insides quaking with emotion so strong she wanted to take a step back from it.

Perla bit her lip. 'Yes, I know he got married last month but I didn't know he was still away… I was hoping he was back…' She drifted to a stop, her gaze trying desperately not to stray over his hauntingly beautiful face. A face that had featured in her dreams more times than she cared to acknowledge even to herself.

'He would've got married sooner. He delayed it because your husband's involvement in the Pantelides oil tanker crash was still under investigation. It would've been in bad taste to celebrate what is supposed to be the happiest day of any man's life with events like that hanging over everyone's head.'

The veiled mockery in his tone made her hackles rise, but it was the memory of his blistering anger the last time they'd met that made her insides quake.

She sucked in a deep breath. 'I apologise for the inconvenience—'

A slashing gesture with his hand stopped her words. 'He'll be back in two weeks. Feel free to come back then.'

The lift doors started to shut. Galvanised into action, she threw out a hand to stop it just as he did the same. Warm fingers grazed hers, sending electricity zapping through her. Perla jumped back and felt her heart thunder as she caught the look he levelled at her.

'I'm…I'm afraid this can't wait. Just point me in the direction of HR and I'll be out of your hair…'

As if reminded of that part of her, he stepped back and his lazy gaze trailed upward to rest on the hair she'd pulled back into a tight bun. Once he'd looked his fill, those hazel eyes, whose mesmerising flecks she recalled so vividly, recaptured hers. 'The whole HR team is on a day's training in Paris.'

Her stomach plummeted with despair. 'You're kidding, right? The *whole* team?'

He raised a brow at her.

'This really is an emergency. I came here specially. I need to talk to someone.'

Just like that, he shrugged, turned and walked away.

With every fibre of her being she wanted to let the doors shut once more and be plunged back to the ground floor, back to safety. But too much depended on her trip here today. Much too much.

So she took one step into Arion Pantelides's vast, opulent domain.

The architecture of the Pantelides Tower had looked formidable and stunning from the outside. Inside his office, the glass, chrome and steel structure blended with earthy tones made the place simply magnificent.

A wide roll-top desk, obviously an expensive antique, took up one corner of the glass-walled room, offering a breathtaking view of the river and the iconic buildings across the water. Under her feet, a deep gold carpet muffled her tentative footsteps.

She managed to take that all in in the handful of seconds before Arion folded his leanly muscled frame behind his desk.

Fighting her rising irritation, she glanced back at him. 'Did you hear what I said? I need to talk to someone. It's important.'

'By all means, if this can't wait, tell me what the problem is and I'll see if I can accommodate you.'

He was toying with her, like a jungle animal toying with his prey. But she would not give him the satisfaction of thinking he could pounce and annihilate her again without consequences.

Even though the need to turn tail and flee stalked through her, she held her ground. Because what other choice did she have? She couldn't exactly flounce out of here. Her situation was too dire. They needed a solution now or Morgan's parents would lose the house in which they'd brought up their son. After what they'd been through, Perla couldn't stand by and do nothing whilst they suffered another blow in addition to the one they'd already been dealt by losing their only child.

Pursing her lips, she reached into her bag and brought out the file she'd compiled. Stepping forward, she slapped it on the table in front of him.

'According to these letters, neither Morgan's parents nor I are entitled to his death-while-employed insurance pay out. That can't be right. I know he signed on for that benefit.'

Arion steepled his fingers and watched her dispassionately over them. 'Ah, so you're here to collect on your husband's death.'

She couldn't stop herself from flinching at his tone. And he saw it because his eyes gleamed with something akin to satisfaction.

She straightened her spine. 'I'm only asking what is rightly due to me as the spouse of a man who died while employed by your brother's company. I've read the small print. I know my rights, so I'd thank you not to make me sound like a vulture, Mr Pantelides.' She kept her voice firm because she sensed that any weakness would be met with scalpel-sharp ruthlessness.

Abruptly, he sat forward. Even across his desk, his imposing figure dominated, enclosing her in his powerful aura and making her pulse race.

Steady breaths. Just breathe.

'Trust me, *glikia mou*. No red-blooded man would look at you and liken you to a vulture. There are other, more exotic creatures perfectly apt to describe you.'

Really? Perla nearly groaned in relief when she realised she hadn't asked the question out loud.

'I'd prefer not to be thought of in terms of creatures great or small. Are you able to help me with this or am I wasting my time here?' she snapped.

Arion shrugged and glanced at his watch. 'Unfortunately, I have a lunch meeting in fifteen minutes.' He reached across and grabbed the papers from the table. 'Are you staying in town?'

She frowned at the unexpected question. 'No, I'm returning to Bath this evening.'

'Then don't let me stop you. Someone will be in touch soon.'

Something in the way he said that made suspicion rise higher. 'And just how soon is *soon?*'

Another careless shrug. 'I can get my brother to email his head of HR and get them to look into it but he's somewhere in the South Pacific. In a state of wedded bliss, who knows how often he checks his emails.' A shadow crossed his face, a tiny hint of what she'd glimpsed that night in the Macdonald Hall car park. Despite the need for self-preservation, her heart twisted.

'Arion…' He immediately stiffened and she bit her lip. *Wrong move, Perla! Keep on point.* 'Mr Pantelides, I don't have the sort of time you're offering. Could you…would you be willing to look into this yourself for me? Please?' she added when he remained frozen.

His eyes hardened. 'Is this where you trot out the for *old time's sake?*'

A heated flush crawled up her neck. 'No, I wouldn't be so crass as to refer to an occasion we'd both prefer to forget…but of course you won't believe that about me so I don't even know why I'm bothering. Look, I'm not sure whether you know about my circumstances, but Morgan and I lived with his parents after we got married. We were always going to move out and get a place of our own but that never happened. Two years ago, his mother was in a bad accident. Terry, Morgan's father, had to give up his job to look after her. Times have been hard for them. Without Morgan's insurance payment, they could lose their house. I know I'm nothing but a piece of trash in your eyes but they don't deserve to lose their home so soon after losing their son.'

She sucked in a breath and risked a glance at him. His expression remained stone-cold. For several minutes he didn't speak. Then he reached into his desk and slid across a small black triangular piece of gleaming plastic.

There were no markings on it. It could've been one of those if-you-had-to-apply-for-it-you-couldn't-afford-it credit cards reserved for multi-billionaires she'd read about in a magazine once. Or it could've been a loyalty card for die-hard coffee addicts. Perla had no way of telling. She looked from the card to Arion's face.

'What's that for?' she asked suspiciously.

'That card lets you into that lift.' He nodded towards the small lift to one side of his office, across from the one she'd come up in. 'The lift will take you straight to my penthouse. You'll wait for me there—'

'No way.' Perla stopped what was coming before he could finish.

His nostrils flared. 'Excuse me?'

'I won't do…whatever it is you have in mind. I know you think I'm nothing but some common whore but you're wrong. What happened between us that night wasn't cheap and it wasn't tawdry. Not for me at least. And I despise you for thinking I'd stoop that low to get you to help me—'

'Shut the hell up for one second and listen.' His rough command dried her words.

Her fist clenched. 'How dare you speak to me like—?'

'You said you have nowhere to stay. I have a meeting

in…exactly eight minutes which will last for five hours. Minimum. Unless you intend to wander the streets in the rain until I'm finished, my offer is the best you're going to get.'

Surprise stamped through her. 'Oh, you mean you want me to go up and just…wait for you?' she asked.

'Why, Mrs Lowell, you sound disappointed.'

Severely taken aback, it took her a minute to regroup. 'I assure you, I'm not.'

He held out the card. 'Good.'

With a hand she cursed for trembling, she took it and headed slowly for the lift, trepidation in her every step.

'Oh, and Perla?' he murmured mockingly.

She stopped and turned back to him. 'What?'

'Don't look so frightened. You're not going up to a den of iniquity. There's more to my apartment than a bed and a pole for you to perform on.'

Her hand tightened on the card. 'Wow, I'm shocked you even have those. The way you've been acting, I'd imagine a torture rack and thumb screws would be more accurate furnishings for the women you send up there.'

His eyes darkened and the hand lying on the table clenched into a fist. She'd scored a point in their battle of wills. Finally. But the victory felt hollow. With every word and every gesture, Arion tainted their one night together, letting bitterness fill the space where she'd known a few hours of joy. If only she could forget. But forgetting was impossible. Not when he sat there, so vital, so impossibly gorgeous.

So infuriatingly captivating.

'I've never invited a woman to my penthouse. Ever.'

'Oh, then I'll consider myself one lucky woman. Don't worry, I'll try not to skip with joy and ruin your priceless floors.' She quickened her steps towards the lift, eager to be out of his sight and escape that merciless tongue. The plastic key slid soundlessly into the designated slot and the lift whispered open. She turned and faced the office, not in the least bit surprised to find Arion's gaze fixed squarely on her.

She wriggled her fingers in a careless wave. 'See you in a few hours, charmer.'

He didn't take his eyes off her, nor did he respond to her mockery as the lift door shut. But the look in his eyes sent a shiver of unease through her.

And with every hour that passed, despite having been whisked up into what felt like the lap of luxury—Ari's personal chef had served her the most delicious three-course meal, after which she'd had a call from the concierge to find out whether she wanted a facial or pedicure while she waited—her tension escalated.

So much so that when she heard the lift whisper open she stopped breathing. She jerked up from the suede sofa and her feet hit the floor with a thud. The magazine she'd been reading—one of many supplied by the concierge—spilled onto the floor. She bent to pick it up and straightened to find him a foot away, those piercing hazel eyes pinned on her.

'You…uh, do you have news for me?' she blurted, more to stem the overwhelming force of his presence than a need for immediate answers.

But then she didn't see the need for pleasantries. They weren't friends. Hell, they weren't even lovers. They were two strangers who'd given in to a mad moment that had returned to haunt them with merciless cruelty.

'Is that how you greeted your husband when he returned from work?' he rasped.

Her shocked gasp made him freeze. She watched a contrite grimace cross his face.

'Forgive me, that was beyond tasteless,' he rasped.

'Not to mention extremely disrespectful. You know

nothing about my life with Morgan.' And she intended it to remain that way.

He clawed a hand through his hair. 'No, I didn't. I'm sorry.'

With jerky movements, he loosened then yanked his tie off and flung it on the sofa where she'd been sitting.

Not expecting his immediate apology, Perla was left floundering. 'Apology accepted,' she murmured, a little absently because suddenly she found herself wondering what it would be like to have a real husband come home to her.

A husband like…Arion?

Hell, no. They would drive each other homicidal within weeks.

But during that time too they would have hot, exquisite, mind-melting sex.

The heat that rushed over her made her take a step back and give herself a mental slap. She wasn't here to reminisce over dreams that wouldn't come true in a million years. She was here to save Terry and Sarah's home—*her home*—before the bank made good on their threat of repossession.

Focus.

But then how could she, when Arion, having discarded his tie, was now in the process of undoing his top buttons, revealing the gloriously sleek muscled chest she'd explored without shame or inhibition a little over three months ago?

He caught her stare and a look passed through his eyes. One she didn't want to interpret. One that made her rush to speech.

'I'm sorry if I seem to be rushing you but I'm hoping to catch the last train back to Bath tonight.'

He sauntered over to the drinks cabinet and poured a large whisky. She shook her head when he indicated the extensive array of drinks with a lifted brow.

She needed to keep her wits about her. The memory of

what had happened the last time she'd shared a drink with him was a reminder never to indulge around him. Ever.

'I had Sakis's people look into it.'

'And?'

He knocked back the drink without taking his eyes off her. 'You said he signed the part of his contract that allows you to receive spousal income on his death?'

'Yes.'

'So you're not aware he signed the Under-Forty waiver thereafter?' he asked.

Unease dredged through her stomach. 'What's an *Under-Forty waiver?*'

'All employees under forty can take the option of death insurance or a yearly double bonus in place of compensation to family on death. Once an employee turns forty the option is no longer available. Your husband was—'

'Morgan was a long way from forty when he died,' she supplied through numb lips.

Ari nodded. 'According to his line manager, he asked for that clause to be amended in favour of receiving the double bonus and he never reinstated the original clause. Therefore, you are not entitled to receive funds.'

Ari watched her expression go from shock to disbelief to anger, then back to disbelief. She opened then shut her mouth. Then her gaze narrowed suspiciously.

'Please tell me you're not toying with me or making this up because…because of…'

'For someone who seems intent on making me believe our incident is behind you, you seem to leap back to it at the slightest opportunity.'

'I wasn't… I just…I can't believe Morgan would do that to his parents.'

To his parents. Not to her. The curious statement set off alarm bells in his brain. He didn't like alarm bells. They reminded him that he'd refused to listen to them clanging long and hard in the years before his father's real character had been brought to light.

They reminded him that in the end he'd lived in false hope that the father he'd looked up to wouldn't attempt to throw him to the wolves to save himself.

'You think that the husband you were so happy to betray was less than honest with you? Need I point out the irony there?' he bit out more sharply than he wanted to, the memory of betrayal and devastation growing rawer by the minute.

'I didn't betray Morgan.' Again an expression a lot like pain crossed her face. He hardened himself against it. Much like he'd hardened himself against thinking about her all the way through his meeting. A meeting he had barely been able to control because he hadn't been able to tear his mind away from the fact that she was here, in his living space, touching his things, leaving the hypnotically seductive scent of her body all over the place.

Theos, what had he been thinking, offering her the use of his apartment when he could just as easily have sent her across the street to the luxury guest apartments they used for visiting executives? Because he hadn't wanted to risk her strutting into another bar, catching the eye of another hungry predatory male and offering them a taste of what she'd offered him.

Stasi!

The admonition did nothing to lift his mood. 'I have no interest in lying to you, nor do I take pleasure in prolonging this meeting. You came here seeking information. I've provided it. What you do with that information is now up to you. I suggest you come clean with your in-laws and find a way around it.'

Her eyes darkened further as she stared at him. '*Find a way around it*, just like that? You think it's that easy?'

He shrugged. 'I fail to see how any of this is my problem.'

She raised both hands and slid them through her long vibrant hair—hair she'd released from its tight bun at some point in the last few hours.

Ari found himself helplessly following the seductive ripple. Heat speared through him as he watched her pace to the window and back to where he stood, her agitated, breast-heaving breathing doing incredibly groin-hardening things to him.

She glared at him, the beginning of fire sparking those amazing green eyes. 'Surely I should've been informed of this change in his contract since I stood to lose from the amendment?' she railed at him.

The blatant statement of avarice made bitterness surge through him. Arion's father had torn their family apart, ripped it from its very foundations. All because of greed for money, carnal pleasure and power.

In the three months since his last encounter with Perla, he'd tried to blot the chaotic memories her actions had brought from his mind. He'd told himself that reacting to her the way he had at Macdonald Hall was because he'd been caught on the raw.

But, watching her now, he felt the same insidious desire creeping through him, damning him for being weak and helpless against his body's reaction to her.

When he'd finally been brought to justice, his father, although he hadn't shown an ounce of contrition, had confessed that he hadn't been able to help himself in the face of temptation.

A wave of despair washed over Ari now as he contemplated that perhaps he had a similar trait.

Hell, no!

But even that thought wasn't enough to stop his gaze from dropping to the hectic rise and fall of Perla's breasts as she paced his living room.

An image of her perfect rosy nipples and how they'd tasted in his mouth smashed through his mind.

Smothering the recollection, he took a few, much needed steps to his bar. 'It is what it is. Have you eaten?' he asked, then wondered why he was prolonging this meeting.

She dropped her hands, her expression incredulous. 'My life is in tatters and you're asking me if I want to eat?'

'Cut the melodrama. I was merely attempting to be courteous. I have nothing else to say to you on the matter of your husband's employment. Feel free to leave. Or stay and join me for dinner.' His hand tightened around the decanter as the invitation slipped out, almost without conscious thought.

'Why do you snarl every time you say the word *husband*? Morgan was your brother's tanker pilot, and I know things didn't end well…'

Ari raised a brow. 'You think things didn't *end well?*'

He knew Sakis had done a stellar job in saving the company's reputation and hidden the true extent of Morgan Lowell's sabotage from the press. But was she also oblivious to her husband's betrayal? Or had she merely blinded herself to her husband's true nature, the way she'd blithely hidden the fact that she was newly widowed when she'd climbed into his bed?

'I'm not trying to belittle what happened. I just don't understand why you look as if you have dog poo on your shoes whenever I use the word *husband!*'

'Perhaps I don't wish to be reminded of the dead.' Death had brought too much suffering, had left devastation in its path, wounds that could never be healed. Knowing it was death that had made their paths cross in the first place didn't ease the vice around his chest.

His answer seemed to sober her. 'No, neither do I,' she said.

Her steps were decidedly less agitated when she went to retrieve her large bag from the corner of his sofa.

She was leaving, walking out of his life again. That single thought sent a spark of fierce rebellion through his stomach. He didn't realise he'd placed himself between the lift and her until she stopped in front of him.

'Thank you for your help, Mr Pantelides.' Her words were polite enough and her eyes were determined enough but he didn't miss the slight wobble to her mouth.

Ari wanted to slide his thumb over that mouth, loosen it until its velvet plumpness slid smoothly against his skin.

'What are you going to do?' he asked.

Her eyes narrowed. 'I thought you didn't care?'

'People tend to get litigious in your circumstances. For your own sake and the in-laws you claim to care about, I would hate for you to take that route.'

She hitched her handbag up onto her shoulder, her eyes back to full glare. 'I detect a veiled threat in there. But, from where I'm standing, I have nothing to lose so I may or may not speak with a lawyer to weigh my options.'

'From where I'm standing, you have none. Do you have a job?'

Her gaze slid away and he got the distinct feeling she was about to be less than truthful. 'Kind of.'

'Kind of? Doing what?'

She carefully avoided his gaze. 'Oh, this and that. Not that it's any of your business.'

'And does *this and that* not provide you with enough to keep a roof over your head?'

Her eyes darted back to his, defiance burning in their depth. 'If you must know, I'm not working at the moment. But I had a job before I got married. Morgan encouraged me to take a leave of absence for a while so his mother wasn't left alone for long periods of time. Terry was a long-haul lorry driver.'

'Right, so your husband convinced you to abandon your career to play babysitter to his mother. And you agreed?'

'There's that tone again. Why the hell am I even bothering?' She tried to move past him. 'Goodbye, Mr Pantelides. I hope you don't get a nosebleed from that super lofty position on your high horse.'

He caught her by the waist. The slide of her cotton shirt over her skin reminded him of how it'd felt to undress her, to bare her softness to his touch. Ari's mouth watered with the fierce need to experience that act again.

Weak... Theos, he was weak, just like his father.

'Let me go.'

'No,' he said, feeling a thread of real fear in that word. He should let her go. Forget about her. Forget how she'd made him feel that night. Because everything that had come after that moment of bliss had brought him nothing but jagged pain.

'Yes! I refuse to talk to you when you act like I'm some lowlife who's wandered into your perfect little world.'

'The circumstances of our meeting—'

'Can be placed squarely at your feet. I told you to leave me alone in that bar. But you were too busy playing the alpha *me-big-man-you-little-woman* role to listen to me. If you'd left me alone to have my drink we wouldn't be in this position.'

He whirled and propelled her back against the wall next to the lift. He didn't like that description of him. Didn't like that he'd seen what he wanted and just gone for it. It struck too close to home, made him too similar to the man he'd desperately tried to forget all these years.

And yet, as if from another dimension, he heard his reply. 'You mean this position when all I can think about is tearing that prissy little skirt off you, yanking aside your panties and slamming inside you?'

Her gasp was hot on his face. He welcomed it. Welcomed the excuse to plunge his tongue between her lips and taste her the way he'd been longing to taste her since she'd walked into his office today.

She pushed frantically at his shoulders but Ari wasn't in the mood to be denied. Not until he'd taken a little bit of the edge off this insane, pulsating need. Besides, her lips had started to cling, to kiss him back.

He groaned as her tongue dashed out to meet his, tentatively at first, then with progressively daring thrusts that made his blood rush south with dizzying speed. He hitched her higher up on the wall, felt her moan vibrate through them as he palmed her breast.

God, she was hot. So damned hot. Her nipples were already hard nubs beneath his thumbs as he teased them. Her cries of pleasure made him thankful she was here with him, not in a bar somewhere being hit on by other men.

Her fingers scraped over his nape and up through his hair, then dropped back down to restlessly explore his shoulders.

Theos, she was as hungry for him as he was for her.

With impatient fingers he slid up her skirt. The scrap of lace he encountered made his blood boil some more. With a rough growl, he shredded them.

'Oh, God! I can't believe you just did that,' she gasped and stared down at the tattered lace in his hand.

'Believe it. My hunger for you is bordering on the insane, *glikia mou*. Be warned.' He took her lips in another kiss, bit down on the plump lower lip and felt her jerk with the sensation.

Without giving her time to think, he sank to his knees and parted her thighs.

Her eyes widened as she read his intention. 'Arion...'

He hadn't had time to explore her like this last time. But this time he fully intended to gorge on her.

'No,' she said, but he could read the excitement in her eyes.

He managed to drag his lips from the velvet temptation of her inner thigh and the seductive scent inches away. 'Why?'

'Because you'll hate yourself if we do this again. And you'll hate me. For whatever trivial reason, you think I soiled something for you by sleeping with you three months ago. Frankly, I don't want to have to deal with whatever that was again.'

The reminder sent a spear of ice and jagged pain through his heart. Before he could stop himself, he rose and his hand slid to her throat.

Her eyes widened, not with fear, but with wariness at the look he knew was on his face. Every condemning thought he was trying to keep at bay came flooding back.

'*Trivial?* You think my reason for blaming you for sullying that day is *trivial?*' Pain made his voice hoarse, his heart thud dully in his veins. He distantly registered the quickening pulse beneath his palm but he was too lost in his own turmoil to react to it.

'I don't know! You never told me why. You were only interested in shredding me for—'

'For sleeping with a soulless wanton and ruining my wife's memory for ever?'

CHAPTER FIVE

PERLA FELT THE blood drain from her face. From head to toe she went numb. So numb she couldn't move. Or speak. Or do anything apart from stare at the pain-racked face of the man who held her upright.

When the full meaning of his words sank in, she jerked from him, pushing him back with a strength that felt superhuman but only made him take one single step back.

'Your *wife?* You…you're *married?*' The word choked out of her throat.

His nostrils flared and the skin around his mouth whitened. 'Was. Same as you. Bereaved. Same as you. The night we met, I was mourning. *Unlike* you.'

The accusation slashed across her skin, waking her numbness. The tingle of pain came with a healthy dose of anger. 'What makes you think I wasn't in mourning too?'

'Let me see, you were discussing cocktails with the bartender and doing nothing to bat off his very clear interest in you.'

'And you think that automatically makes me less of a person? Because I wasn't snarling at a total stranger?'

'Your actions weren't those of a bereaved widow.'

'Everyone handles grief differently. Just because you chose to sit in a corner nursing your whisky and demanding silence doesn't mean you have the monopoly on heartache.'

She watched his face harden further. 'And what of the

events afterwards? Which step of the grieving process did you tick by sharing the bed of a stranger before your husband was even in the ground?'

Despite her reeling senses, she fought to keep her voice steady. 'That's what bothers you, isn't it? The fact that I committed some cardinal sin by seeking solace before I'd buried my husband.'

'Was that what you were doing? Seeking solace?' His gaze bored into her, almost as if he was willing her to answer in the affirmative.

Because that would make him see her in a better light?

She shook her head and started to straighten her clothes. 'Does it matter what I say? You've already judged and found me guilty. I slept with you three days before my husband was in the ground. Trust me, you don't detest me more than I detest myself. But tell me, what's your excuse? Why did you sleep with me, other than that I was a willing body with a fascinating hair colour you couldn't resist?'

Her question made him jerk backward. He frowned and slowly his hand fell away from her throat. Hazel eyes dropped to his hand, and she watched it slowly curl into a fist, then release.

'For some of us, the pain reaches a point when it becomes unbearable. You were there. You offered a willing distraction.'

For some of us...a willing distraction...

Perla wasn't sure which of the two statements hurt deeper. What she was sure of was that Arion believed both statements; believed she'd gone to the bar at Macdonald Hall for her own selfish reasons other than with grief in mind.

And, in a way, wasn't he half right? The actions that had propelled her out of her car had had more to do with her frustration and anger at what Morgan had done to her than with pure grief.

The grief had come later, of course. Because, despite everything else he'd put her through, his loss hurt the two people she'd come to see as surrogate parents.

Terry and Sarah had partly filled a void she'd longed for Morgan to complete. They'd treated her as their own, and for someone who'd known only the coldness of the state foster system for most of her life, it'd been a blessed feeling to finally be part of a loving family. To feel a degree of being wanted she'd never experienced before.

Of course, she couldn't tell Arion that; he wouldn't believe her. She'd all but thrown herself at him in that car park, just after prattling on about Santorini and weddings.

She knew her actions had fallen far short of that expected of a newly bereaved wife. But she refused to let him keep denouncing her as a whore.

'I went into that bar for a drink, nothing else. I've never picked up a man in my life. You were a mistake that shouldn't have happened. But you happened. We had a moment. You can choose to shame me over it for as long as you live if it makes you feel better. I prefer to put it behind me, forget it ever happened.'

Hazel eyes narrowed and her breath caught. She'd been trying to reason with him. Instead, she'd made him angrier.

'If you wanted to forget you shouldn't have come here today. You should've appointed a representative and made them deal with this situation on your behalf. Coming here and parking yourself in my lobby tells me forgetting was the last thing on your mind.'

'You're wrong! Besides, I live in the real world, Mr Pantelides. Representatives and lawyers cost money. Hiring one to do the job I was perfectly capable of doing myself is irrational. The only thing this trip's cost me is a train ticket.'

One smooth eyebrow rose. Then his hand glided back to her neck, then down to her shoulder to rest just beneath her breast. 'Are you sure?' His breathing had grown slightly ragged and his other hand was now flexing through her hair, toying with it.

'Mr Pantelides—'

'You once told me my given name pleases you,' he murmured in that deadly low voice.

Her breath hitched. 'How can I forget if you keep reminding me?'

'Perhaps I don't want you to forget. Perhaps I want you to relive the pain and devastation and the pleasure with me.' One thumb teased her nipple and she felt her knees give way. 'If I have to be like *him,* then maybe I deserve whatever I get.'

The rawness in his voice struck deep inside her. 'Like who?'

He shook his head. 'No one. We've already committed the crime, Perla *mou.* The guilt will never leave us.'

Sensation bombarded and it was all she could do to keep her thoughts straight. 'So your solution is to commit the crime again?'

'If you'd stayed away, that would've ended the matter. But you're here now, front and centre, and I find that I lack the willpower to let you walk away.'

Her shocked laughter scraped her throat. 'You speak as if I have some sort of power over you—'

'You enthralled me from the moment I saw you.' The words were spoken with no pleasure. None. There wasn't even a hint of a compliment in there.

'I'm sorry I affect you that way. Let go of me and I'll remove myself from your presence.'

His laugh was self-deprecatory. 'I've had you wedged against this door for the last twenty minutes. A gentleman would've offered you a drink, shown you the spectacular view from the tower deck, then offered to have you chauffeured home.'

'There's absolutely nothing stopping you from doing that.'

'But there is. Perla, I'm not a gentleman. Your panties are shredded at my feet and in the next sixty seconds I intend to be deep inside you.'

The words murmured, hot and urgent, against her neck made her close her eyes against the drugging inevitability that assailed her. Need, ten times more powerful than she'd experienced the first time with him, shot to her sex, leaving her drowning in liquid heat.

Perla barely managed a squeak when he swung her up in his arms and strode purposefully down a hallway. He stopped at the first door on his right and thrust it open to reveal a large white-carpeted bedroom. Black and chrome stood out in sharp contrast to each other, with no warmth or decorative aesthetics to lighten the mood.

He deposited her on the bed and pulled off her skirt, then froze. His mouth worked soundlessly for several seconds before the groan exploded from his chest.

'I thought I imagined how exquisite you were but I didn't.' Again the words were spoken with a starkness that caused a sliver of ice to pierce her pleasure.

'Arion...'

He rubbed the back of his knuckles across her sex, then stepped back and undressed with swift, jerky movements.

Pulling her thighs wide apart, he muttered something in his native language, his fingers biting into her thighs.

Sucking in a needy breath, she glanced up at him and almost wished she hadn't.

He looked tortured, his face a hard mask of desire as he surged inside her. He'd already damned himself by sleeping with her the first time.

They were caught in a spell neither seemed capable of breaking, and she watched that knowledge eat him alive as he penetrated deeper inside her.

'Ari...' It felt wrong, but it also felt so right, just like it had the first time.

The need to pull him back from his torment, if only for a moment, made her reach for him.

She touched his face and he refocused on her. Hazel eyes stared deep into hers as he increased the tempo of his thrusts. Almost possessed, he took her pleasure to another level. By the time her orgasm tore through her, she believed she'd touched something sacred. With a guttural cry, he followed her into ecstasy. Deep convulsions ripped through him as he collapsed on top of her. Her hand slid from his face to cradle his sweat-slicked neck. She shut her eyes as sensation drifted into calm. She knew it was elusive; that what they'd done was in no way calming or solace-giving.

They'd given in to their animal instincts. Had let that damning temptation run free. And yet...

Before she could complete the thought, he surged upright and swung himself off the bed. Keeping his back turned, he pulled on his boxers and trousers.

'The bathroom's through there. Get dressed and come and find me. We need to talk,' he threw over his shoulder before he left the room.

Dazed and confused, she lay there for several minutes, staring at the beautifully designed chrome ceiling lights. It took several deep breaths and a severe talking-to before she managed to pull herself together.

She returned to the living room to find him at the window, still shirtless and breathtakingly gorgeous.

He turned at her entrance and raked a hand through his hair. 'Are your in-laws expecting you back tonight?' he asked, his eyes exhibiting none of the tormented pleasure she'd witnessed minutes ago.

'Yes,' she responded warily, wondering where he was going with his enquiry.

He nodded. 'Then I'll make it fast. Pantelides Inc. has

been through a lot in the past few years. I don't wish to draw any more unwanted attention to the company.' He went to the desk and picked up a pad and pen.

'Write your account details on here. I'll have funds transferred to your account first thing in the morning.'

The pain she'd been holding in a tight ball since she got up from his bed burst into her chest. 'Excuse me?' she rasped.

'I'm not unsympathetic to the fact that your husband left you in dire straits. I'm trying to make some form of reparation,' he replied, his voice still devoid of emotion.

'By sleeping with me and immediately offering me money afterwards?' Her own voice was sickeningly shaky and pain-filled but she didn't shy away from it. She wanted Arion Pantelides to know exactly what she thought of him. 'Why don't you come right out and book me for a repeat performance next Tuesday?'

His jaw tightened. 'What happened tonight won't happen again.'

'*Hallelujah!* Finally, something we both agree on. I thought you were pretty vile to accuse me of the things you accused me of before. But this…this is a new low.'

His grip tightened around the pad until it buckled beneath his strength. His gaze lowered but the rigid determination in his face didn't abate. 'Okay, perhaps the timing is unfortunate—'

'*You think?*' she snapped.

'But the offer remains. It's your choice whether to accept it or decline.'

'You can shove your offer where the sun doesn't shine!' She stalked past him to where she'd dropped her bag what felt like a thousand years ago. Snatching it up, she marched to the lift and pressed the button. Nothing happened. She stabbed harder, feeling her chin wobble with impending tears.

Dear God, no! No way was she going to cry in front of him.

'You need this.'

She turned. He was holding up the triangular card he'd given her earlier. She went to snatch it from him but he pulled it back at the last second.

'Perla—'

'No, don't say my name. You lost the right to speak to me when you offered me money for sleeping with you, you disgusting bastard.'

'Stop and think for a moment. The two situations have nothing to do with one another. You're being melodramatic again.'

'And you're being a complete ass who is holding me here against my will.'

'Think rationally. It's almost midnight. You're putting yourself in danger by attempting to return home at this time of night.'

'After everything you've said to me, you expect me to believe my safety concerns you?' She gave a very unladylike snort and glanced pointedly at the lift.

'Perla—'

'The only thing I want from you is to make the lift work, Ari. I want to leave. Right now.'

He sighed, and again she heard that weariness in his voice. 'I may not be a gentleman but I'm not averse to being schooled.'

She frowned when she realised he wasn't mocking her. He really meant it.

Turning, she faced him fully. 'First off, I wouldn't force a woman who wants to leave to stay against her will.'

He nodded, came forward and offered her the card. She took it.

'Second, don't ever, *ever* try to give a woman you've

just slept with money. No matter your intention, it comes off as super sleazy.'

Hazel eyes gleamed before his eyelids veiled his expression. 'But your situation still needs to be addressed.'

'It's my problem. I'll take care of it.'

He took a deep breath and she couldn't stop her eyes from devouring the sculpted chest that rose and fell. 'What were your skills before you gave up your career?'

The out-of-the-blue question threw her for a moment. Then she cleared her throat and tore her gaze away from the golden perfection of his skin. 'I was an events organiser for a global conglomerate.' She named her previous employer and his eyes widened a touch.

The fact that she'd managed to impress Arion Pantelides sent a fizz of pleasure through her.

'I'm leaving for LA in the morning but Pantelides Luxe has been on a recruitment drive for the last six weeks.' He scribbled a name and number on the mangled pad and passed it to her. 'If you're interested in interviewing for a job, call this number and speak to *my* head of HR.'

Unsure how to take the offer, she stared at him. 'Why are you doing this?' she finally blurted.

'I'm trying to find an alternative solution to your problem. Is this too not acceptable?' he asked, his face set in its usual world-weary lines.

'It's acceptable but I'm not sure it's the right solution for me.'

He shoved his hands into his trouser pockets. 'From where I'm standing, your options are slim to nil. Don't take too long in deciding or you'll find yourself back to square one.'

'Okay…thanks.' Her limbs felt heavy as she turned away. She told herself it was because she was drained from the head-on collision with Arion, and not the disconcerting realisation that she didn't want to leave. Because *that* would be ridiculous.

She slid the card through its slot and heard the smooth whirring of the lift.

'May I make another suggestion?' he asked. The sensation of his breath on her neck told her he'd moved close. Far closer than was good for her equilibrium.

She glanced over her shoulder. Up close, his sexy stubble made her want to run her hand over his jaw, feel its roughness just one more time. 'What?' She forced herself to speak.

'Allow my driver to get you back home?'

The thought of slogging through the rain to catch the last train to Bath made her waver dangerously. The sudden realisation that she could be doing so minus her panties made her stomach flip over.

She could stand on principle and endure a hugely uncomfortable journey, or she could give in this once. 'Okay.'

'I'll give him a half hour heads-up. It'll give us time to eat something on the tower deck before you leave.'

It took all of two minutes the next day to realise she had zero options. And really, had her head not been full of singeing memories of what she'd done with Ari the night before, she'd have come to that realisation a lot sooner.

But as much as she'd tried to push the shocking events that had stemmed from her complete lack of control from her mind, the more the vivid memories had tumbled forth.

She'd slept with Ari Pantelides for a second time, even after his blistering condemnation of her reasons for doing so the first time. Almost a day later, her internal muscles throbbed with the delicious friction of his possession.

But, even now, it was the vivid memory of his tortured face that haunted her.

Enough!

Perla glanced down at the piece of paper Ari had handed her. A quick call to a local lawyer this morning had reiterated Ari's warning. She had no recourse because Morgan had changed the terms of his contract.

Unless a miracle fell into her lap—and she was cynical enough to realise those were rarer than unicorn teeth—she and Morgan's parents were headed for the welfare office.

While her prior experience had been with only one large chain of hotels, she'd excelled at her job and enjoyed it enough to feel a tiny thrill at being given an opportunity to re-enter the business world again.

As for Ari…

According to her previous search, he was rarely in London and therefore the chances that they would meet again were minuscule.

Ignoring the stab of discontentment that realisation brought, she grabbed the phone and dialled the number before she lost her nerve.

The swiftness with which her previous job history was taken and the interview scheduled left her floundering. As did the realisation that the interview itself would be spread over two days.

Feelings of insecurity started to rush back, a legacy, she knew, from her dealings with Morgan. Although she hated herself, she couldn't stop the feeling from growing.

When she found her fingers hovering over the phone an hour later, contemplating calling back to cancel the interview, she pursed her lips and straightened her spine.

Morgan might have succeeded in whittling away her self-confidence, through threats and blackmail, but giving in now would see her in the far more precarious position of being without means to support herself and his parents.

Besides, she was getting ahead of herself. Maybe she wouldn't even get this job—

No!

She might not believe in unicorns but neither would she succumb to doom and gloom. Taking a deep breath, she stepped back from the phone and went to find her in-laws.

Explaining to them why she had to return to London again so soon was a little delicate, seeing as she'd told them the outcome of her previous visit. She didn't want to get their hopes up because she'd been out of the job market for far too long and knew realistically she could fall flat on her face the first time, positive thinking or not.

'Are you sure that's what you want to do? London is so far away,' Sarah said worriedly.

'Nonsense, it's only a short commute by train. And don't forget, we need all the help we can get right now. We wish you all the best, Perla. Don't we, Sarah?' Terry glanced at his wife.

Sarah smiled, her eyes brightening a little from the devastating sadness still lurking in their brown depths. 'Of course we do. It's just that…we don't know what we'd do without you now that Morgan is…' Tears filled her eyes and she dabbed at them with the hanky Terry slipped into her hand.

Perla felt her throat clog and quickly swallowed. *This* was the reason she'd stayed. The reason she'd kept Morgan's secret and given up her career.

Watching them console each other in their grief, the need to protect them surged higher. From the moment she'd been introduced to Terry and Sarah Lowell, they'd taken her into their hearts. After the devastation of Morgan's revelation, she'd known, just as he'd deviously surmised, that she couldn't turn her back on the only promise of a proper home she'd ever known.

Neither could she reveal the secret that would've destroyed his parents.

The familiar guilt for the secret she carried and could never share made her rise from her seat. 'I...I'd better go and brush up on my interview techniques.'

In the hallway, she paused for a second to steady her breathing. Then she straightened.

Morgan was gone. Terry and Sarah were her responsibility now.

Briskly, Perla entered her bedroom and busied herself sorting through her meagre clothes. Three interviews in two days meant she would have to be inventive with her wardrobe.

The black skirt and satin shirt she'd worn to London would have to make another appearance. As would the black dress she'd worn the night she'd met Ari.

Laying the garments on the bed, she couldn't help the treacherous bite of sensation that nipped at her. Both outfits held memories she'd rather forget, of Ari's hands on her body, undressing her, stripping her bare before taking her with masterful possession.

Heat flared high, making her fingers shake as she scraped back her hair and forced the memories away.

She had no business thinking about another man in this house; in this room. Even if that man was the only person in her life who'd made her feel special and wanted for a brief moment in time. Even if the memory of his face as he'd taken her forced feelings of protectiveness as well as desire to surge into her chest.

It was over and done with. Move on.

'Congratulations and welcome to the company.'

Perla heard the words from far off, still numbly disbelieving that she'd actually got through the gruelling interviews to secure a job on the Pantelides Luxe events management team.

'I…thank you.'

The two other candidates who'd also been offered similar jobs out of the twenty-five candidates wore similar expressions of pleased wonderment.

She'd got the job, with a salary and benefits that had left her mouth agape when she'd read them on her contract. Now she forced herself to focus as the head of HR continued to speak.

'For those who require the option, your first month's salary will be paid to you in advance of month's end. Just tick that option when you sign your contract. But remember if you should decide to leave the company before the first thirty days are up, you will be required to reimburse the company.' He looked directly at her as he said that.

Slowly anger and embarrassment replaced the stunned pleasure.

Had Ari Pantelides been so unprofessional as to share her private financial affairs with others? It was bad enough that she'd seen the morbidly curious looks on a few of the employees' faces as she'd been introduced. She was well aware that the widow of the man whose actions had caused a Pantelides oil tanker to crash and pollute a breathtaking African coast only a few short months ago was the last person they expected to seek employment in this company.

Knowing that her financial dire straits were being shared with others made her skin crawl with shame.

Forcing her head high, she returned the older man's stare, barely hearing the end of his welcome speech as she tried to grapple with her emotions. Fifteen minutes later, contract in hand, she started to leave the room.

The low hum of her mobile had her rooting through her handbag.

'Hello?'

'I understand congratulations are in order.' The voice, deep and gravel-rough, sent a pulse of heat through her belly.

'I...how did you get my phone number?' she blurted to cover her inner floundering.

'You're now my employee, Perla. Prepare yourself for the fact that some of your life is now an open book to me.'

A shiver went through her at the low, dark promise. As much as she tried to tell herself she wasn't affected, his voice did things to her that were indecent. Her hand tightened on the phone. 'So open that you decided to share some of it with your HR director?' she demanded.

'Excuse me?'

'Did you tell your HR director that I needed money?' The very thought of it made her flush with mortification.

'Why would I do that?' He sounded amused. Vaguely it occurred to her that he didn't sound as tormented and as bleak as he had a few days ago. Why that thought lifted her heart, she refused to contemplate as she reminded herself why she was annoyed with him.

'Because he offered a month's salary in advance. I may have been out of the general workforce a while but even I know that salaries don't get paid in advance.'

'Did he offer only you that option?' he asked.

'No, he offered it to the other new employees as well.'

He remained silent for several heartbeats. 'The reason for that perk is because most of the people I hire for the role you're filling are young, dynamic graduates. *Broke*, young, dynamic graduates who I expect to hit the ground running. The last thing I want them to be thinking about is how to pay their rent or feed themselves. If and when I headhunt other talent, I offer them signing-on bonuses too. Either way, everyone gets the same treatment.'

The bruised hurt eased a little. 'Oh, so I wasn't singled out for special treatment?'

'Now you sound disappointed,' he mocked in a low tone that was equally as lethal to her senses.

'I'm not.' And of course, now he'd explained the reason for the stipulation, it made total sense. How better to keep his employees happy and loyal than to ease the one thing certain to add to their anxiety in their first months of employment? Realising there was something else she needed to do, she cleared her throat. 'Thank you…for giving me this opportunity. I promise I won't let you down.'

Again a thoughtful silence greeted her words. 'I'm glad to hear it, Perla, because I'm giving you the chance to prove it sooner rather than later.'

Her heart jumped into her throat. 'What do you mean?'

'It means I'm throwing you in at the deep end. You fly out to join me in Miami after your accelerated orientation tomorrow. My assistant will provide you with the details.'

CHAPTER SIX

T<small>EN</small> VIP <small>GUESTS.</small>

Miami Fashion Week.

What could go wrong? It turned out to be plenty as Perla doused yet another metaphorical fire four days later, this time in the form of a wardrobe malfunction for one of the guests—a social media mogul's wife, minutes before she was due to head down to the Pantelides V3 Hotel & Casino.

She curbed the urge to blurt out that she was an events organiser not a stylist and placed a phone call to summon the harried stylist. Twenty minutes later, after the crisis had been averted, the young blonde cast a grateful glance at Perla as they rode the lift down to the lobby.

'I should've gone for something like what you're wearing instead of this...this thing.' She indicated the blue organza multi-layered dress that showed off more cleavage and bare back than Perla would ever be comfortable showing.

Her own knee-length silk dress, although slashed dramatically at the waist and side, was covered with thin mesh netting that made her feel not quite so...exposed. And the long fitted sleeves made of the softest leather offered further boosting confidence.

'That black totally rocks against the vivid colour of your hair. You must give me the name of your colourist. Everyone tells me red and curly is the new black this season.'

The blonde flicked her straight hair back and offered a brittle smile.

Again Perla bit her tongue, smiled back and discreetly checked her watch. The pre-runway show drinks would be served in exactly six minutes. Although she realised she was probably being rude by not responding and discussing her now extensive wardrobe that had come courtesy of her generous Pantelides clothes expense account, she couldn't think beyond the fact that in a few minutes she'd be coming face to face with Ari for the first time in almost a week.

By the time she'd arrived in Miami, he'd left for New York and she'd been given three days to prep for the arrival of the special guests, who ranged from a young senator to Hollywood royalty.

The earlier sailing trip around Biscayne Bay had been a success despite one guest almost ending up being launched overboard after one too many mojitos.

Keeping her fingers crossed for the same success tonight, she pasted a smile on her face as the lift doors opened onto the foyer that led to the cordoned-off VIP lounges where the runway shows were being held.

Ari Pantelides stood with a group of guests. Head and shoulders above most men, he was the first person she saw when she stepped forward.

The punch to her solar plexus winded her for an instant. Her mouth dried as she took in his imposing shoulders and breathtaking physique.

It really was a sin how one man could possess such a strikingly commanding presence. He turned to another guest and Perla caught a glimpse of that designer stubble. The memory of its roughness against her breasts and thighs sent a pulse of heat straight between her legs.

God, she really needed to get a grip. Like, right now!

Of course, he chose that moment to turn his head towards her.

Hooded eyes speared hers before they rose to rest on her hair. Recalling his fascination with her hair, she fought the foolish urge to touch the elaborate knot she'd worked the tresses into.

You're here to work!

The stern reminder focused her a little.

Turning to the blonde woman at her side, she said, 'I'll be around if you require anything else, Mrs Hamilton. Otherwise, I'll see you at the show in an hour.'

She left Selena Hamilton to find her husband and headed straight for the head waiter. After reassuring herself that everything was running smoothly, she found a quiet corner and activated her mini tablet. Double and triple-checking every detail was essential. The two designers whose shows they would be visiting were temperamental at the best of times and, with runway shows, seating arrangements could descend into chaos with little warning.

'*Kalispera,* Perla.'

Her hand trembled and she nearly lost her hold on her tablet as the deep voice washed over her. Her one visit to Santorini meant she understood the greeting.

Her head snapped up and her eyes collided with steady hazel eyes. 'Good evening, Ar…Mr Pantelides. How was your trip?'

His eyes narrowed slightly at the hasty correction but he didn't comment on it. 'Predictable. You seem to have settled in okay. I hear your boat trip today was interesting.'

It wasn't a question and she had very little doubt that he'd been checking up on her since her arrival.

'Yes, it hasn't been smooth sailing, pardon the pun, but the orientation was very useful. And your head of Events let me shadow him for a day to get the hang of things. That was useful too…' She stopped when she realised she was babbling. But, with him standing so close, she was dealt the full force of his powerful aura and the spicy scent of his aftershave. She'd smelled him up close and personal and knew continuing to breathe him in was not a very wise idea. 'Anyway, I need to get back to work.'

He stopped her with a brush of his fingers down her arm. Electricity shot through her body. 'How did your in-laws take your new status?' he asked.

She froze, looked at him to see if he was being sarcastic but his eyes only held mild interest. 'A lot better than some of the Pantelides employees.' She bit her lip at the slip. She'd meant to let the avidly curious looks and whispers behind her back slide right over her. But it'd been hard not to be affected.

Her stomach hollowed when his eyes narrowed. 'Who's been giving you a hard time?' he asked, his voice low and dangerous enough to send a shiver down her spine.

'Sorry, I didn't stop long enough to take names. Besides, can you really blame them? Morgan's actions nearly brought down your company.'

He stilled. 'So you know the full details of what he did?'

Perla frowned. 'Of course I know. Even though your brother tried to protect me from the whole truth, I got enough from the papers to put the pieces together. Frankly, I was surprised Morgan's benefits weren't stripped from him, all things considered.'

His jaw clenched for a moment before his face cleared. 'Those benefits weren't advantageous to you in the end, though, were they? It must have been upsetting to find out that the man you loved would betray you that way?' This time there was a definite question in his tone. His incisive gaze bored right into her. As if he was trying to understand her. And, more specifically, her actions on the night they'd met.

To admit that she hadn't been thinking straight when she'd slept with him—least of all of her dead husband— would only make things worse. 'It's not easy to find out, no.' But compared to the bombshell she'd received on the night of her wedding it was a walk in the park.

'I'm aware that betrayal has a way of messing with people's minds.' A hint of that torment she'd glimpsed made an appearance. As did the curiously strong need to alleviate it for him.

Brushing it away, she answered, 'Are we talking people generally or do you have personal knowledge of this?'

He stepped closer, blocking out the rest of the room and giving her no choice but to inhale his scent, to look into those unique gold-flecked hazel eyes. 'I've been dealt a few life lessons but I'm talking about you. Was that why you slept with me?' he breathed with a quiet intensity. 'To assuage your sense of betrayal?'

'Why are we going over this again?'

He murmured something pithy under his breath. 'Perhaps I'm trying to make sense of it all. Trying to square things in my mind so I can move on.'

Shame scythed through her as she admitted that she didn't want it squared away. She wanted to remember that night; to treasure it as the special moment in time it'd been for her. Of course, she knew she could never tell him that.

Straightening her spine, she returned his stare. 'Morgan's decisions and actions were his own. For my part, I married him for better or worse; he was the man I'd pledged to honour and cherish. And yes, before you remind me again, I broke that vow before he was even buried. Was I upset that things turned out the way they did? Of course I am.' A trill of laughter from a guest grounded her to where she was. 'I also think that this is the last place we should be discussing this. Frankly, I'd prefer it if we buried the subject once and for all. Can we do that, please?'

He stared down at her for several minutes before he inhaled deeply. He took a single step back and nodded. 'Consider the matter buried.'

She managed to nod before glancing over his shoulder. Several guests were looking their way, no doubt wondering why she'd commandeered Ari's attention. 'I need to get back to work, earn the generous salary you're paying me.'

His lips pursed but he gave her enough room to slide past. 'I look forward to seeing you in action.'

Perla wasn't sure if it was a threat or anticipation. And she couldn't dwell on it because her insides were churning from the exchange. Once again, it had seemed as if her reason for sleeping with him mattered to him.

Far from being a distraction as he'd claimed, it seemed he couldn't stop thinking about that night any more than she could.

Could she trust him not to bring it up again? Could she trust herself not to blurt out that it'd meant more than just a means to alleviate her pain?

She sucked in a deep breath and pinned a smile on her face. She'd survived Morgan and the debacle that had been her marriage.

She was a lot stronger now for it. She just needed to keep reminding herself of it.

Both runway shows went without a hitch. Watching from the back, Perla breathed a sigh of relief when the lights went up and her guests started to finish off their vintage champagne. Another few minutes and she could start herding them back to the limos to return to the Pantelides Casino for the gambling part of the evening. That was the most important part because it was why Ari had organised this event in the first place—

'Relax,' Ari said from beside her. How could a man so big, move so silently? 'You're off to a good start if Selena Hamilton is singing your praises. According to her, the two of you are BFFs now.' He picked up two glasses of pink champagne from a hovering waiter's tray and offered one to her.

'I wouldn't go that far but I'm glad she's pleased.' She took the champagne but didn't take a sip, much as she wanted to. The need for liquid courage was what had placed her in Ari Pantelides's crosshairs in the first place.

She was not going to make the mistake of drinking around him ever again.

'She isn't the only one who is impressed by your efficiency.'

Unable to help herself, she looked up at him. Hazel eyes captured hers and her breath snagged in her chest. 'Oh?'

'Her husband was equally effusive. Twice as much, in fact.' A hard bite had materialised in his tone.

She swallowed. 'What are you implying?'

He shrugged. 'He has wandering hands. Make sure you're not caught between them.'

On the surface, it seemed like a fair warning. Perhaps she was reading more into the situation than was necessary. They stared at each other for several heartbeats before she nodded. 'Thanks for the heads-up.'

His eyes flicked to her hair and again the punch of heat returned. Never in her wildest imagination would she have thought the colour of her hair would produce such a reaction. But every time Ari's gaze slid hungrily over her hair she felt hot, bothered and more than a little on edge. Before she could stop it, a small sound escaped her throat.

His gaze locked on hers once more. The air thickened around them, blocking the sounds of the party and locking them in their own sensual cocoon.

'Please, don't.' She was very much aware that she was begging. For as long as she could remember she'd wanted someone to notice her, give her a little bit of their time and attention. Although she'd found that to some extent with Terry and Sarah, it ultimately wasn't the right kind.

The attention Ari was giving her now *felt* like the right kind. Which was extremely frightening because it was the skull-and-crossbones kind, guaranteed to annihilate her with minimal effort.

'I'm as puzzled by my fascination as you are, *pethi mou*,' he murmured. 'Or perhaps my inner ten-year-old is still reeling from the discovery that his favourite TV actress's red hair came from a bottle,' he said dryly.

'How traumatic for you. Would it be better if I dyed my hair black or shaved it all off?' she half teased.

He sucked in a sharp breath and his grip tightened around his glass. 'I invite you to dare,' he breathed in a low, dangerous voice.

'You know, this would be the moment when I tell you that it's *my* hair, and I can do with it what I choose.'

'And I would in turn threaten to lock you up in a faraway dungeon until you came to your senses.'

Against her will, she felt a smile curve her lips. His mouth twitched too, as if sharing her amusement, but then his face turned serious again, and they went back to staring at each other.

Dirty, delicious thoughts of dungeons and shirtless heroes cascaded through her brain, sending spikes of desire darting through her body.

Realising just how pathetic she was being to take pleasure in the possessive tone in his voice, she cleared her throat. 'Can I make a suggestion?'

He took a sip of his drink without taking his eyes off her. She desperately wished she could follow suit but she needed to stay as clear-headed as possible. 'Go ahead.'

'Perhaps if we agree to stay out of each other's way, this…*thing* will eventually go away.'

'Haven't you heard the new saying? *Abstinence makes the heart grow fonder?*'

'I think we can both agree our hearts aren't the problem here.'

His face slowly froze until it was a hard, inscrutable mask. 'No. They're most definitely not.' The depth of feeling in his voice made something sharp catch in her chest. Again that torment stained his expression.

'You must miss her very much. Your wife,' she blurted before she could stop herself.

His fingers tightened so forcefully around the stem of his glass she feared it would snap. 'Sofia's death is a loss to the world. And to me.' The agony in his voice cut right into her heart.

Unable to look into his face, bleak with pain and guilt, she glanced away. Her own fingers were curled around the warming glass of champagne which trembled wildly, threatening to spill its contents. Hurriedly, she set it down on a nearby table.

'I never got the chance to say it before. I'm sorry…for your loss. Um, please excuse me. I think I'm needed now.'

She hurried away before she could do or say something rash, like ask him to define what that kind of love felt like. Or expose the emotion writhing through her that felt shamefully like jealousy.

She'd wanted a love like that for herself, had built all her hopes around Morgan, who had taken her desperate need and used it to blackmail her. Fate had kicked her in the teeth for daring to hold out her hand and ask.

She wasn't foolish enough to even contemplate asking a second time. The lesson had been well and truly delivered.

Ari watched Perla walk away, stunned by what he'd just revealed. He never spoke about Sofia. Never. Not to his brothers, not to his mother. And certainly not to traitorous strangers he'd made the colossal mistake of sleeping with.

And yet, with one simple sentence, he'd spilled his guts;

would've spilled some more if Perla hadn't rushed away. Because the admission of how Sofia—a warm-hearted, gentle innocent whom he'd ruthlessly clung onto and used to soothe his ravaged soul right after his father's betrayal— had come into his life and ultimately left it, had been right there on his tongue.

Absently nodding to a guest who'd approached and started talking to him, he tried to reel in his flailing senses.

It was unconscionable that he still felt this unrelenting pull towards Perla Lowell. What had happened between them—twice—should've been enough to curb whatever appetites he hadn't even realised were growing until he'd met her.

At first he'd thought his fascination with her was because she was the first woman he'd slept with after Sofia. That had been his excuse in the weeks following his discovery of her real identity.

And the second time?

He gritted his teeth. The second time, their emotions had been running high. So high, he hadn't had the common sense to use a condom. Hell, even that little nugget hadn't hit him until he was halfway across the Atlantic on his way to the US. A shudder raced under his skin at the sheer stupidity of his actions.

How many times, growing up, had he cautioned his brothers on the responsibility of taking care of their sexual health and those of the women they slept with, especially after finding out the bitter and humiliating legacy their father had left behind?

Granted, both Sakis and Theo were old enough now and no longer his responsibility. But for him to have fallen in the same trap, under the same spell that—

Enough. Beating himself up about it would achieve nothing. He smothered his thoughts and concentrated on the

guest next to him, expertly hiding his distaste when he saw
who it was trying to get his attention.

'She's something, your new organiser.' Roger Hamilton's gaze was fixed on Perla as she spoke to his guests,
her smile open and friendly. The clear interest in his eyes
sent a bolt of anger through Ari.

'She's also off-limits.' The snarl in his tone was unmistakable.

Hamilton's eyes widened, then his thin lips curved in
a sly, knowing grin. 'Right, she's marked territory. Got it,
buddy.'

Ari gritted his teeth and opened his mouth to deny the
assertion. 'Very marked. And I'm very territorial. Are we
clear?' *Theos*, where had that come from? He was losing
his mind. There was no doubt about that.

Roger slapped him on the arm. 'As crystal, buddy. But
tell me something; between you and I, is that hair colour
real?'

Ari's fists clenched so hard his knuckles screamed in
protest. From the first, he'd found an almost unholy fascination with Perla's hair. To hear that same fascination in another man's voice made the blackest fury roll through him.

'That, *buddy*,' he breathed, 'is something you'll never
find out.'

From then on, he made sure he kept a room's width between himself and Perla at all times. Not that he actively
needed to. She seemed just as determined to stay away
from him.

A thought that should've pleased him, but only succeeded in darkening his mood further. On impulse, he
pulled his phone out of his pocket and dialled.

Theo answered on the first ring. 'A call from the big
man himself. I haven't been naughty, have I?'

'You tell me. And while you're at it, tell me what the

hell is so captivating about Rio that you can't seem to tear yourself from the place?'

His youngest brother laughed. 'Sun, sea and wall-to-wall gorgeous women. Need I say more?' Despite his tone, there was something cagey that set Ari's radar buzzing.

'Is everything okay, man?' The worry that never abated when it came to his brothers rose higher. Of all his family members, Theo had been the youngest and most vulnerable when their world had unravelled, thanks to his father. That worry had never gone away.

'Of course. How about you? Normally, you send me terse one-line emails asking me to report in.'

'Half of which you never answer. Thought I'd try another means to get your attention.'

Theo remained silent for a minute. 'You sure you're okay, bro?'

A flash of red caught his eye and he tensed further. 'I'm fine. But it would be good to row again, all three of us, some time soon.'

'Ah, you're nostalgic to get your ass whopped. I can oblige. But would this need to burn energy have anything to do with the headache you've created for yourself by hiring the Lowell woman?'

He gave an inward sigh. 'You've heard?'

Theo snorted. 'The whole company's wondering if you've lost your mind. Hell, *I'm* wondering if you've lost your mind. *Theos*, she's not blackmailing you in any way, is she?' he asked sharply.

The tense note in Theo's voice made Ari's hand clench over his phone as a wave of pain swept over him. Theo had been kidnapped as a teenager and their family held to ransom for a tense two weeks before he'd been released, which made the subject of blackmail a very volatile one.

'No, she needed a job, she proved to have the skill and I gave her one.'

'Did you run it past Sakis, because I'm pretty sure he'll blow a gasket once he crawls out of his love cocoon and returns to the real world.'

Ari's jaw tightened. 'I'll deal with Sakis. In the meantime, have your assistant check schedules with mine about our next rowing session. I want to get together sooner rather than later, and get to the bottom of exactly what you're doing in Rio.'

'Dammit, anyone would think I was still twelve instead of a grown man.'

'You'll always be a twelve-year-old to me, brother, simply because you can't help but act like one.' He noticed the gruffness in his voice but couldn't help it.

He hung up to Theo's pithy curse and realised he was smiling. Pocketing his phone, he looked up and found Perla's gaze on him. Wide green eyes held shock and wonder, which she quickly tried to bank. When he realised it was in reaction to his smile, he cursed under his breath.

Was it really so strange that he would smile? Was he such an ogre that he'd given the impression that smiling was beyond him?

Yes...

A lance of pain speared his heart. Smiling and laughter had become a thing of the past for him, ever since he'd lost the most precious thing in his life through hubris and carelessness. He'd believed he'd paid enough, sacrificed enough for his family and deserved happiness of his own. He'd believed he'd bled enough to owe fate nothing else.

He'd been careless with Sofia's health, given in to her penchant to always look on the bright side, when deep down he'd known the bright side rarely existed. Guilt rose to mingle with the pain, wiping away every last trace of mirth from his soul. He had no right to smile or laugh. Not when he had blood on his hands...

Realising Perla was still staring at him, he turned away abruptly. But the unsettled feeling wouldn't go away.

Perhaps Theo had been right. Had he lost his marbles by employing her, despite her obvious talent? He knew had he looked harder, he'd have found someone equally talented to employ who didn't rock the boat or make his male clients salivate just by the sight of her. He pursed his lips. Hell, she herself knew she was distracting enough to have made some of his employees talk, made her own life uncomfortable—

Frowning, he removed his phone from his pocket and dialled his assistant. 'Contact my head of HR—I want a conference call first thing tomorrow. Tell him I want to discuss Perla Lowell.'

CHAPTER SEVEN

'WHY DID YOUR HR director just call to check up on me?
And please don't tell me he does that with everyone else
because I asked David and Cynthia and he didn't call them
so I know I'm the only one he's called.'

Ari continued to admire the stunning penthouse view
from his latest hotel set in the heart of Washington DC and
forced himself not to react to the huskily voiced accusation or the unwanted intrusion. But it was difficult not to
turn around; not to tense against the electricity that zapped
through him at her presence.

It'd been three weeks since Miami, and the last time he'd
seen Perla. He'd left the day after Fashion Week and busied himself with his other casinos and hotels on the West
Coast. But he'd needed to return because Pantelides WDC
was by far his most successful hotel yet and he needed to
throw his every last waking moment into making it the
jewel in the Pantelides Luxe crown.

That he'd spent far too much time thinking about Perla
Lowell was something he preferred to view as simply making sure she wasn't causing any more ruffles in his company. Of course, he'd have preferred if word hadn't got out
that he was doing so but…

He sighed. 'Discretion really seems to be thin on the
ground these days.'

Her gasp sounded just behind his left shoulder. He tensed

further, bracing himself for the impact of the sight and scent of her.

'So you're not denying it? You do realise how you've made me look by doing that, don't you?'

'What exactly did my director say to you?' he asked.

'He asked me how I was getting on with work and with my colleagues.'

'And you immediately jumped to the conclusion that I was trying to undermine you somehow?'

'Did you or did you not ask him to call to check up on me?'

'Perla, you brought a potential workplace problem to my attention. And I took steps to rectify it. I think my director may have taken his directive a little too seriously given who you are. If you think it was an unnecessary step—'

'I do,' she flung at his back.

Ari gritted his teeth and tried to remain calm as she continued.

'Now you've said something—'

'Actually, *you* said something. Had you come to me instead of seeking verification from your colleagues, they would've been none the wiser.'

'So you're saying this is my fault?' Outrage filled her voice. 'And can you turn around when I'm talking to you, please?' she snapped.

With another sigh, he started to turn. 'I think you're blowing things out of proportion—' He stopped dead when he caught his first glimpse of her.

Her hair was a long, dark, *wet* ribbon curling over her naked shoulder. And she wore a black bikini with the thinnest strings that looked as if they were about to succumb to the laws of gravity. Heat punched into his gut so viciously, he had to lock his knees to keep from stumbling backward against the floor-to-ceiling window behind him. Around her waist, a carelessly knotted black sarong rested on her hipbones.

'I'm not blowing things out of proportion. The fact is you've severely undermined me in the eyes of my colleagues.'

'Did it occur to you that singling you out for attention could be for a beneficial reason rather than a detrimental one?'

He couldn't breathe. And he couldn't move. Even though words emerged from his mouth, his tongue felt thick and all his blood was rushing painfully south. In exactly one minute, she'd know the effect she had on him.

The intensely crazy, intensely electrifying effect he'd thought he had under control.

Her mouth dropped open and her eyes widened. 'I… no, I didn't.'

His smile felt a little tight around the edges. 'Perhaps you should've given it a little further thought then. As for David and Cynthia, don't rule them out completely. They may be receiving phone calls as well. You may simply have been lucky number one, this time.' His gaze slid over her once more and he wondered how many other people had seen her in that bikini, her exquisite body on full show? He forced himself not to think about it.

She frowned. 'I find it hard to believe that you check on every single employee…' She stopped and took a breath. 'Ari, why did you really do it?'

The sound of his name on her lips sent hot lust-filled darts to his groin. 'Why does it upset you so much?' he murmured.

Her eyebrows shot up. 'Are you serious? I have to work with these people!'

He shrugged. 'Then I'll leave it in your capable hands to smooth things over, assure your colleagues that my HR director was conducting a simple employee assessment and you jumped to a conclusion. Because that's what really happened.'

'God, you really expect me to believe that, do you?'

'I do.'

'You must think I'm really gullible.'

'If I did, you wouldn't be working for me. And you shouldn't take too much stock in what others think of you. Unless that's the problem here? Are you saying you don't trust your own judgement, Perla?'

She froze. Before his eyes, her face leached all colour. Her fingers twisted around each other in a clearly distressed way that made him curse inwardly. 'Yes,' she whispered raggedly. 'That's exactly what I'm saying. I'm…I'm not a very good judge of character.'

The visible distress made something catch in his chest. Before he could think better of it, he closed the distance between them and took her chin in his hand. This close, the scent of her warm body mingled with the chlorine from her swim hit him in the throat. His blood pounded harder, but Ari consoled himself with the fact that with her gaze on his, she wasn't witnessing what her proximity was doing to him below the waist.

'What makes you think that?'

'I got it spectacularly wrong with you, didn't I?' she asked.

His mouth firmed. 'But I wasn't who you were thinking of just now.' He knew it as certainly as he knew his name.

'What, you read minds now?'

'No. But, unlike you, I can read people. Who was it, Perla?' he asked, although he had a fair idea.

'Does it take a genius to figure out that I misjudged the man I married?' she said, confirming his theory. 'I thought he was someone I could depend on. Instead, he…he…' She closed her eyes and shook her head. The pain in her face and her words struck a dark chord within him. A chord he absolutely did not want struck.

But he couldn't help it as memory gathered speed through his brain.

He'd grown up depending on his father, looking up to him, hanging on his every word. For most of his early years, he'd wanted nothing more than to follow in his father's footsteps, only to find out that they were the shoes of a philanderer, an extortionist and a fraudster. A man who would take his son's idolisation and attempt to use it against him…to manipulate it for his own selfish needs.

His gut tightened against the ragged pain he'd thought long buried but that seemed to catch him on the raw much too often these days. It didn't help his disposition to know that Perla was always present when it happened. That perhaps they shared a connection with hurt and betrayal.

'If you're talking about your husband, he was just one man. Don't let him cloud your judgement about everyone else. Trust your instincts.'

'*Trust my instincts?* I don't think that's a very good idea. My instincts told me *you* were a good guy. But you turned on me like I was some sort of criminal when you found out who I was.'

'I no longer think that, or you wouldn't be here.'

She opened her mouth to speak, paused, then eyed him. 'But that's only half true, isn't it? If you'd thought I could really cope on my own you wouldn't have stepped in.'

He dropped his hand, then immediately flexed it at his side when it continued to tingle wildly. 'You told me how long you'd been out of the corporate world. That, coupled with your husband's activities, placed you in a vulnerable position.'

'And you were trying to *save* me? How unnecessarily noble of you.' The hand she'd placed on her hips drew attention to her pert breasts. Breasts he'd feasted on for a long time that first night. Breasts he wanted to touch, to caress again more than he wanted his next breath.

He whirled away and focused on the views of the GW Monument and Capitol Hill in the distance, lit up beacons of power, hoping his brain would find a different focus other than replaying the sight of her in that pulse-destroying bikini.

'So, are you done berating me?' he asked. He wanted her gone before he did something completely stupid. Like finding out just how robust the wraparound sofa behind him would be with both their weights pounding it.

'No. I don't need saving, Ari.'

'Fine, I won't interfere. Even though you've clearly exacerbated a simple assessment directive, perhaps I should've just let things play out. Let's move on, shall we?'

Behind him, she heard her soft sigh. 'Move on. That's easy for you to say.'

His chest tightened. 'No, actually, it's not,' he said, then froze. *Where the hell had that come from?* Pushing his hands into his pockets, he hoped she would let the careless slip slide.

Instead, she came closer until she stood next to him. 'What do you mean?' she asked with a soft murmur.

He clenched his jaw for several seconds, then felt the words spiral out of him. 'It means I know what it feels like to be under scrutiny. To know that people are looking at you and forming judgements you have no control over. That at best you were being judged with pity and at worst with scorn and malice.'

She sucked in a shocked breath. 'God, who...why...?'

He turned and glanced at her. Her wide eyes were drowning in sympathy and her mouth was parted with agitation. The realisation that she wore that look for him struck him in the gut. 'You don't know about Alexandrou Pantelides, my father?'

She shook her head.

Giddy relief poured through him. 'Then I prefer to keep you in the dark just a little while longer.'

'Was he…was he the one you meant when you said *him* that day in your office?'

Another time, another slip. When it came to this woman, it seemed he didn't know when to shut the hell up. 'Yes,' he confessed.

'And you don't want to be like him? What did he do to you?' she asked, sympathy making her voice even huskier.

'Nothing I wish to share with you.'

Although a tinge of hurt washed over her eyes, she kept her gaze on him. 'Okay. But you know there's nothing to stop me from searching the Web for information the moment I leave here.'

His insides tightened at the thought of Perla knowing just how mired in deceit and humiliation his past was. 'No, there isn't. But it'll be an extra few minutes when I know you're not forming an opinion about me the way you think others are doing about you.'

'But if you know how it feels then why did you contact HR?'

'I saw a potential problem. I stepped in to fix it. It's what I do.' After his father had slashed their lives into a million useless pieces, seventeen-year-old Ari had assumed the role of protector. Protecting his mother and his younger brothers from the press intrusion after Alexandrou Pantelides's sleazy dealings and philandering lifestyle had come to light had, overnight, become his number-one priority.

His brothers, after severely rocky years, had grown into stable, intensely successful individuals. And his mother had eventually found peace. He'd believed his family was safe…

Until fate had shown him otherwise…

Theos, this was too much! Resentment that he'd inadvertently taken a trip down memory lane yet again coiled through him.

Sucking in a deep breath, he faced Perla. 'You've aired your grievance. I've listened. Now don't you have work to be getting on with?'

The harshness of his voice stung. 'It's my day off, but Ari—'

He let his gaze slide down her body, ignoring the fire sizzling through his veins. 'And was this what you meant when you suggested staying away from each other? Because this plan—' he indicated her skimpily clad form '—is a poor attempt at removing temptation from both our paths.'

'I'm sorry. I wasn't thinking… I just reacted—'

'Well, make a better judgement call next time!'

She flinched as if he'd struck her. But he couldn't regret his tone because he was drowning in hell. He'd almost opened up about secrets he shared with no one. And the temptation to unburden had been great. But not to her. Not to the woman whose husband had caused the media to dredge up all the bitterness and humiliation only a few short months ago.

He tightened his jaw and watched, fascinated, as she pulled herself together with a grace and dignity he found curiously admirable.

Crossing her arms round her middle, she glared at him. 'We're weak when it comes to each other. Striking out at me for your weakness is cowardly and beneath you. Stop it. Believe me, I can bite back.'

He felt a wash of heat surge up his cheekbones. 'You need to leave. Now. Before I do something we'll both regret.'

'Ari—'

'A word to the wise. No man likes being told he's weak; it can be misconstrued as a challenge. Leave. Now, Perla, before I invite you to honour your promise of biting me.'

Eyes wide, she backed quickly towards the door. 'We'll need to find a way of working together eventually, Ari.'

'Let's discuss it further when you're not wearing a whisper-thin sarong and a clinging bikini that's just *begging* to be ripped off.'

Perla tried not to count the ways things had gone spectacularly wrong as she left Ari's penthouse. First her headlong flight from the swimming pool, bristling with intense irritation and hurt, had been ill-timed. She should've waited to cool down before confronting him.

And what, in goodness' name, had she been thinking, going into his presence wearing two tiny pieces of Lycra and an even flimsier sarong?

But of all the things slamming through her mind, it was the look on his face as he'd confessed that he'd walked in her shoes that struck deepest and made her kick herself for picking the wrong time to confront him.

His pain had been unmistakable. It was a different sort of pain from when he'd spoken about his wife but the dark torment had been present nonetheless.

Just how much had Arion Pantelides been through? And what the hell had his father done to him?

She reached her suite five floors below and immediately glanced at her laptop set atop the most exquisite console table. She dismissed the voice that whispered that knowledge was power. However foolish it might be, she couldn't forget the relieved look on Ari's face when she'd confessed to not knowing who his father was.

There'd been a point in time a few months ago when she would've given her right arm to remain oblivious to what Morgan had done.

If Ari craved privacy, she would grant him that.

As for his anger at the way she'd gone to him, dressed in only a bikini and a sarong… She glanced down and saw her body's visible reaction to him. Her nipples were sharp points of fierce need and the way her chest rose and fell in her agitation…

God, no wonder he'd been angry!

She sank onto her bed, overwhelmed by her body's turbulent response.

It was clear that staying away from each other the last three weeks had achieved none of the clarity and purpose they'd both sought. If anything, the attraction bit harder, the hunger sharper.

It was also clear that she'd overreacted to the HR director's call and possibly made her work situation worse.

But she was sure she hadn't imagined the cynical looks between her colleagues when all her suggestions on the various stages of the opening night for Pantelides WDC had been accepted without question. Pleased that she was being valued as a hard-working member, she'd put forward more suggestions.

It was why she'd begun questioning herself, and the call coming so close to that had made her storm from the rooftop pool with every intention of confronting Ari and taking him to task.

Of course it had nothing to do with the fact that she'd been unable to stop thinking about the man since Miami; she had found herself growing curiously bereft with his continued absence and the fact that her body seemed to have pulsed to life the moment she'd found out he was back.

She was here to do a job. She seriously needed to focus on that and nothing else.

Let's move on…

Pursing her lips, she pulled off her sarong. Ari was annoyingly right.

They had two weeks before this spectacular hotel set in the heart of America's political and cultural capital opened.

The hotel itself was a jaw-dropping architectural masterpiece, and fully expected to achieve six-star status within the next few weeks. They'd already hosted the industry critics, who'd since given glowing reviews.

With prime views of the Lincoln Memorial and Capitol Hill, the mid-twentieth-century building had been given a multi-million-dollar facelift that had seen it propelled to the realms of untold luxury and decadence.

Marble, slate and gleaming glass were softened by hues of eye-catching red-and-gold furniture and art that captured the imagination, and the five top-class restaurants were already booked well into the new year.

Regardless of her own shaky issues, Perla was hugely excited to be working on the hotel opening.

After showering and slipping on her bathrobe, she ordered room service and pulled open her laptop. Her research into the Washington scene had thrown up a few ideas for the opening. She'd already secured the jazz quartet said to be a favourite of the President to her list and confirmed the special tour of the Smithsonian and the White House for the VIP guests who would be staying overnight. Her idea of a midnight cruise on the Pantelides yacht had also been greeted with enthusiasm.

Feeling her confidence return, she pulled up the details of Oktoberfest on a whim, then immediately discarded it. Somehow she didn't think beer-drinking went well with Ari's vision for his hotel.

But there was nothing wrong with checking it out for herself while she was here. Something to do to take her mind off the fact that Ari was once again within seeing and touching distance…and the knowledge that her pulse skittered every time she admitted that fact.

Her doorbell ringing brought welcome relief from her thoughts. The scent of the grilled chicken and salad made her stomach growl and reminded her she hadn't eaten since a hastily snatched bagel and coffee first thing this morning.

Ravenous, she ate much faster than she should have, a fact she berated herself for when she bolted out of her chair, rushed to the bathroom and emptied the contents of her stomach a mere hour later.

'Are you all right? You look a bit peaky.'

Susan, the assistant concierge, peered at her as Perla waited for the list and notes she'd typed up last night to finish printing.

Perla nodded absently and smoothed her hand down her black skirt and matching silk shirt she'd worn for the meeting with Ari and the rest of the key hotel staff.

Glancing down at herself, she wondered if she'd made the right choice. The shirt hadn't felt this tight across the bust when she'd picked it as part of her work wardrobe a month ago. The gaping between the top buttons had forced her to leave the first and second buttons open and she questioned now whether she shouldn't have changed her outfit altogether.

But after waking up twice more to throw up, she'd eventually fallen into a deep sleep and missed her alarm.

Which was why she was hopelessly late—

'Do you intend to join us for this meeting, Perla?'

Ari stood behind her, tall, imposing, gorgeous beyond words. In the morning sun, the sprinkling of grey at his temples highlighted the sculpted perfection of his face. But it was his unique hazel eyes that made her belly spasm with heat and a whole load of lust.

'I...I was just coming.'

'Good to hear.' He turned on his heel and strode back into the conference room.

'Someone's got an armadillo in their bonnet,' Susan whispered, her eyes wide with speculation.

Perla grabbed the sheets, gave a non-committal smile to

Susan and hurried across the marble floor in her three-inch heels, only to freeze when she entered the room.

The only seat left at the small conference table was next to Ari. She'd have to sit beside him, breathe in his spicy cologne, feel the warmth of him and place herself within his powerful aura for however long the blasted meeting took. Her throat dried as her heart rate roared.

Ari glanced up and sent her another impatient look, one that made her stash her unease and walk to his side.

Ideas for the opening event were discussed and tossed or kept as Ari saw fit. Half an hour later, he turned to her. 'Do you have your list?'

She nodded and passed copies around. 'The top four are secured. The other three are yet to be finalised...'

'*Oktoberfest?*' Ari demanded.

Perla frowned and glanced down at the sheet in her hand. 'Sorry, that wasn't supposed to be on there. It was an idea I thought of floating but I don't think it's the right image for this hotel.'

'You're right. It's not.'

Several of her colleagues exchanged glances. Perla ignored them. Pursing her lips, she met Ari's direct stare. 'Like I said, it wasn't supposed to be on the list—'

'But it would be perfect for the San Francisco hotel.' He put the list down and caught up a pen, flicking it through long, elegant fingers. 'Contact their concierge, tell them to trial it and give us feedback on how it goes. And make sure you take credit for it. As for the rest of the suggestions, I'm on board with the jazz quartet and the White House tour. Add it to the other maybes and we'll discuss a shortlist at the next meeting.'

Warmth oozed through her but her veins turned icy when she spotted the repeated exchanged glances. From the corner of her eye she saw Ari's jaw tighten as he brought the meeting to a close.

In her haste to leave his disturbing presence, she dropped her file. She retrieved it and straightened to find him blocking her path to the door.

Her heart jumped into her throat. 'Did you need something?'

His gaze drifted over her and he frowned. 'Is everything in your wardrobe black?'

'Excuse me?'

'Black doesn't suit you. It makes your skin look too pale.' His eyes dropped lower, the opening of her shirt.

She forced herself not to reach up and button her shirt. Or touch her skin to test if it really was on fire since his gaze burned her from the inside out. 'You stopped me from leaving to disparage my clothes?' She casually leaned against the table and lifted an eyebrow, although casual was the last thing she felt.

He rocked back on his heels and shoved his hands into his pockets. For several seconds he didn't speak. 'I see that I've made things difficult for you here,' he finally said.

The hint of contrition in his tone made her breath catch. Nonchalantly, she tried to shrug it away. 'It's partly my fault. I overreacted. I'll deal with it. As you said, I need to trust my instincts and my talent, and not what other people think.'

He nodded. 'Bravo,' he said. Thinking he would move out of her way, she started to take a step and paused when his mouth opened again. 'And if it doesn't earn me a sexual harassment charge, may I suggest you find a better fitting shirt that doesn't display all your assets?'

Her gasp echoed around the room. 'It's not that bad! And stop talking about my assets or I'll have to point out that shoving your hands in your pockets like that pulls your trousers across your junk and displays *your* assets. Not that I'm paying a lot of attention, of course,' she added hurriedly and felt her face flame.

God, she needed her head examined!

One eyebrow slowly lifted. 'Of course.' He remained planted in front of her, as if he had nothing better to do than to rile her.

Unable to stand his intense gaze, she glanced down and saw just how much cleavage she was displaying. *God!*

'I just…seem to have put on a little weight, that's all. And I was running a little late this morning so there was no time to change…' She grew restive beneath his continued silent scrutiny. 'Seriously, it's not that bad.'

His nostrils flared and a look passed through his eyes that made her think he was toying with the idea of arguing the point. Instead, he opened the door. 'After you,' he said.

Walking in front of him across the large marble foyer felt like walking the plank on some doomed pirate's ship. She was aware of the intensity of his scrutiny on her back, her legs…her bottom. Electricity sparked along her nerves and spread throughout her body.

Slowly she noticed the sound of last-minute preparations in the vast space had gradually faded as people stopped to stare.

David and Cynthia, the two colleagues who'd been recruited the same time as her, stood at the solid wood-carved reception, watching with blatant curiosity. She didn't need to turn around after she passed them to know they were whispering behind her back.

Same as she didn't need to turn around to notice the moment Ari veered off towards his own office. Because her skin stopped tingling and her pulse began to slow.

By the time she shut herself away in the tiny office behind the concierge's station, she was shaking. Going to her coffee stand, she flicked the kettle on and practised her breathing as it boiled. She poured water onto the tea bag, then immediately gagged as the scent of camomile made her stomach roil violently.

Abandoning tea in favour of water, Perla waited for the sickness to subside and threw herself into her work.

She spent the rest of the day finalising catering requirements, confirming bookings and chasing RSVPs. The turkey sandwich she ordered for lunch stayed put and she breathed a sigh of relief. The last thing she needed was to get sick within the first month of starting a new job in which she already felt compromised.

But by six o'clock her feet ached, her head throbbed with a dull ache and the debilitating weakness that had dogged her all day was weighting her limbs. Shutting off her computer, she dug through her bag and located the painkillers she always kept to hand. Swallowing two, she took the lift to her suite, collapsed onto the bed, kicked off her shoes and pulled the covers over her head.

The buzzing of her phone woke her an hour later.

Dazed, she pushed the hair off her face and snagged the handset. 'Hello?'

'Perla.'

Excitement jack-knifed through her body.

God, the way he said her name should be banned. Or she needed to charge for it. Because she was sure she suffered a tiny nervous breakdown every time his voice grated out her name like that.

'Um…hi,' she mumbled, squinting in the darkened room.

'Did I wake you?' There was a frown in his voice.

'No, I was just…no.'

'I've been thinking about your predicament.'

'What predica…? No, I told you, I'll handle it.'

'You may not need to. Have you had dinner yet?' he asked.

She tried to make her brain work. 'No, I haven't.'

'Meet me at the Athena Restaurant in half an hour,'

he said, naming the five-star restaurant on the first floor of the Pantelides WDC, headed by a very sought after Michelin-starred chef.

Perla flicked the bedside lamp on and struggled to sit up. Thankfully, her headache seemed to have disappeared. 'Um…why?'

'I have a proposal to discuss with you. A new opportunity you might be interested in.'

The thought of meeting with Ari so openly again after this morning and being the cynosure of all eyes made her nape tighten. Exhaling, she faced up to the fact she had to deal with that sooner or later. She refused to let gossip rock the self-esteem she was trying hard to rebuild.

She cleared her throat. 'I'd love to hear your proposal but I think the Athena is fully booked tonight. And yes, I know you own the hotel and can chuck someone out but I'd feel bad. Do you think we can order room service instead?'

For a few seconds, silence greeted her suggestion. 'Given our track record, do you think being in a hotel room alone together is wise?' he rasped.

Liquid heat flooded her belly, followed closely by chagrin. 'Um, you're right, it's not. I'll…come to you.'

'Half an hour. Don't keep me waiting.'

She hung up and threw the covers off. Going to the bathroom, she took a quick shower, pleased that she felt a whole lot better now than she had all day.

The dress she chose was functional and stylishly respectable without being overtly sexy. Pulling on the slingbacks she'd discarded earlier, she caught up her black clutch and black wrap and left her room.

Despite telling herself this was just business, butterflies fluttered madly in her stomach as the lift rushed her downward.

She stepped out of the lift and was about to head towards the foyer when her phone pinged.

Come outside. A

Slowly, she swivelled on her heels and headed out into the cool October night. Beneath the elegantly columned portico of the hotel, Ari leaned, cross-legged and cross-armed against a gleaming black sports car.

The sight of him, magnificently imposing, arrestingly gorgeous, was incredibly dangerous to her well-being. He wore a dark blue cotton shirt with black trousers and a matching jacket that hugged his wide shoulders.

The intensity of his stare as it drifted over her made her body grow hot all over. And even though he didn't say anything, by the time his gaze returned to hers she had the distinct impression he was displeased.

But then what else was new? Ari alternated between finding her irritating and being incredibly considerate.

Given the choice, I'd settle for a little bit of peace.

'What did you say?' he asked, straightening from the car to open the passenger door for her.

Realising she'd muttered her thoughts, she blushed. 'Nothing. I thought we were meeting inside?'

He shook his head. 'Change of plan. I thought we could experience what Washington DC has to offer. You had a Greek restaurant on your list. Care to try it?' he asked.

Pleased that he'd remembered, she smiled. 'I'd love to.'

He straightened, waited for her to slide in and shut the door behind her.

Unable to stop herself, Perla watched him round the bonnet. God, even the way this man moved demanded attention. His lean, sinewy grace seemed innate.

The moment he shut the door all her senses flared to life. His scent was intoxicating, addictive in a way that made her want to throw herself across the console and slide her greedy hands all over him.

Expecting him to start the car and drive, she glanced at him and caught his rigid profile. When his fingers wrapped around the steering wheel and gripped tight, she knew he was fighting the same raw need.

She must have made a sound because a choked noise filled the tense space.

'Ari...'

He sucked in a jagged breath. 'We are not teenagers and we are not animals.' His voice was rough, darkly husky. 'We have enough self-control to be able to resist this...this *insanity* between us.'

Her hand tightened around her clutch. 'I agree.' Although fighting it felt like a losing battle right now.

'What happened between us can't happen again,' he continued gratingly. The mild self-loathing in his voice finally pierced the cocoon of sensual delirium.

Stung, she whipped her head to stare out of her window. 'I get the message loud and clear, Ari.'

'Do you?' he demanded, and she knew he was staring at her because she could feel the intensity of his gaze on her skin.

She bit her lip to stop another helpless moan from escaping. 'You hate me because I remind you of something in your past. I don't know what exactly. Maybe it's connected to this insane temptation we can't kill. I could find a reason to hate you too but what good would hate do either of us?'

'I don't hate you,' he growled. 'There are a lot of things I feel but, rest assured, *hate* isn't one of them.'

A little bit of the hurt eased but hearing that self-loathing still present in his voice made her heart lurch. 'That's good to hear.' She took a deep breath and immediately regretted it when his scent filled every atom of her being. 'I'd suggest handing in my notice and finding a new job if I could—' She jumped at the snarl that filled the car. 'But I've only been working a few weeks, and my chances of finding another job are—'

'You're not quitting this job. You're not going anywhere.' He pressed the button that started the ignition but he didn't drive away. 'You signed a contract so you're staying put.'

CHAPTER EIGHT

ARI MADE SURE his words left no room for doubt or ambiguity. Which was laughable, considering he was nowhere near as stalwart under the barrage of the emotions coursing through him.

He'd firmly believed he had regained some control after yesterday's incident. It was the reason he'd called to discuss business with her. He'd been so certain, after seeing her in that bikini and not jumping on her like some hormone-riddled teenager, he could see Perla, be within touching distance of her without experiencing that unbridled depth of yearning that seemed to claw up from his very soul.

A soul he'd believed withered and charred after Sofia… after his father…

But now, with her seductive, addictive warmth so close, her husky voice seeming to caress him whenever she spoke, he knew resisting this insanity wouldn't be as easy as he'd thought.

But resist he had to. The guilt that had ridden him from the very moment he'd slept with Perla still resided beneath his chest. It fought savagely with his intense attraction but it never went away…

I remind you of something in your past…

She had no idea how accurate that was.

'Okay, I'll honour my contract. But, um…do you think

we can get out of here? The valet attendants are beginning to get frantic at the backed-up traffic.'

A quick look in the rear-view mirror confirmed her words. With a twist of the wheel and a foot on the accelerator, he squealed out of his hotel's driveway and onto the freeway. The sound of the throaty engine drowned out his thoughts for the precious few seconds it took to regain a little bit of his control.

Masculine pleasure at the purr of the powerful engine beneath him soothed his turbulent pulse and he inhaled slowly.

Next to rowing, alone or with his brothers, powerful engines like these were his passion. Except he didn't get to indulge enough. It was probably why he'd succumbed to temptation—

Stasi! Enough with the excuses. Perla had hit the nail on the head. They'd been weak with temptation and he'd succumbed. Not once but twice. The only way to avoid being no better than his father would be to make sure it didn't happen again.

'Ari, could you slow down a little, please?'

A quick glance showed her death grip on the bucket seat. He cursed under his breath and eased off the pedal. 'My apologies.'

She nodded and her fingers relaxed. 'What did you want to talk to me about?' she asked as he signalled off Connecticut Avenue and slid to a stop in front of the Greek restaurant. Perla didn't know it but it was one of his favourite restaurants outside of his homeland.

As they were led in, he found himself following the line of her body again. The way her black dress hugged her tight behind, the way her black wrap caressed her shoulders and her black heels made her legs go on for ever.

His thoughts screeched to a halt. She was wearing black

again. And not just a touch here and there but black from head to toe…as if she was making a statement.

Was she?

'You're scowling again.'

They'd reached their table and she was already sitting down, while he stood beside it, arrested by his crazy thoughts. He gritted his teeth, pulled out his chair and sat down.

Business. Focus on business.

'You asked what I wanted to talk to you about.'

She nodded as he beckoned the *sommelier*. She ordered a white wine spritzer and he a full-bodied claret. Once they were alone again, he took out his mini tablet and set it on the table between them. A few swipes and he had the page he was looking for.

'My new resort and casino in Bermuda, set to open in two months.'

Her brow rose. 'Another one?' She leaned closer and swiped through the pictures. Slowly her mouth fell open. 'It's spectacular.'

He allowed himself a small smile. 'I worked closely with the architects to achieve the results I wanted—a private resort which caters to extreme water sports lovers without taking anything away from the signature luxury casino.'

'Water seems to be a major theme for you, doesn't it? Eighty per cent of your portfolio is built on or around water.'

He was impressed that she'd done her homework. 'I grew up around water and started rowing from a very early age.'

'You rowed?' she asked in surprise.

'Competitively for six years, four of those with Sakis and two with Theo.' It had been one of the few ways he and his brothers had coped with their shattered lives.

She played with the beads on her purse. 'Did you win?'

'Of course.'

She laughed, the sound so pure and delightful, his stomach clenched. '*Of course*. How many titles?'

'Five that are worth mentioning. My mother has all my trophies from when I was a child.'

Her head tilted to one side, traces of laughter lingering in her eyes. 'I can't quite picture you as a child. You look as if you were born looking like you do now.'

Against his will, his smile widened. 'For my mother's sake, I'm glad that wasn't the case.'

A sudden wave of anguish passed over her face, erasing the laughter. Then it was gone. Reaching out, she took a slice of bread from the basket the waiter had set between them and broke off a piece. 'Is your mother still around?'

He tried not to let his mixed feelings about his mother show. 'Yes. She lives at the family home in Athens.'

Curiosity built in her eyes. 'Do you see her often?'

He shrugged. 'When I'm in Greece. Which isn't often enough, she tells me.'

'Are you two close?' He detected the faint longing in her voice and wondered at it. It suddenly struck him that, beyond the intense sexual pull and the actions of her dead husband, he didn't know much about Perla Lowell.

'We used to be. There was a time when I shared everything with her. She was my best friend and she encouraged my every dream. Then...my father happened.'

Her breath caught slightly. 'He...*happened?*'

The usual fierce reluctance to revisit the past spiked through him, even though he'd been the one to open the door. Despite his reticence, he found himself nodding. 'A few months before I turned eighteen, a journalist uncovered my father's duplicitous life. Details of fraud, corruption, embezzlement all came to light.' His insides twisted with remembered agony that he hoped his face didn't reflect. 'Overnight, our lives were turned upside down. I was working in one of my father's companies and was in the office with my father when the fraud squad stormed the building.'

Her eyes widened. 'That must have been very difficult to witness.'

'It would've been if I hadn't realised quickly that I would be busy trying to save my own skin.'

'*What?* Why?'

For a moment, he considered not uttering the words. Considered hiding it from her the way he'd hidden this fact from his brothers, from his mother. Only a distant uncle knew what Ari had suffered, and Ari had made sure to enforce the attorney-client privilege that prevented his uncle from ever divulging the truth.

'My father tried to shift some of the blame of his fraudulent activities onto me. He implicated me in a few of his bribery scams and tried to get me to take the fall so his charges could be lessened.'

Her eyes darkened with shock. 'Oh, God! Why would he do that?'

'I was his firstborn son, and had taken a keen interest in the business since I turned sixteen. I had a good head for figures and the authorities knew he'd been grooming me to eventually take over from him. Because I was still under eighteen when he was arrested he figured I would get off easily. For a short while the authorities believed him.'

Her eyes grew dark with sympathy. 'That's horrible. How did your brothers take it? Where was your mother?'

Unable to stop, his lips twisted as old wounds were ripped open. 'Sakis and Theo didn't know... I never told them.'

Her mouth dropped open. 'You didn't?'

He shrugged. 'What good would it have done? By the time we were done with my father, enough devastation had been spread around. It was my duty to protect them from more hurt. Revealing that I possibly faced jail when they were counting on me was not an option.'

'But...you've been carrying it for all this time...'

'Human beings are predisposed to carrying a hell of a lot of baggage,' he answered. 'And I have very broad shoulders,' he added, in the hope of lightening a suddenly heavy atmosphere. But her eyes only grew more solemn, as if she shared his pain, sympathised with his blighted past.

'Broad shoulders or not, you shouldn't have had to bear that on your own. Your mother...'

'Retreated to our villa in Santorini and locked herself away. Her husband's betrayal was too much for her. She couldn't cope.' He'd needed her more than ever in the darkest time of his life. And she'd abandoned him. Just as she'd abandoned Sakis and Theo when they'd needed her the most.

It had taken a long time for Ari to forgive her, a long time to get past his anger and bitterness at her weakness. But he'd learned to smother it. Because he'd needed to get past his personal devastation in order to take care of his brothers. To salvage the charred remains of the family business his father had decimated with his greed and carelessness.

He jerked as Perla's hand touched his in gentle sympathy. 'I'm sorry that happened to you.'

Sincerity blazed from her clear green eyes. Sincerity he wanted to take and wrap around his damaged heart. Instead, he forced himself to nod.

Slowly, he pulled his hand away.

Because, even in the midst of excruciating reminiscing, he could feel that pull again, that potent hunger that lurked like the sweetest siren call, ready to tempt him.

'Why?'

Her fingers curled around her piece of bread. 'Because... because no one deserves to go through what you did.'

Their drinks arrived and he took a healthy gulp of wine,

exhaling in satisfaction as the fire in the alcohol temporarily replaced the fire of lust. 'But I survived. Some would say I triumphed.'

'But you're still affected by it, aren't you?'

He tensed. 'Excuse me?'

'Yesterday you didn't want me to find out what your father had done. Clearly you're still affected by what happened.'

'Are we not all shaped by our pasts to some extent? You're clearly steeped in the past and reacting to your own experiences.'

Her cheeks lost a bit of colour. 'What makes you say that?'

'Yesterday *you* admitted your lack of judgement when it comes to dealing with people. I don't need to be a genius to work out the root cause of it.'

Paling further, she shook her head. 'I…I'm not…'

'Tell me how you met Lowell?' he asked before he could stop himself. 'Of all the men you could've dated, why him?'

'Because I didn't have a crystal ball that could look into the future to see how things would turn out. And you say *of all the men* as if I had hundreds at my feet.'

He barely stopped himself from glancing up at her hair. The idea that no man had shown interest in her was laughable. 'So he was the first man to show his interest?' He tried to force a neutral tone and barely pulled it off.

'He was charming; he paid me the right sort of attention…at the beginning. I believed I was making the right choice, that we had the same goals and that my feelings were reciprocated.'

Anger roiled through his belly. 'Instead, he abandoned you shortly after you were married?'

Shocked eyes met his. 'How did you know that?'

'I'm a major shareholder in the company he tried to de-.

stroy. My brother dealt with the bulk of the investigation but I saw enough.'

Her gaze grew haunted, then it slid away and she reached for the glass of water. After a few sips she set the glass down. 'So you know a great deal about me.'

'Enough to know there are no mention of your parents anywhere on record. You take care of your in-laws but what about your own parents?' he asked, eager to get away from the subject of dead spouses.

The earlier anguish he'd glimpsed returned. 'I don't have… I was placed in the foster system when I was one month old. My birth mother left me in front of the social security office with my first name and my date of birth pinned to my blanket. My birth date could be wrong because there was no birth certificate, although the doctors are fairly sure I was born in the month I was left but there were no hospital records so I don't even know *where* I was born. So no, I have no record of who my parents are,' she murmured in a voice ravaged with pain. 'I'm the child no one wanted.'

His fingers tightened around his glass and he realised he was holding on tight so he wouldn't reach out for her like she'd reached out for him.

Only he wanted to take her face between his hands and kiss away her pain. He wanted to rewind time, take a different track of conversation that was so far off what he'd come here for it was ludicrous. He should've stuck to business, facts, figures.

Not their painful personal pasts. And he should certainly not be sitting here, hanging onto that connection that stemmed from opening up and sharing his desolate history with her.

He wasn't a *sharer*.

'Perla—'

She forced a laugh. 'How do we always end up on the personal when we vow never to again?'

'We're especially bad at pulling the forbidden out of each other.'

'Or exceptionally good?' she joked.

He stared at her. And just like that the madness descended again. He tried to shift away from it but it clawed into him, sank its merciless talons into his gut and held him down. Almost in slow motion, he watched her mouth part, her nostrils quiver delicately as she sucked in a desperate breath.

Theos!

She gave a distressed shake of her head and glanced down at the now powered down tablet. 'The resort. We were discussing the resort,' she said after clearing her throat.

He forced his mind on track. 'Yes. I wanted to float the idea of you handling the pre-opening VIP events for the Bermuda resort on your own. If you agree to take on the task, you'll have to work fast to organise it. The guests arrive at the resort at the end of next week.'

'The pre-opening event is so your A-list clients can experience the resort and spread the word to their other A-list friends by the time the resort opens properly, correct?'

He nodded. 'So it needs to be extra-special. Your input here in Washington has been invaluable and you can choose to stay here if you wish, but I think this is more along the lines of what you used to do in your previous position, only on a much larger scale?'

'Yes, but I've never worked in such an exotic location before.'

'This will be your chance to prove yourself then. I want to see how you fare spearheading a larger project.' He sipped his wine—absently acknowledging he would have to abandon his beloved sports car in favour of another means of transport to return to the hotel—and watched her digest the information.

Slowly her stunning green eyes widened. '*Spearheading?* Are you serious?'

'You can handpick your own team, hire and fire as you see fit. You'll be provided with the initial list of attending guests but you can extend the list if you think you can handle it.'

'You *are* serious!' Shocked happiness erased the last evidence of her bleak foray into the past and, watching her, enchantment eased through him.

Examining himself closer, he realised he felt lighter than he had in a long while. He refused to believe unburdening his past to Perla had succeeded in lightening the heavy load of bitterness and pain, but he had no other explanation for it.

When he found himself smiling in reaction to her still stunned expression, something tugged hard in his chest. 'Serious enough to promise a quick firing and slow roasting if you mess up my opening.'

She popped another piece of bread into her mouth. 'Which is really no better than a slow firing and a quick roasting since both sound horrific.'

He laughed and saw her gaze linger on his face and her eyes darken a fraction.

No, he wasn't going there. *They* were not going there.

He beckoned the hovering waiter and paused as Perla examined the menu. Slowly she pulled her lower lip into her mouth and pondered some more.

'Can I help?' he offered after several minutes.

She looked up in relief. 'Would you? I never know what to order when I go to a restaurant and I always end up hating what I choose and coveting what's on other people's plates.'

'I'll order a variety of dishes and you can decide which ones you like and which ones you don't.'

She smiled. 'That works for me. *Efharisto.*'

He froze, the sound of his mother tongue so erotically charged coming from her that he forgot to breathe. 'You're learning Greek?'

'I work for a Greek company. It seems wise to learn a few essential words like *thank you* and *where the hell is the coffee?* I find some of the pronunciations quite hard, though.'

'Let me know what you have difficulty with and I'll teach you.' Again the words slipped out before he could stop them.

What in heaven's name was wrong with him?

Mentally shaking his head, he recited the dishes he wanted prepared to the waiter and added a command for haste.

They discussed the Bermuda resort and her initial ideas. The passion she exhibited for business made him glad he'd offered her the chance. So much so, he slightly regretted it when their meal arrived and intruded on the atmosphere. Small platters of roasted vegetables, tenderly prepared meats served on a bed of traditional salad, hummus and oven-baked breads.

He watched her dig into the food with the same gusto she'd eaten that night at his apartment in London. Then, as now, he'd found her appetite refreshing.

Recalling her comment earlier about putting on weight, Ari's gaze slid to her breasts. They looked slightly heavier, plumper than they had in London, and her cleavage seemed deeper.

Warmth rushed into his mouth that had nothing to do with the sumptuous textures of the food and everything to do with recalling the exquisite taste of her hard nipples on his tongue. He forced his gaze away. Only to snap it back to her when she made a sound of distress.

Her eyes had widened and she was reaching for her water. 'Um…Ari…I don't feel so good.'

Ari frowned and he jerked to his feet. 'What's wrong? What is it?'

She dropped her glass and water splashed across the table. In one move, he was by her side, pushing her chair back so he could take her face in his hands.

'Perla?'

She jumped up and looked around wildly, drawing the attention of other diners. She must have spotted the signs for the lavatory because she grabbed her bag and lurched forward.

'Excuse me.' She clamped her hand over her mouth and fled.

CHAPTER NINE

THE DEBILITATING WEAKNESS was back again, weighting her limbs down and fanning a dull ache throughout her body.

But it was nothing compared to the crushing weight of suspicion anchoring her heart.

No matter how much she tried to push the thought away, it kept coming back, intruding, demanding to be heard, to be acknowledged.

Perla cast a furtive glance at the man who stood beside her in the hotel lift, his hand gripping her arm. He hadn't said a word since they left the restaurant. He'd been there when she emerged from the Ladies, pale, weak and shaky, barely able to meet his gaze when he'd enquired whether she wanted to leave.

The restaurant staff had been profusely apologetic but she hadn't had the courage to reassure them that what was going on was most likely not the fault of their food. She'd left the soothing of ruffled feathers to Ari, simply because she hadn't been able to think past the stark reality of what she could be facing.

They exited the lift and she followed him numbly. It wasn't until they were inside the suite that was easily three times the size of hers that she realised they hadn't returned to her suite but to his. He bypassed the living room, the study and the master bedroom and entered a second bedroom.

Before her stood what was easily an emperor-sized bed, complete with solid four-posters and cream silk muslin curtains. A bathroom and walk-in closet were visible through a golden-lit arch and beyond the windows Washington DC shone its powerful light over the city.

Her gaze returned from sweeping the room to find Ari standing with his hands on his hips, those mesmerising eyes fixed questioningly on hers.

'There's a new toothbrush through there if you need to use it?'

She nodded, dropped her clutch on the bed and darted into the bathroom. The need to escape was less to do with cleaning her mouth properly and more to do with delaying the inevitable.

Quickly, she brushed her teeth and rinsed her mouth. Then gripped the edge of the sink as a fresh wave of apprehension rolled through her.

Arion Pantelides wasn't stupid. The knowledge in his eyes told her his thoughts had taken the same path as hers.

'Perla.'

She jumped and whirled so fast, her vision blurred.

Callused hands steadied her, one curving around her waist and the other rising to cradle her cheek for a moment before he dropped his hand.

'Come.'

The gentle gesture threatened her equilibrium and she fought not to react as he led her back to the room and sank onto the bed beside her. He'd discarded his jacket and folded back the sleeves of his shirt.

The sight of the silky hairs on his forearm made sensation scythe through her but it was the look in his eyes that stopped her breath.

His fingers trembled as they caught her chin and an emotion moved through her heart she was almost too afraid to examine. 'How do you feel?' he asked in a low, deep voice.

Something in his tone made her glance at him. His face had lost a few shades of vibrancy and in his eyes dark, unfathomable shadows lurked.

Whatever was ahead of them, Perla knew it wouldn't be an easy road.

'I…I'm…' Her throat felt swollen and scratchy so she stopped.

'Here, have some water.' He passed her a glass and waited while she took a few sips. His gaze never left her and, feeling her hands begin to shake, she put the glass down.

Trepidation welled up inside her. 'Ari…'

More colour leached from his face. 'Before you say anything, Perla, I need you to be one hundred per cent sure.'

The depth of emotion in his voice made her heart flip over, then thunder with enough force to threaten her ribs. 'Why?' she asked before she could stop herself.

'Because the ramifications would mean more than you could ever imagine.' The roughness in his voice and the faint trembling of the hand still at her waist made her insides quake.

Incomprehensible emotions swirled around inside her. Unbidden, tears welled up in her eyes and slipped down her cheeks.

'*Theos*, do not cry. Please,' he ordered raggedly.

'Sorry, I'm not normally a crier,' she muttered, then cringed as more tears fell. 'I just can't seem to help myself.'

He gritted his teeth and brushed her cheeks with his thumbs, then stared down at her with dark eyes but said nothing as the tears continued to fall.

The knock on the door made him turn away but not before she caught another glimpse of jagged torment in his eyes. 'The doctor's here.'

'The *doctor?*' When had he even called him? 'Ari, I don't need a doctor. I feel fine.'

He stood and stared at her for a long moment before he shoved his hands into his pockets. 'I can send him away if that's what you want. But I think we need to make absolutely sure that you're not coming down with an illness. *That* is not negotiable. So we can do it now or we can do it tomorrow. Your choice.'

She gripped the covers, the feeling of hurtling towards the unknown growing by the second. But Ari was right. They needed to be sure nothing else was wrong before they went any further.

She nodded. 'Okay, we do it now.'

He left the room and returned moments later followed by a tall, lanky man with brown hair and serious brown eyes. He proceeded to look her over and fire questions at her that made her cringe. Ari stood, hand in his pocket next to the bed the whole time, his eyes never leaving her.

'The headache and fatigue worries me a bit, and your glands are slightly swollen,' the doctor finally said. 'My advice is to rest for a few days—'

'Yes, she'll do that—'

'No, she won't,' she countered sharply with a frown which he returned twice as hard and twice as dangerous. 'I'm not sick, Ari. Seriously, I'll be fine by morning.'

The doctor looked between them, clearly sensing the undercurrents. 'Or I can give you a flu shot just in case? Head it off at the pass?'

At her nod, he opened his bag and took out the needle. She tensed and tried to curb her nerves but Ari's narrowed gaze told her he'd seen her reaction.

Rounding the bed, he slid in beside her and pulled her close, his warm, hard body a solid comfort. 'You fear needles and yet you're refusing the simple alternative.'

'I'll take a small prick any day compared to days lazing about in bed.'

The small charged silence that followed gave her time

to hear her words echo in the room. Then a fierce blush washed over her face.

The doctor hid a smile as he focused on preparing the syringe. Ari's mocking laughter lightened the tense atmosphere a touch, although she could feel his tension. 'It's not gentlemanly to laugh at a harmless *double entendre*. Especially when it comes at the patient's expense.'

He blinked and his gaze dropped to her mouth.

This close, his designer stubble was within touching distance and the gold flecks in his eyes and the sensual curve of his mouth were even more mesmerising. The hand he'd slipped around her tightened, drawing her infinitesimally closer to his body. Heat oozed through her, breaking loose that wild yearning she seemed to be useless at keeping sealed up.

The doctor clearing his throat made her jump. The needle filled with liquid was poised against her skin. 'Stop! Will this harm a pregnancy?' she blurted.

Beside her, Ari tensed.

The doctor frowned. 'Are you pregnant, Miss Lowell?'

'It's Mrs…actually,' she murmured absently as her gaze swung and collided with Ari's. In that moment, she *knew*.

And so did he.

The doctor moved. With a swiftness that stunned the breath out of her, Ari grabbed the doctor's needle-holding hand and held it in a death grip. All without taking his eyes from hers.

'So you're sure?' he rasped.

She nodded.

Wordlessly he let go of the doctor's wrist. Lines of torment bracketed his mouth as he left the bed.

She was pregnant. With Ari's child. The two thoughts tumbled over one another in her brain, one seeking dominance over the other and neither coming out the victor. Because both thoughts were equally mind-boggling.

Vaguely, she heard him dismiss the doctor and leave the suite.

But all too soon he was back. Tall, imposing, bristling with emotions she was too cowardly to try and name.

For several minutes, he paced the room. Then he finally stopped at the foot of the bed. 'Did you know you were pregnant?' His voice was gritty with emotion.

'No, I didn't. I didn't even guess.'

'Not even when you were late? How late are you?'

The date flared like a beacon in her mind. 'Almost two weeks.'

He muttered a word she didn't need translation for. '*Theos!*' Running a hand through his hair, he resumed pacing. 'And it didn't raise any alarms?'

'No. My period has always been irregular.'

She thought back to that night and felt shame crawl over her skin when she remembered she'd been so into it, too far gone with delirium that she hadn't stopped to think about safe sex that second time.

And now she was pregnant.

Tiny waves of joy slowly spread through her stunned senses.

A child of her own. To cherish and love. And, if she was lucky, a child who would love her back.

She jerked upright, her hand rushing to cover her stomach. 'Oh, God, I took some painkillers this afternoon!'

His gaze sharpened on her. 'What did you take?'

She told him. 'W…would it have harmed the baby?'

He shook his head. 'The doctor told me which medicines are okay to take during pregnancy.'

Relief poured through her. 'You asked him?'

Ari stilled. 'Of course. This baby is mine too,' he grated out.

But it didn't take a genius to see that he wasn't thrilled

about it. Pain and hurt scythed through her joy. A second later a rush of protectiveness enveloped her.

'I realise this is unexpected. I don't want you to think that you need to be involved in any way...'

'Excuse me?' His voice was a rasp, his eyes dark with thunder as he stared at her.

Perla licked her lips, contemplated taking a sip of water and discarded the idea. She was too shaken not to pour it all over herself.

'I mean this wasn't planned or anything, so don't feel as if you have to participate in any decision-making. I'll take care of it.'

'You'll *take care of it?*'

The skin-flaying fury in his voice made her realise that once again she'd chosen the wrong words.

'No! I meant I'll take care of him or her after the birth.'

Dark implacable eyes bored into hers. 'So, just so we're clear, you intend to keep the baby?'

'Of course! I'd never, ever dream of...' She raised her chin. 'Yes, I intend to have this baby. What I meant was that I'll take sole responsibility so you don't have to worry.' Her eyes dropped to her stomach. This child was hers and she intended to protect him or her with her last breath.

'What gives you the right to assume sole responsibility for the child? Sexual responsibility is a two-way street.'

'I know, but I participated too without giving a thought to protection. Arion, all I'm trying to say is there's no need to get all macho and blame yourself for something that involved both of us.'

'Perla, look at me.' The order was soft, deadly.

She dragged her eyes from where she'd been staring at her stomach in silent wonder. The resolution and implacable determination in his eyes made her shiver.

'Do I look like the sort of man who would leave his child to be brought up by another man? And I assume you don't intend to remain single for the rest of your life? That you will seek another relationship at some point in the future?'

That thought was so unlikely she wanted to laugh. Except the look on his face told her he wouldn't find it funny. So she shrugged. 'I don't know. Maybe.'

'Let's try something else much simpler.' He drew closer to the bed. His hands hung loose at his sides and his open-legged stance was unthreatening. But she didn't fool herself for one second that Ari wasn't seething beneath that calm exterior. 'Do I look like I'm going anywhere?'

'Ari—'

'*Do I?*'

'No. You don't.' And she wasn't sure whether to be pleased or frightened by that admission.

If Ari wanted this child and, from his stance, she concluded he did…for now…it would mean she would have him in her life for the foreseeable future.

Her childhood in foster care had opened her eyes to the fact that not all children were wanted. No matter what the circumstances of conception, there came a point in time where some parents simply abandoned their children and walked away.

She had no intention of ever doing that to her child. But she couldn't speak for Ari. His childhood had created deep scars that rippled through his every decision. He'd been let down by the people who should've been there for him. In a way it was worse than never having felt the love of two devoted parents. She hadn't experienced that particular devastation because she hadn't had the fantasy in the first place. To know that he'd had parents who'd let him down, who'd let him shoulder the responsibility of caring for his brothers on his own was too distressing to bear.

A wave of despair swept over her. Would Ari let go of his pain long enough to let himself love a child?

'Good, I'm glad we've established that fact.' He stepped

back from the bed and turned towards the door. Without speaking another word, he left.

He returned less than ten minutes later with a tray of food which he set on her lap. The simple ham and cucumber sandwich made her stomach rumble and she remembered she'd barely eaten a few mouthfuls of dinner before her attack.

'I prepared it myself. Until I find you a personal chef who will be apprised of all your dietary requirements, I'll prepare all your meals myself.'

Her mouth dropped open for several seconds before she managed to snap it shut. 'Wait… What?'

He poured a glass of orange juice and handed it to her. 'Which part needs explanation?'

'The part…all of it. You don't have to do this, Ari.'

'Yes, I do. You're carrying my child. I absolutely have to do this.'

Again, the depth of emotion behind the words made her eyes widen. But when she looked at him, his eyes were veiled and his face inscrutable.

'Eat,' he instructed.

In silence she ate because as much as she wanted to argue with him, probe behind his words, she was starving. And she needed to do everything in her power to keep her baby healthy and safe.

She forced herself to eat slowly this time. She accepted a second glass of orange juice. Once she'd drained it, Ari set the tray aside.

'How do you feel?' Again there was that concern in his voice. But, coupled with that, there was a thin vein of anxiety that made her heart skitter.

'I'm fine. Right now I'm more interested in how *you* feel.'

He rose with the tray. 'My feelings are irrelevant. Get some sleep. We'll talk in the morning.'

She wanted to ask what exactly they would be talking about, but he was already leaving, his shoulders and back set in tense lines that made her nervousness rise higher.

Her hand slid down to rest on her abdomen.

Whatever it was, she could handle it. As long as it didn't interfere with the welfare of her baby.

He was having a child.

Ari barely managed to set the tray down before it slid out of his useless grip.

Shaking from head to toe, he gripped the edge of the granite counter in the suite's kitchen and tried to breathe.

He was having a child!

The self-indulgent need to rail at fate was so strong the growl bubbled up through his chest before he managed to swallow it down. He stalked to the living room and contented himself with a fiery shot of single malt Scotch. Except he was no better equipped to handle the bone-crushing fear gripping him. It writhed like a poisonous snake inside him before sinking its merciless fangs into his heart.

Was he doomed to fail at this task too, the way he'd failed Sofia? He'd single-handedly taken care of his brothers and his mother, had ensured they were protected as much as possible from the fallout of his father's misdeeds.

And yet he hadn't been able to save his wife.

Or his unborn child.

Was fate taunting him again? Willing him to fail again? *No!*

His fist tightened around the glass and he set it aside before it shattered. This time things would be different. Because anything else was unthinkable.

He moved restlessly across the room, willing his pulse to slow, his insides to stop churning viciously with the acrid mix of guilt and fear.

He was going to be a father. His steps slowed and he

stopped in front of the view. Funny, he'd stood here just two days ago thinking he was in control of his world. It had been in the moments before Perla burst in and accused him of controlling her life.

Now he barely felt in control of his.

Whirling round, he walked out of the living room and entered his study. It might be the middle of the night in Washington, but it was still a working day in London and the rest of Europe.

His first call was to the Pantelides headquarters in London, where he gathered all the pertinent information he needed. Next he placed a call to his lawyers in Greece. His dealings with them so far had been purely business so he wasn't surprised at their thinly veiled shock as he outlined his wishes.

By the time he finished his calls, the horizon was lightening with the coming dawn.

Ari rubbed a hand across his jaw and rested his head against his seat.

He had no idea how Perla would take the conversation he intended to have with her come morning. There could potentially be many obstacles to getting his way but he intended to smash them all aside.

Because one thing had become clear in his mind from the second he'd found out Perla was carrying his child.

The welfare of his child was the most important thing in his life.

She was already up when he knocked on her door just after seven o'clock. Up, showered and dressed.

In black. Only the flame of her hair provided vivid colour in the harsh landscape. And she was in the process of coiling it into a tight bun when she followed him out to the dining room, where he'd set her breakfast tray.

Ari resisted the urge to pull her hands away from her

task. He also resisted the urge to command her to change her clothes.

She finished securing her hair and turned to him. Her gaze met his for a moment before travelling over his body.

Noting his attire, she looked back up. 'Have you slept at all?'

'No,' he replied, vaguely disturbed by his anger at her choice of clothes.

A look of concern crossed her eyes. He allowed it to touch him for a second, two seconds, before he looked away.

'Sit down. Drink your tea and have some of those dry crackers. They'll calm any nausea that triggers morning sickness.'

She looked at the tray and wrinkled her nose. 'Too late. I've already thrown up twice.'

He forced away the anxiety that tightened his nape. 'Drink it anyway.'

She sat and he poured her tea and passed it to her, noting the anxious glances she sent his way. Part of him wanted to reassure her. He curbed the feeling because he knew the road ahead wouldn't be easy.

'Aren't you having anything?'

'No. Until we find out which smells trigger your nausea, I'll eat my meals separately.'

'How come you know so much about morning sickness and nausea triggers?'

Ice formed in his belly, stealing his breath. But it was nothing compared to the pain that ripped through his heart as the guilt and fear returned twice as forcefully.

He looked up and saw the anxiety stamped on her face. 'Ari?'

'I know because my wife was four months pregnant with our first child when she died.'

Her cup clattered onto the saucer and her features

paled. 'Oh, my God. I'm… I don't know what to say. I'm sorry for—'

He slashed a hand through the air, unwilling to dwell on the past, unwilling to let her see the devastation that still had the power to shred his insides.

They had more important things to discuss than the subject of his hubris.

'Drink your tea, Perla. We have a lot to discuss.'

The shock of his revelation still clear in her eyes, she slowly picked up her cup and took another tiny sip. He waited until she'd eaten a cracker before he spoke.

'Do you have any health issues that I should know about?'

She placed her cup down. 'I'm allergic to shellfish but, aside from that, I've always been healthy and Morgan's health insurance provided me with annual check-ups. They always came back clean.'

The mention of her husband's name made his fists clench but he forced the feeling away. He needed to get over the fact that she'd been another man's wife only a short time ago.

'Good. Then we'll postpone a thorough health check until we return to London.'

Her eyes connected with his. 'We're returning to London?'

'Yes.'

'Why?'

'Because London is where we will be married.'

CHAPTER TEN

'No.'

'You've already said that. Twice.'

'I believe in making things crystal-clear so there's no misunderstanding. I won't marry you.'

Perla watched his nostrils pinch in that way that told her he was hanging onto his control by a thread. But the emotions coursing through her eroded any concern for his control or lack thereof.

Who would've believed that a proposal of marriage could bring so much pain? But devastating pain was exactly what ravaged her as they faced each other across his wide living room like two boxers about to engage in a fight.

'You've yet to give me a reason why not.'

'And you've yet to give me a valid reason why I should. Presumably it's because I'm pregnant. Regardless, the answer is still no.'

'Perla—'

'No is no, Ari.' Her hands shook as she thought back to what she'd been through the last three years. 'I got married under false pretences three years ago. I won't do it again, no matter the reason.'

His eyes sparked with curiosity. 'Explain.'

She paused. Could she reveal the final humiliation? 'I've already told you my marriage was…difficult. I also know how you feel about me and the circumstances under which we met. No matter how much you try to deny it, I know you despise what happened between us. Trust me, losing my virginity to a man who's mourning his dead wife on the anniversary of her death is bad enough. I refuse to become trapped in another sham of a marriage where I'm second best.'

She ground to a halt at his white-faced shock.

'Your *virginity?*' he rasped in a tone that could've flayed stone.

Perla flinched. Of course. Of all the things she'd said, that was the one he'd have picked up on. Turning around, she squeezed her eyes shut as the familiar shame dredged through her stomach.

'Perla.' He was right behind her, standing so close his breath washed over her exposed nape, making a shiver course through her. 'Did you just say you were a virgin when we slept together?' he asked, his voice spiked with emotions she couldn't name.

Clenching her hands into tight fists, she struggled to breathe. 'Yes.'

'Turn around.'

'No.'

'You really need to stop defying me so much. There are some things I will let slide. This isn't one of them. Turn around,' he demanded, more forcefully this time.

Heart in her throat, she opened her eyes and turned. The gold flecks in his eyes stood out with the intensity of his stare. 'You were married for three years. How were you still a virgin on your husband's death?'

She affected a shrug that felt far from casual. 'We never got round to it, I guess.'

He gripped her shoulders in an implacable hold. 'This is not the time to be facetious. Tell me how Lowell could have a woman such as you in his bed and walk away. Why a woman who could drive any red-blooded man to his knees with just one look could remain a virgin for so long within the bounds of marriage.'

'Because I did nothing for him!'

He frowned. 'You refused to sleep with him?'

She laughed, or rather she attempted to laugh. The sound scraped her throat and emerged a ragged croak. 'On the contrary, I threw myself at him. Hell, I even tried to seduce him *before* and after we were married. He suggested we wait. Stupid me, I thought it was the height of *romantic*; that he was being *noble!* But it turned out he didn't want me. You want to know why? Because my husband told me on our wedding night that he was gay!'

Hazel eyes widened. 'Lowell was gay?'

'I'm surprised you don't know, considering where he was when your investigators found him in Thailand.'

'We knew he'd taken residence in a disreputable part of Bangkok when he was found but I assumed...'

'He was whoring it up with women? No, Ari, the man I married was probably shacked up with a boyfriend when your men caught up with him. I didn't need to be a genius to read between the lines. And I don't need a crystal ball to know he changed the terms of his contract and plotted to crash the Pantelides tanker because he needed money to fund his secret life and the drug habit that killed him.' Raw humiliation threatened to consume her whole, especially when he let out a crude curse.

'Perla *mou*...'

'No, I don't want to talk about this any more. And I don't want to discuss marriage. You're proposing because I'm pregnant but nothing will ever convince me to get married again.'

'Not even the welfare of your child?'

She paled and he let out another curse. Swinging her into his arms, he walked to the sofa and sat down with her in his lap.

'This child means everything to me. I intend to give it everything it needs,' she whispered fiercely.

'Except a stable home and the unity of both parents.'

'That's a low blow, Ari. You had that for a while. But it didn't turn out great for you either, did it?' She regretted her answer but she had to fight back. She was no longer fighting for just herself. She had her baby to think of.

Ari's arms tightened around her. 'Our marriage will be different.'

'You cannot possibly know that.'

'I'm determined to win this fight, Perla.'

'Why does it have to be a fight?'

'Because you're resisting my every effort to make you see sense.'

'Just because I don't see things your way doesn't mean it's nonsense. If this hadn't happened, would *you* have ever remarried?'

The tightening of his jaw and the way his eyelids swept down gave her the answer she needed. 'So why does it have to be different for me?'

'Because this is no longer just about you.'

Simple words that made her breath catch. 'I know. But this is emotional blackmail.' And she refused to succumb to blackmail of any sort ever again.

'It's the truth. Tell me what your plan is for our child. Do you intend to return to your former in-laws after he or she is born, live with Lowell's parents with another man's child?'

A shiver went through her. 'Of course not. I'll find another place to live.'

'And when the child is older? What then?'

'I'll find adequate childcare and continue my career. Millions of women do it every day. Why should I be any different?'

'Because this child is not just any child. It is a Pantelides.

Whether you want to admit it or not, that makes it different from any other child.'

'I know you like to think you're special but—'

'No buts, Perla. I've lost one unborn child.' His gaze dropped to her flat stomach and he swallowed hard. 'If I'm lucky enough to become a father for a second time, nothing and no one will keep me from my child.'

A stalemate.

Despite knowing it was temporary, she hung onto the stalemate as Ari's private jet raced them towards Bermuda and the Pantelides resort project she'd undertaken what seemed like a thousand years ago.

It was hard to fathom that it'd been barely eighteen hours since she'd discovered she was carrying Ari's child.

Even harder to believe she'd agreed to give him an answer in the time the marriage licence would take to be ready.

But the look on his face when he'd made his vow had shaken her to the core. Shaken her into considering the fact that he meant it when he said he wanted a full-time role in their child's life.

After what she had been through, shoved from foster home to foster home and then eventually spat out at eighteen, did she not owe it to her child to give it the best care possible?

But then could she bear to tie herself to another man who clearly did not want her for herself? Morgan had used her to hide his true sexual orientation from those he believed would judge him.

With Ari, it was simply the fact that she carried his heir.

A wave of sadness washed over her and the tablet she was supposed to be using to jot down ideas for the resort opening blurred as tears welled in her eyes.

Tears. Another symptom of her pregnancy she couldn't

seem to stem. She brushed them away and looked up to find Ari watching her.

'What's wrong?'

'I seem to have discovered the pregnancy hormone that lets me cry at the drop of a hat. I should hire myself out to Hollywood.'

He stood from his wide leather seat and approached her with one hand outstretched. 'Come with me,' he commanded.

'Where are we going?' she asked, although she found herself putting her hand in his, allowing him to draw her up.

'We don't land for an hour and a half. You should take the time to rest.'

She stopped. 'I'm pregnant, not sick. I don't need to rest.'

'But you will. Or I'll turn this plane around and we can head to London.'

'I have work to do, Ari—'

'You were staring at a blank screen on your tablet.'

'I was *strategising*.'

'Yes, and it was so effective you were in tears.' He placed a firm hand on her waist and propelled her forward. He opened the cabin door and she entered a large, sumptuously appointed bedroom. The gold-and-blue décor screamed opulent sophistication but it was the bed that drew her attention. King-sized and high, it was piled with pillows and covered with a gold silk spread that begged to be touched.

Moving forward, she did just that, then went one better and sat on the edge of the bed. The firm mattress gave a little beneath her and, on a whim, she kicked off her shoes and scooted backwards just as a large yawn caught her unawares.

She looked up to find Ari regarding her with an amused expression. 'Fine. I can probably do with a little rest.'

He moved forward and started removing the cufflinks

from his shirt. As he folded the sleeves back, he toed off his shoes.

'What are you doing?'

'What does it look like?'

'But…' She stopped as she recalled that he'd been up all night. It suddenly struck her that he'd taken care of her all through the shocking discovery of her pregnancy and afterwards while he'd neglected his own needs.

She could insist he return to the cabin but that would be unnecessarily mean and, really, there was more than enough room on the bed for both of them. It wasn't as if he was about to tear her clothes off and make mad, passionate love to her.

They'd moved past that.

She pushed away the ache that lodged in her heart at the thought and lifted the cover.

The smile he gave her didn't quite reach his eyes and she noticed the tension lines around his mouth when he got into bed.

Expecting him to relax against the pillow, she held her breath when he turned sideways and propped his head on his curved arm. Hypnotic eyes travelled over her hair. 'You'll be much more comfortable if you take your hair down.'

'I don't think so. My hair has got me into too much trouble around you and your inner ten-year-old. It's staying up.'

Her hair had been an explosive subject between them. Far be it from her to tempt fate. Or, worse still, for her to tempt fate only to find fate couldn't care less.

His mouth twisted. 'Please yourself.' He relaxed against the pillows, crossed his hands over his chest and closed his eyes. Within minutes, his even breathing echoed softly through the room.

She stared because she couldn't help herself. And because, like the first time she'd watched him sleep, Ari's transformation in repose was breathtaking.

But now she knew the reason behind the constant torment that lurked in his eyes and the bone-deep weariness etched into his face, she was thankful he received peace in sleep.

For the first time since he'd told her, she let herself think of just what Ari had lost. Losing his wife was devastating enough, but his unborn child, too? Was it any wonder he'd been so desolate that day at Macdonald Hall?

Was it any wonder he'd wanted to find oblivion? Her heart ached and tears clouded her eyes all over again.

God, this needed to stop or she'd be a basket case long before this child was born. She couldn't afford to be a basket case. Couldn't afford anything other than her complete wits about her, her mind *and* her heart intact. She'd been through too much to put her emotions on the line again. Until she could find a way to guarantee that, there was no way she could consider Ari's proposal.

Because there were times when he showed her kindness that her foolish heart believed he could care for her.

And that was a slippery slope to heartache she had no intention of skidding down...

She woke to the sound of a steady heartbeat beneath her ear and a warm, familiar scent in her nostrils. But it was the fingers splayed over her stomach that made her eyes slowly drift open.

Ari was awake, his gaze fixed on her flat belly. She must have curled closer to his side of the bed in her sleep because he had one arm clamped around her while his other rested on her stomach.

As she watched him, a wave of despair washed over his face. The emotion was so strong her breath caught. He heard it and his eyes flew to hers. He started to withdraw, but she held his hand in place.

'What happened to her?' she asked softly.

He froze and his features shuttered. For several minutes she thought he wouldn't answer. 'She had a weak heart. The doctors were divided on whether she could carry a child to term without it causing a severe strain on her heart. I warned her it was too risky. She chose to side with the more optimistic doctors. Her heart gave out in her second trimester.'

The naked devastation in his voice slashed her insides. 'And you blame yourself.'

That was why the news of her pregnancy didn't bring joy. The look on his face had been one of deep, wretched torment.

His smile was grim as his eyes were bleak. 'Despite my fears, I let myself be convinced she would be all right. That our child would be all right. They both died.'

'Ari, you can't—'

He pulled away and got out of bed. 'We are not having this conversation now, Perla. It's time to leave the plane. We landed ten minutes ago.'

The Pantelides Bermuda was another architectural work of art. The blueprints and plans Ari had shown her at the restaurant were nowhere near as awe-inspiring as the real thing.

The long, palm-tree-lined drive along a private road gave way to six sprawling buildings linked together by curved wooden bridges.

Multi-roomed suites, each one containing a wide wooden deck, an infinity pool and a luxurious spa, faced a stunning private white-sanded beach. Four-poster beds built with local carved wood soared up to vaulted ceilings and crown mouldings that lent an air of old-world elegance, blending old and new in exquisite symmetry.

The exclusive three-storey casino made entirely of triple-paned glass was set away from the main resort on giant transparent stilts and accessed by private boats manned by discreet security guards. From the resort, the building seemed to be floating on water.

Once their luggage was loaded into an air-conditioned SUV, Ari turned to her. 'We'll take the full tour later. Right now I'll introduce you to your chef.'

'As long as it's not to another bed and a command to "rest", we're okay.'

His lips twisted but he said nothing as he climbed in beside her and drove them to their villa at the southernmost point of the resort.

The sight of the turquoise waters gave her another idea for the opening. 'I think I'll add scuba-diving to the activities.'

'Great. Consider rowing too.'

'Rowing?'

'Sakis and Brianna are joining us for a couple of days before the guests arrive. Sometimes the waters around here get a little choppy but I intend to row with Sakis. I'll let you know how I rate it.'

'That would be great, thanks.'

There was no sign of the ragged pain she'd seen on his face on the plane. He was back to Arion Pantelides, luxury hotel mogul and master of all he surveyed.

She held her breath when they reached the villa and the staff asked where to place their luggage.

'I'll take the smaller suite. You take the master suite,' Ari said.

Perla wasn't sure why her stomach fell with disappointment. Had she really thought he would insist on joint sleeping arrangements? Nothing had changed since yesterday aside from the fact that their indiscretions had resulted in a child. Sexually, they were done with each other.

Still she couldn't suppress her rising desolation as he

walked away. With two personal butlers seeing to the unpacking, Perla changed into the only bikini she owned and
walked from room to room, acquainting herself with the
layout of the villa. It was as she entered the solarium that
she noticed the repeating item in each room.

She turned as Ari walked in. 'You've had an epi pen
placed in each room?' she asked, her heart flipping over
when she noticed he'd changed into khaki shorts and a
white T-shirt.

'Yes,' he answered simply.

The thoughtfulness behind the gesture was so alien, she
blurted, 'Why?'

He paused on the way to the French windows that led to
the teak-floored deck, changed course and came to stand
in front of her. This close, his proximity wreaked havoc
with her pulse rate. Reaching out, he brushed his fingers
down her cheek.

'I'm not taking any chances this time, Perla. Not with
you, not with this baby.' His voice was a solid, solemn vow
that struck deep into her heart.

Her eyes prickled and she sniffed hard. 'Are you determined to make me cry again?'

He grimaced and dropped his hand. 'Perhaps I need to
learn to accept that tears are par for the course. Come and
meet Peter, your chef.'

Slowly she followed him outside into the sunshine, desperately trying to get her wayward emotions under control.
'I really don't need a personal chef.'

'It is already done, *glikia mou*, so you have to live with
it.'

She was trying to decipher the Greek endearment when
a man dressed in chef whites stepped forward from behind
the table where he'd been slicing fresh fruit.

'Your fruit platter is coming right up. And for lunch

I have some freshly grilled chicken kebabs with a green salad. If you need anything else, let me know.'

Ari steered her towards twin loungers by the pool. As they sat down, his phone pinged. The huge smile that split his face as he read the text made her breath catch.

'Theo is coming down too. He'll be here at the end of the week.'

A pang of envy spilled into her heart. 'You're very close, aren't you?'

He looked up and shrugged. 'They're my family. They mean everything to me.'

The simple statement made more tears prickle her eyes. He saw it and frowned. 'Perla?'

'You're so lucky. I mean…you've had tragedy, of course, but you've remained close with your family and that's… that's…'

He watched her with keen eyes. 'It's something you've never had.'

'No.'

He set his phone aside. 'Marry me and you can have it too.'

Her heart lurched and temptation shot hope into her heart. But still her instincts shrieked dire warning.

'It's not that simple. I can't…'

His face hardened. 'For the sake of this child we have to make sacrifices, Perla.'

'What do you mean?'

'I mean we both agree we're not an ideal match but we need to look beyond that to what's best for our child. Whatever lofty ideas you have of being an ideal single parent will always pale in comparison to what we can provide as a united family. That is the bottom line.'

'That may be your bottom line. It's not mine. I think it's more important that this child grows up in a loving environment.'

His face hardened further. 'And you don't think we can provide that?'

She held her breath until Peter had delivered the fruit platters and returned to the far side of the deck where he was preparing their lunch. 'Come on, Ari. After what you've been through, what we've both been through—'

'My past has nothing to do with this.'

Her heart sank. 'If you believe that then I'm going to need even more time to consider your proposal.'

'What the hell are you saying, Perla?'

'I'm saying you've been hurt and devastated. We've both been. We need to factor that into how much that will impact our child's welfare.'

'So you want me to spill my feelings to you before you consider marrying me.'

'No. But we need to get past the bitterness and deal with the pain before we can move on. That aside, we've barely spent more than forty-eight hours in each other's company.'

His eyes gleamed. 'And a good portion of that time we spent having sex. At least we know we're compatible in the bedroom.'

Heat crawled over her skin and burrowed inside to sting parts of her body she didn't want to think about right now. 'How does that help in bringing up a child?'

His gaze drifted over her flushed skin, and his smile held a great deal of mockery. 'You'd be surprised how compliant a well-sated man can be.'

She speared a piece of papaya with her fork as her face flamed. 'Well, I wouldn't know. I didn't succeed in that department during my marriage.'

He stiffened. 'You were wasting your passion on the wrong man. Our marriage will be different.'

'So…so you intend for us to…'

'Have sex? Yes, Perla. I have no intention of living like a monk.'

So she had an answer as to how the physical part of their marriage would be. But no clue as to the emotional. Could she contemplate a future with him, knowing he would never be emotionally available?

No. Sex, as she'd discovered, was great. But it would never be enough in the long run.

Despite losing her appetite, she forced herself to eat a few more chunks of fruit and summoned a smile when the staff cleared away their plates.

She looked up to find Ari staring at her, the question clear in his eyes. 'We agreed to a week, Ari.'

His lips compressed. 'What will be different in a week's time that we can't resolve today?'

Her hands shook and she took a sip of water. 'Maybe I can convince you to talk to me a little bit more.'

His eyes narrowed. 'And will this therapy session be a two-way thing?'

She'd already told him the most humiliating secret, but the deeper secret, the yearning for a connection, to belong… It was that deep yearning that had swayed her into Morgan's path in the first place. Could she share that with Ari?

She took a deep breath. 'I'm willing to try if you are. But we both have to be committed to try.'

'Perla…' His voice held mild disgruntlement.

'We agreed on a week. All I'm doing is adding a tiny addendum. You owe our child, at the very least.'

Ari felt his insides tighten and fought the need to demand an answer right there and then. With each minute that ticked past, he felt more and more on edge, as if some unforeseen wrecking ball hovered just beyond the horizon, ready to smash through the quiet joy bubbling beneath his skin.

Perla was right. He'd never intended to marry again, but waking up next to Perla on the plane to find her curled up so trustingly against him, he'd begun to dare to believe that he could have another chance to reclaim what he'd lost.

A part of him had died with Sofia and their unborn child. But he could forge a new family, be the father he'd always wanted to be, the one his own father had failed so comprehensively to be.

But in this he knew he had to be patient, no matter how much it killed him.

'I'm not a patient man.'

His chest tightened as her mouth curved in a tiny relieved smile. 'I'm learning that. Maybe I should also confess I'm a stubborn woman.'

His gaze flew to her hair and his groin tightened. He wryly admitted that his need to speed things up also stemmed from the fact that as a married man he wouldn't have to hold back on the need that clawed relentlessly through him day and night.

'Fine. I agree that we use this week to learn some more about each other.'

She smiled at Peter as he delivered their main course. Then her eyes returned to Ari. 'Does that mean I can ask you whatever I want?'

He'd opened that particular door. Attempting to slam it shut now would only make things worse. He gave a single curt nod and saw the speculative smile that curved her full mouth.

'Word of warning, though. I give as good as I get. And I don't always play fair.'

Her smile disappeared and Ari couldn't stop the laugh that rumbled out at her startled look.

He tore into his lunch and watched with satisfaction as she consumed hers. They were polishing off the last of the salad when she glanced furtively at him.

'Do your brothers know that I'm…pregnant?'

'No, I haven't told them yet. Ideally, I'd like to announce the pregnancy and our intended marriage at the same time.'

Her gaze slid from his and he forced himself not to react. 'Um…okay.'

Feeling the restlessness that had taken up residence in his body clamouring through him again, he got up. 'Time for the full tour, then I'll let you get to work.'

CHAPTER ELEVEN

THE DAYS PASSED in a blur of activity and by the time Sakis and Brianna arrived on Thursday afternoon, Perla had everything in place in anticipation for when the VIP guests arrived on Sunday.

Unlike their first meeting, Sakis Pantelides's smile was openly friendly if a lot speculative. She read the same keen interest in Brianna's stunning blue eyes.

'Ari tells me you're putting on a spectacular list of events for the opening.'

'He should know. He's been slave-driving me up the wall with his endless demands for perfection. Perhaps now you're here, you can get him out of my hair for an hour or two.'

Brianna laughed as she hugged her husband's arm. 'That seems to be a common trait amongst the Pantelides men. They never know when to leave well enough alone and trust us women to get on with it.'

Her husband sent her an indulgent smile so full of adoration Perla's heart snagged in her chest then dropped to her stomach in envy.

'Asking me to leave you alone is like asking the lark to stop singing first thing in the morning. It's simply impossible, *agapita*.'

A blush raced up her face and the powerful passion that arced between them made Perla look away.

Sakis turned to her. 'Where is my brother, anyway?'

'He's getting the scull ready for your rowing session this afternoon. I believe he wants to hit the water the moment Theo arrives,' she said.

What she didn't add was that Ari had been growing steadily more restless as the days had progressed this week. This morning they'd snapped at each other over breakfast, after which he'd disappeared with a curt instruction for her to take things easy. Or else…

God, why had she deluded herself into thinking they'd learn *nice* things about each other this week? So far she'd learned that even though he'd stated that he was happy for her to carry on working, he intended to keep a close eye on her at all times.

She only had to think of a need for it to materialise. Meals and snacks appeared minutes before cravings hit and there was always someone with a golf buggy, a wide-brimmed hat or a cool drink nearby.

That he also fully intended to extract a *yes* from her as soon as he could was also clear. As for the heated looks he'd sent her whenever she walked into his presence…

She shook her head and focused to find two pairs of eyes trained on her. 'Um…the concierge's assistant will escort you to your villa and I'll let Ari know you're here.'

With a smile she knew was a little strained, she walked away. After triple-checking everything on her list and clucking with impatience because she knew she was daw-dling, she jumped into her allotted SUV and drove down to their villa.

Ari was in the middle of a phone call when she walked into the cool, brightly lit living room. He advanced until he stood in front of her but carried on his conversation, one hand idly playing with her loose hair.

She'd started their stay by wearing it up but Ari had

found every opportunity to free it until she'd given up. There were some fights that just weren't worth the effort.

She didn't follow his conversation because it was conducted in rapid-fire Greek. But even if he'd spoken English, she wouldn't have followed it because of the feverish emotions coursing through her at his touch.

Each day since they arrived at the resort he'd laid assault to her senses like this, touching her whenever she was within a few feet, grazing his fingers over her stomach in a possessive move that sent her emotions into free fall every time. That had been when he wasn't snapping at her.

To say their time together so far had been a roller coaster would be an understatement.

She heard him end the call as his thumb traced over her mouth. Slowly he lowered the phone and his head began to descend.

'Were you looking for me?' he murmured.

'Yes. Your brother and Brianna are here.'

'I know. Sakis called me ten minutes ago.' His head moved closer. 'Theo is also on his way from the airport. He'll be here in less than ten minutes. He wants to row straight away so I've had the equipment sent down to the water.'

His lips flitted over hers and she tried to pull back. 'Ari…don't.'

He stiffened slightly. 'I've been a bear towards you all week. Let me apologise,' he coaxed in that deep, hypnotic voice.

Her breath gushed out of her as he sealed her lips with his. Their mingled groan echoed around the room, then faded away to be replaced with harsh breathing. They strained towards each other until she could feel the solid imprint of his body and the even more rigid outline of his arousal against her belly.

The need that tore through her made her spear her hands

through his hair. With a deep groan he picked her up and carried her to the sofa without breaking their kiss.

He was kissing his way down her neck when she finally came to her senses.

'No. Stop!'

He raised his head slowly, his eyes sizzling pools of need and frustration. 'Why the hell should I?' he growled.

'We can't…you can't use sex to apologise. Saying you're sorry is enough.'

A mirthless smile tilted one corner of his mouth. 'You really are naïve, aren't you?'

She blushed fiercely. 'Perhaps, but I also know that sex can confuse issues. You've been grumpy for days because you weren't getting your way. Sex will not achieve what you want.'

His eyes gleamed as he reared back. 'But it will make me feel a whole lot better. And you can deny it all you want but it will make you feel better too.'

She couldn't deny it but neither was she going to admit it. She sat up and straightened her clothes. The black sundress wasn't exactly appropriate for the tropics but it seemed black was all she'd packed. 'Anyway, we can't. We have guests who require our attention. But don't think I haven't noticed that every time I try to get you to talk to me like we agreed, you find something else for me to do!'

He stiffened and jerked to his feet. 'You're asking a man who has kept his innermost thoughts hidden most of his life to bare his soul, *glikia mou*. It's not as simple as hitting play on a machine,' he said, his voice charged with the echo of painful memory.

Her heart twisted for him, but she pressed on. Deep inside, she'd begun to hope that this would be the way to reach him, the way they could both move forward and begin the tentative steps to building a solid platform for their child.

'I know that. Of course I know that. But, as difficult as it is, we have to give it a shot, Ari.'

Slowly, he inhaled. Then he nodded and held out his hand to her. 'We will. Before we leave here. Now, you can come and watch me row my sexual frustration away. That will be your entertainment for the afternoon.'

She let herself be pulled up and felt some of her trepidation melt away. Immediately, thoughts that had hovered on the edge of her mind crowded in. Thoughts that involved whether she and Ari could make a marriage work despite all their baggage. That he seemed to believe it was possible had slowly eroded her own scepticism as the week had crept on.

The way Ari had taken care of her since her pregnancy came to light, she didn't doubt now that he would provide a parent's utter devotion and stability. And perhaps, over time, that devotion would spill onto her.

Her heart lurched painfully.

Morgan had shaken the foundation of her beliefs. But she'd discovered in the last few weeks that he hadn't totally annihilated her self-confidence. It was that renewed self-confidence that made her want even better for herself and her child.

At least, with Ari, she knew the lay of the land going in. The events of his past might mean he never cared deeply for her. So the only thing that she needed to be sure of was whether she could live without the love she'd been so desperate for the first time round.

Before we leave here...

She pushed away the lingering trepidation and concentrated on getting in the electric buggy that would take them down to the water, although it was hard not to keep glancing at Ari's bare thighs as he drove.

The youngest Pantelides was already on the waterfront with Sakis when they arrived.

Theo Pantelides was as tall as Ari but broader-shouldered with the same jet-black hair, although his bore no hint of the grey sprinkled at Ari's temples.

Equally as gorgeous, his eyes were several shades lighter than Ari's hazel and held the same speculation as Sakis's when they rested on her.

'So I finally meet the woman who's caused quite the stir at Pantelides HQ.'

'Theo…' Ari growled a mild warning.

Theo's smile was unrepentant as he held out a closed fist to her. A smile twitching at her lips, she touched her knuckles to his in a bemused fist bump.

'About time someone shook him out of his doldrums,' he added with a wink.

Sakis laughed and Brianna grinned but Ari's narrow-eyed stare held no mirth.

'Tell me you're ready to get your ass whipped and I'll happily oblige you,' he said through clenched teeth.

'Any time, old man.'

Ari's jaw clenched harder but the hand he clamped on his brother's shoulder to push him towards the boat was so affectionate it brought a lump to Perla's throat. He disappeared into the specially built boathouse and emerged minutes later dressed in a dark gold rowing suit that moulded to his body.

Perla tried not to stare at the perfect specimen of man that was Arion Pantelides but when he grabbed the end of the scull and hefted it over his shoulders, she struggled to get air past her restricted throat into her lungs.

Purely for self-preservation, she looked away. Then immediately looked back.

'God, don't even try to resist that. Don't get me wrong, I think Sakis is the best-looking of the bunch, but the three of them together like this, even I find it hard to breathe, never mind keep my eyes solely on my husband,' Brianna muttered.

She grinned at Perla's shocked laugh, fanned herself and moved closer to the edge of the viewing bench to watch the men set their scull on the water and climb in.

Sakis took the front seat, Theo the middle and Ari the last. They sank their oars into the water. Theo rolled his shoulders and laughed when Ari admonished him to be still.

Their chests rose and fell in rhythm, once, twice. Then they struck away from shore in flawless synchronicity.

'Wow.'

'I know, right? I've watched them row many times but I never get over how perfect they look together.'

Again Perla felt that tiny pang of jealousy. But she couldn't help but wonder if this could be her baby's life if she agreed to what Ari wanted. Her child, and by definition she, could be a part of this…togetherness. She didn't have to be on the outside looking in like she had her whole life. She could give her baby a ready-made family who would cherish him or her.

She watched the men row, her eyes continually drawn to Ari, who now had a grin on his face despite the determination in his eyes.

'Ari seems different.'

Perla jumped and turned to Brianna to find those incisive blue eyes on her. 'Um…is he?'

Brianna nodded. 'At the funeral he seemed ready to smash everyone's head in. Today he looks as if the only person whose head is in danger is Theo, which, considering that's par for the course, is worth mentioning.'

'And you think I have something to do with that?'

'Definitely. You and…that, I'm guessing.'

She followed Brianna's gaze to where her hand rested on her stomach. With a gasp, Perla snatched her hand away but not before Brianna gave her a sympathetic smile.

'I…no one knows,' she said hurriedly.

'Don't worry, your secret's safe with me.' Her hand rose to rest over her own stomach. 'I have a secret of my own. Although I have a feeling it won't remain a secret for long. Sakis has been bursting to tell the whole world. But I'm guessing he'll start with his brothers for now.'

'Congratulations,' Perla offered. Then curiosity made her blurt, 'How do you feel?'

'Frankly? Scared out of my mind. I didn't have the best of childhoods so I don't have a role model to fall back on. Sakis tells me I'll be a great mother but I think he's hopelessly biased.' Her smile was tinged with anxiety but full of love as her gaze swung back to the men. 'What about you?'

'Honestly, between Ari's determination to get me to marry him and the job I have to do here, I haven't had time to be scared, but—'

'Ari asked you to marry him?' Brianna's eyes were wide with surprise. 'That's huge! I presume he's told you what happened to his wife?'

Perla nodded.

'He wouldn't have made the decision easily.'

'He only wants to marry because of his child.'

Brianna frowned. 'I don't think so. I don't want to scare you but the reality is that every one in four pregnancies ends in miscarriage. If all he wanted was to give the baby respectability, he'd have waited until it was born to ask you to marry him.'

Perla shook her head, refusing to even begin to hope. 'Besides the baby, there's really nothing like that between us.'

'But there is *something*. There's incredible chemistry. Don't knock the power of great sex.'

She gasped. 'That's what he said,' she said then blushed as she realised what she'd let slip.

Brianna laughed. 'I knew there was an alpha horn dog

beneath all that suave Pantelides exterior. Now let's go and cheer our boys home before I give in to the urge to ask for details I have no business knowing.'

She jumped up and headed towards the waterfront. Perla followed at a slower pace and got there in time to see the brothers embrace at the news of Brianna's pregnancy.

Ari's gaze drifted to her as Sakis pulled his wife close and kissed her. His gaze dropped to her stomach but he said nothing, only helped his brothers stow the scull and oars in the boathouse before they all piled into the buggies to head back to their villas.

Dinner that evening turned into a family celebration, one that hammered home to Perla just what she could be missing out on if she refused Ari's proposal. All through the evening his eyes kept straying to her, the intent in their depths clear and determined.

By the time she excused herself and returned to her suite, her mind was in turmoil.

That turmoil continued for the next three days. Thankfully, she had no time to think.

From the moment the first luxury SUV rolled in with the guests her days turned manic. She barely saw Ari because he was equally busy entertaining guests in the plushly equipped casino while she dealt with organising the guests and directing the activities she'd planned for them.

She was busy sorting out the sky-diving group and pairing them with their instructors and guests on the last day when she heard a familiar voice.

She looked up to see Selena Hamilton heading towards her.

Perla's mouth dropped open before she could stop herself.

'So, what do you think?' Selena trilled, patting her new russet-coloured curls.

Perla forced a smile. 'You look great.'

Selena's smile slipped a fraction. 'I'm glad you think so. Roger thinks I look awful. What does he know, right?' She forced a laugh that didn't touch her curiously over-bright eyes.

Roger Hamilton strolled in at that moment. He completely ignored his wife and, grabbing Perla, kissed her on both cheeks.

'Sign me up for whatever you're organising, darling! I'm all yours.'

Behind him, Ari entered the room and froze to a halt. The thunderous look in his eyes made her stomach flip but she managed to keep the smile on her face as he walked to where she stood. Seeing the look he directed at Roger, she glared at him and shook her head once. His jaw clenched but he exchanged pleasantries until the instructor called for them to suit up.

Ari's hand slid over her nape and tilted her head up to meet his descending kiss. It was hard and quick. 'You take care of Hamilton, *glikia mou*. Or I will,' he muttered. Then he was gone.

Breathing a sigh of relief, she turned around just as Selena returned to her side. Before she could utter a word, Selena grabbed her arm. 'I think Roger is going to leave me,' she whispered fiercely.

'Are you sure?'

Her frenzied nodding made her curls bounce wildly. 'I think he's having an affair.' Her scarlet-painted lips wobbled and her eyes widened.

'You could be wrong…'

'What if I'm not? I can't live without him. He's everything I've ever wanted but I can see him slipping away from me.' Tears filled her green eyes.

'Selena, I don't think you should go sky-diving if you're feeling like that.'

She swiped her tears with perfectly manicured fingers.

'Nonsense. Roger wants to go sky-diving so I'm going with him.'

But a glance at Roger, who was busy flirting with a female instructor, suggested he had no interest in what his wife wanted. Perla glanced at Selena again and worry gnawed at her. Selena's glazed eyes suggested she was under the influence of something other than unhappiness. But there was no diplomatic way to ask without causing offence.

Gnawing at her bottom lip, she followed the guests out to the air-conditioned buses that would take them to the airstrip. Then climbed in with them.

'*Where the hell is she?*' Ari demanded for the fifth time. The concierge manager paled and reached for his phone again.

'I'm sorry, sir, but we think she may have joined one of the guest events.'

'You *think*? Try her phone again.'

The manager hurried to do his bidding. When he shook his head regretfully, Ari curbed the need to punch a hole in the desk.

'Giving your staff hell?' came a droll voice from behind him.

'Not now, Sakis.'

'Why? What's wrong?'

'I'm trying to find Perla. No one's seen her in the last hour.'

'And this is worrying because…?'

Ari pursed his lips. 'She's supposed to be at the villa, having lunch.'

He looked up as the assistant manager hurried forward. 'Mr Pantelides, I've just been told by one of the drivers that Mrs Lowell joined the sky-diving guests.'

For a moment, he couldn't compute the information. 'She *what?*'

The voices that responded were drowned out by the blood thundering in his ears. When his arm was grabbed in a firm hold and he was propelled down a hallway, he did not protest.

He heard a door shut behind him seconds before Sakis pushed him into a seat.

'Talk to me, Ari. What the hell is going on?'

He speared both hands into his hair and tried to stem the terror rushing through him. 'It's probably nothing. She can't possibly have gone *sky-diving…*'

'Yeah…that's what your man said.'

He tried to swallow. 'Well…she can't have.'

'Why not? If she's qualified—'

'Sakis. She's pregnant.'

His brother's mouth dropped open seconds before the colour leached from his face. They both leapt for the phone on his desk but Ari was quicker. 'I need your fastest driver out front in the next ten seconds.'

Sakis wrenched the door open. They passed Theo in the hallway and one dark look from Ari and his brother stemmed whatever wisecrack he'd been about to utter.

In silence, he fell into step beside them.

The journey to the airstrip was the longest of Ari's life.

Horrific scenarios he couldn't stem tumbled through his mind and the fingers that continually clawed through his hair shook uncontrollably.

Brightly coloured parachutes slowly loomed into view as their SUV roared down towards the designated area on the edge of the parachute landing site.

Theos, surely she hadn't…

Ari was out of the car before it'd come to a screeching halt. He heard the thunder of running feet behind him as his brothers followed him.

One by one he watched the eight parachutes drop lower, his heart hammering as he rushed from one to the other.

None of them were Perla.

'Ari?' He whirled round to find her stepping down from the air-conditioned bus, Selena Hamilton following behind her. Relief was followed closely by volcanic anger. This time, there were no feet thundering behind him as he sprinted to the bus.

He skidded to a halt in front of her. She started to speak. '*Not. One. Word.*'

Her mouth dropped open. Without giving her a chance to respond, he swung her up in his arms and marched her to the SUV parked a hundred yards away.

'Out,' he growled. The driver jumped out and held out the keys. He placed her in the passenger seat, secured her seat belt and ignored his brothers as he got in and slammed the door.

'I'm guessing we have to find our own ride back?' Theo quipped to Sakis.

Ari turned the ignition and peeled out of the airstrip, his heartbeat a deafening roar in his ears.

The journey to the villa took less than ten minutes. This time he didn't help her out. He headed straight into the villa and sought out the butler.

'I want you and your staff to take a break. Don't return until I tell you to.'

He returned to the living room to see the staff hurrying out and Perla standing in the hallway, her face pale and her teeth worrying her lower lip.

'Ari, please. You're scaring me.'

He threw the car keys across the room and watched them hit the wall and bounce on the marble floor.

'*I'm* scaring *you?*'

Her arched brows spiked upward. 'Can we try less snarling and more coherence?'

'You left the resort without telling anyone, without tell-ing *me*. I thought you'd gone *sky-diving!*'

She started to laugh, then stopped. 'Wait, seriously? Why on earth would I? Anyway, I texted you to tell you that I didn't think Selena Hamilton should be on her own. I think she might have taken something. Luckily, I eventu-ally managed to talk her out of sky-diving—'

'I didn't receive a text and you seem to be missing the point here.'

'Which is what, exactly? That I have to report my every move to you now? Well, you'll be happy to know that, aside from talking his wife down from a possibly fatal jump, I warned Roger Hamilton that if his eyes strayed to my cleav-age one more time I'd gouge them out. I was very diplo-matic about it, of course.' She smiled sweetly. 'Was there anything else you wanted to know?'

Ari couldn't believe his ears. He'd been scared out of his wits. And she was giving him sass. 'Are you serious?'

He watched her walk towards him until he could smell her. He raked a hand through his hair as she tilted her head and regarded him with steady eyes.

'Ari, you're seriously overreacting here. You can't molly-coddle me through this pregnancy. I know what this child means to you but I won't be wrapped up in cotton wool until the baby's born'

He whirled from her and paced to the window. 'You think I'm only concerned about the baby?'

'Come on, be honest—would you be this worked up if it was just me on that plane?'

The air drained out of him and he reeled from the ac-cusation thrown at his feet. He opened his mouth but no words came out. Because the realisation that was dawn-ing on him—had been dawning on him all week—felt too overwhelming to make sense of.

'Perla…'

'You know what I was thinking when I was on the bus?'

Slowly, he shook his head.

'I started off thinking perhaps I should count my blessings. My first husband was physically and emotionally unavailable but I *could* graduate to a physically available but emotionally unavailable one. And maybe, if this one doesn't work out, I might strike it lucky third time round—'

'There won't be a next time. If you marry me, you'll be stuck with me for this lifetime and the next.'

'Let's not get ahead of ourselves here. What I didn't say was that the thought of an emotionally unavailable husband would never work for me. Not now. I'm learning very fast that I'm an all-in kind of girl. So I'm not willing to risk my future happiness on a man who won't open up to me even a little.'

The emotion that slashed through him made his gut clench hard. He couldn't breathe. Could only remain still as she stared defiantly back at him, dared him to react to the gauntlet she'd thrown down.

He opened his mouth; no words came out.

He shook his head, damning himself for ten kinds of a fool when pain rolled over her face.

'Or you could just get lucky. Since you're so determined to hammer home just how incompetent I am at taking care of myself, maybe I'll just die and save you the trouble.'

Perla heard the words tumble from her lips and felt shock bolt through her.

Ari's face whitened and he actually stumbled back a few steps. Horror gripped her at how callous she'd been.

'Oh, God, I'm sorry.' She rushed to him but he flung out his hand to stave her off. 'Arion, I didn't mean it.'

His hand slowly lowered and he stared at her as if she was a monster. Perla's insides shredded as he took another step back.

'I'm sorry,' she repeated. Her stomach went into free fall when he remained silent. 'Please, say something.'

'Get out.'

'No, Ari. Please—'

He jerked forward and caught her to him. The kiss he delivered was harsh and pain-filled and devastatingly breathtaking. But it lasted less than ten seconds before he pushed her away and strode from the room.

She refused to shed another tear even though her throat thickened painfully with the need for release.

Going to her bedroom, she sank onto the bed, tried to make sense of what had just happened.

Pain had made her lash out in the worst possible way and strike Ari where it'd hurt the most. She'd gone too far. She had to fix it.

She rose, smoothed her hand down her dress and left her room.

He was in his study, his shoulders rigid, fists clenched as he stared at the ocean.

'Ari, we need to talk.'

He stiffened but didn't turn around. Grateful for not being thrown out, she stepped further into the room.

'We've both been through a lot. And our past is always going to be there. You were taking care of me the only way you knew how. I shouldn't have said what I said.'

He remained silent for a full minute. Then he turned. 'You want to know about my past? About Sofia?'

Heart in her throat, she nodded.

'My father fought for years to stay out of jail. He used lawyers and manipulated the system to try to escape justice. But the authorities were equally determined. The economy was in the toilet and he'd been lining his pockets with ill-gotten gains. They were slavering to make an example of him. Just when I thought it was ending, some other charge would be added to the list and the circus would begin all over again. The only people who mattered were my brothers and my mother. But even I couldn't protect them from the cruelty of the media and their so-called friends. Watching them suffer made me hate my father even more. Then he was convicted. Finally, I thought I could get some closure for my family. Before we could take a breath, he was gone.'

Perla frowned. 'What do you mean, gone?'

'He died in jail months into his thirty-year sentence.'

'How?'

'He caught pneumonia and refused treatment.' He gave a sharp laugh. 'After the chaos he'd caused, he went out with barely a whimper.'

'And you felt cheated?'

'I felt more than cheated. I wanted to hunt him down in the afterlife and strangle him all over again. I went on a month-long bender. I was on a very fast downward spiral when I met Sofia.' His eyelids descended, veiling his expression. But she saw his hands form fists. 'She…saved me.'

Perla's breath stopped. 'Oh…'

When he looked up again, his eyes were the darkest green, shadowed with pain. 'She brought me back from the brink of rage and despair. And I rewarded her by ignoring all the danger signs.'

'Surely, she must have known the risks of getting pregnant if she had a weak heart?'

'She knew. But she was convinced she would survive it. She was an eternal optimist.'

'Ari, you can't keep blaming yourself for what happened to Sofia. You got her the medical care she needed and she made a choice. The outcome was unfortunate but—'

'I could've insisted. I could've—'

'Ordered her about, just like you're trying to do to me?'

Colour slashed his cheeks and he looked away. 'You

can't control everything, Ari. Sometimes you have to let go and let things play out.'

'Is that what you're suggesting I do with you? Let you run around until something unforgivable happens?'

'You're assuming that you're the only one who cares for the welfare of this baby. But I want this baby more than anything else.' It wasn't strictly true. There was *one* thing she wanted equally as badly. 'But in order to give this baby what it needs, we need to put the past behind us and move on or it'll keep tripping us up, dictating our lives.'

'Move on. Just like that?' he asked through gritted teeth.

'No, not just like that. It's hard, I know, but I'm willing to give it a try.'

'You're willing to try when you're pregnant with my child but can't even move on from wearing funeral black every day?'

Shocked, she stared down at her clothes. The idea that her all-black wardrobe was sending a particular message hadn't even crossed her mind.

'Moving on isn't as easy as you think, is it, Perla?' he queried in a soft voice lined with steel. 'Come and talk to me about moving on when you change the colour of your wardrobe.'

'I'm talking to you now. And I didn't choose this wardrobe. You gave me a little more than a day to join you in Miami when I started this job. The stylist knew my history and she assumed I'd want to be decked out in black all the time because I was a widow, and frankly I didn't think it mattered in the grand scheme of things.'

His jaw tightened. 'It mattered.'

'They're just clothes, Ari. The fact of the matter is I want love. I wanted it when I married Morgan and I want it now.'

His gaze lasered on her. 'Why did you stay married to him after you found out he was gay?'

Ice welled through her veins. 'He told me on our wedding night that he'd married me because he didn't want anyone to find out. Especially not his parents.'

'The ones you continue to look after?'

She gave a slight nod. 'They worshipped him but he knew they wouldn't accept his sexual orientation. And… he knew how much I cared for them. I'd told him about my childhood and the foster system and he…he told me I could still have a family, provided…'

'You kept his secret?' he finished harshly.

'Yes. I begged him to come out. I even fooled myself into thinking I was getting through to him last Christmas.'

Ari's gaze sharpened. 'How?'

'He told me he was thinking about telling his parents. That he just needed time to sort out a few things first. Now, I realise he was probably planning something else.'

'Something like what?'

She gave a jagged laugh. 'Oh, I don't know, maybe he was planning to emigrate to Timbuktu? Or New Zealand? He took a bribe to crash Sakis's tanker so, whatever it was, it must have been worth the risk to him.'

He walked slowly towards her until he stood in front of her. His eyes were still shadowed but the agony had lessened. 'He took advantage of your kind heart and your unfortunate past to prey on you. The bastard didn't deserve you. You know that, don't you?'

'I know but it doesn't mean the need I have has abated. It's still there, Ari. The need to be loved. But I know you can't give me that. Am I right?'

Hazel eyes darkened and he looked away.

She tried to ignore the sharp stab of pain in her heart and forced herself to continue. 'I told you I'd make a decision once we talked.'

He tensed. 'And have you?'

She ignored all the self-preservation signs and blurted, 'Yes, I'll marry you.'

His head snapped back. 'You will?'

She nodded. 'I can choose to live in a fantasy where I get everything I want delivered to me on a silver platter. Or I can live in the real world where I get the baby and the family I've always yearned for. Two out of three will have to be enough.'

He caught her chin and raised her head so he could look into her eyes. 'You will marry me. You're sure?' His eyes blazed with an intensity that drilled to her soul.

Nervously, she swallowed. 'I'm sure.'

He gave a single nod. 'I'll put the arrangements in place.' He headed towards the door.

'Ari?'

He looked over his shoulder.

'About…what I said earlier…'

He shook his head. 'Forget it. We have more important things to deal with now.' He strode out of the room without another word.

Shaky legs carried her to the window as the tears she'd fought so hard against slid down her cheeks.

Against the stunning backdrop, the sun blazed down, uncaring that she'd given Ari the answer he'd been clamouring for, and yet she felt as if she was still slipping down a slope, destined for failure and heartache.

Her hand drifted over her stomach. For better or worse, she'd made the decision for her and her baby. She had to learn to live with it.

Three Pantelides jets flew out of Bermuda three days later, all headed for Greece and Ari's private island off the coast of Santorini.

Ari had announced that morning over breakfast that they were to be married in two days at his island home.

The news had been greeted with joy from Brianna but with more restraint from the two brothers. That neither of them looked surprised told her they'd been fully aware of the reason for Ari's mad dash to the sky-diving site yesterday.

Perla took the first opportunity to escape to the cabin bedroom. Ari was busy on the phone, presumably putting the arrangements he'd told her about in place.

The irony of it didn't escape her.

She was an events organiser who didn't even have a say in her own wedding. At this moment she didn't even know who would be attending; whether it would be a large ceremony or a hole in the wall with a priest and his brothers as witnesses.

She fell into a deep, disturbed sleep and woke to find Ari next to her. He was wide awake, staring down at her with a look on his face that stopped her breath.

Before she could speak, he cupped her face in his hands and slanted his mouth over hers. It was rough. It was deep. And her soul sang with the feverish joy of it. She was completely unprepared when he wrenched his lips away seconds later.

'Arion?'

In silence, he climbed out of bed and began to undress.

Perla watched him, mesmerised by the dark beauty of him and the stark need in his eyes that so echoed the one in her heart.

She shook as he came back and stretched out next to her. Naked, gloriously aroused, his eyes intent on hers.

'Do you really think we can move on from the past?' he grated out, his voice little more than a whisper.

An egg-sized lump wedged in her throat. 'We can work at it, give it everything we have. Brianna told me she didn't have a smooth childhood either.'

'She didn't.'

'And I don't think Sakis escaped your family's devastation but they seem incredibly happy now.'

He continued to stare at her, his eyes glinting with a sheen that made her heart twist for him.

She didn't utter a word when he reached for her, slid down the zip of the light grey dress she'd bought from the resort shop that morning, and pushed the straps off her shoulders. Her panties and bra came next. Then he untied her hair from its loose knot and spread it over his pillow.

He kissed her mouth, her neck, her breasts, all the way to the heart of her, each touch, each kiss making her tremble and moan, and fight back scalding tears.

With just his mouth he brought her to a shuddering climax, then kissed his way back up her body.

Then he tilted her head up to meet his gaze.

'What you said…about dying…take it back. Take it back now, Perla,' he commanded, his eyes dark with torment, his voice gruff with pain.

Her hand settled on his chest, felt his heart thunder unevenly beneath her touch. 'I take it back. I never should've said that.'

He entered her with a guttural groan that filled the room. With each thrust her heart filled with emotions she dare not let out, emotions she'd always dreamed of voicing to that one special person. The knowledge that they wouldn't be well-received made her bite her lip.

He hooked his arms under her knees and surged deeper inside.

Ecstasy mushroomed through her. 'Arion!'

The sound of his name on her lips seemed to shatter him. Caught in the vicious web of passion, he climaxed with a tormented groan, brutally ripped from his soul.

It took several minutes for their heartbeats to slow, for total silence to return to the cabin. But just when she thought he'd drifted off to sleep, he turned towards her.

'We may not love each other but I promise to take care

of you, and to care for you. And I will guarantee you this. Every night. Every day. For the rest of our lives.'

Her heart lurched. Would that be enough?

It didn't matter. It was too late. Because she knew without a shadow of a doubt that she was in love with Arion Pantelides.

CHAPTER TWELVE

SANTORINI WAS JUST as magical as she remembered, even viewing it from onboard Ari's immense yacht moored half a mile away from the capital, Fira.

Far from thinking she would be spending the day before her wedding in Ari's villa, he'd brought her straight to his yacht once they'd landed.

Granted, the luxury that seemed an extension of the Pantelides name was everywhere her eyes touched.

But the feeling that she wasn't good enough to spend time in his family home refused to leave her. It didn't help that Brianna had been roped into keeping her company and was determined to cheer her up. It also didn't help that another stylist had turned up that morning with three full rails of brightly coloured designer clothes.

In a fit of anger and misery, Perla had sent the stylist away. She was perfectly well-equipped to choose her own clothes. Except now she refused to wear black or the grey dress she'd bought before they left Bermuda.

Leaving the suite that seemed to close in on her, she went along the wide galley and knocked on the door.

Brianna answered with a smile. 'I was just coming to find you. Oh, I thought you were getting dressed?' she said as she took in Perla's silk dressing gown.

'I was, but everything I have in my wardrobe is black.

I was wondering whether I could borrow something from you?'

Brianna's smile widened, and she stepped back. 'Of course. Help yourself.' She waved her towards the walk-in closet. 'And shoes too, if you want. I think we're the same size.'

Perla gaped at the sheer number of clothes, her eyes widening as she spotted some seriously expensive labels.

'Yeah, it's something you're going to have to get used to. I sent my stylist away a few times in the beginning too. Then I realised I was just delaying the inevitable. Our lives are too busy to accommodate spur of the moment shopping trips, and things will only get worse time-wise once the babies are born, especially if you want to continue working.'

Perla bit her lip. 'I don't know what will happen. I don't know where we'll live or even if we'll live together. Because Ari has chosen not to discuss it with me.' Tears surged in her throat and she whirled away from Brianna's concerned stare. Blindly, she reached for the first thing that came to hand and pulled out a burnished orange slip dress. 'This one?'

Brianna nodded. 'It's the perfect thing to go shopping in.'

Perla froze. 'Shopping?'

'You're getting married tomorrow. The least you can do is invest in some knock-out lingerie that'll blow Ari's mind. A woman can't have too many weapons in her arsenal.'

'That depends on what she's fighting for,' Perla murmured. Dropping her dressing gown, she slipped the dress over her head. The cotton felt cool against her skin and the colour lifted her spirits a fraction.

'Don't give up so easily, Perla. You've come too far to stop now. If you want Ari, make him stand up and take notice. Sometimes it's the only way to win against strong-willed men.' Her expression held a determination Perla couldn't help but admire. 'Are you ready?'

With a last look in the mirror, she pursed her lips. 'Almost.' She dashed back to her room and dug through her handbag until she found it. Uncapping the scarlet lipstick she'd worn the night she met Ari, she boldly smoothed it over her lips.

Brianna was waiting for her on the deck. Her eyes widened, then her smile grew. '*Now*, you're definitely ready. Let's go.'

The shops weren't as sophisticated as those on the mainland but they provided an eclectic mix that satisfied her immediate needs.

Perla bought two sundresses, one yellow, one green, and a pair of low-heeled sandals. Against her protests, Brianna dragged her to a wedding shop with every intention of forcing her to buy lingerie.

But Perla froze as she spotted a dress on the hanger. The simple cream Greek goddess-style dress could pass for evening-wear or wedding dress. The front was plain and sleeveless and its halter neck design would keep her cool in the Santorini heat. But it was the back that took her breath away.

The lace pattern travelled down the middle of the back and held the skirt that hugged the hips and flared to the floor in a tiny train.

'Wow. With your hair caught up, that dress would look gorgeous on you. Provided, of course, you want to look fabulous for your wedding day,' Brianna teased.

Curbing her indecision, Perla bought the dress. 'Can we go now?'

'Just one more stop.' They went two doors away and entered the most unique shop Perla had ever seen. Scent candles in all shapes and colours stood on pedestals while incense burned from assorted sticks. 'Sakis calls this my *juju* shop. I tend to get my way a lot when I burn a few candles on certain nights.' She laughed.

Forcing a smile, Perla felt herself sinking deeper into misery.

Leaving Brianna to make her selection, she browsed the shop. As she made her way to the front, she met a woman in her early thirties. The hostile look she sent her stopped Perla in her tracks.

A torrent of Greek followed, to which Perla shook her head and shrugged.

Brianna turned sharply and frowned. The woman continued to speak, her voice growing louder.

'I'm sorry, I don't understand.'

Brianna rushed forward and grasped her hand. 'Come on, let's go.'

'What's she saying?'

Brianna shook her head. 'It doesn't matter.' She hurried out of the shop.

'Yes, it does. You know what she was saying.'

'My Greek isn't that great,' she said, but Perla caught her guilty look.

She came to a dead stop on the pavement. 'But you understood enough. Tell me, please.'

Brianna's lips pursed and a look of unease crossed her face. 'The whole island knows that Ari is getting married again. His wife, Sofia, was from a large family here in Santorini. I think that woman was her cousin. They know he's marrying a redhead and I guess she thought it was you.'

'Well, she was right. What exactly did she say?'

Brianna grimaced. 'I think she said… God, if I get this wrong and Ari finds out, not even Sakis can save me.'

Ice trailed up Perla's spine. 'What did she say?' she demanded.

'She said Ari and Sofia's love was a match made in heaven; the love of the century. She said…'

'What?'

'She said Ari will never love you the way he loved her.'

The sob that rose from her soul shattered her heart on its way up. She saw Brianna pale and reach for her hand but Perla shook her away. 'If I'd understood that was what she was saying, I could've saved her the trouble. I already know Ari doesn't love me. He never will.'

'You need to get over here, fast.'

Fear spiked through Ari at Sakis's tone. 'What's wrong? Is Perla okay?'

'Yes, she's fine physically but something happened when she went out with Brianna… Look, just get yourself over here, pronto, *ne?*'

Ari ended the call and glanced at the chaos all around him. Carpenters and decorators rushed to do his bidding, to set up the place for what most couples would deem the most important day of their lives.

But, deep down inside, he knew the most important day of his life had come and gone. The most important day of his life had happened when he'd thought he was too mired in guilt and grief to ever function properly.

Even when he'd looked up from his drink at Macdonald Hall and his world had shifted he'd refused to acknowledge the importance of it.

She's fine physically…

His breath shuddered out of him as he grabbed his jacket and ran for the door of his villa. Every day since he'd met Perla Lowell had been important but he'd been too damned afraid to admit it to himself.

Well, it was time to stop hiding and dare to be as brave as Perla had been. It was time to take care of the single most precious thing in his life *emotionally.*

He reached his yacht in record time. Sweat poured off his temples as he flew down the stairs, barely acknowledging Brianna's anxious look or Sakis ushering her away as he headed down the galley towards his suite.

He turned the doorknob and found it unyielding. He bit back a curse and swallowed down the fear climbing into his throat.

'Perla, open the door.'

'No.' Even through the closed door he heard the pain in her voice and his chest tightened.

'*Glikia mou*, open the door now. I'm not going anywhere until you do.'

'Go back to the island where you belong. There's nothing for you here.'

'You're wrong. Everything I want is right here. This is where I belong.'

The silence that greeted him tore at his insides. He leaned his forehead against the door and fought the urge to smash it in. 'Open the door, Perla. *Please.*'

Another minute went by, then he heard the scrape of the lock.

The moment it opened a crack, he slipped inside. The sight of her tear-ravaged face eviscerated him. He started to reach for her but she pulled away sharply. He clenched his fist to stop from grabbing for her. He didn't like the hollowness filling his soul.

'Tell me what happened today.' He'd already heard the gist of it from Sakis when he'd called from the car after leaving the villa.

'It doesn't matter what happened. I thought I could do it, Ari, but I can't.'

His heart plunged to the bottom of his feet. 'You can't do what?'

'Marry you. I thought I could but I can't.'

'Not even for the sake of our child?' He hated to play that card, but he was desperate.

The misery when she glanced up at him made his heart bleed.

'I thought I could but I will not come second best for anyone.'

He frowned. 'Second best? Who told you you were second best?'

'No one needed to. I have eyes and a brain. You brought me here and you stashed me on your boat. Out of sight, out of mind. The moment I ventured off the boat I was reminded why I'll never be good enough for you.'

'What the hell are you talking about?'

'Sofia, your wife, will always be the love of your life. The woman at the shop called it the love story of the century. I thought I could live with that, but I can't…'

He ventured forward and exhaled in relief when she didn't cringe away from him. More than anything he wanted to reach for her but he stopped himself. She could bolt, and that would destroy him.

'I loved her, I won't deny that. She saved me from a dark, bleak place and brought me back from the brink. But I wasn't the best husband to her that I could be. I failed to save her the way she'd saved me. I should've been stronger for her sake.'

'Every time you talk about her, I hear the pain in your voice.'

'Because, despite knowing that she had the best medical care, a part of me still feels I let her down by not insisting she take the right advice.'

'So it's guilt that's been eating at you?'

'It was before, but not so much any more. As much as I regret what happened, I can't undo the past. You've taught me that I need to look to the future, to let go of things I can't change. And I have to believe that Sofia would want that for me too.'

'Then why did you stash me on the boat?' Her hurt was unmistakable.

'I'm sorry. I wanted to spare Sofia's relatives unnecessary pain, yes, but I also wanted to make sure the villa was ready for you. For our wedding. I haven't lived here for three years, and it was nowhere near as ready as I wanted it to be.'

Her fingers twisted round the tissue in her hand and his heart twisted along with it. 'But why here? We could've married anywhere else in Greece.'

He frowned. 'You don't remember what you said to me when we met?'

Confusion marred her forehead. 'What I said?'

'At Macdonald Hall, you said your first trip to Greece was to Santorini. That you'd always dreamed you'd get married here.'

Realisation dawned and her eyes grew wide.

'Yes, *glikia mou*, I wanted to give you that wish.'

'Why?'

'Because your happiness means the world to me.'

She sucked in a breath. 'Please don't say that. Please don't make me hope.'

'Why not?'

'Because you'll make me want the impossible.'

'What do you want, Perla? Tell me what you want and you might be surprised by how motivated I am to give it to you.'

When she said nothing, he ventured closer. The orange sundress she wore made her golden-hued skin glow. Unable to resist, he reached out and took her hand in his.

The shiver that coursed through her echoed through him.

'Please tell me what you want, *agape mou*.'

Green eyes rose to his. In their depths he saw courage, determination, naked longing and another emotion he hoped to God was what he imagined it to be.

'I want you. To love me.'

'Only if you love me half as much as I love you, Perla *mou*.'

She gasped. 'What?'

He kissed her knuckles and closed his eyes for a second when her fingers trembled against his lips.

'I love you. I knew from the first that what I felt for you went beyond mere desire, but I fought it because…well, you know why.'

'But on the plane you said—'

'Something stupid about us not loving each other? That was pure self-protection speaking. I thought I could have what I wanted while protecting my heart.' He shook his head. 'The truth is, I don't need to protect my heart; not from you. Yes, what I feel scared the life out of me but what you and I have also fills me with joy even while making me a little crazy. Every time I look at you, I crave you. Every time I make love to you, I want to do it all over again, immediately. It makes me insane but it also makes me feel more alive than I have in the longest time. I never want to lose you because I intend to drive myself insane for a lifetime. If what I had with Sofia is being described as the love of the century then ours will be the love story of the millennia.'

Her eyes filled with tears he didn't hesitate to kiss away. 'Oh, Arion. I thought you were doing all this for the baby.'

'When I wasn't sure you'd take me as I was I admit I tried to use our baby to sway you.'

'And I let myself be swayed because I didn't see any other way to be with you. Now I can tell you that I love you too, without being scared it'll push you away. Tell me you love me again, Arion.' Her eyes shone with a brilliance that stopped his heart.

Happiness rushed into his chest and he had no problem uttering the words. 'I love you. I wish I'd admitted that to us both sooner. But I intend to make up for lost time. You have my promise on that.'

He kissed her for a long time, only raising his head when they ran out of air.

'The house is almost ready. But you have a free hand to change anything you want before the wedding tomorrow.'

She licked lips swollen from his kisses, making him groan. 'Um, can I practise a woman's right to change her mind? Blame it on all the pregnancy hormones rushing through my body right now.'

'What do you want to change?'

She touched his face, leaned forward until their foreheads touched. Ari knew he wouldn't like what was coming but he didn't care. 'The wedding date. The venue. The guest list. *Everything?*'

She stopped his groan of protest with her mouth. And he let her.

EPILOGUE

'Is this better?'

Perla placed her hand over her swollen stomach and sighed with happiness. 'Much better. I don't even miss the fact that I can't have champagne at my own wedding.' She glanced down at her hand and watched her new platinum wedding ring gleam in the setting Bermudan sun. The flash of her heart-shaped ruby engagement ring also caught the rays as Ari lifted her hand and kissed the back of it.

'You delayed us getting married for four months then refused to wait another two until the baby was here.'

'I thought I could hold out but the thought of calling you my own got too overwhelming.'

The look that crossed his face was one she'd seen on his brother's face as he gazed at Brianna. At that time she'd envied it. Right now, she basked in it and sent a prayer of thanks for her very own fantasy coming true.

'You've owned me since the moment I saw you, wearing that lipstick you're henceforth banned from ever wearing in public again. I just didn't know it yet.'

'Better late than never, I guess.'

He laughed and they both turned when Sakis and Brianna entered with their three-week-old baby. Dimitri Pantelides was fast asleep in his father's arms, one fist curled around Sakis's forefinger.

Brianna arranged his blanket more snugly around him,

then looked up with a cheeky smile. 'Did you guys see the woman Theo came with? She's stunning!'

'But she also looks as if this is the last place she wants to be,' Sakis added, his tone displaying a keen speculation that made Ari shake his head.

'And Theo the last person she wants to be seated next to. The spark between them could've rivalled last night's pre-wedding firework display.'

'Anyone know who she is?' Brianna asked.

Perla shook her head and looked at Ari, who shrugged. 'He introduced her as Inez da Costa, a business associate from Rio.'

'If she's a business associate, then I'm Santa's Little Helper!' Sakis said.

Ari grinned. 'Think we should go jerk his chain a little?'

'You stay here with your new wife. I'll go put my son to bed and then I'll get right on it. I owe him big for the ribbing he gave me during the Pantelides Oil party on my island.' Sakis grinned with unabashed relish. He walked off and Brianna rolled her eyes and followed him.

Ari leaned down and kissed the side of Perla's neck. 'Before you think of leaving me because of my crazy brothers,' he said gruffly, 'let me tell you again how much I love you. How much I'm honoured to have you in my life and how much I adore you for giving me a chance at true happiness.'

Her heart soared, and she gasped as their baby kicked in approval.

'I love you too, Arion. You've given me the same chance too and there's nowhere else I'd rather be.'

* * * * *

What The Greek Wants Most

DEDICATION

To my editor, Suzanne Clarke,
for your unfailingly brilliant insight and support!

CHAPTER ONE

THEO PANTELIDES ACCELERATED his black Aston Martin up the slight incline and screeched to a halt underneath the portico of the Grand Rio Hotel.

He was fifteen minutes late for the black tie fund-raiser, thanks to another probing phone call from his brother, Ari.

He stepped out into the sultry Rio de Janeiro evening and tossed the keys to an eager valet who jumped behind the wheel of the sports car with all the enthusiasm Theo had once felt for driving. For life.

The smile that had teased his lips was slowly extinguished as he entered the plush interior of the five-star hotel. Highly polished marble gleamed beneath his feet. Artistically positioned lighting illuminated the well-heeled and threw the award-winning hotel's design into stunning relief.

The hotel was by far the best of the best, and Theo knew the venue had been chosen simply because his hosts had wanted to show off, to project a false image to fool him. He'd decided to play along for now.

The right time to end this game would present itself. Soon.

A sleek designer-clad blonde dripping in diamonds clocked him and glided forward on sky-high stilettos, her strawberry-tinted mouth widening in a smile that spelled out a very feminine welcome. And more.

'Good evening, Mr Pantelides. We are so very honoured you could make it.'

The well-practised smile he'd learnt to flash on and off since he was eighteen slid into place. It had got him out of trouble more times than he could count and also helped him hide what he did not want the world to see.

'Of course. As the guest of honour, it would've been crass not to show up, no?'

She gave a little laugh. 'No, er, I mean yes. Most of the guests are already here and taking pre-dinner drinks in the ballroom. If there's anything you need, anything at all, my name is Carolina.' She sent him a look from beneath heavily mascaraed eyelashes that hinted that she would be willing to go above and beyond her hostess duties to accommodate him.

He flashed another smile. '*Obrigado*,' he replied in perfect Portuguese. He'd spent a lot of time studying the nuances of the language.

Just as he'd spent a lot of time setting up the events set to culminate in the very near future. For what he planned, there could be no room for misunderstanding. Or failure.

About to head towards the double doors that led to the ballroom, he paused. 'You said most of the guests are here. Benedicto da Costa and his family. Are they here?' he asked sharply.

The blonde's smile slipped a little. Theo didn't need to guess why. The da Costa family had a certain reputation. Benedicto especially had one that struck fear into the hearts of common men.

It was a good thing Theo wasn't a common man.

The blonde nodded. 'Yes, the whole family arrived half an hour ago.'

He smiled at her, effectively hiding the emotions bubbling beneath his skin. 'You've been very helpful.'

Her seductive smile slid back into place. Before she could grow bolder and attempt to ingratiate herself further, he turned and walked away.

Anticipation thrummed through his veins, as it had ever

since he'd received concrete evidence that Benedicto da Costa was the man he sought. The road to discovery had been long and hard, fraught with pitfalls and the danger of letting his emotions override his clear thinking.

But Theo was nothing if not meticulous in his planning. It was the reason he was chief troubleshooter and risk-assessor for his family's global conglomerate, Pantelides Inc.

He didn't believe in fate but even he couldn't dismiss the soul-deep certainty that his chosen profession had led him to Rio, and to the man who'd shattered what had remained of his tattered childhood twelve years ago.

Every instinct in his body yearned to take this to the ultimate level. To rip away the veneer of sophistication and urbanity he'd been forced to operate behind.

To claim his revenge. Here. Now.

Soon...

He grimaced as he thought of his phone call with his brother.

Ari was beginning to suspect Theo's motives for remaining in Rio.

But, despite the pressure from his family, neither Ari nor Sakis, his older brothers, would dare to stop him. He was very much his own man, in complete control of his destiny.

But that didn't mean Ari wouldn't try to dissuade him from his objective if he'd known what was going on. His oldest brother took his role as the family patriarch extremely seriously. After all, he'd had to step up after the secure family unit he'd known for his formative years had suddenly and viciously detonated from the inside out. After his father had betrayed them in the worst possible way.

Theo only thanked God that Ari's radar had been momentarily dulled by his newfound happiness with his fiancé, Perla, and the anticipated arrival of their first child.

No, he wouldn't be able to stop him. But Ari...was Ari.

Theo shrugged off thoughts of his family as he neared

the ballroom doors. He deliberately relaxed his tense shoulders and breathed out.

She was the first thing he saw when he walked in. His lips started to curl at his clichéd thought but then he realised she'd done it deliberately.

The dress code for this event had been strictly black and white.

She wore red. And not just any red. Her gown was blood-red, provocatively cut, and it lovingly melded to her figure in a way that made red-blooded males stop and stare.

Inez da Costa.

Youngest child of Benedicto. Twenty-four, socialite… seductress.

Against his will, Theo's breath caught as his gaze followed the supple curve of a breast, a trim waist and the flare of her hips.

He knew each and every last detail of the da Costas. For his plan to succeed, he'd had to do what he did best. Dig deep and extract every last ounce of information until he could recite every line in the six-inch dossier in his sleep.

Inez da Costa was no better than her father and brother. But where they used brute force, blackmail and thuggery, she used her body.

He wasn't surprised lesser men fell for her Marilyn Monroe figure. A true hourglass shape was rare to find these days. But Inez da Costa owned her voluptuousness and confidently wielded it to her advantage. Theo's gaze lingered on her hips until she moved again, dropping into conversation with the consummate ease of a practised socialite. She had guests eating out of her hands, leaning in close to catch her words, following her avidly when she moved away.

As he advanced further into the room, she turned to speak to another male guest. The curve of her bottom swung into Theo's eye line, and he cursed under his breath as heat raced up through his groin.

Hell, no.

His fists curled, willing his body's unwanted reaction away. It had been a while since he'd indulged in a mindless, no-holds-barred liaison. But this was most definitely not the time for a physical reminder, and the instigator of that reminder was most definitely not the woman he would choose to end his short dry spell with.

He exhaled in a slow, even stream, letting the roiling in his gut abate and his equilibrium return.

As he made his way down the stairs to join the guests, the deep-seated certainty that he was meant to be here—in the right place at the right time—flared high.

If Pietro da Costa's love of excess hadn't led him down the path of biting off more than he could chew, this time in the form of commissioning a top-of-the-line Pantelides super-yacht he could ill afford, Theo wouldn't have flown down to Rio to look into the da Costas' finances three years ago.

He wouldn't have become privy to the carefully hidden financial paper trail that had led right back to Athens and to his own father's shady dealings almost a decade and a half ago.

He wouldn't have dug deeper and discovered the consequences of those dealings for his family. And for him personally.

Memory stirred the unwanted threads of anxiety until it threatened to push its way under his control like Japanese knotweed. Gritting his jaw, he smashed down on the poisonous emotion that had taken too much from him already. He was no longer that frightened boy unable to stem his fears or chase away the screaming nightmares that plagued him.

He'd learned to accept them as part of his life, had woven them into the fabric of his existence and in doing so had triumphed over them. Which wasn't to say he wasn't determined to make those who'd temporarily taken power from him pay dearly for that error. No, that mission he was very much looking forward to.

Focusing his gaze across the room to where Benedicto and his son held court among Rio's movers and shakers, he strategised how best to approach his quarry.

Despite the suave exterior he tried to portray with his tailor-made suit and carefully cropped hair, Benedicto could never mask his lizard-like character for very long. His sharp, angular face and reptilian eyes held a cruelty that was instinctively felt by those around him. And Theo knew that he honed that characteristic to superb effect when needed. He bullied when charm failed, resulting in the fact that half of the people in this room had attended the fund-raiser tonight just to stay on Benedicto's good side.

Five years ago, Benedicto had made his political aspirations very clear, and since then he'd been paving the way for his rise to power through mostly unsavoury means.

The same unsavoury means Theo's own father had used to bring shame and devastation to his family.

Grabbing a glass of champagne, Theo sipped it as he slowly worked his way deeper into the room, exchanging pleasantries with ministers and dignitaries who were eager to find favour with the Pantelides name.

He noticed the moment Benedicto and Pietro zeroed in on his presence. Bow ties were surreptitiously straightened. Smiles grew wider and spines straighter.

He suppressed a smile, deliberately turned his back on the father and son and made a beeline for where the daughter was smiling up at Alfonso Delgado, the Brazilian millionaire philanthropist, who was her latest prey.

'If you want me to host a gala for you, Alfonso, all you have to do is say the word. My mother used to be able to throw events like these together in her sleep and I've been told that I've inherited her talent. Or do you doubt my talents?' Her head tilted in a coquettish move that most definitely would've made Theo snort, had his eyes not been drawn to the sleek line of her smooth neck.

Alfonso smiled, his expression beginning to closely re-semble adoration.

Forcing himself not to openly grimace, Theo took an-other sip of champagne and brushed off an acquaintance who tried to catch his eye.

'No one in their right mind would doubt your talent. Per-haps we can discuss it over dinner one night this week?'

The smile that started to curve her full, glossy lips forced another punch of heat through him. 'Of course, I would love to. We can also discuss that pledge you made to support my father's campaign…?'

Theo moved closer, deliberately encroaching on the space between the two people in the centre of the room.

Alfonso's attention jerked towards him and his smile changed from playboy-charming to friendly welcome.

'*Amigo*, I wasn't aware that you had returned to my be-loved country. It seems we cannot keep you away.'

'For what I need to achieve in Rio, wild horses couldn't keep me away,' he replied, deliberately keeping himself from glancing at the woman who stood next to Alfonso. He breathed in and caught her scent—expensive but subtle, a seductive whisper of flowers and warm sunshine.

His friend's eyes gleamed. 'Speaking of horses—'

Theo shook his head. 'No, Alfonso, your racehorses don't interest me. Speedboat racing, on the other hand… Just say the word and I'll kick your ass from one end of the Copa-cabana to the other.'

Alfonso laughed. 'No can do, my friend. Everyone knows underneath that tuxedo you're part shark. I prefer to take my chances on land.'

A delicate clearing of a throat made Alfonso turn, a smile of apology appearing on his face as he slipped back into playboy mode. For the ten years that Theo had known him, Alfonso had had a weakness for curvy brunettes.

Inez da Costa had curves that required their own danger

signs. His friend risked being easy prey for whatever the da Costas had in mind for him.

'Apologies, *querida*. Please allow me to introduce you to—'

Theo stopped him with a firm hand on his shoulder. 'I'm perfectly capable of making my own introductions. Right now, I think you're needed elsewhere.'

Alfonso's eyes widened in confusion. 'Elsewhere?'

Theo leaned and whispered in his friend's ear. Shock and anger registered on Alfonso's face before his jaw clenched and he reined his emotions back in. His gaze slid to the woman next to him and returned to Theo's.

Taking in a deep breath, he held out his hand. 'I guess I owe you one, my friend.'

Theo took the proffered hand. 'You owe me several, but who's counting?'

'And I shall repay you. *Até a próxima.*'

'Until next time,' Theo repeated. He heard the disbelieving gasp from Inez da Costa as Alfonso walked away without another glance in her direction.

A thread of satisfaction oozed through him as he tracked his friend to the ballroom doors. Scanning the room, he saw Pietro da Costa's thunderous look in his sister's direction.

Theo lifted his glass to his lips and took a lazy sip then turned his attention to Inez da Costa.

Her large brown eyes were filled with anger as she glared at him.

'Who the devil are you and what did you say to Alfonso?'

CHAPTER TWO

THEO DIDN'T LIKE the idea that he'd been less than one hundred per cent thorough in covering every angle in his investigations.

His surveillance of Inez da Costa had been from afar simply because until recently he'd deemed her involvement in his investigation peripheral at best.

The extent of her role in her father's organisation had only come to light a few days ago. But even then he should've recognised her power.

Now, at the first proper sight of what was turning out to be the jewel in Benedicto da Costa's crown, the essential cog in the sinister wheel that his enemy was intent on using to his full advantage, he experienced a pulse of heat so strong, so powerful, he sucked in a quick breath.

Up close, Inez da Costa's heart-shaped face was flawless…breathtaking, her skin a silky, vibrant complexion even the best cosmetics couldn't hope to produce.

Not that she hadn't attempted to enhance her beauty even further. Her make-up was impeccable, her lids smoky in a way that drew attention to her wide, doe-like stare.

Long-lashed eyes that bored into him with unwavering demand and a healthy dose of suspicion. Her nose flared with pure Latin ire and her full lips parted as she released another agitated breath.

The pictures in his dossier did her no justice at all. Flesh and blood wrapped in red silk from cleavage to toe, she made his senses ignite in a way he hadn't felt in a long time. The earlier pull deep in his groin returned. Harder.

'I asked you a question.' Her voice held a hint of dark sultriness that reminded him of a warm Santorini evening spent drinking ouzo on a deserted beach. And the mouth that framed her words, painted a deep matt red, reminded him of what happened on the beach after the ouzo had been consumed and inhibitions were at their loosest.

She glanced over his shoulder and Theo's jaw clenched at the thought that she was more concerned with the departing Alfonso than she was with him.

'Why is one of my guests walking out the door right this moment?'

'I told him that if he didn't want a noose slipped around his neck before he was ready to be hog-tied, he needed to stay away from you.'

Her parted mouth gaped wider, showing a row of perfect white teeth. *'Excuse me—?'*

'You're excused.'

Eyes the colour of dark caramel flashed. 'How dare you refer to me as such—?'

'Careful, *anjo*, you're causing a scene. *Pai* would not be happy to see his event ruined by a tantrum now, would he?'

Her eyes didn't stray from his, her stare direct and cutting in a way that made it difficult for him to look away. Or maybe it was because, despite the boldly challenging stare, he spied a quickly hidden vulnerability that tweaked his radar?

'I don't know who you think you are but perhaps you need to be educated in the etiquette of social gatherings. You don't deliberately set out to insult your host or—'

'My intention was quite simple. I wanted to get rid of the competition.'

'The *competition?*'

The doors to the larger ballroom where the dinner fund-raiser was to be held were thrown open. Theo turned to her. 'Yes. And now Alfonso's gone, I have you all to myself. And, as to who I am, I'm Theo Pantelides, your VIP guest of honour. Maybe you should add another bullet point to your rules of etiquette. That the hostess should know who her most important guests are?'

Her mouth started to drop open but she caught her reaction and pursed her lips.

'You're Theo Pantelides?' she muttered.

'Yes, so I suggest you make nice with me to stop me from leaving. One high net worth guest departing before dinner may be excusable. Barely. Two will certainly not go down well with your crowd. Now, smile and take my arm.'

Inez reeled under the steely punch packed behind the suave, sophisticated exterior and charming smile.

Theo Pantelides.

This was the man her father and Pietro had talked about. The one who would be taking over majority shares in Da Costa Holdings until after the elections. The one her brother Pietro had referred to as an arrogant bastard.

Well, he certainly was arrogant all right. The swiftness with which he'd dispatched Alfonso and assumed he could control her confirmed that assertion. As to whether he was a true bastard…well, that was something to be determined. But so far all signs pointed in that direction.

What she hadn't been aware of was that the man spoken of with such scorn would be so…visually breathtaking.

'I thought you would be older.' The words tripped from her tongue before she could stop herself.

'As opposed to young, virile and unbelievably handsome?' he drawled.

Shock jolted though her at his unapologetic, irritatingly justified confidence. Because he undeniably was. A full head of vibrant jet-black hair was common enough among her countrymen. Even his hazel eyes, sculpted cheekbones and square jaw were conventional in the polo-loving jet set crowd her father and brother encouraged her to associate with.

On this man, though, the whole combination had been elevated several hundred notches to an entirely different level of magnetism that demanded attention and got it. There was a quality about the way he carried himself, his broad shoulders unyielding, that spelled a tough inner core anyone would be foolish to mess with.

And yet that danger Inez could feel rising off him was… compelling. Alluring.

She found her gaze drifting over his face, past the tiny dimple in his chin to the dark bronze throat as he lazily swallowed a mouthful of champagne.

She inhaled a sharp dart of air as she watched his Adam's apple move. Then jerked back when her fingers flexed suddenly with the urge to touch him there.

Santa Maria!

She fought to remember her anger at this stranger. As much as she detested her role in tonight's events—the blatant begging for campaign funds disguised as a charity event—she couldn't let opportunities slip through her fingers.

It was the deal she'd made with her father.

An education in return for serving her time. In six short weeks she would be free to pursue her dreams. Free of her father's influence, of the sleazy, horrifying rumours that had been part of her childhood and what had driven her mother to quiet despair when she thought she wasn't being observed.

She needed to focus, not moon over how coarse this arrogant stranger's faintly stubbled jaw would feel against her skin.

'*Make nice?* After you rudely interrupted my conversation and sent my guest for the evening running without so much as a goodbye?'

'Think about that for a minute. Do you really want a man who would abandon you so easily on the strength of a few whispered words?'

Genuine anger replaced the momentary sensory aberration. 'That you needed to whisper those words instead of state them in my hearing makes me wonder just how confident you are of your manhood.'

Inez was used to being the butt of male jokes. Pietro and her father had mocked and dismissed her career ambitions until the day she'd picked up her suitcase and threatened to leave home for good.

But she was still shocked when the man in front of her threw back his head and laughed. Even more so when the sight of his strong white teeth and the genuine twinkling merriment in his eyes sent her pulse racing. An alien tingling started in her belly and spread outward like fractured lightning.

'Did I say something funny?'

Light hazel eyes speared hers. 'I've been challenged on a lot of things, *querida*, but never over my manhood.'

The political career her father so desperately craved produced men who could fake confidence with the best of them. She'd seen political candidates on a clear losing streak fake bravado until they were on the verge of looking totally ridiculous.

This man oozed confidence and power so very effortlessly it was like a second skin. Couple those two elements with the dangerous magnetism she could feel and Theo Pantelides was positively lethal.

Over her thundering heartbeat, she heard the master of ceremonies announce that the fund-raiser she'd so carefully orchestrated—the platform that would see her achieve her freedom—was about to begin.

Beyond one broad shoulder of the man who seemed to have sucked the air from the large ballroom, she saw her father and Pietro heading towards her.

Her father would want to know what had happened to Alfonso. The Brazilian businessman had promised to host a polo match on his large ranch where he bred the finest thoroughbreds. Securing a time and a date and a campaign donation had been her job tonight.

A much needed win this man had cost her.

Frustrated anger flared anew.

'This can be resolved very easily, Inez,' Theo Pantelides murmured in her ear. His voice was deep. Alluring. To hear him use her given name, the version her half-American mother had so lovingly bestowed on her, made her momentarily lose her bearings. A state that worsened when his hot breath washed over her neck.

Barely managing to suppress a shiver, she snapped herself back into focus. 'Don't say my name. In fact, don't speak to me. Just…just go away!'

Inez knew she was on the verge of displaying childish behaviour but she needed to regroup quickly, find a solution to a situation that had been so cut and dried fifteen minutes ago.

She watched her father and brother approach and the dart of pain that resided beneath her breastbone twisted. For a long time she'd yearned for a connection with them, especially after *Mãe* had been so cruelly ripped from their lives following a fall from a racehorse a week before Inez's eighteenth birthday. But she'd soon realised that she was alone in the pain and loneliness brought on by the loss of the mother who'd been her everything. Pietro had been given no time to grieve before their father had stepped up his grooming campaign. As for Benedicto himself, he'd barely finished burying his wife before resuming his relentless pursuit of political power.

The only other male she'd foolishly thought was honourable had turned out to be just as ruthlessly power-hungry as the men in her family.

Constantine Blanco—one lesson well and truly learned.

'I see the rumours were false after all,' the man who loomed, large and imposing, in front of her drawled in that deep voice of his, capturing her attention so effortlessly.

She pushed down the bitterness that swirled through her at the thought of what she'd allowed to happen with Constantine. How low she'd sunk in her need for love and a desire for a connection.

'What rumours?' She infused a carelessness in her voice she was far from feeling.

'The ones that said you exhibit grace and charm with each bat of your eyelids. At the moment all I can see is a hellcat intent on scoring grooves into my skin.'

'Then I suggest you stay away from me. I wouldn't want to ruin your *unbelievably handsome* face now, would I?'

She hurried away from his magnetic presence towards where the tables had been set out with highly polished sterling silver cutlery and exquisitely cut crystal. At twenty thousand dollars a plate, the event was ostensibly to raise money for the children trapped within Rio's *favelas*, a cause dear to her heart.

Shame it had to be tainted with power-hungry sharks, mild threats to secure votes and…devastatingly handsome rogues with piercing hazel eyes who made her breath catch in a frighteningly exciting way…

The direction of her thoughts made her stumble lightly. Catching herself, she smiled at a guest who slid her a concerned glance.

Each table was set for eight. Her father had insisted their table was placed in the centre, where all eyes would be on them.

With Alfonso's unexpected departure, the empty seat would stick out like the proverbial sore thumb once the Secretary of State and his wife and the other power couple had taken their places.

She had no choice but to bump someone to the high table. All she needed to figure out was who—

'Staring at the empty seat will not make your departed guest suddenly reappear, *senhorita*,' the deep voice uttered from behind her.

That hot shiver swept up her spine again.

Before she could summon an appropriately scathing retort, her chair and the one bearing Alfonso's name were pulled back.

'What are you doing?' she demanded heatedly under her breath. She continued to stare down at the place setting, unwilling to look up into those hazel eyes. Something in their light depths made her hyperaware of her body, of her increased heartbeat. As if she was prey and he was the merciless predator.

It was preposterous. She didn't like it. But it was undeniable.

'Saving your skin. Now, smile and play along.'

'I'm not a puppet. I don't smile on command.'

'Try. Unless you want to spend the rest of the evening sitting next to the equivalent of an elephant in the ballroom?'

Something in his voice made her forget her vow not to look into his eyes. Something…peculiar. Her head snapped up before she could stop herself.

Their eyes clashed. And she found herself in that hyperaware state again. She forced herself to breathe through it. 'You created the very situation you now seem intent on fixing. Why don't you save us both time and state what your agenda is?'

A look passed over his face. Too quickly for her to decipher but whatever it was made her breath catch in a totally different way from before. Warning spiked the hairs on her nape.

'I merely want to redress the situation a little. And, as talented as you seem to think you are at hiding it, I can see my actions caused you distress. Let me help make it better.'

'So you cause me grief then swoop in to save me like a knight in shining armour?'

'I'm no one's knight, *senhorita*. And I prefer Armani to armour.'

He pointedly held out her seat.

Casting a swift glance around, Inez saw that they were attracting attention. Short of causing a scene, there was nothing she could do. Willing her facial muscles to relax into a cordial smile, she slowly sat down and watched as Theo Pantelides folded himself into the seat next to her.

He reached for his champagne at the same time as she reached for her water glass. The brush of his knuckle against her wrist made her jump.

'Relax, *anjo*. I've got this,' came the smooth, deep reassurance.

A hysterical laugh bubbled up her throat, curbed at the last minute by a cough. 'Pardon me if that assurance brings me very little comfort.'

He lifted the glass she'd abandoned and held it out to her. 'Tell me, what's the worst that could happen?'

She took the glass and stared into the sparkling water. The need to moisten her dry throat had receded. 'Believe me, the worst already has happened.'

For a long time she'd hidden from the truth—that her father had his heir, and she was a useless spare part.

Pain writhed through her and her breath grew shaky as her throat clogged with anger and bitterness.

'Get yourself together. Now isn't the time to fall apart. Trust me, Delgado may be a good friend but he has a wandering eye.' The hard bite to his tone cut a path through her emotions.

Setting the glass down, she faced him. 'I have been toyed with enough to last me a century, and I know your business here tonight has nothing to do with me, so do me a favour, *senhor*, and tell me straight—what do you want?' she whispered fiercely. She noted vaguely that her heartbeat was once again on rapid acceleration to sky-high. Her fingers shook and her belly churned with emotions she couldn't have named to save her life.

'First of all, cut out the *senhor* bit. If you want to address me in any way, call me Theo.'

'I will address you how I see fit, Mr Pantelides. And I see that once again you have failed to give me a straight answer.'

'No, I've failed to jump when you say. You need to be taught a little patience, *anjo*.'

She lifted a deliberately mocking brow. 'And you propose to be the one to teach me?'

That wide, breathtaking smile appeared again. Just like that, her pulse leapt then galloped with a speed even the finest racehorse would've strained to match.

What was going on here?

'Only if you ask nicely.'

She was searching for an appropriately cutting response when her father reached the table with the rest of the guests.

He cast her a narrow-eyed glance before his gaze slid to Theo Pantelides.

'Mr Pantelides, I had hoped for a few minutes of your time before the evening started properly,' her father said as he took his seat across the table.

Inez wasn't sure whether she imagined the slight stiffening in the posture of the man beside her. Her senses were too highly strung for her to trust their accuracy. Searching his profile as he stared at her father, nothing in his face gave any indication as to his true feelings.

'I'm all for mixing business with pleasure. However, I draw the line at mixing business with the plight of the poor. Let the *favela* kids have their cause heard. *Then* we will attend to business.'

The firm put-down sent an arctic chill around the table. The Secretary's wife gave a visible gasp and her skin blanched beneath her overdone make-up. Pietro, who'd just approached the table as Theo replied, gripped the back of his chair, anger embedded in his face.

Silence reigned for several fraught seconds. Her father flicked a glance at Pietro, who yanked back his seat and sat down. The hands her brother placed on the table were curled into fists and for a moment Inez wondered if his famous temper was about to be let loose on their guests.

Benedicto smiled at Theo. 'Of course. This cause is extremely dear to my heart. My own mother was brought up in the *favelas*.'

'As indeed you were, no?' Theo queried silkily.

Again, the Secretary's wife gasped. She reached for her wine glass and took a quick gulp. When she went to take another, her husband surreptitiously stayed her hand and sent her a stern disapproving look.

Her father nodded to the waiter, who stood poised with a bottle of the finest red wine. He took his time to savour his first sip before he answered.

'You are quite mistaken, Mr Pantelides. My mother managed to escape the fate most of her lot failed to and bettered her life long before she bore me. But I inherited her fighting spirit and her determination to do what I can for the bleak place she once called home.'

Theo's eyebrow quirked. 'Right. I may have been misinformed, then,' he said, although his dry tone suggested otherwise.

'I assure you misinformation is rife when it comes to the ploys of political opponents. And I have been told more than once that only a foolish man believes everything he reads in the papers.'

Theo slashed a smile that had a definite edge to it across the table. 'Trust me, I know a thing or two about what lengths newspapers will go to achieve a headline.'

'We seem to have lost Alfonso. Would you care to explain his absence, Inez?' Pietro's voice slid through the conversation.

Anger still rippled off him and Inez was acutely aware that he hadn't directly addressed Theo Pantelides.

Before she could speak, the man in question turned to her brother. 'He was called away suddenly. Emergency business elsewhere. Couldn't be helped. Since I was there when he took his leave, your sister offered me his seat and I graciously accepted, didn't you, *anjo*?'

She saw Pietro's eyes visibly widen at the blatant endearment. Just as swiftly, they narrowed and she could almost see the wheels spinning in a different direction as his gaze swung between her and Theo Pantelides.

No! Never! Her fingers curled into fists and she glared at him until he looked away.

'Well, perhaps Delgado's loss is our gain, *sim*?' her father prompted.

Again Theo smiled. Again her heart thudded hard at the sheer magnetism of his smile, even though it sorely lacked any humour.

The man was an enigma. He'd inveigled his way onto the top table, then proceeded to insult his host, just as he'd insulted her.

Inez had little doubt her father would unleash his anger at the slight later.

But right now she was more puzzled by the man next to her. What was his game plan? If he was in a position to acquire a controlling share of their company then clearly he was a man of considerable means. But he wasn't Brazilian. That much she knew. So why was he interested in her father's political ambitions?

She realised she was staring when that proud head turned and gold-flecked hazel eyes captured hers, one eyebrow quirked in amusement.

Hastily averting her gaze, she picked up her glass and took another sip.

Thankfully, the master of ceremonies chose that moment to climb onto the podium to announce the first course and the first speaker.

Inez barely tasted the salmon mousse and the wine that

accompanied it. Nor did she absorb the speech given by the health minister about what was being done to help the poor.

Her hyperawareness of the man beside her interfered with her ability to think straight. The last time she'd felt anything remotely like this, she'd wandered down a path she'd hated herself for ever since. She'd almost given herself to a man who had no use for her besides using her as a pawn.

Never again!

Six more weeks. She needed to focus on that. Once her father was on his campaign trail, she could start her new life.

She'd heard the rumours about her father's ruthless beginnings when she was growing up; a couple of her school friends had whispered about unsavoury dealings her father had been involved in. Inez had never found concrete proof. The one time she'd asked her mother, she'd been quickly admonished not to believe lies about her family.

At the time, she'd assured herself that they weren't true. But the passage of time had whittled away that assurance. Now, with each day that passed, she suspected differently.

'You look as if the world is coming to an end, *anjo*,' the man she was desperately trying to ignore murmured. Again the endearment rolled off his tongue in a deep, seductive murmur that sent shivery awareness cascading over her skin.

'I hope you're not going to ask me to smile again, because—' She gasped as he took her hand and lifted it to his mouth.

Firm, warm lips brushed her skin and Inez's stomach dipped in sensual free fall that took her breath away. Desperately, she tried to snatch her hand back.

'What the hell do you think you're doing?' she snapped.

'Helping you. Relax. If you continue to look at me like you want to claw my eyes out, this won't work.'

'What exactly *is* this? And why on earth should I play along?'

'Your brother and father are still wondering why Delgado

left so abruptly. Do you want to suffer the third degree later or will you let me help you make it all go away?'

She eyed him suspiciously. The notion that there was something going on behind that smooth, charismatic façade didn't dissipate. In fact, it escalated as he stared down at her, his features enigmatic save for that smile that lingered on his wide, sexy mouth.

'Why do you want to help me?' Again she tried to take back her hand but he held on, one thumb smoothing over her inner wrist. Blood surged through her veins at his touch, her pulse racing at the spot that he so expertly explored.

'Because I'm hoping it would persuade you to have lunch with me tomorrow,' he replied.

His gaze flicked across the table. Although his expression didn't change, she again sensed the tension that hovered on the edge of his civility. This man didn't like her family. Which begged the question: what was he doing here investing in their company?

He swung that intense stare back to her and she lost her train of thought. Grabbing it back, she shook her head.

'I'll have to refuse the lunch offer, I'm afraid. I have other plans.'

'Dinner, then?'

'I have plans then, too. Besides, don't you have business with my father tomorrow?'

'Our business won't take longer than me signing on a dotted line.'

'A dotted line that gives you a permanent controlling share in my family's company?'

His eyes gleamed. 'Not permanent. Only until I have what I want.'

CHAPTER THREE

'AND WHAT IS it you want?'

'For now? Lunch. Tomorrow. With you.' Another pass of his thumb over her pulse.

Another roll of sensation deep in her belly. The temptation to say yes suddenly overcame her, despite the warning bells shrieking at the back of her mind.

She forced herself to heed those warning bells. Her painfully short foray into a relationship had taught her that good looks and charm often hid an agenda that would most likely not benefit her or her heart. And Theo Pantelides had metaphorical skull and crossbones stamped all over him.

'The answer is still no,' she replied, a lot sharper than she'd intended.

His lips compressed but he shrugged. As if her answer hadn't fazed him.

And it probably hadn't. He was one of those men who drew women like bees to pollen. He could probably secure a lunch date with half of the women in this room and tempt the other married half into sin should he choose to.

With his dark, exquisite looks and deep sexy voice, he could have any woman he chose to display even the mildest interest in.

The thought that he would do just such a thing punched so fierce a reaction in her belly that she suppressed a shocked gasp.

What on earth is wrong with me? She needed to get herself back under control before she did something foolish—like discard her plans for tomorrow in favour of spending more time with this infuriatingly self-assured, visually stunning man.

Giving herself a fierce pep talk, she pulled her hand from his grasp.

She folded her hand in her lap and wrapped her other hand over her wrist. But suddenly her own touch felt…inadequate.

She was saved from exploring the peculiar feeling when the lights dimmed and the projector started reeling pictures of miles and miles of rusted shingle roofs that formed the world famous Rio *favelas*.

Her father climbed onto the podium to begin his speech.

The tale of despair-driven prostitution, violence, gang warfare and kidnapping of innocents, and the need to do whatever was needed to help was one she'd heard at many fund-raisers and charity dinners.

She clenched her fist. Knowing that half the people in here, dripping in diamonds and tuxedos worth several thousand dollars, would've forgotten the plight of the *favela* residents by the time dessert was served made her silently scream in frustration.

The need to get up, to walk out almost overwhelmed her but she stayed put.

There would be no running. No walking away from the work she'd committed herself to, nor walking away from the formative minds that were depending on her.

Fierce pride tightened her chest at the part she was playing in the young lives under her charge. And the fact that she'd managed to change that part of her own life without her father or brother's interference.

She refocused as her father finished his speech to rousing applause. The projector was shut off and the lights grew brighter.

She reached forward for her glass of wine and noticed that she was once again the focus of Theo's gaze.

'Should I be offended that I'm being so comprehensively ignored?' he asked.

'It's not a state you're used to, I expect?' With her surroundings once more in focus, she noticed the looks he was getting from women on other tables. She didn't delude herself that any of them were interested in his views on politics or world peace. No, each and every one of them would vie for much more personal, much more physical contact with the lean, broad-shouldered man next to her, whose hands casually caressed his wine glass stem in a way that made her think indecent thoughts.

She noticed the young famous actress on the next table where Theo should have been sitting gazing over at him, and again felt the sharp edge of an unknown emotion pierce her insides.

His smile grew hard. 'You'd be surprised.'

Curiosity brought her gaze back to his. 'Would I? How?'

'That question makes me think you've formed an opinion of me.'

'And that answer convinces me that you're very good at deflecting. You may fool others, but you do not fool me.'

He stared at her for a moment before one corner of his mouth lifted. Abruptly, he stood and held out his hand. 'Dance with me, *anjo*, and enlighten me further as to what you think you know about me.'

The demand was silky and yet implacable. In full view of the other guests, her refusal would be extremely discourteous.

Her heart hammered as she slowly slid her hand into his and let him draw her to her feet.

Emotions she was trying and failing to suppress flared up at the warmth and firmness of his grip. Fervently, she prayed for time to speed up, for the evening to end so she could be free of this man. Her reaction to him was puzzling in the extreme and the notion that she was being toyed with unsettled her more with each passing second.

As they skirted the table to head for the dance floor, her gaze met her father's. Expecting approval for accommodating the man whose business he was so obviously keen to garner, she was taken aback when she saw his icy disapproval.

Through the elite Rio grapevine she knew Alfonso Delgado's net worth and knew he couldn't afford to acquire a controlling share of Da Costa Holdings. So why did her father disapprove of a man who was clearly superior in monetary worth to Alfonso?

'You really have to do better with your social skills than this. Or I'll have to do something drastic to retain your attention.' The hard bite to Theo's voice slashed through her thoughts. 'Or were you really that into Delgado?'

'No, I wasn't.'

Her immediate denial seemed to pacify him. 'Then tell me what's on your mind.'

Inez found herself speaking before she could snap at him not to issue orders. 'Have you ever found yourself in a position where everything you do turns out wrong, no matter how hard you try?'

'There have been a few instances.' He pulled her close and slid an arm around her back. Heat transmitted to her skin via the soft material of her dress and flooded through her body. This close, his scent washed over her. Strong but not overpowering, masculine and heady in a way that made her want to draw even closer, touch her mouth to the bronze skin just above his collar.

Deus!

'You think this is one of those occasions for you?'

'I don't think; I know.'

'Why?'

Her laugh grated its way up her throat. 'Because I have a perfectly functioning brain.'

'You're worried because your father and brother are displeased with you?'

'Everything else this evening has gone according to plan except…'

'Delgado. You're worried that your father offered you up on a silver platter because he seems to think you're a prize worth winning and now he'll demand to know what you did wrong.'

Her eyes snapped to his, the insult surprisingly painful. 'What do you mean by *seems to think*? What do you know about my father? Or about me, for that matter?'

Theo forced himself not to tense at the question. Or let the fact that her body seemed to fit so perfectly in his arms impact on his thinking abilities. 'Enough.'

'Do you always go around making unfounded remarks about someone you've just met?'

He let a small smile play over his mouth. 'Enlighten me, then. Are you a prize worth winning?'

'There's no point enlightening you because it will serve no useful purpose. After tonight you and I will never meet again.'

She took a firm step back. Attempted to prise herself out of his arms. He held her easily, willing back the thrum of anger and bitterness that rose like bile in his throat.

'Never say never, *anjo*.'

Her fiery brown eyes glared at him. 'Don't.'

He feigned innocence. 'Don't what?'

'Don't keep calling me that.'

'You don't like it?'

'You have no right to slap a pet name on someone you just met.'

The hand holding hers tightened. 'Calm down—'

'No, I won't calm down. I'm not an angel. I'm certainly not *your* angel.'

'Inez.' A warning, subtle but effective.

Inez's pulse stalled, then thundered wildly through her veins.

'Don't,' she whispered again. Only this time she wasn't sure what she pleaded for.

He leaned closer until his mouth was an inch from her ear. When he breathed out, warmth teased her earlobe. 'Don't use your given name? It's either that or *anjo*. All the other words are only appropriate for the bedroom.'

Heat flamed through her belly as indecent thoughts of rumpled sheets, sweaty bodies and incandescent pleasure reeled through her mind.

She shook her head to dispel the images and heard his low laugh.

When she stared up at him, his eyes blazed down at her with a hunger that smashed through her body. Her nipples slowly hardened and the fire raged higher as his lips parted on another heart-stopping smile. Unable to help herself, her eyes dropped to the sensual curve of his mouth.

'I think it's my turn to say *don't*. Not if you don't want to be thrown over my shoulder and raced to the nearest cave.'

She forced a laugh despite the sensations rushing through her. 'This is the twenty-first century, *senhor*.'

'But what I'm feeling right now isn't. It's very basic. Primeval, in fact.'

He swerved her out of the path of another couple and used the move to draw her even closer. At the fierce evidence of his arousal against her stomach, Inez swallowed hard.

Her confusion escalated.

Constantine had been charismatic and breathtaking in his own right. But he'd never made her feel like *this*, not even in the beginning...before everything had gone disastrously wrong.

Thinking of the man who'd broken her heart and betrayed her so cruelly threw much needed ice over her heated senses. She'd made a fool of herself over one man. Foolishly believed he was the answer to her prayers. She was wise enough now to know Theo Pantelides wasn't the answer to any prayer, unless it was the crash and burn type.

'I believe I've fulfilled my obligatory dance duty to you. Perhaps you'd like to find a more unwitting female to club over the head and drag to your cave?' She injected as much indifference into her voice as possible.

'That won't be necessary. I've already found what I'm looking for.'

Theo watched several emotions chase over her features before Inez da Costa regained her impeccable hostess persona.

Although he silently cursed himself for his physical reaction, he was thankful she realised her effect on him.

Let her think she held the power. Allow her to believe that he could be manipulated to her advantage. Or, rather, her father's advantage.

Her reaction to Delgado's departure had shown him that fulfilling her role as her father's Venus flytrap was most important to Inez da Costa. Or was it something else? Did she hope to bag *herself* a millionaire while serving her father's purpose? She came from a family ruthless in its pursuit of wealth and power. Was that her underlying agenda?

That knowledge demanded that he rethink his strategy. The conclusion he'd arrived at was surprising but easily adaptable.

He had an opportunity to kill a few more birds with one stone. With any luck, he would conclude his business in Rio in a far shorter time than he'd already anticipated if he played his cards right.

Inez tried to wrench herself from his grasp once more. The primitive feelings he'd mentioned so casually a moment ago resurfaced. When she tugged harder, he forced himself to release her. Her soft hand slid from his, leaving a trail of sensation that made his groin pound and his blood heat.

The plan he'd hatched solidified as he gazed down into

her heart-shaped face, saw her fighting to stop her clear agitation from messing with her breathing.

Theo hid a smile.

Either she was offended at his primitive declaration or she was turned on by it. Since she wasn't slapping his face, he concluded that it was the latter.

His gaze dropped lower, and the sight of her tightly beaded nipples against her gown made his own breathing stall in his chest. Lower still, her tiny waist gave way to those tempting hips that his palms ached to explore.

Even as he talked himself into believing his reaction would ultimately serve his purpose, a part of Theo was forced to acknowledge that he hadn't reacted this strongly to a woman in a very long time. Everything about her brought his senses to roaring life in a way only the thought of revenge had for the past decade.

Revenge...retribution over the person who had created such chaos in his life.

He gritted his teeth as the sound of tinkling laughter and animated conversation refocused his mind to his task and purpose.

'Good evening, Mr Pantelides. I hope you enjoy the rest of your evening,' Inez said stiltedly.

She turned and walked off the dance floor before he could reply. Not that he felt like replying. Although he'd mostly kept on track throughout the evening, a large part of him had become far too consumed by her seductive presence.

Inez da Costa was only one part of the game. To keep on track he needed to keep his head in the *whole* game.

He headed for the bar and sensed the moment Benedicto and his son halted their conversation and moved pincer-like towards him.

Dreaded anxiety washed over his senses but he forced himself to breathe through it.

I am no longer in that dark, cold place. I am in light. I am free…

He tersely repeated the short statement under his breath as he tossed back the shot of vodka and set it down with cold, precise care.

He was no longer weak. No longer helpless.

And he most certainly would never be put in a position to beg for his life. Ever again.

By the time they reached him, he'd regained control of his body.

'Senhor Pantelides—'

'We're about to become business partners—' his gaze slid over Pietro's head to where Inez was holding court in a group of guests; the sleek line of her neck and the curve of her body sent another punch of heat straight to his groin '—and hopefully a little bit more than that. Call me Theo.'

The younger man looked a little taken aback, but he rallied quickly, nodded and held out his hand. 'Theo…we wanted to hammer down a time to discuss finalising our agreement.'

He took Pietro's hand in a firm grip. Benedicto started to offer his hand. Theo deliberately turned away. Catching the bartender's eye, he held up his fingers for three more drinks. By the time he faced them again, Benedicto had lowered his hand.

Theo breathed through the deep anger that churned through his belly and smiled.

'Tomorrow. Ten o'clock. My office. I'll have the documents ready for us to sign.'

This time it was Benedicto who looked taken aback. 'I was under the impression that you wanted to iron out a few more details.'

Theo's gaze flicked back to Inez. 'I had a few concerns but they no longer matter. Your campaign funds will be ready in the next twenty-four hours.'

Father and son exchanged triumphant looks. 'We are pleased to hear it,' Benedicto said.

'Good, then I hope the three of you will join me for dinner tomorrow evening to celebrate our new deal.'

Benedicto frowned. 'The three of us?'

'Of course. I expect that, since this is a family company, your daughter would wish to be included in the celebrations? After all, the company was her mother's family's business before it became yours, Senhor da Costa, was it not?' he queried silkily.

The older man's eyes narrowed and something unpleasant slid across his face. 'I bought my father-in-law out over a decade ago but yes, it's a family business.'

Bought out using money he'd obtained by inflicting pain and merciless torment.

The bartender slid their shots across the polished counter.

Theo picked up the nearest shot glass and raised it. 'In that case, I look forward to welcoming you all as my guests tomorrow evening. *Saúde.*'

'*Saúde,*' Benedicto and his son responded.

Theo threw back the drink and this time didn't hold back from slamming it down.

Again he saw father and son exchange looks. He didn't care.

All he cared about was making it out of the ballroom in one piece before he buried his fist in Benedicto da Costa's bony face. The urge to tear apart the man who'd caused his family, caused *him*, so much anguish reared through him.

The sound of his phone vibrating in his jacket pocket brought a welcome distraction from his murderous thoughts.

'Excuse me, gentlemen.' He walked away without a backward glance, gaining the double doors leading out to the wide terrace before activating his phone.

'Heads up, you're about to get into serious trouble with Ari if you don't fess up as to why you're really in Rio,' Sakis, his brother, said in greeting.

'Too late. I've already had the hairdryer treatment earlier this evening.'

'Yeah, but do you know he's thinking of flying down there for a face-to-face?'

Theo cursed. 'Doesn't he have enough on his hands being all loved up and taking care of his pregnant fiancé?' He wasn't concerned about a confrontation with Ari. But he was concerned that Ari's presence might alert Benedicto to Theo's true intentions.

So far, Benedicto da Costa was oblivious as to the connections Theo had made to what had happened twelve years ago. The older man had been very careful to erase every connection with the incident and sever ties with anyone who could bear witness to the crime he'd committed. He hadn't been careful enough. But he didn't know that.

Having another Pantelides in Rio could set off alarm bells.

'You need to stall him.'

'He's concerned,' Sakis murmured. Theo heard the same concern reflected in his brother's voice. 'So am I.'

'It needs to be done,' he replied simply.

'I get that. But you don't need to do it alone. He's dangerous. The moment he guesses what your true intentions are—'

'He won't; I've made sure of it.'

'How can you be absolutely certain? Theo, don't be stubborn. I can help—'

'No. I need to see this through myself.'

Sakis sighed. 'Are you sure?'

Theo turned slowly and surveyed the ballroom. Rio's finest drank and laughed without a care in the world. In the centre of that crowd stood Benedicto da Costa, the reason why Theo couldn't sleep through a single night without waking to hellish nightmares; the reason anxiety hovered just underneath his skin, ready to infest his control should he loosen his grip for one careless second.

Inexorably, his eyes were drawn to the female member of the diabolical family. Inez was dancing with a man whose blatant interest and barely disguised lust made Theo's fist curl over the cold stone bannister.

His stomach churned and adrenaline poured through his system the same way a boxer experienced a heady rush in the seconds before a fight. This fight had been long coming. He would see it through. He had to. Otherwise he feared his demons would never be exorcised.

He'd lived with them for far too long, and they needed to be silenced. He needed to regain complete, unshakeable hold of his life once more.

His other hand tightened around his mobile phone, his heart thundering enough to drown out the music. He spoke succinctly so his brother would be in no doubt that he meant every word.

'Am I sure that I need to bring down the man who kidnapped and tortured me for over two weeks until Ari negotiated a two million ransom for my release? *Hell, yes*. I'm going to make him feel ten million times worse than what he did to me and to our family and I don't intend to rest until I bring all of them down.'

CHAPTER FOUR

'A DOUBLE-SHOT AMERICANO, *por favor*.' Inez smiled absently at the barista while she tried to juggle her sketchpad and fish out enough change from her purse to pay for the coffee.

It was barely nine o'clock and yet the heat was already oppressive, even more than usual for a Thursday morning in February. Normally, she would've opted for a cool caffeine drink but her energy levels needed an extra boost this morning.

She'd slept badly after the fund-raiser last night. And what little sleep she'd managed had been interspersed with images of a man she had no business thinking, never mind dreaming, about.

And yet Theo Pantelides's face had haunted her slumber...still haunted her, if truth be told.

The last time she'd seen him he'd been leaning against the terrace bannister outside the ballroom, his eyes fixed firmly on her. Inez wasn't sure why her attention had been drawn outside. All she knew was that something had compelled her to look that way as she danced with a guest.

Even from that distance the tension whipping through his frame had been unmistakable, as had the blatant dark promise in his eyes as his gaze raked her from head to toe.

More than anything she'd wished she could lip-read when she'd watched his lips move to answer whoever was at the other end of his phone conversation.

That last look plagued her. It'd held hunger, anger and another emotion that she couldn't quite decipher. Brushing it off, she smiled, accepted her coffee and headed outside. She was a little early for her class with the inner city kids but she hadn't wanted to spend another moment at the tension-fraught breakfast table with her father and brother this morning.

In contrast to Pietro's third degree as to what exactly had happened with Alfonso Delgado, her father had been cold and strangely preoccupied. The moment he'd stood abruptly and left the table, she'd made her excuses and walked away.

Even Pietro's reminder that they had a dinner engagement she couldn't recall making hadn't been worth stopping to query. All she'd wanted was to get out of the mansion that felt more and more as if it was closing in on her.

'*Bom dia, anjo.*' The deep murmured greeting brought her thoughts and footsteps to a crashing halt.

Theo leaned casually against a gleaming black sports car, a pair of dark sunglasses hiding his eyes from her. But her full body tingle announced that she was the full, unwavering focus of his gaze. Her breath stalled, her heart accelerating wildly as her pulse went into overdrive.

'What the hell are you doing here?' she blurted before she could stop her strong reaction.

Aside from the devastation his tall, lean suited frame caused to her insides, the thought that he could discover where she was headed or what she did with her Tuesday and Thursday mornings made her palms grow clammy. By lunchtime today, if Pietro were to be believed, Theo would be firmly entrenched as a business partner in her family's company. Which meant constant contact with her family. Which meant he could disclose parts of her life she wasn't yet ready to disclose to her family.

'Are you following me?' she accused hotly as she approached him, her senses jumping with the possibilities and consequences of her discovery.

'Not today. My trench coat and fedora are at the laundry.'

'Keep them there. In this heat, you'd boil to death.'

A smile broke across his face. 'Do I detect a little un-ladylike relish in your voice, *anjo*?'

'What you detect is high scepticism that you're here by accident and not following me,' she snapped.

'You give me too much credit, *agape mou*. I asked for the best coffee shop in the city and I was directed here. That you're here too merely confirms that assertion. Unless you go out of your way to sample bad coffee?'

Before she could respond, he straightened and reached for the hand wrapped around her coffee. Curling his hand over hers, he brought his lips to the small opening on her coffee lid and tilted the cup towards him.

He savoured the drink in his mouth for a few seconds before he swallowed.

Inez fought to breathe as she watched his strong throat move. The slow swirl of his tongue over his lower lip caused darts of sharp need to arrow straight between her legs.

'Delicious. And surprising. I would've pegged you for a latte girl.'

'Which goes to show you know next to nothing about me,' she retorted.

He slowly raised his sunglasses and speared her with his mesmerising eyes. Although a smile hovered over his sensual lips, some unnameable tension hovered in the air between them. A charged friction that warned her all was not as it seemed.

Hell, she knew that. Theo Pantelides spelled danger. Whether smiling or serious, dallying with him was akin to playing with electricity. Depending on his mood, you could either receive a mild static frizzle or a full-blown electro-cution. And she had no intention of testing him for either.

'*Sim*, I don't know enough about you. But I intend to remedy that situation in the near future.'

She shrugged. 'It is your time to waste.'

He merely smiled and turned towards his car.

'I thought you came to get coffee?' she probed, then bit her lip for prolonging a meeting she wanted over and done with. Last night she'd told herself to be thankful that she would never see this man again. And yet, here she was, feeling mildly bereft at the notion that he was leaving.

He paused and his gaze slid over her. Immediately, she became supremely conscious of the white shorts and blue tank top she'd hurriedly thrown on this morning. Her hair was caught up in a ponytail because it helped keep it out of the way during her class. Her face was devoid of make-up except for the light sunscreen and the gloss she'd passed over her lips. All in all, she projected a much different image this morning than the sophisticated hostess she'd been last night.

Catching herself wondering whether he found her wanting now, she mentally slammed the thought down. She didn't care what Theo thought of her.

'I have the kick I need to keep me going. See you tonight.'

'Tonight? Why would you be seeing me tonight?' she demanded.

His smile slowly disappeared as his gaze slid over her again. This time, his hot gaze held an element of possessiveness that made her fight to keep from fidgeting under his keen scrutiny.

Stepping back, he activated a button on his car key and the door slid smoothly upward. She watched, completely captivated, as he lowered his tall masculine frame inside the small space. A touch of a slim finger on a button and the engine roared to life.

'Because I want to see you. And I always get what I want, Inez,' he said cryptically, his tone suddenly hard and biting. 'Remember that.'

I always get what I want.

Another shiver of apprehension coursed down her spine. All through the two art and graphic design classes she taught from ten till midday, the infernal words throbbed through her head as if someone had set them on repeat.

She managed to keep her focus, barely, as she demonstrated the differences between charcoal and pencil strokes to a group of ten-year-olds. Once or twice she had to repeat herself because she lost her train of thought, much to the amusement of her pupils, but the satisfying feeling of imparting knowledge to children who would otherwise have been left wandering the streets momentarily swamped the roiling emotions that Theo had stirred with his unexpected appearance this morning.

The suspicion that he had been following her didn't go away all through her hurriedly taken lunch and the meeting she'd scheduled with the volunteer coordinator at the centre.

Her decision to forge her own path by seeking a permanent position at the centre had solidified as she'd tossed and turned through the night.

Seeking her independence meant finding a paying job. To do that she needed more experience, which she hoped her longer hours spent volunteering would give her.

Thanks to her father's interference, all she had was one semester at university. It wasn't great but, until such time as she could further her education, it was better than nothing. That plus her volunteering was a starting point.

A starting point that was greatly enhanced when the co-ordinator agreed to increase her hours to three full days.

She was smiling as she activated her phone on the way to her car after leaving the centre.

The first text was from Pietro, reminding her that they were dining out that evening. With Theo Pantelides.

The unladylike curse she uttered won her a severe look of disapproval from an elderly lady walking past. The urge to text back a refusal was immediate and visceral.

After last night and this morning, exposing herself to the raw emotions Theo provoked was the last thing she needed.

And even more than her suspicions this morning, she

had a feeling he'd engineered this dinner. Hell, he'd as much as taunted her with it with his last words to her this morning.

As much as she tried to think positive and hope that the dinner would be quick and painless, a premonition gripped her insides as she slid behind the wheel and headed home.

'*Filho da puta.*' Her brother's habitual crude cursing wasn't a surprise to her. That it had seemingly come out of no-where was.

'What's wrong?' She eyed him as they stepped out of the car at the marina of the exclusive Rio Yacht Club just before seven p.m.

She pulled down her box-pleated hem and wished she'd worn something a little longer than the form-fitting mid-thigh-length royal-blue sleeveless dress. The traffic had been horrendous and she'd arrived home much later than planned. The dress had been the nearest thing to hand. Now she stared down at the four-inch black platform heels she'd teamed with it and grimaced at the amount of thigh and legs on show.

The light breeze lifted a few strands of her loose hair as she turned to her brother and saw him jerk his chin to-wards the largest yacht moored at the far end of the pier. 'Trust Pantelides to rub my nose in it,' he said acerbically.

She looked from the sleek black, gold-trimmed vessel back to her brother. 'Rub your nose…what are you talk-ing about?'

With a sullen look, he strode off down the jetty. 'That's my boat.'

'*Yours*? When did you buy a boat?'

'I didn't. I couldn't. Not after the mess up with *Pai*'s last campaign. That boat was supposed to be mine!' Dark anger clouded his face.

Her heart jumped into her throat. 'Pietro, a boat like that costs millions of dollars. Besides that very unsubtle hint that

I in any way stood in the way of your acquiring it—which is preposterous, by the way—there's no way you could ever have afforded a boat like that, so—'

'Forget it. Let's go and get this over with. It's bad enough *Pai* pulled out of coming tonight. Now I have to schmooze for both of us. You have to play your part, too. It's clear Pantelides's got a thing for you.'

Disgust and anger rose in her and she snatched her hand away from Pietro when he tried to lead her down the gang-plank.

'I won't participate in another of your soulless schemes. So you may as well forget it right now.'

'Inez—'

'No!' Feelings she'd bottled up for much longer than she cared to think about rose to the surface. 'You keep asking me to throw myself at prospective investors so you can fund *Pai*'s campaign. You're his campaign manager and yet you can't seem to function without my help. Why is that?'

Pietro's eyes darkened. 'Watch your mouth, sister.'

'Show me some respect and I'll consider it,' she challenged.

'What the hell has got into you?'

'Nothing that hasn't always been there, Pietro. But you need me to point it out to you so I will. I'm done. If you want me to accompany you as your *sister* to Theo Pantelides's dinner, then I will. If you have another scheme up your sleeve, then you might as well forget it because I am not interested.'

Her brother's lips pursed but she saw a hint of shame in his eyes before his gaze slid away. 'I don't have time to argue with you right now. All I ask, if it's not too much, of course, is that you help me secure this deal with Pantelides, because if we lose his backing then we might as well pack up and head back up to the ranch in the mountains.' He set off down the jetty.

She hurried to keep up, picking her way carefully over

wooden slats. 'But I thought everything was done and dusted this morning?' she asked when she caught up with him.

Anxiety slid over Pietro's face. 'Pantelides cancelled the meeting. Something came up, he said. Except I know it was a lie. I have it on good authority he was parked outside a coffee shop chatting up some girl when he was supposed to be meeting us to finalise the agreement.'

Inez stumbled, barely catching herself from toppling headlong into the water a few feet away.

'You're having him watched?' How she managed to keep her voice even, she didn't know.

Petulance joined anxiety. 'Of course I am. And I'd bet my Rolex that he's doing the same to us.'

The thought of being the subject of anyone's surveillance made her skin crawl, even though a part of her had reluctantly accepted the truth: that her father's business dealings weren't always legitimate. But hearing her brother admit it made her stomach turn.

And if that was the way Theo Pantelides conducted his business as well...

She pressed her lips together and looked up as Pietro strode past the potted palm lined entrance to the Yacht Club.

'Aren't we dining in there?'

He shook his head. 'No. We're dining on my...on *his* boat,' he tossed out bitterly.

Inez glanced at the yacht they were approaching.

This close, the vessel was even more magnificent. Its sleek lines and exquisite craftsmanship made her fingers itch for her sketching pad. She was so busy admiring the boat and yearning to capture its beauty on paper that she didn't see its owner until she was right in front of him.

Then everything else ceased to register.

He wore a black shirt with black trousers, his dark hair raked back from his face. Under the soft golden lights spilling from the second deck his sculpted cheekbones and strong jaw jutted out in heart-stopping relief.

At the back of her mind, Inez experienced a bout of irritation at the fact that he captured attention so exclusively. So effortlessly.

Even as he shook hands with Pietro and welcomed him on board the *Pantelides 9*, his eyes remained on her. And God help her, but she couldn't look away.

On unsteady feet, which she firmly blamed on the swaying vessel, she climbed the steps to where he waited. When his eyes released hers to travel over her body, she grappled with controlling her breath. She reached him and reluctantly held out her hand in greeting.

'Thank you for the dinner invitation, Mr Pantelides.'

With a mocking smile, he took her hand and used the grip to pull her close. Despite her heels, he was almost a foot taller than her, easily six foot four. Which meant he had to lean down quite a bit to whisper in her ear, 'So formal, *anjo*. I look forward to loosening your inhibitions enough to dissolve that starchy demeanour.'

Her pulse, which had begun racing when his palm slid against hers, thundered even harder at his words. 'I can see how not having a woman fall at your feet the moment you crook your finger can present a challenge, *senhor*. But you really should learn the difference between playing hard to get and being plainly uninterested.'

His eyebrow quirked. 'You fall into the latter category, of course?' he mocked.

'*Sim*, that is exactly so.'

He looked towards where Pietro had accepted a glass of champagne from a waiter and was admiring the luxuriously decorated deck, at the end of which a multi-coloured lit jet pool swirled and shimmered.

When his gaze re-fixed on hers, there was a steely determination in his eyes that sent a shiver down her spine. All the earlier alarm bells where Theo was concerned clanged loudly in her brain.

'Then I will have to get a little more inventive,' he murmured silkily before dropping her hand.

Inez clenched her fist and fought the urge to rub the tingling in her palm. She didn't want him getting inventive where she was concerned because she had a nasty feeling she wouldn't emerge unscathed from the encounter.

But she kept her mouth shut and followed him onto the deck. The cream and gold décor was the last word in luxury and opulence. Plump gold seats offered comfort and a superior view onto the well-lit marina and the open sea to their right. To their left, the lights of Rio gleamed, with the backdrop of the huge mountain, on top of which resided the world-famous Cristo Redentor.

A sultry breeze wafted through the deck as a waiter served more flutes of champagne. She took a glass as Pietro rejoined them. His glass was already half empty and she watched him take another greedy gulp before he pointed a finger at Theo.

'I wish you'd given me the chance to make you another offer for this boat before you pulled the plug on our sale agreement, Pantelides.'

Theo's jaw tightened before he answered. 'You had several opportunities to make good but you failed to close the deal. So I cut my losses.' He shrugged. 'Business is business.'

Pietro bristled. 'And cancelling our meeting today? Was that for business too, or pleasure?'

Theo's eyes caught and held hers. Inez held her breath, wondering if he was about to give her up. His eyes gleamed with a mixture of danger and amusement. Somehow he'd sensed that he held her in his power. And he relished that power. Her hand trembled slightly as she waited for the axe to fall.

'I'm not in the habit of discussing my other business interests, or my pleasurable ones, for that matter. But, suffice it to say, what kept me away from our meeting was very much worth my time.' His gaze swept down, lingering over her breasts and hips in a blatant appraisal that made her breathing grow shallow. When his eyes returned to hers, Inez was sure all the oxygen had been sucked out of the atmosphere.

'Our business together should be equally worth your time,' Pietro countered.

Theo finally set her free from his captivating gaze. Narrow-eyed, he glanced at Pietro.

'Which is why I rescheduled for this evening. Of course, your father chose not to grace us with his presence. So the song and dance continues, I guess.' The hard edge was definitely in his tone again, prompting those alarm bells to ring louder.

Pietro muttered something under his breath that she was sure wasn't complimentary. He snapped his fingers at the waiter and swapped his empty glass for a full one.

'Well, we'll be there at the appointed time tomorrow. We can only hope that you will not be delayed…elsewhere.'

The upward movement of Theo's mouth could in no way be termed a smile. His eyes flicked back to her. 'Don't worry, da Costa, I intend to hammer out the final points of our agreement tonight. When I turn up to sign tomorrow, it will be with the knowledge that all my stipulations have been satisfied.'

The firm belief that his statement was connected to her wouldn't dissipate all through dinner. As a host, Theo was effortlessly entertaining. He even managed to draw a chuckle from Pietro once or twice.

But Inez couldn't shake the feeling that they were being toyed with. And once or twice she caught the faintest hint of fury and repulsion on his face, especially when her father's name came up.

She shook herself out of her unsettling thoughts when the most mouth-watering dessert was set down before her.

Whatever Theo was up to, it was nothing to do with her. Her father had managed their family business with enough savvy not to be drawn into a scam.

With that comforting thought in mind, she picked up her spoon and scooped up a mouthful of chocolate truffle-topped cheesecake.

Her tiny groan of delight drew intense eyes back to hers. Suddenly, the thought of dishing out a little of the mockery he'd doled out to her tingled through her. Keeping her gaze on his, she slowly drew the spoon out from between her lips, then licked the remnants of chocolate with a slow flick of her tongue.

His nostrils flared immediately, hunger darkening his eyes to a leaf-green that was mesmerising to witness. With another swirl of her tongue, she lowered the spoon and scooped up another mouthful.

His large fist tightened around the after-dinner espresso he'd opted for and she momentarily expected the bone china to shatter beneath his grip. But slowly he released it and sat back in his chair, his eyes never leaving her face.

'Enjoying your dessert, *anjo*?' he asked in that low, rough tone of his.

She hated to admit that the endearment was beginning to have an effect on her. The way he mouthed it made heat bloom in her belly, made her aware of her every heartbeat... made her wonder how it would sound whispered to her at the height of passion. *No!*

'Yes. Very much.' She fake smiled to project an air of nonchalance.

He smiled at her mocking formality. 'Good. I'll make a note of it for the next time we dine together.'

Before she could tell him she intended to move heaven and earth to make sure there wouldn't be a next time, Pietro lurched to his feet. 'I never got the chance to inspect my…this boat before the opportunity to buy it was regrettably taken away. You won't mind if I take a look around, would you?' he slurred.

Theo motioned the hovering waiter over. He murmured to him and the waiter went to the deck bar and picked up a handset. 'Not at all. My skipper will give you the tour.'

A middle-aged man with greying hair climbed onto the deck a few minutes later and escorted a swaying Pietro towards the stairs.

Inez watched him go with a mixture of anxiety and sympathy.

'He's drunk.' Her appetite gone for good, she set her spoon down and pushed the plate away.

'You say that as if it's my fault,' he replied lazily.

'Did you really have to do that?' She glared at him.

He raised a brow. 'Do what, exactly?'

'This was supposed to be Pietro's boat.' No matter how unrealistic that notion had been, her brother didn't deserve to be humiliated like this.

'*Supposed* being the operative word. We had a *gentleman's* agreement.' That hard bite was back again, sending trepidation dancing along her nerve ends. 'He didn't hold out his end of the deal.'

'Regardless of that, do you have to rub his nose in it like this?' she countered.

'As I said before, I'm a businessman, *anjo*. And I currently have a yacht worth tens of millions of dollars that needs an owner. The Boat Show starts next week. I relocated aboard in order to get it in shape for prospective buyers, otherwise our dinner would have taken place at my residence in Leblon and your brother's delicate feelings would've been spared.'

She frowned. 'You're selling the boat?' The thought of the beautiful vessel going to some unknown, probably pompous new owner made her nose wrinkle in distaste. The design was exquisite, unique…sort of like its owner.

As hard as she tried to imagine it, she couldn't see anyone else owning the boat besides Theo. Not even Pietro. Its black and gold contrasts depicted darkness and light in a complementary synergy—two fascinating characteristics she'd glimpsed more than once in Theo.

'Needs must.'

She looked around the beautiful deck, imagined its graceful lines awash with sunlight, and sighed.

Theo's eyes narrowed as he stared across at her. 'You like the boat.'

'Yes, it's…beautiful.'

He watched her for a few minutes then he nodded. 'Let's make a date for Sunday afternoon. We'll take her out for a quick spin.'

She laughed. 'Unless I'm mistaken, this is a four hundred foot vessel. You don't just take her out for a *quick* spin.'

'A long spin, then. I need to make sure it runs perfectly. If you still like it when we return to shore, I'll keep it.'

Her heart lurched then sped up like a runaway freight train. 'You would do that…for me?'

'*Sim*,' he replied simply.

Genuine puzzlement, along with a heavy dose of excitement she didn't want to admit to, made her blurt, 'Why?'

He strolled lazily to where she stood. This close, she had to tilt her head to catch his gaze. *Darkness and light.* He might have been smiling but Inez could almost reach out and touch the undercurrent of emotions swirling beneath his civility. She jumped slightly when he brushed a forefinger down her cheek.

'Because I intend to keep you, *anjo*. And while you will not have a lot of choice in the matter, I'm willing to make a few adjustments to ensure your contentment.'

CHAPTER FIVE

THEO WATCHED HER grapple with what he'd just said. Unlike her brother, she wasn't inebriated—she'd barely touched her glass of the rich Barolo 2009 he'd specially chosen for their dinner.

She shook her head in confusion. 'You intend to *keep* me?'

Her skin, satin-smooth beneath his touch, begged to be caressed. He gave in to the urge and traced her from cheek to jaw. When she withdrew from him, he followed. He stroked the pulse beating in her neck and pushed back the need to step closer, touch his mouth to the spot.

He'd learnt two things last night.

The first was that Benedicto da Costa, for all his cunning and veneer of sophistication, was still a greedy, vicious snake who thought he could con millions of dollars out of an unsuspecting fool like him.

The second was that Inez da Costa could be a key player in the slow and painful revenge he intended to exact for the wrong done to him. It didn't hurt that the chemistry between them burned the very air they breathed.

In the past Theo had made several opportune decisions by switching tactics at the last minute and making the most of whatever situation he found himself him.

With the newfound information at his fingertips, he'd found a way not only to end the da Costas once and for all, but also to make a tidy profit to boot.

He barely stopped himself from smiling as he looked down into Inez's face. She really was stunningly beautiful. With a mouth that begged to be explored.

'Mr Pantelides?'

'Theo,' he murmured, anticipating her refusal to use his first name.

She blew out an exasperated breath. 'Theo. Explain yourself.'

The unexpected sound of his name on her lips sent a pulse of heat through his body. Followed swiftly by a feeling he recognised as pleasure.

With a silent curse he dropped his hand. Pleasure featured nowhere on his mission to Rio. Nor was standing around, gazing into the face that reminded him of the painting of an angel that used to hang in his father's house.

Pain. Reparation. Merciless humiliation. Those were his objectives.

'There's no hidden message in there, *anjo*. For the duration of my stay in Rio I expect you to make yourself available to me, day and night.'

Her genuine laughter echoed around the open deck. When he didn't join in, she quickly sobered. 'Oh, I'm sorry. But I believe you have me confused with a certain type of woman you must encounter on your travels.'

Theo let the insult slide. He'd told his skipper to take his time with the tour, but even his trusted employee couldn't keep Pietro away for ever. And it looked as if he needed to step up this part of his strategy in order to forward his overall objective.

'I was supposed to sign documents that guaranteed your father's campaign funds this morning but I didn't turn up. Aren't you even a little bit curious as to why?'

A touch of confusion clouded her brown eyes but she shrugged one silky-smooth shoulder that shimmered softly under the deck lights. 'Your business with my father is not my concern.'

A little of that control he kept under a tight leash threatened to slip free. 'You don't care where the money comes from as long as you're kept in the style to which you've grown accustomed, is that it?'

Her eyes widened at the acid leaching from his tone. 'You may think you know me but, I assure you, you've got things wrong—'

'Have I? From where I'm standing it's very evident you're the bait he uses to trap weak, pathetic fools into opening their wallets.'

Her ragged gasp accompanied a look of outrage so near authentic Theo would've believed her reaction had he not seen her in action with Delgado last night.

'If it is your intention to be offensive to show your *machismo*, then *bravo*, you've succeeded,' she threw at him and whirled away.

He caught her wrist before she could take a step.

'Let me go.'

'I've yet to outline my plans, *anjo*.'

'I think you've *outlined* enough. I won't stand here listening to your unfounded insults. I'm going to find Pietro. And then we're leaving.' She tried to free herself. He tightened his grip until he could feel her pulse under his fingers. Furious. Passionate.

His groin stirred and he forced himself to ignore the throb of arousal determined to make itself known. 'You're not leaving here until we have this discussion.'

'What we're having is not a discussion, *senhor*. What you're doing is holding me captive, torturing me with—'

She broke off, no doubt in reaction to his hiss of fury and the flash of icy memory that made his whole body go rigid for one long second.

Theo released her, turned away sharply and shoved his hand through his hair. He noted his fingers' faint trembling and willed himself to stop shaking.

'Th…Theo?' Her voice came from far away, filled with confusion and a touch of concern.

He willed away the effect of the trigger words and forced himself to breathe. But they pounded through his brain nonetheless—*captive, prisoner, torture, darkness…*

Fingers closed over his shoulder and he jerked around. '*Don't!*'

She jumped back, snatching back her hand. It took several more seconds for him to recall where he was. He wasn't in some deep, dark hole in a remote farm in Spain. He was in Rio. With the daughter of the man who continued to cause his recurring nightmares.

'What's…what's wrong with you?' she asked with a wary frown.

He drew in a steady breath and gritted his teeth. 'Nothing. I'll get to the point. The agreement was that I'd take control of Da Costa Holdings and keep a fifty per cent share of the profits in exchange for liquidated funds to finance your father's political campaign. However, the papers your father had drawn up contain a major loophole that I can easily exploit.'

Slowly, his panic receded and he noticed she was absently rubbing her wrist. He quickly replayed his reaction to her touch and breathed a sigh of relief when he confirmed to himself that he hadn't grabbed her in his panic.

She continued to rub her skin and slowly another earthy emotion replaced his roiling feelings. He welcomed the pulse of arousal despite the fact that he had no intention of falling prey to the easy wiles of Inez da Costa. No matter how mouth-watering her body or how angelic her face.

'Shouldn't you be telling my father this, give him a chance to fix the loophole before you sign?'

He smiled at her naiveté. 'Why should I? I stand to gain by signing the agreement as it's drawn up.'

Her brow creased. 'Then why tell me about it? What's

to keep me from telling my father about it the moment I leave here?'

'You won't.'

One expertly plucked eyebrow lifted. 'Again, I think you underestimate me.'

He strode to the extensively stocked bar and poured himself a shot of vodka. 'You won't because if you do I won't sign the agreement in any form. And the offer of financial backing vanishes.'

All trace of colour left her face. 'So this is a blackmail attempt. To what purpose?'

'The purpose needn't concern you. All I want you to know is that there is a loophole which I can choose to exploit or leave alone, depending on your cooperation.'

'But what is to stop you from going ahead with whatever you have planned after I've cooperated with...what exactly is it you want from me?'

'That's the simple part, *anjo*. I want to keep you. Until such time as I tire of you. Then you will be set free.'

When the full meaning of his words finally became clear, ice cascaded down Inez's spine. Despite the warm temperature, she shivered.

Oh, how easily he said the words. As if her answer meant nothing to him. But of course it did. He'd been planning this for a while. The meeting this morning outside the coffee shop—which she was now certain hadn't been coincidental—the dinner invitation that he'd probably known her father wouldn't be able to attend due to his long-standing monthly dinner with the oil minister, the invitation to the yacht, which was sure to cause a reaction in her brother, letting Pietro drink far more than he should've so he'd get her alone...

'You planned this,' she accused in a hushed tone because her throat was working to swallow down her rising anger.

'I plan everything, Inez,' he replied simply.

She looked into his face. The indomitable determination stamped on his harsh features sent a wave of anxiety through her.

She started to speak, to say the words that seemed unreal to her and her mouth trembled. His gaze dropped to the telling reaction and she immediately clamped her lips together. Showing weakness would only get her eaten alive.

Not that she wouldn't be anyway. A bubble of hysteria threatened. She swallowed and held his gaze.

'You want me to be your *mistress*?'

He laughed long and deeply. 'Is that what you would call yourself?'

She flushed. 'How else would you describe what you've just demanded of me? This *keeping* me? What you're suggesting is archaic enough to be described as such. Or does *plaything* more suit your pseudo-modernistic outlook?'

'No, Inez. I don't like the term plaything either. I have no intention of playing with you. No, what I foresee for us is much more grown up than that.' The sexual intent behind the statement was unmistakable.

Rather than being offended or shocked, Inez found herself growing breathless. Excited.

No!

'Yes,' he murmured as if he'd read her mind.

'Whatever term you slap on your intentions, I refuse to be a part of it. I'm going to find my brother—'

He slowly sank onto the plush seat, curved his hand along the back of the chair and levelled one ankle over his knee. 'And tell him that you've dashed his hopes of a possible high profile position in your father's administration because you couldn't take one for the team? I don't think you're in a position to refuse any demands I make, *anjo*.'

'Stop calling me that! And I won't be a pawn in whatever game you're playing with my father and brother. Pietro is well aware of that.'

'Really? Since when? Wasn't serving on your father's

campaign the reason you dropped out of university? Clearly, you play a part in your father's political ambitions or you wouldn't have been trying to fleece poor Alfonso. Why stop now when you're so close to achieving your goals? And why claim innocence when it's something you've done before?'

The hurt that scythed through her was deep and jagged. She wasn't aware she'd moved until she stood over him, glaring down at the arrogant face that wore that oh, so self-assured smile.

'I've never wanted to be this…this person you think I am. I was merely trying to help my family. I misjudged the situation and—'

'You mean you fell in love with your mark.'

She swallowed. 'I don't know what you're getting at.' But deep down she suspected.

'I mean you were set a target and you fell in love with your target. Isn't that what happened with Blanco?'

Light-headedness assailed her as he confirmed her suspicion. 'You know about Constantine?'

'I know everything I need to know about your family, *anjo*. But by all means enlighten me as to why you've been so misjudged.'

His cynicism raked her nerves raw. 'I made a mistake, one that I freely admit to.'

'What mistake do you mean, *querida*? I want to hear it.'

'I misjudged a man I thought I could trust.'

'You mean you meant to use him but found out he intended to use you too?' he mocked. 'Some would call that poetic justice.'

Recalling Constantine's public humiliation of her, the names he'd called her in the press, her stomach turned over. 'You're despicable.' She raised her chin. 'And assuming you're even close to being right, won't I be a fool to repeat that mistake again?'

'No.'

'No?'

His eyes fixed on hers. Serious and intense. 'Because this time you know exactly what you're getting. There will be no delusions of love on either of our parts. No pretence. Just a task, executed with smooth efficiency.'

'But you intend to parade me about as your…lover? What will everyone think?'

He shrugged. 'I don't care what everyone thinks. And I don't much think that bothers you either.'

She shivered. 'Of course it bothers me. What makes you think it won't?'

'You're the ultimate young Rio socialite. You have a dedicated following and young impressionable girls can't wait to grow up and be you.' His mockery was unmistakable.

Heat crept up her cheeks. 'That's just the media spinning itself out of control.'

'Carefully fuelled by you to help your father's status. You're always seen with the right offspring of the right ministers and CEOs. You're the attraction to draw the young voters, are you not?'

She couldn't deny the allegation because it was true. Nor did she want to waste time straying away from the more serious subject of the demand he was making of her.

The demand she wouldn't—*couldn't*—consent to.

But there was something about him…a reassurance… and expectation of acquiescence that made the hairs on her nape stand on end.

'What happens if I refuse this…this sleazy proposal?'

'I sign the agreement then use the company as I wish. I could dismantle it piece by piece and sell it off for a neat profit. Or I could just drive down the share price and watch the company implode from the inside out. But that's all boring business. What do you care?'

Her fists clenched. 'I care because my grandfather built that company from nothing.'

'And now your father's willing to hand it over to a complete stranger just so he can further his political career.'

She pursed her lips and fought not to react. She'd been deeply concerned when she'd first heard how her father planned to raise funds for his campaign. Concerns that had been airily brushed away with reassurances of airtight clauses.

Clauses which Theo had apparently easily loopholed.

Maybe it wasn't too late. She could tell him to go to hell and warn her father and brother about the danger their proposed business partner presented and advise them to walk away. Surely that would be better than admitting the lion into their midst and letting him wreak havoc at whim?

Light hazel eyes watched her with a predatory gleam. 'If you're thinking of warning your family, I'd think twice. Remember how easily I dispatched Delgado?'

She stiffened, recalling how a few whispered words had caused one investor in her father's campaign to walk away. 'You don't mean that,' she tried.

He slowly rose from the chair and towered over her. Every protective instinct screamed at her to step back but she stood her ground. Any show of weakness would be mercilessly pounced on.

'Do you want to test me, *anjo*?' The blade of steel that hovered over the endearment sent a shiver down her spine.

She slowly uncurled her fists and forced herself to breathe. 'What do you expect me to do?'

His smile was equally as predatory as the look in his eyes. 'You will inform your father and brother tomorrow that you and I are an item—our meeting last night sparked a chemistry so hot we couldn't *not* be together.'

A tiny sliver of relief eased her constricted chest. 'If that's all you want, I'm sure I can convince them—'

His mocking smile stopped her words.

'After you tell them that, you'll pack your bags and move in with me.'

Shock slammed her sideways. 'Are you serious?'

He gripped her chin and held her pinned under his gaze. 'I've never been more serious in my life.'

'But...why?'

'My reasons are my own. You just need to do as you're told.'

Do as you're told. Constantine had tried to blackmail her with those very words. When she'd refused he'd spread rumours about her in the newspapers.

Anger grew in her belly. But it was a helpless anger born of the knowledge that there was nothing she could do. Once again she was trapped in a hell that came from trying to do what was right for her family.

Only this time she was to truly pay with her body. In a stranger's bed. Her heart tripped before going into fierce overdrive.

She gazed at Theo's face, then his body. A body she would in the very near future become scorchingly intimate with. The horror she'd expected to feel oddly did not materialise.

'How long exactly will I be expected to *do as I'm told*?' she snapped.

'Until after the elections.'

A horrified gasp escaped her throat and she forcibly wrenched herself from his grip. 'But...that's...the elections are *three months* away!'

'*Sim*,' he replied simply.

'*Sim*? You expect me to put my life on hold for the next three months, just like that?' She clicked her fingers.

He raised an eyebrow. 'Do you want me to repeat the part about you not having a choice?'

She searched his face, trying to find meaning behind his intentions. 'What did my father do? Did he best you at a deal? Bad-mouth you to investors? Because I can't see what would make you want to go down this path of trying to get your own back.'

She watched his eyes darken, and his nostrils flare. All

traces of mockery were wiped from his face as he stared down at her. Only she was sure he wasn't really seeing her.

His usual intense focus dulled for several seconds and his jaw clenched so tight she feared it could crack. Whatever memory he was reliving caused volcanic fury to bubble beneath the harsh, ragged breath he expelled and this time she did take that step back, purely for self-preservation.

Voices sounded on the deck below. In a few minutes Pietro and the skipper would return from their tour. Inez wasn't sure whether to be grateful for the disruption or frustrated that her opportunity to find out Theo's reasons for demanding her presence in his bed had been thwarted.

His gaze sharpened, flicked towards the steps and back to her.

'It's time for your answer. Do you agree to my terms?'

She shook her head. 'Not until you tell me— *what are you doing*?' she blurted as he snapped out an arm and tugged her close.

One large bold hand gripped her waist and the other speared through her hair. Completely captured, she couldn't move as he angled her face to his. The unsettling fury was still evident in his darkened eyes and taut mouth. Despite the heat transmitted from his grip, she shivered.

'You seem to think you can talk or question your way out of this, *anjo*. You can't. But perhaps it was a mistake to expect a verbal agreement. Perhaps a physical demonstration is what's best?'

Despite his rhetorical question, she tried to answer. 'No…'

'Yes!' he muttered fiercely. Then his mouth smashed down on hers.

She'd been kissed before. By casual boyfriends in her late teens who she'd felt safe enough with.

By Constantine, in the beginning, before he'd revealed his true ruthless colours.

Nothing of what had gone before prepared her for the power and expertise behind Theo's kiss. Her world tilted beneath her feet as his tongue ruthlessly breached the seam of her lips. Hot, erotically charged and savagely determined, he invaded her mouth with searing passion. Bold and brazen, he flicked his tongue against hers, tasting her once and coming back for more.

The shocked little noise she made was a cross between surprise and her body's stunned reaction to the invasion.

The hand at her waist pressed her closer to his body. Whipcord strength, sleek muscles and his own unique scent brought different sensations that attacked her flailing senses.

Fire lashed through her belly as liquid heat pooled between her thighs. Her breasts, crushed against his chest, swelled and ached, her nipples peaking into demanding points with a swiftness that made her dizzy.

Deus!

Feeling her world career even faster out of control, she threw up her hands. Hard muscle rippled beneath her fingers. The need to explore slammed into her. Before she could question her actions, she slid her hands over his warm cotton-covered shoulders to his nape, her fingers tingling as they encountered his bare skin.

He jerked beneath her touch, pulled back with a tug on her hair. Breathing harshly, he stared into her eyes for several seconds. Hunger blazed in his, turning them a dark, mesmerising molten gold that stole what little breath she had from her lungs. Then his eyes dropped lower to her parted mouth.

A rough sound rumbled from his throat. Then he was kissing her again. Harder, more demanding, more possessively than before.

Inez pushed her fingers through his hair as arousal like she'd never experienced before bit deep. This time, when his tongue slid into her mouth, she met it with hers. Boldly, she tried to give as much as she got, although she knew she was hopelessly inadequate when it came to experience.

The hand around her waist tightened and she was lifted off her feet. Seconds later, she found herself on the bar stool, her legs splayed and Theo firmly between thighs exposed by her stance. He came at her again, the force of his sensual attack tilting the stool backwards.

She threw out her hands onto the counter to keep from toppling over. Theo growled beneath his breath, his hands moving upward from her waist to cup her breasts. He moulded her willing, aching flesh so expertly she whimpered and arched into his hold. Beneath her clothes, her tight nipples unfurled in eager anticipation when his thumbs grazed over them. The deep pleasurable shudder made him repeat the action, eliciting a soft cry of pleasure from deep inside her.

'*Inez!*'

The rapier-sharp call of her name doused her with ice-cold water. She wrenched herself from Theo's hold...or at least she tried to.

The hands that had dropped from her breasts to her waist at the sound of Pietro's return stayed her desperate flight.

'What the *hell* do you think you're doing?' Pietro growled, no longer looking as drunk as he'd been half an hour ago.

'If you need it explained to you, da Costa, then I'm wondering who the hell I'm getting into business with.'

Her brother flushed in anger. 'I wasn't talking to you, Pantelides. But maybe I should ask you what you're doing, pawing my sister like some mad animal.'

Inez desperately tried to pull her dress down. But Theo stood firmly between her thighs, making the task impossible. Her sound of distress drew his attention from Pietro. He stared down at her for a second before he adjusted his stance. But although he allowed her to close her legs and pull her dress down, his hands didn't drop from her waist.

If anything, they tightened, their hold so possessive she fought to breathe.

'Inez was going to tell you tomorrow. But I guess to-night's as good a time as any.'

Pietro's gaze shifted from Theo's face to hers. 'Tell me what?'

'Do you want to do the honours, *anjo*? Or shall I?' he queried softly.

Her heartbeat accelerated but not with the arousal pounding through her bloodstream. She heard the clear warning in Theo's tone. Anything short of what he'd demanded of her would see her family ruined completely.

She opened her mouth. Closed it again and swallowed hard.

A trace of fear washed over Pietro's face. Despite their strained relationship, there'd been times in the past when they'd been close. She knew how much a political career of his own some day meant to him. How much he was pinning his hopes on what her father's campaign would mean to him personally.

She tried again to speak the words Theo demanded she speak. But her vocal cords wouldn't work.

'Would someone hurry up and tell me what's going on?'

Fierce hazel eyes drifted over her face in a look that spelled possession so potent her breath caught.

Theo curled his arm over her shoulders and pulled her into the heat of his body. He drifted his mouth over her temple in an adoring move so utterly convincing she reeled at his skilful deception.

She was grappling with that, and with just how much of the kiss they'd shared had been an exercise in pure ruthless seduction on his part, when he spoke.

'Your sister and I have become…enamoured with each other. We only met last night but already I cannot bear to be without her.' His voice held none of the mockery from before, sparking another stunned realisation of his skill. He stared down at her and she caught the implacable determination in his eyes.

When his gaze reconnected with Pietro's she stared, mesmerised, at his profile then shivered at the iron-hard set to his jaw.

'Tomorrow she will be moving out of your home. And into mine.'

CHAPTER SIX

'*LIKE HELL YOU are*,' Pietro repeated for the hundredth time as their chauffeur-driven car stopped outside the opulent Ipanema mansion she'd grown up in.

She quickly threw open the door and hurried up the steps leading to the double oak front doors although she knew escape wouldn't be easy. Pietro was hard on her heels.

'Did you hear what I said?' he demanded.

'I heard you loud and clear. But you fail to realise I'm no longer a child. I'm twenty-four years old—well over the age when I can do whatever the heck I want.'

He slid a hand through his hair. 'Look, I know I may have pushed you into playing a greater part in *Pai*'s fund-raising campaign. But…I don't think getting involved with Pantelides is a good idea,' he said abruptly.

Inez's heart lurched at his concern but she couldn't reassure him because she herself didn't know what the future held. 'Thank you for your concern but like I said, I'm a grown up.'

He swivelled on his heel in the vast entrance hall of the villa. 'Are you really that into him? I know what I saw on his deck tells its own story but you only met him last night!'

'I hadn't met Alfonso Delgado before last night either and yet you expected me to charm him.'

'*Charm* him, not move in with him!'

'There's no point arguing with me. My mind is made up.'

Pietro's face darkened. 'Is this some sort of rebellion?'

Inez sighed. 'Of course not. But I'd planned to move out anyway, once you and *Pai* started on the campaign trail.'

'Move out and go where? This is your home, Inez,' he replied.

She shook her head. 'My world doesn't begin and end in this house, Pietro. I intend to rent an apartment, get a job.'

'Then don't start by ruining yourself with Pantelides.'

Her throat clogged. 'My reputation is already in shreds after Constantine. I really have nothing left to lose.'

She turned to head up the grand staircase that led to the twin wings of their villa. Behind her, she could still hear Pietro pacing the hallway.

'This doesn't make any sense, Inez. Perhaps a good night's sleep will bring you to your senses.'

She didn't answer. Because she didn't want to waste her time telling him the decision had already been made for her.

For Theo to have gone to the effort of staging that kiss and paving the way for the lies she had to perpetuate, she knew without a shadow of a doubt that his demands were real.

He'd gone to a lot of trouble to set up tonight's meeting. She would be a fool to bait him to see if he would carry out his threat.

Her heart hammered as she undressed and stepped beneath the shower. Slowly soaping her body, she found her mind drifting back to their kiss. The incandescent delirium of it was unlike anything she'd felt before.

Her fingers touched her lips, and they tingled in remembrance.

Tomorrow she was inviting herself into the lion's den to be devoured whole for the sake of her family.

A hysterical laugh became lost in the sound of the running water.

Pietro was finally showing signs of being the brother she remembered before their mother died. Shame that she'd had to sacrifice herself on the altar of their family's prosperity before he'd come round. As for her father…sadness engulfed her at the thought that even if he knew of her sacrifice, he probably wouldn't lift a finger to shield her from it.

Theo's gaze strayed to his phone for the umpteenth time in under twenty minutes and he cursed under his breath.

He'd called Inez this morning and they'd agreed a time of eleven o'clock, two hours before he was due to sign the documents at her father's office.

It was now eleven twenty-five and there was no sign of her. No big deal. She was probably stuck in traffic. Or she hadn't left her home on time, especially if she was packing for a three-month stay.

Besides, women are always late.

Even as a child he'd known this. His mother had never been on time for a single event in her life.

His mother…

Memory rained down vicious blows that had him catching his breath. His mother, the woman who'd been nowhere in sight, either before or after he was kidnapped and held for ransom by Benedicto da Costa's vicious thugs.

For weeks after he'd been rescued and returned home, broken and devastated by his ordeal, he'd asked for his mother. Ari had made several excuses for her absence. But Theo had been unable to reconcile the fact that the mother who'd once treated him as if he'd been the centre of her world suddenly couldn't even be bothered to pick up the phone and enquire about her mentally and physically traumatised child.

No. She'd been too preoccupied with wallowing in her misery following her husband's betrayal to bother with her own children.

Ari had been the one to hold them together after their family was shattered by the press uncovering their father's many shady dealings and philandering ways.

For a very long time he'd laboured under the misconception that out of the three brothers he was the most special in their father's eyes. That just because he was the miracle baby his parents had never thought they'd have, he was their favourite. His kidnapping and what he'd uncovered since had mercilessly ripped that indulgent blindfold away.

Finding out that his father had known about Benedicto da Costa's escalating threats and that he'd done nothing to warn or protect him had forced the cruellest reality on him.

And his mother's response to all that had been to abandon him, together with her other two children, and go into hiding.

Hearing of his father's eventual death had made him even angrier at being robbed of the chance to look his father in the eye and see the monster for himself.

Because, even now, a pathetic part of him clung to the hope that maybe his father hadn't known the full extent of the kidnapping threat; hadn't known that Benedicto da Costa's reaction to being thwarted out of a business deal would be to kidnap a seventeen-year-old boy, and have his torture photographed and sent to his family to pressure them into finding the millions of dollars owed to him.

His phone rang, wrenching him out of the bitter recollections. Glancing down at the number, a bolt of white-hot anger lanced through him. He forced himself to wait for a couple more rings before he answered it. 'Pantelides.'

'*Bom dia.* I've just had a very interesting conversation with my daughter.' Theo detected the throb of anger in Benedicto da Costa's voice and a grim smile curved his own lips. 'She seems determined to pursue this rather *sudden* course of action where you're concerned.'

'Your daughter strikes me as a very determined woman who knows exactly what she wants,' he replied smoothly.

'She is. All the same, I can't help think that this decision is rather precipitate.' There was clear suspicion in Benedicto's voice now.

'Trust me, it's been very well thought through on my part. Tell me, Benedicto, has she left yet?'

'*Sim*, against my wishes, she has left home,' he replied, his voice taut with displeasure.

A wave of satisfaction swept through Theo. 'Good. I'll await her arrival.'

'I hope this will not delay our meeting,' the older man enquired.

'Don't worry. The moment I welcome your daughter into my home, I'll head to your offices.'

An edgy silence greeted his answer and Theo could sense him weighing his words to perceive a possible threat. Finally, Benedicto answered, 'We should celebrate our partnership once the documents are signed.'

Theo's mouth twisted. Benedicto had already moved on from the subject of his daughter. And he noticed there had been no admonition to treat her well, *or else…*

But the knowledge that Benedicto had intensely disapproved of Inez's intentions and had called him to air that disapproval was good enough for him.

'Great idea. Unfortunately, I'll be busy for the next few nights. Perhaps some time next week Inez and I will have you and Pietro over for dinner.'

The fiery exhalation that greeted his indelicate words made Theo's grin widen.

'Of course. I'll look forward to it. *Até a próxima,*' Benedicto said tightly.

Theo ended the call without responding. He absorbed the pulse of triumph rushing through his bloodstream for a pleasurable second before he exhaled.

His plan was far from being executed. But this was a brilliant start.

He looked out of the floor to ceiling window at the sparkling pool and the beach beyond and tried to push away the images that had visited him again last night and the single hoarse scream that had woken him.

A full body shudder raked his frame and he shoved a hand through his hair. Although he'd long ago accepted the nightmares as part of his existence, he loathed their presence and the helplessness he felt in those endless moments when he was caught in their grip.

The single therapy session he'd let Ari talk him into attending had mentioned triggers and the importance of anxiety-detectors.

He laughed under his breath. Putting himself within touching distance of the man responsible for those nightmares would be termed as foolhardy by most definitions.

Theo chose to believe that exacting excruciating revenge would heal him. *An eye for an eye.*

And if he had to suffer a few side-effects during the process, then so be it.

He tensed as his security intercom buzzed. Crossing the vast sun-dappled room, he picked up the handset.

'*Senhor*, there's a Senhorita da Costa here to see you.'

A throb of a different nature invaded his bloodstream. 'Let her in,' he instructed.

Replacing the handset, he found himself striding to the front door and out onto his driveway before he realised what he was doing.

Hands on his hips, he watched her tiny green sports car appear on his long driveway. The top was down and the wind was blowing through her loose thick hair. Stylish sunglasses shielded her eyes from him but he knew she was watching him just as he was studying her.

She brought the car to a smooth stop a few feet from him and turned off the ignition. For several seconds the only sound that impinged on the late morning air was the water cascading from the stone nymph's urn into the fountain bowl. Then the sound of her seat belt retracting joined the tinkling.

'You're late,' he breathed.

She pulled out her keys and opened her door. 'It took

a while to uproot myself from the only home I've ever known,' she said waspishly.

A touch from a well-manicured finger and the boot popped open. He strolled forward, viewed its contents and his eyes narrowed.

'And yet you only packed two suitcases for a three-month stay?' he remarked darkly. 'I hope you don't think you can run back to *Pai*'s house each time you need a new toothbrush?'

She got out of the car.

From across the width of the open top, she glared at him. 'I can afford to buy my own toothbrush, thanks,' she retorted.

Theo nodded. 'Good to hear it.' Unable to stop himself, his gaze travelled down her body.

Faded jeans moulded her hips and her cream scooped-neck silk top left her arms bare. Its short-in-the-front, longer-at-the-back design exposed a delicious inch of golden, smooth midriff when she turned to shut her door and the air lifted the light material.

Heat invaded his groin, once again reminding him of their kiss last night.

The kiss that had blown him clean away and rendered him almost incoherent by the time her brother had rudely interrupted them.

Hell, she'd been so responsive, so intoxicatingly passionate, she'd gone to his head within seconds. What had set out as a hammering-a-point-home exercise to convince her he meant business had swiftly morphed into something else. Something he'd still been struggling to decipher when she'd been hustled off his boat by her suddenly protective brother.

One thing he'd been certain of was that had Pietro been a few more minutes returning to the top deck, Theo was sure he would've had his hands on her bare skin, exploring her in a more earthy way, propriety be damned.

Luckily, he'd come to his senses. And, from here on in, he intended to focus on his plan and his plan alone.

She went to the boot and bent over to lift the first case. The sight of her rounded bottom made a vein throb in his temple.

He stepped forward, grabbed the cases from her and handed them to his hovering butler. 'I'm running late for my meeting. We should have done this last night like I suggested.'

He'd tried. But she'd stood her ground and he had quickly decided that there was nothing to be gained from getting into a slanging match with Pietro da Costa. That he'd also realised that his change of timing was to do with that kiss and nothing to do with his carefully laid plans had had him sharply reassessing his priorities.

'I'm here now. Don't let me stop you from leaving if you wish to.'

He smiled at the undisguised hope in her voice. 'Now what kind of host would I be if I desert you the moment you turn up?'

'The same as the one who blackmailed me into this situation in the first place?' she replied caustically.

There was a thread of unhappiness in her voice that grated at him.

'This will go a lot easier if you accept the status quo.'

'You mean just shut up and *do as I'm told*?' she snapped bitterly as she slammed the boot shut and walked towards him.

Unease weaved through him. With restless shoulders, he shrugged it away. 'No. You can protest all you want. I just want you to be aware of the futility of it.'

She snorted under her breath, a sound that made his smile widen. She had spirit, and wasn't afraid to bare her claws when cornered. Which made him wonder why she withstood the unreasonable control from her father. Were material benefits so important to her?

The heavy glass front door slid shut behind them and he watched her reaction to his house. It was an architectural masterpiece, and had featured in several top magazines before he'd bought it a year ago and ceased all publicity of the award-winning design.

'Wow,' she breathed. 'This place must have cost you a bomb.'

Theo had his answer. Disappointment scythed through him as he watched her move to the bronze sculpture he'd acquired several weeks back.

'I saw the exhibition on this two months ago. This piece is worth a cool half million,' she gasped in wonder. 'And that one—' she pointed to another smaller sculpture he'd commissioned by his favourite New York artist '—is an exclusive piece, worth over two million dollars.'

His lips twisted. 'Should I be worried that you know the monetary value of every piece of art in my house?'

She whirled to face him. 'Excuse me?'

'I hope we can engage in more meaningful dialogue than how much everything is worth. I find the subject of avarice…distasteful.'

Her gasp sounded genuinely hurt-filled. 'I wasn't…I'm just…that's a horrible thing to say, Mr Pantelides.'

His eyebrow lifted. 'I thought I kissed all the formality out of you last night?'

She flushed a delicate pink that made her skin glow. Her expressive brown eyes slid from his and she turned back to examine the room.

It was then that he noticed the faint bruises on her left arm. He was striding to her and lifting her arm to examine the marks before his brain had connected with his body.

'Who did this to you?' he demanded.

Her surprised gaze snapped from his to her arm. Her flush deepened as she swiftly shook her head. 'I…it doesn't matter; it's nothing—'

He swallowed hard. 'Like hell it is.' The idea that his de-

mands on her might have caused this to happen to her made
a thread of revulsion rise in his belly. He forced it down and
concentrated on her face. 'Tell me who it was.'

She swallowed. 'My father.'

Pure fury blurred his vision for several seconds. 'Your
father did this to you?'

She gave a jerky nod.

Why the hell was he surprised? 'Has he done anything
like this before?' he bit out.

She pressed her lips together in a vain attempt not to
answer. A firm grip of her chin, tilting it to his gaze, convinced her otherwise. 'Once. Maybe twice.'

His vicious curse made her shiver. Theo examined
the marks, which would grow yellowish by nightfall, and
pushed down the mounting fury. 'That son of a bitch will
never touch you again.'

Shock made her gasp. 'That *son of a bitch* is my *father*.
And I've given you what you wanted, so I expect you to
hold up your end of the bargain.'

He frowned with genuine puzzlement. 'Why do you tolerate this, Inez?' He glanced from the bruises to her face.
'You're more than old enough to live on your own. Hell, if
money and a rich lifestyle are what you crave, you're suffi-
ciently resourceful to find some wealthy guy who would—'

She snatched her arm from his grasp. It was then that he
realised he'd been caressing her soft skin with his thumb.
He missed the connection almost immediately.

'I certainly hope you're not about to suggest what I think
you are?'

Keen frustration rocked him into movement. 'I'm curious, that's all.'

'I'm not here to satisfy your curiosity. And perhaps you've
been lucky enough to be granted a perfect family but not
everyone has been afforded the same luxury. We made do
with what we… Did I say something funny?' she snapped.

He cut off the mirthless laughter that had bubbled up at

her words. 'Yes. *You're damned hilarious*. You obviously don't know what you're talking about.'

She stared at him with confusion and a little trepidation. 'No. But how can I? We only met two nights ago. And now I'm here, your possession for the foreseeable future.'

The simple statement twisted like live electricity between them. The look in her eyes said she was daring him to react to it. But the off-kilter emotions swirling through his chest made him back away from it. He shouldn't have dealt with her so soon after speaking to Benedicto. He should've left Teresa, his housekeeper, to see to her needs.

He turned and headed for the door. 'I'll show you upstairs. And then I need to go.'

Striding into the hallway, he started up the grand central stairs that led to the upper two floors of his house. After a few steps, he noticed she wasn't behind him.

Turning, he found her paused on the second step, her gaze once again wide and wondrous as she stared around her.

'What?'

'There are no concrete walls.' She looked up at the all-encompassing glass around her. 'Or ceilings.'

He resumed climbing the stairs. 'I don't like walls. And I don't like ceilings,' he threw over his shoulder.

She hurried after him and caught up with him as they neared the first suite of rooms. She regarded him for a few seconds then bit her lip.

He paused with a hand on the doorknob. 'What?' he asked again, trying and not succeeding in prising his gaze from her plump lips.

'I'm not sure whether to take that as a metaphor or not.'

'*Anjo*, there's no hidden meaning behind my words. I literally do not like concrete walls or ceilings.'

She frowned in puzzlement. 'I don't understand.'

'It's very simple. I don't like being closed in.'

'You're…*claustrophobic*?' She whispered the word as if she wasn't sure how to apply it to him.

He shrugged and hurriedly threw open the door, a part of him reeling at what he'd just admitted. 'We all have our flaws,' he retorted.

'Were you born with it?'

His jaw clenched once. 'No. It was a condition thrust upon me quite against my will.'

'But…you seem…'

'Invincible?' he mocked.

Her lips pursed. 'I was going to say self-assured.'

'Appearances can be deceptive, *querida*. After you.' He indicated the door he'd just opened.

She stopped dead in the middle of the room. From where he stood, Theo could see what she was seeing. With the glass walls and white carpet and furnishings and nothing but the view of the blue sky and sea beyond, the vista was breathtaking.

'*Deus*, I feel as if I'm floating on a cloud,' she murmured with an awe-filled voice.

'That is the primary aim of the property. Light, air, no constrictions.'

He'd learned to his cost that constrictions triggered his anxiety and fuelled his nightmares. Which was why every single property he owned was filled with light.

'It's beautiful.'

The strong pulse of pleasure that washed through him had him stepping back. Things were getting out of hand. He needed to walk away, go to his meeting with Benedicto and remind himself why he was in Rio. This need to bask in Inez's presence, touch her skin, indulge in the urge to taste her sensual lips once more needed to killed. He had to stick to his game plan.

'Make yourself at home. I'll be back later. We're going out this evening. Dinner at Cabana de Ouro, then probably clubbing. Wear something short and sexy.'

Her eyes widened at his curt tone but he was already turning away. He didn't stop until he reached the landing.

On a completely unstoppable urge, he looked over his shoulder. Through the glass walls, he saw her frozen in the middle of her suite, her eyes fixed on him.

She looked lost. And confused. And a little relieved.

With grim determination he turned and headed down the stairs. And he hated himself for needing the reminder that Benedicto da Costa had damaged not just him, but his whole family.

The payback should be equal to the crime committed.

The black satin boy shorts she chose to wear were plenty stylish and sexy. They also moulded her behind much more than she was strictly comfortable with but everything else she'd hastily packed was too formal for dinner at Cabana de Ouro, the trendy restaurant and bar in Ipanema. Coupled with the dark gold silk top, with her hair piled on top of her head and gold hoops in her ears and bangles on her wrist, she looked good enough for whatever club Theo intended to take her to after dinner.

Clubbing wasn't strictly her entertainment of choice. But since, for the next twelve weeks, Theo expected her to obey his every command, the least she could do was learn to pick her battles. And she'd already endured one battle this morning in the form of confrontation with Theo. And found out he was claustrophobic.

He'd been right; she'd secretly imagined him to be invincible. The way he carried himself, the innate authority and self-assurance that seemed part of his genetic make up, she'd had no trouble seeing him best each situation he found himself him.

Hearing him admit to a deep flaw that most grown men would be ashamed of had floored her. Coupled with his concern when he'd seen the marks her father had inflicted when she'd announced she was moving in with Theo, she'd been seriously floundering in a sea of uncertainty by the time he'd left her bedroom.

She examined the marks on her arm now and released a shaky breath to see that they were fading. She was shrugging on the shoulder-padded waist-length leather jacket that went with the outfit when she heard Theo's Aston Martin roar into the driveway.

Her fingers trembled as she fastened the long-chained gold medallion necklace at her nape.

He'd left her so abruptly this morning she hadn't had the time to question him about sleeping arrangements. A closer examination of her suite after he'd left had revealed no presence of another occupant, and after talking to Teresa, his housekeeper, she'd found out that the *senhor*'s suite was directly above hers, taking up the whole glass-roofed top floor of the house.

The fact that she wouldn't be expected to share his bed immediately should've pleased her. Instead she was more on edge than ever. Or maybe that was what he wanted? That she should be kept guessing, kept on a knife-edge of uncertainty like some sort of game?

Deus!

She'd barely spent one day under his glass roof and already she was being driven mad. His response to her admiring his sculptures had been too infuriating for her to explain how she'd come to acquire such knowledge of sculptures—her late mother's talent. If he wanted to believe Inez appreciated beautiful art purely with dollar signs in her eyes, that was his problem.

Her breath caught as she heard distinct footsteps in the hallway. Teresa had shown her how to shroud the bedroom glass for privacy and she'd activated it before she'd gone in to take a shower. It was still shrouded now although she could make out a faint outline of the towering man who knocked a few seconds later.

'Come in.' She cringed at the husky breathlessness of her voice.

The heavy glass swung back and Theo stood framed in the doorway.

Light hazel eyes locked on her with the force of a laser beam for several seconds before they travelled slowly down her body.

Before meeting him, Inez would've found it hard to believe she could physically react so strongly to a look from a man. Constantine, with all his misleading smiles and false charm, had never affected her like this, not even when she'd believed herself in love with him.

With Theo the evidence was irrefutable—in the accelerated beat of her heart, the tightening and heaviness of her breasts and the stinging heat that spread outward from her belly like a flash fire.

She watched his mouth drop open as his gaze reached her shorts and her own mouth dried at the look that settled on his face.

'What the hell are you wearing?'

'What? I'm wearing clothes, Mr Pantelides,' she snapped, once she was able to get her brain working again.

He stepped into the room and the door slid shut behind him. All at once, she became aware of the sheer size of him, of the restriction in her breathing and the fact that her eyes were devouring his magnificent form.

'Let's get one thing straight. From now on you'll address me as Theo. No more *senhor* and no more Mr Pantelides, understand?'

'Is that an order?' She tilted her chin to see his face as he stopped before her.

'It's a friendly warning that there will be consequences if you don't comply.'

'What consequences?' she huffed.

'How about every time you call me *senhor* I kiss that sassy mouth of yours?'

CHAPTER SEVEN

'Excuse me?' Her voice was a little more breathless. With excitement. *Deus*, what was wrong with her? This man was threatening her family, was effectively turning her life upside down for the sake of some unknown grudge. And all she could think of was him kissing her again.

'No, you're not excused. Use my first name or I'll kiss it into you. Your choice. Now tell me what the hell you're wearing.' His gaze dropped back to her shorts, his eyes glazing with hunger so acute, her heart hammered.

'These are shorts. You said "short and sexy".'

His mouth worked for a few seconds before he nodded. 'I said short, but I don't think I meant that short, *anjo*.'

Heat raced up her neck and she barely managed to stop her hand from connecting with his face. 'They are not that bad.'

His rasping laugh made her face flame. 'Trust me, from where I'm standing, they're lethal.'

'I have nothing else to change into. Everything else is too formal for a club.'

Dark eyes rose, almost reluctantly, to clash with hers. 'I find that very hard to believe.'

'It's true. I didn't have enough time to pack properly. Besides, I didn't take you for...'

His eyes narrowed. 'Didn't take me for what?'

She shrugged. 'You don't strike me as the clubbing type.'

One corner of his mouth lifted. 'Have you been forming impressions about me, *anjo*?'

She kicked herself for that revelatory remark. 'Not really.'

He looked down at her shorts one more time and he turned abruptly for the door. 'I'll be ready to go in fifteen minutes. You can tell me what other impressions you've formed about me at dinner.'

Inez exhaled and realised she hadn't taken a full breath since he'd walked into her presence. Her whole body quivered as she shoved her feet into three-inch platforms and made sure her cell phone and lipstick were in the black and gold clutch.

She caught sight of herself in the hallway mirror as she made her way down and cringed at the feverish look in her eyes.

Reassuring herself firmly that it was anger at Theo for his overbearing treatment of her, she made her way to the living room.

Floodlights illuminated the pool and gardens in a stunning display of shimmering light and shrubbery. Like every single aspect of the building, the sight was so breathtaking her fingers itched with the need to draw.

Setting her clutch down, she went to the large duffel bag she'd brought down this afternoon and took out her sketchpad and pencil.

She was so lost in capturing the vista before her, she didn't sense Theo enter the room until his unique scent wrapped itself around her.

She jerked around to see him standing close behind her, his eyes on her picture.

'You draw?' he asked in surprise.

Unable to answer for the loud hammering of her heart, she nodded.

He reached forward and plucked the pad from her nerveless fingers. Slowly, he thumbed through the pages. 'You're very talented,' he finally said.

Expecting a derogatory remark to follow, like his comment on his art this morning, her eyes widened when she realised he meant it. 'You really think so?' she asked.

He closed the pad and handed it back to her, his eyes speculative as they rested on her face. 'I wouldn't say it otherwise, *anjo.*'

Pleasure fizzed through her. 'Thank you.' She smiled as she stood. Crossing over to her duffel bag, she bent to place the pad back into it.

'*Thee mou!*'

She dropped the pad and hastily straightened. 'What?'

'You bend over like that while we're out and I will not be responsible for my actions, understood?' he growled.

Her mouth dropped open at the dark promise in his voice. A shudder ran through her body as hunger further darkened his eyes. She licked her lip nervously as the atmosphere thickened with sensual charges that crackled and snapped along her nerves.

'We…we don't have to go out if what I'm wearing offends you…Theo,' she ventured hesitantly, sensing that he held himself on the very edge of control.

He inhaled deeply, his chest expanding underneath the dark green shirt and black leather jacket he wore with black trousers. 'That's where you're wrong. What you're offering doesn't offend me in the least. But I'm a red-blooded, possessive male who is finding it difficult not to roar out his primitive reaction to the idea of other men looking at you.' He said it so matter-of-factly she couldn't form a decent response. 'But I'll try to be a *gentleman.* Come.' He held out his arm.

With seriously indecent thoughts of Theo fighting to the death for her flitting through her mind, she crossed the room to his side.

He led them out and held the passenger door of his car open. The first few minutes of the ride to Ipanema was conducted in silence. Every now and then, he raked a hand through his hair and slid a glance at her naked thighs. Each time, he exhaled noisily.

A wild part of her wanted to flaunt herself for him, revel in his very physical reaction to her attire. Another part of her wanted to run and hide from the volatile emotions swirling through the enclosed space of the luxurious sports car.

By the time they drew up in the car park of the exclusive restaurant her pulse was jumping with anxiety. She forced the feeling down and followed him into the restaurant. Finding out they were dining in the even more exclusive upper floor led to all sorts of renewed anxiety as she preceded him up the steps.

The moment they were seated, he leaned forward. 'The moment we return home, I'm burning those shorts.'

She glared at him. 'No, you are not, *senhor!* They're my favourite pair.'

'Then frame them and mount them on a wall. But you most definitely will not be wearing them out again.'

That wild streak widened. 'I thought you would be man enough to handle a little…challenge. Are you saying you're not?'

His eyes narrowed. 'Don't bait a hungry lion, *querida*, unless you're prepared to be devoured,' he grated out.

'Did you tell your last girlfriend how she should dress too?' she challenged.

His mouth compressed. 'My last girlfriend was under the misconception that the more frequently she walked around naked the more interested I would be in her. She lasted ten days.'

Inez's curiosity spiked, along with an emotion she was very loath to name. 'How long did your longest relationship last?'

'Three weeks.'

Her breath caught. 'So why three *months* with me?' she asked.

He looked startled for a moment then he shrugged. 'Because you're not my girlfriend. You're so very much more.'

Inez was struck dumb by his reply. A small foolish part of her even felt giddy, until she reminded herself that she was intended to be nothing but his *mistress*. Again unfathomable emotions wrapped themselves around her heart. She cleared her throat and fought to keep her voice even. 'Why *misconception*?'

'Very few women manage to catch and keep my interest for very long, *anjo*.'

'Because you get bored easily?' she dared.

His lashes swept down for a few seconds before they rose again to capture hers. 'Because my demons always win when pitted against the rigours of normal relationships.'

'*Demons?*'

'*Sim, anjo*. Demons. I have a lot of them. And they're very possessive.' A wave of anguish rolled over his face, then it was gone the next instant. He nodded to the hovering *sommelier* and ordered their wine. Another pulse of surprise went through her when she noticed it was the same wine she'd served at the fund-raiser and her favourite.

'The burning is now off the table. Hell, you can even keep the damn shorts. But, for the sake of my sanity, can we agree that you don't wear them outside?' he asked with one quirked eyebrow.

She pretended to consider it. 'What is your sanity worth to me?'

'You think you're in a position to bargain with me, Inez?' he asked, his voice deceptively soft.

'I never pass up an opportunity to bargain.'

He regarded her silently for several minutes. Then he shrugged. 'As long as I achieve my goals in the end, I see no reason why the road to success shouldn't be littered with minor obstacles. Tell me what you desire.'

'Is that what I am, a minor obstacle?'

'Don't miss your opportunity with meaningless questions.'

The need for clarity finally forced her to speak. 'I wish to know exactly what you want of me.'

'Sorry, I cannot answer that.'

She frowned. 'Why not?'

'Because my needs are…fluid.' The peculiar smile accompanying his answer sent a tingle of alarm down her spine.

'So I am to live in uncertainty for the next three months?'

'The unknown can be challenging. It can also be exciting.'

'Is that why you came to Rio? To seek challenge and excitement?'

For several seconds he stared at her. Then he slowly shook his head. 'No, my reason for being in Rio is specific and a well-planned event.'

Inez shivered at the succinct response. 'I can't help but be frightened by your answer.'

Her candid admission seemed to surprise him. 'Why is that?'

'Because I have a feeling it has something to do with my family. Pietro has his flaws but he's never done anything without my father's express approval. Besides, you're much older than him, which makes it unlikely that he's the one you came here for. You're here because of my father, aren't you?'

It took an astonishing amount of control not to react to her simple but accurate summation of the single subject that had consumed him for over a decade.

Thinking back, he realised he'd given her several clues to enable her to reach this conclusion. Somehow, in the mere forty-eight hours that he'd known her, Inez had managed to slip under his guard and was threatening to uncover his true purpose for being in Rio.

He also realised that he'd given her much more leeway than he'd ever intended to when he'd formulated his plan. Inviting her to compromise? Inviting her to state her desires with the knowledge that he was seriously considering granting them?

After his hasty departure this morning he'd realised that he'd let those marks on her arms sway him into going easy on her. *Because he hadn't wanted her to think he was a monster like her father?*

The man who hadn't so much as asked after his daughter when Theo had attended his office to sign the agreement papers?

The man whose eyes had shone with greed and triumph even before the ink had dried on the documents?

No, he was nothing like Benedicto da Costa. He wasn't about to lose any already precious sleep wondering about that little statement.

What he had to be careful of was that his enemy's daughter didn't guess his intentions. He was so very close to having Benedicto right where he wanted him. He couldn't afford to be swayed by a heart-shaped face or the most sinfully sexy pair of shorts he'd ever seen in his life, no matter how acute the ache in his groin.

'Will you please tell me why you're after my father?' she implored softly. The concern on her face appeared genuine and he suddenly realised that, despite Benedicto's treatment of her, Inez cared for her father.

His nostrils flared as bitterness rocked through him. He'd once been in that same position, foolishly believing that the father he'd idolised and loved beyond reason cared just as deeply for him. That he wasn't the fraudster and philanderer the press were making him out to be.

Now, he wanted to rip the blindfold from her eyes, make her see the true monster in the man she called *Pai*. Make her see that her love was nothing but a manipulative tool that would be used against her eventually.

Except he had a strong feeling she already knew, and chose to overlook it. Which made his blood boil even more.

'Why, do you plan to sacrifice yourself to save him?' he taunted.

She gasped, dropping the sterling silver fork she'd been nervously toying with. 'So, it *is* my father!'

He cursed under his breath. 'If you so much as breathe a word in his direction about your suspicions, I'll make sure you regret it for the rest of your life.'

She paled. 'You really expect me to sit back and watch you destroy him?'

'I expect you to hold up your end of the bargain we struck. Live under my roof in exchange for me leaving the loophole in the contract alone. Are you prepared to do that or do I need to plot another plan of action?' he asked, not bothering to hide the threat in his voice.

She stared back at him apprehensively. Her chin rose and her brown eyes burned holes in him but she nodded. 'I'll stick to our agreement.'

When their wine was served, he watched her take a big gulp and curbed the desire to follow suit. He was driving and needed to restrict his drinking. Nevertheless, a sip of the Chilean red went a way to restoring a little order to his floundering thoughts.

Thee mou, he hadn't even fired the first salvo and things were getting out of hand. Why on earth had he shared the presence of his demons with her? And that comment about her being so much more than a girlfriend? He silently shook his head and sucked in a control-affirming breath.

Their dinner progressed in near silence. Theo reminded himself that his main reason for bringing her out hadn't been for conversation. When she refused dessert, he settled the bill quickly and rose to help her out of her seat.

Fire shot through his groin, hard and fierce, as he was once again confronted with the risqué shorts. While they'd been seated, he'd managed to tamp down the effect of those shorts on his raging libido.

Now, as she walked in front of him, he was treated to a mouth-watering sight of her deliciously rounded bottom and stunning legs. With each sway of her hips, he grew harder until he wondered if he had any blood left in his upper extremities that hadn't migrated south.

He was reconsidering his decision not to burn the shorts at the earliest opportunity when he caught a male diner staring in blatant appreciation at her legs.

His growl was low but unmistakable. The man hastily averted his gaze but Theo was still simmering in primitive emotions when they reached the car park.

He followed her to the passenger side but, instead of opening the door for her, he braced his hand on either side of her and leaned in close. With her front pressed against the door, her bottom was moulded into his groin in such a way that she couldn't fail to notice his state of arousal.

Her breathing quickened, but she stayed put. 'What are you doing?'

'Delivering the punishment I promised.'

'Sorry?'

'You called me *senhor* when we were in the restaurant.'

She tried to turn around but he pressed her more firmly against the car. 'I…don't remember.'

'Of course you do. You also thought I wouldn't act on my promise in full view of other diners, didn't you?'

'No, I wasn't—'

'Maybe you were right. Or maybe we both knew I'd want to do more than just kiss you.'

'You're wrong…'

'Am I?'

'Yes…'

'So you'd prefer I let this one slide?' He rocked his hips against her bottom and her breath hitched. 'You won't think me weak?'

Her shocked laugh heated the air around them. 'Only someone foolish would think you weak.'

'I'm not sure whether there's a compliment in there. Is there?'

Her head fell forward, exposing the seductive line of her neck. 'Am I to pander to your ego too, Theo?'

He laughed. 'How can you appear submissive and yet taunt me at the same time?'

She lifted her head and turned to stare at him. Whatever she saw in his face made her squirm harder. Provocatively. Her gaze dropped to his mouth and Theo could no more resist the temptation than he could breathe.

Fingers sliding beneath her knotted hair to hold her still, he caught her mouth in a fierce kiss. Every emotion he'd experienced since waking that morning was delivered in that kiss—passion, arousal, confusion, anxiety and anger. He pinned her against the car so she couldn't move, couldn't put those seductive hands on his body.

Although he missed her touch, a part of him was thankful because, had she had access, he would've lost even more of his mind than he suspected he was losing.

He registered the brief flashes behind his closed eyelids but didn't break the kiss. He suspected Inez had no idea what had just happened. And even if she had, she wouldn't have suspected the true reason behind the paparazzi shots because she was used to being the darling of the press.

Well, she was in for a rude awakening...

She started to open her mouth wider, to return his demanding kiss.

He slowly lifted his head. When she made a tiny sound of protest and tried to recapture his mouth, he forced himself to step away. He'd achieved one part of what he'd set out to do. The second part was a short drive away.

Curving his arm around her waist, he peeled her away from the door, opened it and deposited her inside, all the time trying not to stare down at her legs and imagine how they would feel wrapped around his waist.

He swallowed hard as he rounded the hood and slid behind the wheel.

'Time to head to the club before I give in to the urge to deliver more punishment.'

Her eyes dropped to his mouth and he barely suppressed a groan as she licked her lips.

'For your mercy, I will teach you how to samba like a true Brazilian,' she replied huskily.

Inez lay among the white sheets the next morning, trying hard not to relive the events of the night before but it was as futile as trying to stop a tidal wave.

They'd eventually emerged from the nightclub at two in the morning. She'd been flushed and sweaty from being plastered to Theo's superb body for three straight hours. But the wild racing of her heart had nothing to do with her exertions on the dance floor and everything to do with the man who'd focused on her as if she was the only woman in the whole club.

And *Deus*, had he danced like a dream? Far from tutoring him on the correct steps of her native dance, she'd found herself following his lead as he'd moved expertly on the dance floor.

When he'd caught her to him, her back to his front and replayed the scene in the car park, but this time to music, she'd seriously feared her heart would beat itself to expiration.

In that moment, she'd forgotten that there was a sinister purpose to Theo's plan; that he'd all but admitted she was being used as a pawn in some deadly game he was playing with her father. When he'd laid his stubbled jaw against her cheek and hummed the sultry samba music in her ear, she'd closed her eyes and imagined what it would be like to belong—truly belong—to a man like Theo.

Turning over in bed, she groaned in disbelief at how

susceptible she'd been to his hard body and magnetic charisma. *Santa Maria*, she'd been all but putty in his hands.

Luckily, the fresh air and the long drive back had hammered some sense into her. The moment they'd returned, she'd bidden him a curt *boa noite*, left him standing in the hallway and retreated as fast as her sore feet would carry her.

And she intended to carry on like that. She might not know what his end game was, but she refused to be a willing participant in his campaign.

The last thing she wanted to do was to fall for another manipulator like Constantine.

She was here only because she had no choice but she didn't intend to idle away her time in this house. Theo expected her to stay here for three months, which meant whatever he had planned was not to be executed immediately. Perhaps she could convince him to change his mind in that time.

Yeah, and fairy tales really did come true...

Or she could find out exactly what his intentions were.

She'd seen the look in his eyes when he spoke about her father. Whatever vendetta he'd planned, he intended to see it through.

Helplessly, she rolled over in bed and her eyes lit on the bedside clock. She jerked upright and threw the sheet aside. She might not have anywhere to be on this Saturday morning but lazing about in bed past ten o'clock wasn't her style.

She jumped into the shower, shampooed her hair and washed her body with quick, regimented movement ingrained in her from her time at the Swiss boarding school her father had sent her to just to impress his friends.

Leaving her damp hair to dry naturally, she pulled on an aqua-coloured sundress and slipped her feet into low-heeled thongs. Smoothing her favourite sunscreen moisturiser over her face and arms, she left her room and headed downstairs.

Teresa was crossing the hallway carrying a *cafetière* of freshly made coffee and indicated for Inez to follow her.

She led her out to the terrace that overlooked the immense square infinity pool. Light danced off the water but her attention was caught and held by the man seated at the cast iron oval breakfast table.

His white short-sleeved polo shirt did amazing things to his eyes and olive-toned skin. And loose green shorts exposed solid thighs and lightly hair-sprinkled legs that made her mouth dry before flooding with moisture that threatened to choke her.

'*Bom dia, anjo.* Are you going to stand there all morning?' he mocked.

She forced her legs to move and took the chair he indicated to his right.

'Coffee?' he asked, his voice deep and low.

'Yes, please.' Her voice had grown husky and emerged barely above a whisper.

He nodded to Teresa who smiled, filled her cup then made herself scarce.

Inez sipped the hot brew just as a delaying tactic so she didn't have to look at him.

So far she'd seen Theo in formal evening wear and smart casual and each look had threatened to knock her sideways. But seeing him now, with so much of his vibrant olive skin on show, threatened to topple her completely. She took another hasty sip and choked as the liquid scalded her mouth.

Grabbing the napkin to stop herself from dribbling like an idiot, she looked up and caught his mocking smile. 'You'd rather blister yourself than converse with me?'

She swallowed and fought to present a passable smile. 'Of course not. I was just enjoying the…view.' She indicated beyond his shoulder, where the garden extended beyond the pool and sloped down to the sandy white beach and sparkling ocean.

With a disbelieving smile, he picked up the paper next to his plate and shook it out. 'If you say so—'

Her horrified gasp made him lower the newspaper. 'Something wrong?'

'Is that a picture of *us*?' she demanded through a severely constricted throat. The question was redundant because the picture taking up the whole of the front page was printed in vivid Technicolor.

He'd already seen it, of course, so he didn't bother to glance where her appalled gaze was riveted. 'Yes. Fresh off the morning press.'

'*Meu deus!*' She reached out and snatched the broadsheet out of his grasp. It was even worse up close. 'It looks as if…as if—' Disbelief caught in her throat, eating the rest of her words.

'As if I'm taking you from behind?' he supplied helpfully.

Humiliating heat stained her cheeks. '*Sim*,' she muttered fiercely. 'With your jacket covering me that way it looks as if I'm wearing nothing from the waist down! It's…it's disgusting!'

He plucked the paper from her hand and studied the picture. 'Hmm, it certainly is…*something.*'

'How can you sit there and be so unconcerned about it?' The picture had been taken with a high-resolution camera but, with the low lighting in the car park, the suggestiveness in the picture could be misinterpreted a thousand ways. None of them complimentary.

'Relax. We weren't exactly having sex, were we?'

'That's not the point.' She grabbed the paper back and quickly perused the article accompanying the gratuitous picture, fearing the worst. Sure enough, her father's political campaign had been called into question, along with an even more unsavoury speculation on her private life.

If this is what they do in public we can only imagine what they do in private…

Her hands shook as she threw the offending paper down. 'I thought this was a reputable paper.'

'It is.'

'Then why would they print something so...offensive?'

'Perhaps because it's true. We were kissing in the car park. And you were pushing your delectable backside into my groin as if you couldn't wait till we got home to do me.'

She surged to her feet, knocking her chair aside. Her whole body was shaking with fury and she could barely grasp the chair to straighten it.

'We both know I was not!'

'Do we? I told you those shorts were a bad idea. Do you blame me for getting carried away?'

'Oh, you're *despicable!*'

'And you're delicious when you're angry,' he replied lazily, picked up the paper and carried on reading.

The urge to drive her fist through the paper into his face made her take another hasty step back.

She abhorred violence. Or at least she had before she'd met Theo Pantelides. Now she wasn't so sure what she was capable of...

'Aren't you going to eat, *anjo*?' he asked without taking his eyes off the page.

'No. I've lost my appetite,' she snapped.

She fled the terrace to the sound of his mocking laughter and raced up to her room, her face flaming and angry humiliation smashing through her chest.

He found her on the beach an hour later. She heard the crunch of his feet in the warm sand and studiously avoided looking up. She carried on sketching the stationary boat anchored about a mile away and ignored him when he settled himself on the flat rock next to her.

He didn't speak for a few minutes before he let out an irritated breath. 'The silent treatment doesn't work for me, Inez.'

She snapped her pad shut and turned to face him. His

lips were pinched with displeasure but his eyes were focused, gauging her reaction…almost as if her reaction mattered.

'Having my sex life sleazily speculated about in the weekend newspaper doesn't work for me either.' She blinked to dilute the intense focus and continued. 'I agree that perhaps those shorts were not the best idea. But I saw the other diners in that restaurant. There were people far more famous than I am. But still the paparazzo followed us into the car park and took our picture.'

Inez thought he tensed but perhaps it was the movement of his body as he reached behind him and produced a plate laden with food. 'It's done. Let's move on.'

She yearned to remain on her high horse, but with her exertions last night, coupled with having eaten less than a whole meal in the last twenty-four hours, it wasn't surprising when her stomach growled loudly in anticipation.

He shook out a napkin and settled the plate in her lap. 'Eat up,' he instructed and picked up her sketchpad. 'You have an hour before the stylist arrives to address the issue of your wardrobe.'

She froze in the act of reaching for the food. 'I don't need a stylist. I can easily go back home and pack up some more clothes.'

'You'll not be returning to your father's house for the next three months. Besides, if your clothes are all in the style of heavy evening gowns or tiny shorts, then you'll agree the time has come to go a different route?'

She mentally scanned her wardrobe and swiftly concluded that he was probably right. 'There really is no need,' she tried anyway.

'It's too late to change the plan, Inez.'

And, just like that, the subject was closed. He tapped the plate and, as if on cue, her stomach growled again.

Giving up the argument, she devoured the thick sliced beef sandwich and polished off the apple in greedy bites.

She was gulping down the bottled water when she saw him pause at her sketch of a boat.

'This is very good.'

'Thank you.'

He tilted the page. 'You like boats?'

'Very much. My mother used to take me sailing. It was my favourite thing to do with her.'

He closed the pad. 'Were you two close?'

'She was my best friend,' she responded in a voice that cracked with pain. 'Not a day goes by that I don't miss her.'

His fingers seemed to tighten on the rock before they relaxed again. 'Mothers have a way of affecting you that way. It makes their absence all the harder to bear.'

'Is yours…when did you lose yours?' she asked.

He turned and stared at her. A bleak look entered his eyes but dissolved in the next blink. 'My mother is very much alive.'

She gasped. 'But I thought you said…'

'Absence doesn't mean death. There are several ways for a parent to be absent from a child's life without the ultimate separation.'

'Are you talking about abandonment?'

Again he glanced at her, and this time she caught a clearer glimpse of his emotions. Pain. Devastating pain.

'Abandonment. Indifference. Selfishness. Self-absorption. There are many forms of delivering the same blow,' he elaborated in a rough voice.

'I know. But I was lucky. My mother was the best mother in the world.'

'Is that why you're trying to be the best daughter in the world for your father, despite what you know of him?'

His accusation was like sandpaper against her skin. 'I beg your pardon?'

He shook his head. 'Don't bother denying it. You know exactly what sort of person he is. And yet you've stood by him all these years. Why—because you want a pat on the head and to be told you're a good daughter?'

The truth of his words hit her square in the chest. Up until yesterday, everything she'd done, every plan of her father's she'd gone along with had been to win his approval, and in some way make up for the fact that she hadn't been born the right gender. She didn't want to curl up and hide from the truth. But the callous way he condemned her made her want to justify her actions.

'I'm not blind to my father's shortcomings.' She ignored his caustic snort. 'But neither am I going to make excuses for my actions. My loyalty to my family isn't something I'm ashamed of.'

'Even when that loyalty meant turning a blind eye to other people's suffering?' he demanded icily.

She frowned. 'Whose suffering?'

'The people he left behind in the *favelas* for a start. Do you know that less than two per cent of the funds raised at those so-called charity events you so painstakingly put together actually make it to the people who need it most?'

She felt her face redden. His condemning gaze raked over her features. 'Of course you do,' he murmured acidly.

'It happened in the past, I admit it, but I only agreed to organise the last event if everything over and above the cost of doing it went to the *favelas*.' At his disbelieving look, she added, 'I do a lot of work with charities. I know what I'm talking about.'

'And did you ensure that it was done?'

'Yes. The charity confirmed they'd received the funds yesterday.'

One eyebrow quirked in surprise before he jerked to his feet. Thrusting his hands into his pockets, he turned to face her. 'That's progress at least.'

'Thank you. I don't live in a fairy tale. Trust me, I'm trying to do my part to help the *favelas*.'

'How?'

She debated a few seconds before she answered. 'I work at an inner city charity a few times a week.'

His gaze probed hers. 'That morning outside the coffee shop, that was where you were going?'

'Yes.'

'What does your father think?'

She bit her lip. 'He doesn't know.'

His mouth twisted. 'Because it will draw attention to his lies about his upbringing? Everyone knows he was born and raised in the *favelas*.'

'It's part of the reason why I didn't tell him, yes. But he denies his *favela* upbringing because he's…ashamed.'

'And yet he doesn't mind anyone knowing about his mother?'

'He thinks it gives him a little leverage with the common man to be indirectly associated with the *favelas*.'

'So he likes to rewrite his history as he goes along?'

'Perhaps. I don't delude myself for one second that my father doesn't bend the rules and the truth at times.'

His harsh laugh made her start. 'Right. Are you talking about, oh, let's see…doing ninety on a sixty miles per hour road, or are we talking about something with a little more…teeth?'

That note she'd heard before. The one that sent a foreboding chill along her spine, that warned her that something else was going on here. Something she should be running far and fast from. 'I…I'm not sure what you're implying.'

'Then let me spell it out for you. Are we talking about harmless anecdotes or are we talking about actual deeds? You know—broken kneecaps? Ruptured spleens. *Kidnap for ransom*?'

Her hand flew to her mouth. 'What the hell are you talking about?'

'Come on, you know what your father is capable of. Do

I need to remind you of what he did to you when you displeased him?'

She followed his gaze to the marks on her arm and slowly shook her head. 'I don't excuse this but I refuse to believe he's the monster you describe.'

His mouth twisted. 'I'll let you enjoy your rosy outlook for now, *querida*. I, too, felt like that once about my own father.'

'Is that what you're going to do to my father? Make him accountable for the things he's done?'

For several heartbeats she was sure he wouldn't answer her, or would change the subject the way he'd done in the past. But finally he nodded.

'Yes. I intend to make him pay for what he took from me twelve years ago.'

Her breath froze in her lungs. 'What did he take from you?'

He turned abruptly and faced the water, his stance rigid and forbidding. But Inez found herself moving towards him anyway, a visceral need driving her. She reached out and touched his shoulder. He tensed harder and she was reminded of his reaction to her touch on his boat. 'Theo?'

'I don't like being touched when my back's turned, *anjo*.'

She frowned. 'Why not?'

'Part of my demons.'

Her gut clenched hard at the rough note in his voice. 'Did...did my father do that to you?'

'Not personally. After all, he's an upright citizen now, isn't he? A man the people should trust.' He whipped about to face her.

'But he had something to do with your claustrophobia. And this?'

'Yes.'

'Theo—'

'Enough with the questions! You're forgetting why you're here. Do you need a reminder?'

She swallowed at the arctic look in his eyes. All signs of the raw, vulnerable pain she'd glimpsed minutes ago were wiped clean. Theo Pantelides was once again a man in control, bent on revenge. Slowly, she shook her head. 'No. No, I don't.'

CHAPTER EIGHT

THEIR CONVERSATION AT the beach set a frigid benchmark for the beginning of her stay at Theo's glass mansion.

The next two weeks passed in an icy blur of hectic days and even more hectic evenings. They'd quickly fallen into a routine where Theo left after a quick cup of coffee and a brief outline of when and where they would be dining that evening.

On the second morning when she'd told him she was heading for the charity, he'd raised an eyebrow. 'What sort of work do you do there?'

'Whatever I'm needed to do.' She'd been reluctant to tell him any specifics in case he disparaged her efforts as a rich girl's means of passing the time till the next party.

He'd returned to his coffee. 'Your time is your own when I'm not around. As long you're back here when I return, I see no problem.'

That had been the end of the subject.

After repeating his warning not to mention anything to her father he'd walked away. The man who'd shown her his pain and devastation had completely retreated.

His demeanour during their time indoors was icily courteous. However, when they went out, which they did most evenings, he was the attentive host, touching her, threading his fingers through her hair and gazing adoringly at her.

It was after the fifth night out that she realised he was

pandering to the paparazzi. Without fail, a picture of them in a compromising position appeared in the newspapers the very next morning.

But while she cringed with every exposing photo, he shrugged it off. It wasn't until her third weekend with him, when the newspapers posted the first poll results of the mayoral race, that she finally had her suspicions confirmed.

He was swimming in the pool, his lean and stunning body cutting through the water like the sleekest shark. The byline explaining the reasons behind the voters' reaction had her surging to her feet and storming to the edge of the pool.

'Is this why you've been taking me out every night since I moved in? So I'd be labelled the slut daughter of a man not fit to be mayor?' She raised her voice loud enough to be heard above his powerful strokes.

He stopped mid-stroke, straightened and slicked back his wet hair. With smooth breaststrokes he swam to where she stood barefoot. Looking down at his wet, sun-kissed face, she momentarily lost her train of thought.

He soon set her straight. 'Your father isn't worthy to lead a chain gang, never mind a city,' he replied in succinct, condemning tones. 'And before I'm done with him, the whole world will know it.'

Despite seeing the evidence for herself two weeks ago at the beach, despite knowing that whatever her father had done to him had been devastating, she staggered back a step at that solid, implacable oath.

He planted his hands on the tiles and heaved himself out of the water. It took every ounce of her self-control not to devour him with hungry eyes. But not looking didn't mean not feeling. Her insides clenched with the ever-growing hunger she'd been unable to stem since the first night he'd walked into her life. And, with each passing day, she was finding it harder and harder to remain unaffected.

It seemed not even knowing why she was here, or the full extent of how Theo intended to use her to hurt her father, could cause her intense emotional reaction to his prox-imity to abate.

Which made her ten kinds of a fool, who needed to pull her thoughts together or risk getting hurt all over again.

'So you don't deny that you used me as bait to derail my father's campaign?'

Hazel eyes, devoid of emotion, narrowed on her face. 'That was one course of action. But you haven't been la-belled a slut. I'll sue any newspaper that dares to call you that,' he rasped.

Her laughter scraped her throat. 'There are several ways to describe someone without using the actual derogatory word, Theo.'

He paused in drying his hair and looked at her. Slowly, he held out his hand. 'Show me.'

She handed the paper over. He read it tight-jawed. 'I'll have them print a retraction.'

Dismay roiled through her stomach, along with a heavy dose of rebellious anger.

'That's not the point, though, is it? The harm's already done. You know this means I'll have to stop volunteering, don't you? I can't bring this sort of attention to the charity.'

He frowned and she caught a look of unease on his face. 'I'll take care of this.'

'Forget it; it's too late. And congratulations; you've achieved your aim. But I won't be paraded about and pawed in public any more, so if you're planning on another night on the town you'll have to do it without me.'

His gaze slowly rose to hers and he resumed rubbing the towel through his hair. 'Fine. We'll do something else.' He threw the paper on the table.

She regarded him suspiciously. 'Something like what?'

'I promised you a trip on the yacht. We'll sail this eve-ning and spend tomorrow aboard. Would you like that?'

At times like these, when he was being a courteous host,

she found it hard to believe he was the same man who was hell-bent on seeking revenge on her father for past wrongs.

She'd given in to her gnawing curiosity after his revelations on the beach and searched the Internet for a clue as to what had happened to him. All she'd come up with were scant snippets of his late father's dirty dealings before Alexandrou Pantelides had died in prison. As far as she knew, there was no connection between Theo's family and hers. The Pantelides brothers, one of whom was married and recently a parent, and the other engaged to be married, were a huge success in the oil, shipping and luxury hotel world. Theo's job as a troubleshooter extraordinaire for the billion-dollar conglomerate meant he never settled in one place for very long. An ideal job for a man whose personal relationships were fleeting at best.

And a man tormented by a horde of demons.

She looked closer at him, tried to see the man behind the wall, the man who'd bared his soul for a brief moment when he'd spoken of his mother's abandonment.

But that man was closed off.

'What does it matter what I want? Frankly, I'm surprised my father hasn't been in touch about this.'

'He has. I refused to take his calls.'

'I didn't mean you. Since I was also the subject in these photos, I'm surprised he hasn't called me to vent his anger.'

His eyelids swept down and shielded his gaze from her. Apprehension struck a jagged path through her. 'He has, hasn't he?'

'He tried. I suggested that perhaps he refrain from contacting you and concentrate on kissing babies and convincing little old ladies to cast their ballot in his favour.'

Shock rooted her to the ground. 'How dare you take control of my life like this?'

'Would you rather I gave him access so he airs his disappointment?'

'What do you care? It's a little late to protect me, don't you think?'

His jaw tightened. 'For as long as you remain under my roof, you're under my protection.'

'*Meu deus*, please don't pretend you care!'

She realised how close she was to tears and swallowed hard. Fearing she would break down in front of him, she whirled round, intent on heading for her room. She made it two steps before he stopped her.

Flinging away the towel, he cupped her cheeks with both hands. 'Stop getting yourself distressed about this.'

'Is that another command?'

His eyes narrowed. 'You're angry.'

'Damn right I am. I wish I'd never set eyes on you. In fact I wish—'

His mouth slanted over hers, hot, hungry and all consuming. Her groan of protest was less than heartfelt and devoured within a millisecond.

A part of her was furious that he'd resorted to kissing her to shut her up. But it was only a minuscule part. The rest of her body was too busy revelling in the feel of his warm bare back and the fine definition of muscles that rippled beneath her caress.

His hands speared into her hair, imprisoning her for the invasion of his tongue as he took the kiss to another level.

His first kiss over two weeks ago had been a pure threat and the two that followed a show of mastery. This kiss was different. There was hunger and passion behind it, but also a gentleness that calmed her roiling emotions and slowly replaced them with a different sensation. Need clamoured inside her; a need to be closer still to his magnificent body; a need to dig her hands into his back and feel him shudder in reaction.

His groan was smothered between their melded lips as she dug her fingers even deeper. Power surged through her when he jerked again.

One hand dropped to her bottom and yanked her lower body into his groin. His erection was unmistakable. Bold, thick and hot, it pressed against her belly with insistent power that made her heartbeat skitter out of control.

She wanted him. Above and beyond all sense, she wanted this man. Her willpower, when it came to the chemistry between them, was laughably negligible.

But she couldn't give in. *Couldn't*...

The gentleness she'd sensed in him was false, she reminded herself fiercely. The bottom line was that in a few short weeks he would walk away. Leave her and her family devastated.

'I'm losing you. Come back, *anjo*,' he murmured seductively against her mouth. He ran his tongue over her lower lip and her knees weakened.

When he cupped her bottom and squeezed, she desperately summoned all her resolve and pushed against his chest. 'No.'

He raised his head and she saw behind the wall. He was as caught in this insane chemistry as she was. A little part of her felt better.

'I can change your mind, Inez. Regardless of what I intend for your father, what is between us is undeniable.'

'Do you hear yourself? You think I should forget everything else and sleep with you just because you made me feel a certain way?'

'That's generally the reason why men and women have sex.'

'But we're not just any man and any woman, Theo, are we?'

He stiffened, and a hard look entered his eyes. 'Are you saying that you've been in love with every man you've slept with?' he queried.

She froze and prayed her humiliation wouldn't show on her face as she tried to stem the memory of Constantine's treatment of her.

His cruel rejection was still an ache beneath her breastbone.

'Inez?' Theo interjected harshly.

'My past relationships are none of your business.'

His slightly reddened mouth twisted. 'Far be it for me to request to be lumped in with your other lovers, but isn't it a touch hypocritical to apply one criteria to me that you haven't done with one of your lovers, in particular?'

'If you're referring to Constantine, let me assure you that you have no idea what you're talking about.'

His hand tightened around her waist. 'Then enlighten me. Why did he dump you?'

Inez broke free. 'We weren't compatible.'

'Or he found out the true reason you were with him and wanted nothing to do with you?'

'No. That wasn't why…' She screeched to a stop as the words stuck in her throat.

'So what was it? Did you really love him or did you convince yourself you did in order to achieve your aims?'

She bit her lip as he shone a light on the stark question. Had she blown her feelings out of proportion? Constantine had been charismatic, yes, but he'd never created the decadent chaos that Theo created in her.

When she'd imagined love, she'd always imagined passion, hunger and a keen pleasure even the slightest thought of that special someone brought. She'd believed herself in love with Constantine and yet she'd never experienced those emotions.

Well, she most definitely wasn't feeling them now.

'I believed my emotions were genuine at the time. But he didn't. He believed I was using him to further my father's campaign.'

'What did he do?' he asked. She looked into his eyes and fooled herself into thinking she saw a thawing of the hardness there.

'He made painful digs at me whenever he gave inter-

views. He made the tabloids call my character into question…much the same way you're doing now.'

He dropped his hand. 'It's not the same—'

'Yes, it is. Look Theo, I just want to be left alone to do
my time.'

He paled. 'You're not in prison, Inez.'

She put much needed distance between them. 'Am I not?
How else would you describe my presence here?'

Theo watched her walk away and curled his fists at his sides.
The urge to call her back was so strong he forced himself to
exhale slowly to expel the need. Her reference to her presence under his roof as a prison sentence had stung badly.

But hell, the truth was irrefutable. He'd forced her to
make a choice, and no amount of dinner dates or designer
shopping sprees would gloss over the fact that he'd set the
tabloids on her as a way to dismantle her father's campaign.

Witnessing her clear distress just now had made his chest
ache in a way that confused and irritated him.

Perhaps he needed to step up his agenda, end this dangerous game once and for all and move on with his life.

His brothers would certainly agree. He'd been avoiding
their calls for the best part of a fortnight, replying only by
email and with curt one-liners that he knew would only go
so far before something gave.

He gritted his teeth against the prompt to deliver a swift
killing blow to Benedicto da Costa.

His own ordeal hadn't been swift. It'd been long and
tortuous. The punishment should fit the crime. Any hesi-
tation on his part now merely stemmed from the afterglow
of the chemistry between him and Inez. He freely admitted that theirs was a strong and potent brand, more intense
than anything he'd ever experienced before.

It was messing with his mind, the same way the thought
of her ex-lover had made him see red for several long seconds. But there was no way he was letting it impede his goal.

Which meant he had to come at this problem from another angle.

He swallowed the acrid taste in his mouth at the thought that Inez had put him into the same class as Constantine Blanco.

Slowly walking back indoors, he turned over the dilemma in his mind. By the time he reached his suite and changed out of his swimming trunks, a smile was curving his lips.

An hour later, he watched her descend the stairs, her duffel bag slung over her shoulder and an overnight case in her hand.

'Did Teresa tell you to pack your swimming gear?'

She regarded him warily. 'Yes. But I thought we were just taking the boat out?'

He shrugged. 'I thought you would welcome the opportunity to sunbathe away from the prying lenses of the paparazzi? There are several decks on the yacht that you can sunbathe on. Or we can swim in the sea, dine alone under the stars. Would you like that?' he asked, then felt a jolt at how much he wanted her to answer in the affirmative. In the past, he'd never taken the time to seek out what pleased his girlfriends beyond the usual gifts and fine dining. It was why he operated his relationships on a strict short-term basis with as little maintenance as possible.

Inez was far from low maintenance. And yet he found himself even more drawn to her.

She glanced pointedly over his shoulder. 'I'll think about it and let you know.'

His unsettled feelings escalated. He reminded himself that they were heading for his boat. She liked his boat. Perhaps she would relent enough to forget that she was angry with him. Forget about Blanco and forget that she was being blackmailed.

Theo was still debating why her feelings meant so much to him when he pulled up at the marina.

* * *

'You've been smiling ever since we set sail.'

Her voice was full of heavy suspicion. Theo's smile widened as he tilted his face up into the sunshine. 'Have I? It must be the weather.'

'The weather has been the same for the last month,' she replied sourly.

He slowly lowered his head and captured her gaze with his. 'Then it must be the company.'

A delicate wave of heat surged up her neck into her cheeks, making him wonder, as he had more than once these past two weeks, how she could have been involved with someone like Blanco and still blush like a schoolgirl.

Theo had looked into Constantine Blanco and had not been surprised to find that he was cut from the same cloth as Benedicto. It was perhaps why Da Costa had chosen to ally himself with the younger man politically. He'd sent his daughter to spy on Blanco and had been double-crossed in the bargain.

Theo's smile slipped as he recalled her hurt when he'd thrown her relationship with Blanco at her. He reached for the glass of wine that had accompanied their late afternoon meal and took a large gulp.

The guilt tightening in his chest since her accusation at the pool squeezed harder.

What the hell was going on with him?

'Have you decided whether you're selling the boat or not?' she asked.

In the sunlight, her black hair gleamed like polished jet, making him burn to feel its silkiness beneath his fingers.

He stared into his drink. 'Maybe. I'll have to weigh up practical usage versus the desire to hang on to something beautiful.'

'But you're a billionaire. Isn't collecting toys part and parcel of your status?'

'I wasn't always a man of means. In fact my brothers and

I worked our backsides off to achieve the level of success we enjoy now.' His smile felt tight and strained.

'Your brothers…Sakis and Arion…'

He looked up in surprise. 'You've been playing around on the Internet, I see.'

She raised her chin. 'I thought it wise to learn a little bit more about my enemy.'

The label grated. Badly. 'What else did you try to discover while you were rooting around my family tree?'

'Your brother Sakis had some trouble with a saboteur on one of his oil tankers.'

He nodded. 'We dealt with that quite satisfactorily.'

'And now your brother Ari is engaged to the widow of the man who tried to throw your company into chaos?' She frowned.

A reluctant grin tugged at his mouth. 'What can I say; we thrive on interesting challenges.'

'You also seem to make enemies with the people you do business with. So far you've led me to believe it was my father who wronged you. How do I know it's not the other way round? That you're not here because you deserved everything you got?'

The stem of the wine glass snapped with a sickening crack. Even then it took the cold wine seeping into his shirt to realise what he'd done.

The top part of the glass landed on the table, rolled off and smashed onto the deck.

Inez gasped. 'Theo, you're bleeding!' She surged to her feet and sprang towards him.

'Stop!'

'But your finger…'

'Is nothing compared to what will happen to your foot if you take another step.'

She glanced down at the broken glass an inch from her bare foot and glanced back at his bleeding forefinger. Anguish creased her pale features.

'Sit down, Inez,' he instructed tersely.

'Please, let me help,' she implored.

Gritting his teeth, he grabbed a napkin and formed a small tourniquet around the gaping wound. 'It's not deep but will need to be cleaned properly. There's a first aid kit behind the bar.'

She nodded, slipped on her sandals and dashed for the bar. Theo stood and moved from the dining table to the wraparound sofa to give the crew member who'd arrived on deck room to sweep up the broken glass. He glanced up as Inez rushed back and set the kit on the coffee table.

Her eyes were turbulent with worry as she glanced from his face to the blood-soaked napkin.

'Are you going to stand there staring at me all evening? I'm bleeding to death here.'

With a hoarse croak, she jerked into action. She carefully cleaned the wound with antiseptic and applied gauze before securing it with a plaster. All through the procedure, she darted quick, apologetic glances at him.

As he stared at her, he felt a different sort of jolt run through him. One he hadn't been aware he was missing until he felt it.

Care. Concern. Fear for him.

When was the last time anyone besides Ari and Sakis had felt like that about him? When was the last time his own mother lavished such attention on him? Inez slid him another worried glance and his breath shuddered out.

'Calm yourself, *anjo*. I'll live. I'm sure of it.'

She exhaled noisily and her agitated pulse pounded at her throat. '*Sinto muito*,' she said in a rush.

'Don't apologise. It wasn't your fault.'

'But…if I hadn't accused you of…'

'You're operating in the dark and want to find out the truth. I respect that. But I can't tell you what my business with your father is until I'm ready. You have to respect that.'

'But…this…' She glanced down at his finger and shook

her head. 'Your reaction…the claustrophobia and the touch-ing thing…I can't help but fear the worst, Theo,' she whis-pered.

Against his will, his chest constricted at the anguish in her voice. He wanted to comfort her. Wanted to take that look of anticipated pain from her face. He wanted to kiss her until they both forgot why she was his prisoner and why he was beginning to dread the day he had to set her free.

He swallowed hard.

'Let's make a deal. For the next twenty-four hours, no talk of your father or the reason why I'm in Rio. Agreed?'

Her mouth wobbled and her teeth worried her bottom lip as she glanced back at his finger. Her eyes were no less turbulent when they rose to his but he saw determination flare in their depths. 'Agreed.'

Theo stood at the railing on the third floor deck and watched her swim in the pool on the second deck the next morning. She moved like a water nymph, her long black hair stream-ing down her back as she scissored her arms and legs un-derwater.

He gripped the rail until his knuckles turned white but still he couldn't take his eyes off her.

'I'm waiting for an answer, Theo,' came the weary voice at the end of the line.

Theo sighed. 'Sorry, remind me again what the ques-tion was.'

Ari grunted with annoyance. 'I asked you why I couldn't have one peaceful breakfast without opening the papers to find you wrapped around some poor girl. Seriously, my di-gestive system has sent me a stern memo. Either I treat it better and not subject it to such images or it goes on per-manent vacation.'

Theo heard Perla, his soon-to-be sister-in-law, laughing in the background.

'The answer is simple. Don't read the papers.'

Ari sighed. 'How long is this going to go on for?'

'Everything should be signed, sealed and delivered in a week or two,' he responded, rolling his shoulders to ease the tension tightening his muscles. Another sleepless night, plagued with nightmares. He'd given up on sleep somewhere around three a.m.

'You sound very sure.'

His grip tightened around the phone. As he'd lain awake he'd briefly toyed with the idea of ending this vendetta sooner. And he'd been stunned when the idea had taken firm hold. 'I am.'

'And nothing you're doing down there will affect the wedding? Don't forget it's in two weeks. If you can prise yourself away from that piece of skirt for long enough—'

'She's not a piece of skirt,' he snarled before he could catch his response. Ari's silence made him hurry to speak. 'I'll be at your wedding.'

'Good, since you've missed most of the rehearsals, I'll send you the video of what you need to do. Make sure you get it right; we'll do a quick rehearsal when you get here. I'm not having you mess things up for Perla.'

'Sure. Fine,' he murmured.

He followed the curvy, sexy shape underneath the water and held his breath as Inez broke the surface and rose out of the pool. Dripping curves and sun-kissed skin made his body clench unbearably. He wanted to trace every single inch of her with his hands, his mouth, his tongue. 'Oh, and tell Perla I'm bringing a guest.'

His brother muttered a curse and relayed the message. Theo heard Perla's whoop of delight. 'The love of my life grudgingly agrees but suggests that perhaps, next time, you could be courteous enough to give us a heads-up sooner?'

'Next time? You mean you'll be getting married for a third time?'

He hung up to more pithy curses ringing in his ears and found himself smiling. Without taking his eyes off the figure below, he descended the spiral staircase and walked towards the bikini-clad goddess reaching for the towel on the shelf next to the pool.

Her back was turned and he slowed to a stop as the sight of her tiny waist and curvy hips made blood rush through his veins. Lust twisted through his gut, hard and demanding.

Hell, this was getting unbearable.

He threw his cell phone on the breakfast table and watched her jerk around to face him. The towel she was holding to her hair stilled.

'Hi.'

'Good morning. Enjoy your swim?'

'It was very refreshing,' she replied huskily, her eyes following him warily as he strode towards her. 'So, what's the plan for today?' she asked.

I want to haul you off to my bed and keep you underneath me until we both pass out from the pleasure overload.

He wrenched his gaze from her full breasts, lovingly cupped by damp white triangles, and concentrated on breathing. 'We're headed for Copacabana. We'll stop for something to eat then head back tonight. Or if you want we can stay on the boat and leave in the morning?'

She thought about it for a second and nodded. 'I'd love to draw the boat in the moonlight.'

'Then that's what you shall do.'

Her gaze turned puzzling, weighing.

'What's on your mind?' he asked.

She shook her head slightly and slowly folded the towel. 'Sometimes I feel as if I'm dealing with two people.'

Something hard tugged in his chest. 'Which one do you prefer?'

'Are you joking? The person you are now, of course.'

He froze as the tug tightened its hold on him. His breath came in short pants as he closed the distance between them. 'I thought we weren't going to delve into our issues today.'

'You asked me what was on my mind.'

He nodded. 'I guess I did.' He stared into the pure, make-up-free perfection of her face and something very close to regret rose in his gut.

'Now it's my turn to ask you what's on your mind, Theo,' she murmured thoughtfully.

'It's completely pointless, of course, but I'm wishing we'd met under different circumstances.'

Her mouth dropped open. 'You are?'

The urge to touch grew, and he finally gave in. He traced his thumb over her lips and felt them pucker slightly under his touch. 'As I said, it's pointless.'

'Because you would've been done with me within a week?' she ventured.

'No. I would've kept you for much longer, *anjo*. Perhaps even for ever.'

He forced himself to step away. Once again she'd slid so effortlessly under his skin, opened him up to wishes and possibilities he'd forced himself never to entertain after what their respective fathers and his mother had done to him. She was making him believe in impossible dreams, feelings he had no business experiencing.

He strode quickly towards the pool. A cold dip would wash away the fiery need and alien emotions tearing his insides to shreds. He hoped.

He emerged twenty minutes later to find her polishing off the last of her scrambled eggs and coffee. Over the past fortnight he'd noticed that she ate with a gusto that triggered his own appetite. Or *appetites*.

As he poured his coffee and helped himself to fruit, she reached for the ever-present duffel bag and pulled out her sketchpad.

'Have you thought of doing something with your talent?' he asked.

A shadow passed over her face before she tried to smile through it, but he guessed the reason behind it. Her father.

'I will once I resume my education. I put pursuing my degree on hiatus for a while.'

He didn't need to ask why. 'Until when?'

She shrugged and searched for a fresh page in her pad. 'I haven't decided yet.'

Theo tried not to let his anger show. They'd called a truce for twenty-four hours.

'What will you study when you return?'

'I love buildings and boats. I may go into architecture or boat design.'

He glanced from her face to the pad. 'Boat design, huh?'

She nodded.

He picked up his coffee and regarded her over the rim. 'Why don't you design me one?'

'You want me to design a boat for you?'

'Yes. I'm sure your research showed you what sort of designs we specialise in. It has to be up to the Pantelides standard. But use your own template. Make it state-of-the-art, of course.'

'Of course,' she murmured but he could see the gleam of interest in her eyes as she stared down at her pad.

Her pencil flew across the paper as he devoured his breakfast. She didn't look up as he rose and rounded the table to where she sat. He didn't glance down at her drawing; he was too absorbed with the sheer joy on her face as she became immersed in her task.

Even when his finger drifted down her cheek to the corner of her mouth she barely glanced up at him. But her breath hitched and she jerked a tiny bit towards his touch before he withdrew his hand.

As he walked away, Theo marvelled at how light-hearted he felt.

CHAPTER NINE

THEY DROPPED ANCHOR about a mile away from Copacabana Beach and took a launch ashore.

Inez looked to where Theo stood, legs braced, at the wheel of the launch. The wind rushed through his dark hair, whipping it across his forehead. Stupid that she should be jealous of the wind but she clenched her fingers in her lap as they tingled with the need to touch him.

I would've kept you for much longer, anjo. *Perhaps even for ever.*

Try as she had for the last few hours, she couldn't get his words out of her head. They struck her straight to the heart in unguarded moments, made her breath catch in ways that made her dizzy. Every time she pushed the feeling away. But, inevitably, it returned.

She was in serious trouble here…

A shout from nearby sunbathers drew her attention to the fact that they were not alone any more.

She watched the surge of people and the noise of tourists enjoying a Sunday stroll along the beach roads and suddenly felt as if she was losing the tenuous connection she'd made with Theo last night and this morning. Which was silly. There was no connection. Just a precarious truce.

And an exciting task designing a Pantelides boat, which had made joy bubble beneath her skin all day.

He brought the launch to a smooth stop at the pier and

turned off the engine. Jumping out with lithe grace, he held out his hand to her, the smile on his face making her breath stutter in her chest as she slipped her hand into his.

'I'm in the mood for some traditional food and I know just the place for it. You happy to trust me?'

Safely on solid ground, she glanced up and found herself nodding. 'Yes.'

His eyes darkened. 'It's a bit of a walk.' He glanced at her high-heeled wedges with a cocked eyebrow.

'Don't worry about me. I was born in heels.'

'Then I pity your poor *mãe*.'

She laughed and saw his answering smile.

Gradually they fell silent and his gaze drifted over her face, resting on her mouth for a few seconds before he tugged on her hand. 'Come on, *anjo*.'

He led her along the pier and towards the streets. Ten minutes later, she stared in surprise when they stopped outside a door with a faded sign and a single light bulb above it.

'I hear they serve the best *feijoadas* in Rio,' he said, his gaze probing her every expression.

Inez forced the lump in her throat down as she stared at the sign that had been very much part of a long ago, happier childhood. 'It's true. I…how do you know about this place?'

The hand he'd captured since they alighted from the boat meshed with hers, causing her heart to flutter wildly as he brought it to his lips and kissed the back of it. 'I made it my business to find out.'

Again tears choked her and she couldn't speak for several moments. 'Thank you.'

He nodded. 'My pleasure.'

They stopped in the doorway to allow their eyes to adjust to the candlelit interior.

'*Pequena estrela!*' A matronly woman in her late forties approached, her face lit up with a smile.

After exchanging hugs, Inez turned to introduce Theo.

'Camila and my mother were best friends. I used to have supper here many times after school when I was a kid.'

Theo responded to the introduction in smooth, charming Portuguese that had the older woman blushing before she led them to a table in the middle of the room.

'You want the usual?' Camila asked after she'd brought over a basket of bread and taken their wine order.

Inez glanced at Theo. 'Will you let me choose?'

He sat back in his chair, his gaze brushing her face. 'It's your show, *anjo*.'

She rattled off the order and added a few more dishes that had Camila nodding in approval before she bustled off.

Alone with Theo, she tried to calm her giddy senses. Not read too much into why he'd brought her here of all places. But her emotions refused to be calmed.

He was making her feel things she had no business feeling, considering their circumstances. Her heart was very much in danger of being devastated. And this time the danger signs were not disguised as they'd been with Constantine. She was walking into this with her heart and eyes wide open…

'You're frowning too hard, *querida*.'

Plucking a piece of bread from the basket, she fought to focus on not ruining their truce. 'I think I may have ordered too much food.'

'You have a healthy appetite. Nothing wrong with that.'

'It's that healthy appetite that keeps me on the wrong side of chubby.'

'You're not chubby. You're perfect.'

Her hand stilled on the way to her mouth. In the ambient light, she witnessed the potent, knee-weakening look of appreciation on his face. The look slowly grew until hunger became deeply etched into his every feature.

Desire pounded through her, sending radial pulses of heat through her body to concentrate on that needy place between her legs. '*Obrigado*,' she murmured hoarsely.

He nodded slowly, leant forward and took the piece of bread from her hand. Tearing off a piece, he held it against her mouth. When she opened it, he placed it on her tongue and watched her chew.

Then he sat back and ate the remaining piece.

She eventually managed to swallow and cast around for a safe topic of conversation that didn't involve her father or the dangerous emotions arcing between them.

Whether he noticed her floundering or not, she smiled gratefully when he asked, 'Did your mother grow up around here?'

'No, both she and Camila grew up near the Serra Geral, although she spent part of her childhood in Arizona where my grandmother was from. Their fathers were ranch-owning *gauchos* and neighbours but after they both married they moved to Rio and stayed in touch. Camila is like a second mother to me...'

'Da Costa Holdings isn't a cattle business, though,' he replied, then stiffened slightly.

She smiled quickly, wanting to hold onto the animosity-free atmosphere they'd found. 'No, after my grandfather died, my mother sold the ranch and let my father expand the company instead.' She breathed in relief when Camila returned with their wine and first course.

The older woman's warm smile and effusive manner further lightened the mood. By the time she took her first sip of the bold red wine the slightly chilly interlude had passed.

Theo complimented her on the food choice and tucked into the grilled fish starter. The conversation returned to safer topics and eventually turned to his previous career as a championship-winning rower.

'Why did you stop competing?'

He shrugged. 'I tried a few partners after Ari and Sakis retired. The chemistry was lacking. In a sport like that chemistry is key.' He topped up her wine and took a sip of his own.

MAYA BLAKE   505

'You've been lucky to have had the opportunity to do something you loved,' she replied wistfully.

His smile looked a little taut around the edges. 'Luck is a luxury that normally comes along as a result of hard work.'

She glanced down into her wine. 'But sometimes, no matter how hard you try, fate has other ideas for you.'

His eyes narrowed into sharp laser-like beams. 'Yes. But the answer is to turn it to your advantage.'

'Or you can walk away. Find a different option?'

One corner of his mouth lifted. 'Walking away has never been my style.'

She slowly nodded. 'You wouldn't have won championships if you were a man who walked away.'

His expression morphed into something that resembled gratitude. She couldn't claim she understood all his motives but she was beginning to grasp what made Theo tick. As long as he could see a problem in any area of his life, he would not walk away until it was resolved. It was why he was the troubleshooter for Pantelides Inc.

She'd watched footage of him rowing. His grit and determination had held her enthralled throughout the feature and she would be lying now if she didn't admit it was a huge turn-on.

'But there's also strength in walking away. You walked away from rowing rather than risk partnering up with the wrong person.'

He stiffened. 'Inez…'

She fought the urge to back down. 'I don't want to mess up our truce but I want you to just think about it. There's no shame in forgiving. No shame in letting the past *stay* in the past.'

His eyes grew dark and haunted. 'What about my demons?'

'Do you have a cast-iron guarantee that they will be vanquished by the path you've chosen?'

He frowned for several seconds before his eyes narrowed. 'You're right. Let's not mess up the truce, shall we?'

'Theo…'

'*Anjo*. Enough. Have some more wine.' He smiled.

And, just like that, her pulse surged faster. Hell, everything he did made her pulse race. She took a sip and licked her lips as the languorous effect of the wine and the captivating man sitting opposite her took hold.

She really needed to stop drinking so much. She pulled her gaze from the rugged perfection of his face as Camila returned to offer them coffee.

Inez declined and looked over to see his eyes riveted on her.

'I think we need to get you back to the boat.'

Laughter that seemed to be coming easier around him escaped her throat. 'You make me sound as if I've been naughty,' she said after Camila collected their empty plates and left.

'Trust me, I would tell you if you'd been.'

'Well, the night is still young and I'm not ruling anything out.' She laughed again.

His mouth curved in one of those devastating smiles as he reached for his wallet and extracted several crisp notes.

'I say it's definitely time to get you back and into bed.'

Her breath caught. He didn't mean what she thought he meant. Of course he didn't. But images suddenly bombarded her brain that had her blushing.

As she said goodbye to Camila and headed outside, she prayed he wouldn't see her reaction to his words.

'Hey, slow down, you'll break your ankle rushing in those heels.' He caught up with her outside and slid a hand around her waist.

The warmth of his body was suddenly too much to bear. 'It's okay, I'm fine.' Her voice emerged a touch too forceful and he glanced sharply at her.

'What's wrong?'

She raked an exasperated hand through her hair and tried to stem the words forming at the back of her mind. They came out anyway. 'You're supposed to be my enemy. And yet you brought me to one of my favourite places in the world. You're being so kind and attentive and I can't help... I...I want you.'

The transformation that occurred sent her senses reeling. From the charming, desirous dinner companion, Theo turned into a hungry predatory beast in the space of a heartbeat.

He pulled her into a dark alley between two high-rises. Her heart hammered as he held her against the wall and leaned in close.

'You don't want to say things like that to me right now, Inez,' he grated harshly.

His mouth was so tantalising close, she shut her eyes to avoid closing the gap between them and experiencing another potent kiss. 'I don't want to be saying them either. I can't seem to stop myself because it's the truth.'

'That's just the wine talking,' he replied.

She nodded then groaned when he leaned in closer. Heat from his body burned hers and his breath washed over her face. When his stubbled jaw brushed her cheek, she bit hard on her lower lip to stop another groan from escaping.

'Open your eyes, Inez.'

She shook her head. '*Nao...por favor...*'

'What are you begging me for?' he whispered in her ear.

A deep shudder coursed down her spine. 'I don't know...' She stopped and sucked in a desperate breath. 'Kiss me,' she pleaded.

With a dark moan, he touched his mouth to the corner of hers. Fleeting. Feather-light. Barely enough.

Her hands gripped his waist and held on tight. '*Please*,' she whispered.

'*Anjo*, if I start I won't be able to stop. And neither of us wants to spend the night in jail for lewd behaviour.'

She finally opened her eyes. He stood, tall, dark, devastatingly good-looking and tense, with a hunger she'd never seen in a man's eyes. That it was directed at her made her pulse race that much harder.

'Theo.' Her fingers crept up to his face, dying to touch his warm olive skin. 'Let it go. Whatever my father did, revenge would only bring you fleeting satisfaction.'

His jaw tightened but he didn't look as forbidding as he'd looked before. 'It's the only thing I've dreamed about for the last twelve years.'

Her hand crept up to settle over his heart. 'Have you stopped to think that obsessing about it may just be feeding the demons?'

One large hand settled over hers and he stared fiercely down at her. 'Are you offering me another way to quiet them, *anjo*?'

'Maybe.'

He captured her hand and planted a kiss in her palm. When he glanced down at her, a feverish light burned in his molten eyes. 'He doesn't deserve to have you as a daughter.'

'I can say the same about your parents but we play the hand that is dealt us the best way we can. And when it gets really bad I try to remember a happier time. Surely you must have some happy memories with your mother? And was your father really all bad?'

His mouth tightened. Then, slowly, he shook his head. 'No. It wasn't always bad.'

'Tell me.'

He frowned slightly. 'They thought Sakis would be their last child. I came as a surprise, or so my mother tells me. She used to call me her special boy. My father…he took me everywhere with him. He had a sports car—an Aston Martin—that I loved riding in. We'd take long drives along the coast…' He stopped and his eyes glazed over.

She kept silent, letting him relive the memories, hoping that he would find a way to soften the hard ache inside him. But when his eyes refocused, she saw the raw pain reflected in them.

'I'm not a father, and I probably never will be. But even I know those things are easy to do when life's a smooth sail. The true test comes when things get rough. I find it hard to believe that my brothers and I were ever in any way special to our parents when they turned their backs on us when we needed them most. He could've saved me, Inez—' He stopped abruptly and her heart clenched with pain for him.

'How?'

'One simple phone call to warn me and I wouldn't be here…I wouldn't be afraid of going to sleep each night because of hellish nightmares…' A deep shudder raked his tall frame.

'Oh, Theo,' she murmured. He leaned into the hand she placed on his cheek for several seconds then he pulled away and tilted her chin up.

The vulnerable man was gone. 'This changes nothing. I am what I am. Do you still want me?'

She swallowed. 'Yes.'

Something resembling relief swept through his eyes. 'You have half an hour and a lot of head-clearing air before we're back on the boat. I suggest you use that time to think carefully about whether you want this to go any further. Because, once we cross the line, there won't be any going back.'

CHAPTER TEN

THEO THREW THE reins of the launch to the waiting crew member and turned to help her out. Her bare feet hit the landing pad and she swayed a little when the boat rocked.

Contrary to her thinking he would rush her back to the boat after his pronouncement, Theo had taken his time walking her back down the streets to the promenade and onto the beach that led to the pier.

Hell, he'd even taken the time to help her out of her shoes so they could walk along the shore.

But the plaguing doubt that perhaps he didn't want her as much as her screaming senses craved him evaporated the moment she looked into his eyes.

Burnt a dark gold by volcanic desire, he stared down at her for several seconds before he demanded in a hoarse voice, 'Well?'

She licked her lips and watched his agitated exhalation. 'I still want you.'

'Are you sure? There will be no room for regret in the morning, Inez. I won't allow it.'

'I'm not drunk, Theo. Besides, I wanted you this morning and I wasn't drunk then. Or last week, or the first night we met.'

His nostrils flared as he dragged her close on the deserted lower deck. 'That first night, you felt what I felt?'

An impossible attraction that had no rhyme or reason? 'Yes,' she answered simply.

He swung her up in his arms and strode into the galley and down the steps into his large, opulent suite. Somewhere along the line, her shoes fell from her useless hands. She knew they had because her fingers were buried in his hair, and her mouth was on his by the time he kicked the door shut behind them.

Their tongues slid erotically against each other as they explored one another, his forceful, hers growing bolder by the second. Because she knew he liked it, she nipped his bottom lip with her teeth.

His deep growl echoed inside her before he pulled away. Eyes on hers, he slowly lowered her body down his sleek length. Hard muscles and firm thighs registered against her heated skin and even after her feet hit the plush carpet she held onto him, fearful she'd dissolve into a pool of need the moment she let go.

'I need to undress you,' he said raggedly.

Unable to look away from him, she nodded. The dark purple knee-length dress was form-fitting and secured by a side zip. After a couple of minutes of frustrated searching, she laughed and pointed to the hidden zip beneath her arm.

With a dark curse, he lowered it and tugged the dress over her head.

He dropped the dress. He swallowed. Then he stared so hard she stopped breathing.

'*Thee mou*, you're so beautiful,' he groaned.

The feeling suffusing her was different from her reaction to the incandescent hunger in his eyes. It was pleasure that he liked what he saw, that he might well pardon her for her inexperience.

Eager to experience more of the feeling, she reached for her bra clasp.

'No,' he commanded. He grabbed her hands and placed them on his chest. 'That's my job. *You* don't move.'

He drifted his fingers up her sides, eliciting a deep shiver that brought a satisfied smile to his lips. Her bra came undone a second later and he glanced down at her heavy breasts.

'Do you know how long I've waited to taste these?' He cupped one globe in his hand, lowered his head and flicked his wet tongue repeatedly over her nipple.

Fire scorched through her veins and her head fell back as pleasure surged high.

'Theo,' she gasped as he delivered the same treatment to her other nipple. Caught in the maelstrom of sensation, she wasn't aware her nails were digging into his pecs until he hissed against her skin.

'Take my shirt off, *querida*. I want to feel those nails on my bare skin.'

Fingers trembling, she complied with his demand, pulling the shirt off his broad shoulders and down his arms before giving in to the need to caress his bronzed skin. Heated and satin-smooth, his muscles bunched beneath her touch as she explored him.

But, much too soon, he was pulling her hands away, catching her around the waist and striding to the bed.

Depositing her in the middle of the king-sized bed, he stood staring down at her, one hand on his belt. The power and girth of him knocked the breath out of her lungs and a momentary unease sliced across her pleasure.

So far, Theo hadn't commented on her inexperience but the evidence would become glaringly apparent in a few minutes. She opened her mouth to tell him but he was crawling over the bed towards her, his intense focus paralysing her to everything but the pleasure his eyes promised.

He kissed her again, deeper, more forceful than all the times before. She gave in to her need and buried her hands in his hair, scraped her nails along his scalp and won herself a deep groan of pleasure from him. His lips moved along her jaw to nip her earlobe before going lower to explore her neck and lower.

Once again, he suckled her breasts and once again she lost the ability to think straight.

'You love that, don't you?' he observed huskily when he raised his head.

'*Sim*,' she groaned.

'There are many more pleasures, *anjo*. So many more.'

His lips trailed down her midriff...he kissed his way to the top of her panties before he gripped the flimsy material in his hands. Expecting them to be ripped off—a notion that made her wildly breathless—she was surprised when he slowly and gently lowered them down her legs and drew them off.

Equally slowly, taking his time to savour her, he kissed her from ankle to inner thigh. When his mouth skated over her secret place, her hips arched off the bed in delirious anticipation.

She'd never imagined she'd want a man to go down on her but now she couldn't imagine *not* feeling Theo's mouth on her heated core.

At the touch of his mouth, she cried out, her body twisting as pleasure scythed through her. He tasted her so very thoroughly, his tongue, teeth and lips working in perfect harmony to drive her straight out her mind.

She slid ever closer to breaking point, both fearing and yearning for what lay ahead.

Theo slipped his hands beneath her bottom and pulled her even closer to his seeking mouth. With quick expert flicks of his tongue, he sent her careening over the edge.

Her scream was an alien sound, hoarse and pleasure-ravaged, her grip on the sheets tight as she was buffeted by blissful sensation.

He continued to kiss her until she calmed, then kissed his way up her body to seal her mouth with his.

The earthy taste of her surrender seemed to trigger an even more primitive reaction in him. By the time he lifted his head, his eyes were almost black with hunger.

'Did Blanco make you feel like this?' he grated.

She shook her head. 'No.'

Satisfaction gleamed in his eyes. 'By the time I finish making you mine, you will not remember anyone else who came before me.'

Knowing he would discover her inexperience in a matter of minutes, she took a sustaining breath and blurted, 'I never slept with Constantine. Theo, I'm a virgin.'

He froze in the act of reaching for a condom. Several expressions raced over his face before he spoke. 'So I'm to be your first lover?'

She gave a jerky nod. 'Yes.'

Theo absorbed the news and tried to weigh which was the greater emotion swirling through him—shock or elation. The shock was understandable. But the elation, the fact that he was *pleased* he was to be her first? It'd never crossed his mind that she would be a virgin. But suddenly a few things fell into place. Her blushes, her furtive innocent looks, her surprise at his demanding kisses.

Another feeling rose to curl itself around his chest. Possessiveness.

The fact that he was to be her first made him want to beat his chest like a wild jungle animal. He ripped the condom packet open and stared down at her.

The look of apprehension forced him to slow down. He was moving too fast, possibly scaring her. Time to turn it down a notch.

'I'll go as slow as you want, *querida*, but I won't stop,' he warned. He couldn't. He'd come too far. He wanted her too much.

I would've kept you... Perhaps even for ever.

His own words echoed in his head and yet another emotion swept over him. If they'd met in another time, would she be the one? The idea of Inez as his wife, the mother of his children if he'd been normal, washed over him. His heart raced as he stared down at her, so beautiful, so giving.

Thee mou, what the hell was he doing wishing for the impossible? He wasn't normal…

'I don't want you to stop,' she replied. Then she performed one of those actions that illuminated her inexperience. Her gaze flicked down to his groin and she bit her lip. She had no idea how hot that little gesture made him.

A groan ripped from his chest and effectively wiped away the useless yearning.

Planting his hands on either side of her, he parted her thighs with his and settled himself at her entrance.

'Hold onto me, and feel free to dig your nails into my back if it all gets too much.' He attempted a smile and felt a touch of relief when she returned it.

The seductive bow of her mouth called to him and, leaning down, he drove his tongue between her lips. Gratifyingly, she opened up to him immediately. He deepened the kiss and swallowed her groan.

Carefully, he nudged her entrance, fed himself slowly into her wet heat.

He froze as she tensed. 'Easy, *anjo*. Relax,' he murmured soothingly against her mouth.

With a rough little sound she complied. Except now the tension was channelled into him. The feel of her closing around him threatened to tear him apart. Lying in the cradle of her hips, a sense of wonderment stole over him he'd never felt before. And he wasn't afraid to admit it scared the hell out of him.

'Theo.' She said his name with a touch of imploration and frustration that ramped up his tension. Never had he wanted to make it more right for a sexual partner.

He pushed deeper and felt the resistance of her innocence. Those nails dug in. Pleasure roared through him as he pulled back and looked into her beguiling face.

A face that held a touch of apprehension and breathless anticipation.

'Please, Theo. I want you.'

Her husky entreaty was the final straw. With a hoarsely muttered apology, he breached the flimsy barrier and buried himself deep inside her.

She made a sound of pain that pierced his heart then her head was rolling back on a long moan that echoed around the room. He waited until she had adjusted to him. Then he pulled out and rocked back in.

'*Meu deus*,' she voiced her wonder.

'Inez…' he waited until her glazed eyes focused on him, then he repeated the move '…tell me how you feel.'

'*Fantastico*,' she groaned, and Theo was sure she didn't realise she spoke her native tongue.

Her fingers spiked into his hair and when he thrust into her, she met him with a bold thrust of her own. His breath hissed out.

'You're a fast learner, *querida*.' He increased the tempo and gritted his teeth for control when she immediately matched his pace.

All too soon her back arched off the bed, her chest rising and falling in agitation as she neared her climax. Hot internal muscles rippled along his length and he shut his eyes for one split second to rein in his failing grip on reality. Leaning lower, he took one tight nipple and rolled it in his mouth. Her cry of pleasure was music to his ears. He treated its twin to the same attention then lowered himself on her. Sliding his arms under her shoulders he brought her flush against him and thrust in fast, deep movements.

She screamed once before her teeth closed over the skin on his shoulder. Deep shudders rocked through her as her bliss pulled her completely under.

She bit him harder, her nails scouring his back as she rode the unending wave.

When her head fell back towards the pillow, he raised his

head and looked at her face. The expression of wonder and ecstasy sheening her eyes finally sent him over the edge.

With a roar torn from deep inside him, he gave into the shattering release.

He clamped his mouth shut as new, confusing words threatened to burst free. Praise? Gratitude? Hell, *adoration*? When had he ever felt those emotions in connection to a woman he'd just bedded?

He buried his face in her neck and let the ripples of pleasure wash him away in silence. Until he could fathom just what the hell was going on beyond the chemical level with Inez, he intended to keep his mouth shut.

Inez slowly caressed her hands down his back, not minding at all that she was pinned to the bed by his heavy, muscled weight. Right at that moment, she couldn't think of a better way to suffocate to death. The thought made her giggle.

Theo turned his head and nuzzled her cheek. 'Not the reaction I expect after a mind-blowing orgasm but at least it's a happy sound.'

Immediately her mind turned to the dozens of women he'd pleasured before her. Hot green jealousy burned through her euphoric haze and her hands stilled.

'Hey, what did I say?' His voice rumbled through her. When she didn't immediately answer, he raised his head and stared down at her. 'Inez?'

'It's nothing important,' she replied. And it wasn't.

Earlier this evening, she'd tried to make him see a different way. But he'd refused. This thing between them would last until his vendetta with her father was satisfied. She had no business thinking about what women had come before her or who would replace her once he was done with her family and with Rio.

She endured his intent gaze until he nodded and rose. The feeling of him pulling out of her created a further emptiness inside that made her heart lurch wildly.

Deus, she needed to get a grip. Her hormones were a little askew because she had experienced her first sexual act.

No need to descend into full melt-down mode.

She watched him leave the bed, his body in part shadow in the lamp-lit room. He entered the bathroom and returned a minute later with a damp towel. When she realised his intention, she surged up and tried to reach for the towel.

'No,' he murmured softly. 'Lie back.'

Her face heating up, she slowly subsided against the pillows and allowed him to wash her.

Incredibly, the hunger returned as he gently saw to her needs and when he finally glanced back at her his nostrils were flared, a sign she'd come to recognise as a control-gathering technique.

Her nipples puckered and her body began to react to the look on his face.

'You need time to recover.'

Her body refuted that but her head knew she needed to take time to regroup. When she nodded, he looked almost disappointed. He returned the towel to the bathroom but left the light on as he came back to bed. Getting into bed, he pulled the covers over their bodies and pulled her into his arms.

She settled her hand over his chest and felt his steady heartbeat beneath her fingers. They lay there in silence until another giggle broke free from her jumbled thoughts.

'I'm beginning to get a complex, *anjo*.' He brushed his lips over her forehead.

'I believe this is the part where we make small talk after sex but I can't come up with a single subject.'

She felt his smile against her temple. 'Wrong. Normally this would be the part when I either leave or do what I just did to you all over again.'

Her heart caught. 'And?'

'I'm trying to rein in my primal instincts and not flatten you on your back again.'

Feeling bolder than was wise, Inez opened her mouth to tell him that he needn't hold it back for much longer. Instead a wide yawn took her unawares.

It was his turn to laugh. 'I think the decision on small talk has been shelved in favour of sleep.' He turned her face up to his and pressed his mouth to hers. Within seconds the kiss threatened to combust into something else. He pulled back with a groan and tucked her against him. 'Sleep, Inez. Now,' he commanded gruffly.

With a secretly pleased smile, she slid her arm around his waist, already feeling the drowsy lure of sleep encroaching.

She woke to moonlight streaming through the windows. The bedside lamp glowed and she judged that she'd been asleep for a few hours.

Beside her, Theo lay on his side, tufts of sleep-ruffled hair thrown over his forehead. In the soft lighting he looked younger and peaceful but still so damn sexy her breath caught just looking at him.

She suddenly needed to commit his likeness to paper. Her pad was next door in her suite. Slowly extracting herself from the arm he'd thrown over her, she pulled on his shirt and went to retrieve it.

Returning just as quietly, she settled herself cross-legged at the foot of the bed and began to draw. Every now and then she paused and took a breath, unable to fathom the circumstances she found herself in.

She was in bed with a man who was bent on destroying her family. And yet the overwhelming guilt she expected to feel was missing. Instead she yearned to save him from the demons that she'd glimpsed in his eyes when he spoke of his nightmares.

She swallowed as a well of sadness built inside her. Despite his outward show of invincibility she'd seen his battle. A battle he believed only revenge would win for him...

She froze as Theo made a sound. It was somewhere between a moan of pain and the bark of anger. His hand jerked out and then closed into a tight fist.

His whole body tensed for a breathless second before his chest started to rise and fall in agitated pants.

She dropped the sketchpad. 'Theo?'

'*No. No! No! Thee mou, no!*' The words were hoarse pleas, soaked with naked fear.

Both hands shot out in a bracing position and his head twisted from side to side.

'Theo!' She rose to her knees, unsure of what to do.

'No. Stop! *Arghh!*' With a forceful lunge, he jolted upright with a blood-curdling cry. Sweat poured down his face and he sucked in huge gulping breaths.

'*Deus*, are you okay?' The question was hopelessly inadequate but it was all she could manage at that moment. Because her heart was turning over with pain for what she'd just witnessed him go through.

She reached out and he jerked back away from her. 'Don't touch me!'

'Theo, it's me. Inez.' Tentatively, she reached out and touched his arm.

He shuddered violently and lurched away from her, staring blankly at her for several seconds before his face grew taut and haunted.

'Inez,' he said with a dark snarl. 'I fell asleep?' There was self-loathing in the question, as if he hated himself for having lowered his guard enough to let the demons in.

Her stomach flipped and her fingers curled into her palm. 'Yes. You…you had a nightmare.'

His mouth twisted with a cruel grimace. 'No kidding. What the hell are you doing here?' he snapped, looking around the room with unfocused eyes.

She frowned. 'We…um, we fell asleep together after…' She stopped as heat rushed up her face.

He turned back to her and his gaze slowly travelled over her. He brushed the hair out of his eyes and gradually the dull green lightened into golden hazel. 'We had sex. I remember now.'

She flinched and watched him with wary eyes.

With sure, predatory moves, he lifted the tangled sheet off his body and prowled to where she was poised on her knees. He stopped a hairsbreadth from her.

'Can I…can I touch you?' she asked, unwilling to have him pull away from her, but a part of her longed to soothe the turbulent blackness in his eyes.

His mouth pinched and he took several steadying breaths before he spoke. 'You want to comfort me?'

'If you'll let me.'

Another deep shudder and he closed his eyes. His head lowered until his forehead rested between her breasts. His arms closed around her and tightened so hard she couldn't move. They stayed like that until his breathing steadied.

'Theo?'

'Hmm?'

'Tell me about your dream.'

He tensed immediately and she bit her lip. He raised his head and stared at her.

'Take my shirt off,' he commanded, his voice hardly above a tortured whisper.

Concern spiked through, despite the heat his words generated. 'Theo, you just had a nightmare—'

'One I want to forget.' His hands were on the back of her thighs, hard and demanding as they caressed up to her bottom. He cupped the globes with more roughness than before but there was no pain in the caress. 'Inez, if you want to help me, do it.'

She drew the shirt over her head and dropped it. His eyes devoured her breasts and his tongue darted out to rest against his bottom lip.

Between her legs, liquid heat dampened her folds and he groaned in dark appreciation as his seeking fingers found her core.

'So ready. So tight,' he rasped. With almost effortless ease, he picked her up, pivoted off the bed and sat on the side. Grabbing a condom, he slipped it on and positioned her legs on either side of him.

'You will *make* me forget.' The words were almost a plea but with a promise of things to come. 'Yes?'

Before she could do so much as nod, he pressed her down on top of him. She cried out as he filled her with his hot, heavy length. His hard grip on her hips controlled the rhythm, which grew more frantic with each thrust.

'Theo,' she gasped as pleasure scalded her insides and rushed her towards ecstasy.

'Shh, no talking,' he instructed.

Biting her lip, she stared into his face.

Torment, anger, pleasure and more than a dose of anxiety mingled into an oddly fascinating tableau. He was still caught up in the hell of his nightmare and her heart broke over his anguish.

She tried to catch his gaze, to transmit a different sort of comfort from the carnal that he clearly sought but he avoided her eyes. Instead he buried his face between her breasts and mercilessly teased her nipples until she whimpered at the torture.

He increased his thrusts, bouncing her on top of him with almost superhuman strength that had her reeling.

Her orgasm crashed into her, flattening her under its fierce onslaught before proceeding to completely drown her.

Through the thunderous rush in her ears, she heard his guttural roar as he achieved his own ruthless release.

Sweat slicked their skin and their breaths rushed in and out in frantic pants. This time, though, there were no pleasurable caresses and giggling was the last thing she felt like doing.

With lithe grace, he twisted around and deposited her on the bed. Without speaking, he strode into the bathroom.

Inez lay on the bed, grappling with what had just happened. In the last twenty-four hours she'd glimpsed the man tortured by his nightmares, had seen a side to Theo she was certain very few people saw. Instead of guarding her own heart, she wanted to open herself up even more to him, find a way of taking away his pain and torment.

Had she not learnt her lesson with Constantine?

No, Theo was nothing like that man who'd taken delight in humiliating her. The retraction Theo had promised had appeared in the online evening edition of the newspaper and she was sure she'd seen a look of contrition in his eyes when he'd watched her read it.

Darkness and light.

She was deeply, almost irreversibly attracted to both. Again her heart twisted and she looked towards the bathroom.

A crash came a second later, followed by a pithy curse. She was off the bed and running into the bathroom before she could think twice.

'I'm fine!' he ground out.

She hesitated in the doorway and watched him. His fingers were curled around the marble sink and his head was bent forward. 'What's wrong, Theo?'

'Dammit, woman, I'm not made of glass. And I've been grappling with my nightmares long before you came along, so leave me alone!'

Hurt shredded her inside. 'Don't push me away.'

He locked eyes with her in the mirror and sighed. 'You're too stubborn for your own good, you know that?'

'Maybe, but before you throw me out I need the bathroom,' she lied.

'Fine; it's all yours.'

He started to turn. That was when she saw his scars. '*Meu deus*, what happened to you?' she whispered raggedly.

His glance ripped from her face to where she pointed to his left hip. The marks were puckered and too evenly spaced and shaped to be an accident. But still her mind couldn't grasp the idea that someone had deliberately inflicted pain on him.

'You mean you haven't guessed already, *querida*? *Your father* happened.'

CHAPTER ELEVEN

INEZ STAGGERED BACKWARDS until her legs hit the vanity unit and she collapsed onto it. 'I don't…you're saying my *father* did this to you?' She shook her head in fierce disbelief.

Theo's mouth twisted. 'Not personally, no. He hired thugs to do it.'

She felt the blood drain from her head. Had she not been seated, she would've swayed under the unbelievable accusation.

'But…why?'

He grabbed a towel and secured it around his waist. 'You did your research on my family. You know what happened to my father.'

She nodded. 'He was indicted for fraud, bribery and embezzlement.'

'Among other things. He was also involved with some extremely shady people.'

He turned and strode from the bathroom.

She followed him, the fear she'd harboured for a long time blooming in her chest. 'And my father was one of these shady people?'

Theo turned and watched her. Shocked knowledge flared in her eyes. For a brief moment, he sympathised with what she was going through. Having the truth blown up in front of you wasn't easy.

In his deepest, darkest moments he still couldn't believe how painfully raw he felt at his father's abandonment.

'My father owed him a lot of money on some crooked scheme they were working on when he was arrested and all our assets were frozen. Your father took exception to being out of pocket. When he realised he wouldn't be paid, he decided to pursue a different route.'

Her haunted eyes dropped to the scars covered by the towel and quickly looked away.

'So I'm here to pay for my father's sins,' she whispered raggedly.

That had initially been his plan. Somewhere along the line that particular plan had become questionable. But he'd be damned before he'd admit that.

'Your father made me pay for my father's. Money and power were his bottom line, and he wanted payback. Nothing else mattered to him, not even the tortured screams of a frightened boy…'

He compressed his lips as her mouth dropped open and anguish creased her face. 'How old were you?'

He raked a hand through his hair. Even as a voice shrieked in his head to stop baring his raw wounds, he was opening his mouth.

'I was seventeen. I was returning from a night out with friends when his goons grabbed me. He had me smuggled from Athens to Spain and threw me into a hole on some abandoned farm in Madrid. Ari found me there two weeks after I was taken. After he damned near bled every single cent he could find from every relative and casual acquaintance in order to stump up the two million dollars ransom that your father demanded.'

Her hands flew to her head, her fingers spiking through the long tresses to grip them in a convulsive stranglehold. 'Please tell me when you say a *hole*…you don't mean that *literally*?' The words were a desperate plea, as if she didn't want to believe how real the monster that was her father.

His smile cracked his lips. 'Oh, yes, *anjo*. A twelve-foot-deep *literal* hole in the ground with vertical sides and no hand or footholds. No light. No heat. One meal a day with a bucket for my necessaries.'

'No…'

'*Yes!* And you know what his men did for *fun* when they were bored?'

She shook her head wildly, her eyes wide and horror-struck as he loosened the towel from around his waist and exposed his puckered skin. 'Cigar tattoos, they called them.'

Tears welled in her eyes and fell down her cheeks. Still shaking her head, she walked to the bed and sank down on it. She buried her face in her hands and a gut-wrenching sob ripped from her throat. After the first one, they came thick and fast.

His chest tightened with emotions he was very loath to name. Each sob caught him on the raw, until he couldn't bear to hear another one.

'Inez! Stop crying,' he instructed hoarsely after five minutes.

She shook her head and sniffled some more.

'Stop it or I'll throw you overboard and you can swim to shore.'

That got her attention. She brushed her hands across her cheeks and speared him with wide, imploring eyes.

'If the only people you saw were his men, how did you know it was my father?'

He couldn't fault her for trying to find a different reality to the one he'd smashed her world with. Hell, he'd done that for a long time after his father had been indicted. 'I followed the money.'

She frowned. 'What?'

'I traced the ransom my brother paid through dummy corporations and offshore accounts. It took a few years but I finally found where it ended up.'

'In my father's account?'

'Yes. And since then I've made it my business to find out how every single cent was spent.'

Her shoulders slumped and tears welled again. He could tell the ground had well and truly shifted beneath her feet.

After several seconds, she raised her head.

'Okay. I'll do whatever you want. For however long you want.'

It was his turn to feel the ground shift under his feet. Shock slammed through him as he realised just how much he wanted to take her. To hang onto her.

But not for the sake of revenge. For an altogether different reason; because he wanted her. Not for her father but *for her*.

He shook his head. 'Inez…'

'I can never buy back those two weeks that were taken from you or the horror you've had to live with. But I can try and find a way to make up for what was done to you.'

'How? By giving me your body whenever and wherever I ask for it?'

She paled a little. But the brave, spirited woman he'd come to see underneath all that false gloss raised her chin. 'If that's what you want.'

His mouth twisted. 'I don't want a damned sacrificial lamb. And I sure as hell don't want you throwing yourself on your sword for that bastard's sake!'

'Then what do you want? You have his company. His campaign is falling apart. He will be left with nothing by the time you're done with him. How much more suffering do you need before you let go of this anger? When will you feel pacified?'

Theo started to answer, then realised he had no answer. The satisfaction he'd thought he'd feel was hollowly absent, as was the deep-seated sense of triumph he'd always thought he would feel when this moment came.

Looking into her face, he saw the pain and confusion reflected there and his puzzlement increased. The ground

was still tilting beneath his feet but he'd been on this path
for too long to let go.

Hadn't he?

He forced his gaze to meet hers.

'I will let you know when I'm adequately appeased.'

Over the next week, she watched as he slowly dismantled
her father's campaign piece by piece. Allegations of impro-
priety surfaced, triggering an investigation. Although nothing was found to indict Benedicto, his credibility suffered
a death blow and any meaningful points he'd managed to
retain in the polls dropped to nothing.

On the Monday morning after returning from their sailing trip, the calls to her cell phone started. Both her father
and Pietro bombarded her with messages and texts, demanding to know what was going on.

She hadn't needed Theo to warn her not to take their
calls. After his revelation, each time she saw her father's
name pop up on her screen, her stomach churned with pain
and disgust.

Although she'd long suspected that her father's business
dealings weren't as pure as the driven snow, she'd never in
her wildest dreams entertained the idea that he would con-
done the brutality that Theo had described. Each time she
saw his scars—and she'd seen them every night since their
return, when he'd moved her into his suite—a merciless
vice had squeezed her heart.

And that vice had tightened every time he'd cried out in
the middle of the night after another nightmare.

She'd been surprised that first night after their return
when he'd pulled her close after a fiery lovemaking and
instructed her to go to sleep.

When he kept her with him the following night, she'd
boldly asked him why.

'I don't want to be alone,' he'd stated baldly. And each
time he'd come awake he'd reached for her, wrapping his

trembling body around her and holding on tight until his
nightmare receded and his breathing returned to normal.

More and more, her foolish heart had begun to believe
that her presence was making the nightmares, if not any
less horrific, then at least tolerable.

Or she could just be living in a fantasy land where her
mind and heart had no idea what language the other was
speaking. Because she was beginning to believe that her
heart was more involved in Theo's welfare than was wise.
And yet she couldn't control it enough to make it stop
wrenching in pain when he suffered another nightmare,
or soar with joy when he took her to the heights of ecstasy.
Even the knowledge that some time in the very near future, after his goal to destroy her father was achieved, Theo
would pack up his bags and leave Rio for good, made her
heart ache in a way that was almost a physical pain.

Santa Maria, she was losing her mind—

'There you are. Teresa told me you're still here. I thought
you'd be at the centre by now.' She'd shared more details of
her volunteer work with him during the times when he'd
been *Normal Theo*, not *Revenge Theo*. And she'd been ridiculously thrilled when he hadn't been judgemental or con-
descending.

She looked up as he entered the living room and crossed
to where she sat, applying finishing touches to the sketch
she'd been working on since breakfast an hour ago. She'd
thought he'd left for the day but obviously she'd been mistaken.

Glancing up at his lean, solid frame and gorgeous face,
her heart performed that painfully giddy flip again and
she glanced away. 'I took a day off. I'm…I'm still thinking of resigning.'

He stilled then dropped to his haunches in front of her.
'Why?'

She struggled to breathe as his scent surrounded her,
making her yearn to lean in closer. 'This whole thing with

my father has brought unwanted attention to people who are already struggling with life's difficulties. I don't think it's fair on the children.'

A look resembling regret passed through his eyes before he blinked it away. After a full minute, he murmured, 'No, it's not. But you won't resign.'

Her heart caught. 'Why not?'

'Because I won't allow you to give up something you love doing. The publicity about your father will go away. I'll make sure of it.'

She met mesmerising hazel eyes. 'Why are you doing this?'

He shrugged. 'Perhaps I'm beginning to realise that I was mistaken about how much collateral damage I was prepared to accept.'

Collateral damage. She was grappling with that when he spoke again.

'I have something for you.'

She glanced warily at him. 'Beware of Greeks bearing gifts. I'm sure I've read that warning somewhere.'

His smile held a certain chill but was heart-stopping nonetheless. 'For the most part, I'd urge you to heed that warning. But this one is completely harmless.' He pulled something from his back pocket and presented it to her. The look in his eyes made her stomach flip as she glanced from his face to the box.

'What is it?' she asked.

'Open it and see.'

She opened the velvet case and gaped at the platinum-linked, three-tiered diamond choker nestling between the two catches.

'Are you trying to make some sort of *macho* statement?'

He shook his head in confusion. 'Sorry, *anjo,* you've lost me.'

'This is a *choker*. You want everyone to see that you own me?'

He frowned. 'What the hell are you talking about?'

'Why a choker? Why not a simple diamond pendant?'

'I asked my jeweller to send a few pieces. I liked the look of that one. So I chose it. No big deal, no mind games. I thought you'd like it,' he finished tersely.

She bit her lip and wondered if she was reading too much into it. Much like she was reading far too much into her feelings for Theo and what would happen when things ended.

'It's a beautiful piece of jewellery. But frankly it's a bit ostentatious for my taste.' She snapped the box shut and held it out to him. 'Besides, since my role as paparazzi bait is over, I don't see where I would wear something like that.'

His jaw tightened and he pushed the box back at her. 'I was just coming to that. Ari is getting married next weekend. You're coming with me as my plus one.'

She couldn't stop her mouth from gaping open any more than she could stop breathing. 'You want me to drop everything and fly to Greece with you?'

'I'm sure you can work something out with the charity. I'm happy to make a donation to cover your absence if you like.'

'I…'

'And we're not going to Greece. Ari and Perla are getting married at their resort in Bermuda.'

'Different continent, same response.'

His eyes narrowed. 'Do I need to remind you that we're only three weeks into our agreement?'

Her fingers trembled and she threw the box down on the sofa. 'No, you don't need to remind me. Call me foolish, but I thought we were getting beyond that.'

'I'm trying to, Inez.'

'Then ask me nicely. For all you know, I may be busy next weekend and would need to rearrange my plans for you.'

He raised an eyebrow. 'Busy doing what?'

'Splitting the atom. Shaving my legs. Rehearsing to join a

circus troupe. What does it matter? You didn't bother to ask. You only brought me trinkets and ordered me to be ready to fly off to Bermuda.' Her mouth trembled and she firmed it.

'You're angry.'

'You're very observant.'

'Tell me why.'

She laughed. Even to her ears it sounded as if it could've easily cut glass. His eyes narrowed as she shook her head. 'What would be the point?'

'The point would be that I would listen.'

She placed her feet on the carpet and tried to stand. He caught her hips and kept her seated in front of him.

This close she could see the hypnotic gold flecks in his eyes. She wanted to drown in them. Wanted to drown in him. She tried to calm her racing pulse.

His gaze dropped to her mouth, then down to her chest and a different sort of fever took hold of her.

'That necklace—'

'Is just a necklace. I thought I'd give it to you now so you could get an outfit to match for the wedding.'

'And the trip?'

'I need a plus one. I need *you*. And you can hate me if you want but I'm not prepared to leave you here so Benedicto can hound you.'

'I can take care of myself.'

His eyes narrowed. 'I don't doubt that. But can you tell me that he won't view your refusal to take his calls this last week as a betrayal?'

Her heart skittered. 'And you think he'll harm me in some way?'

He glanced meaningfully at her arm, then back to her face. 'Sorry, *anjo*, I'm not prepared to take that chance.'

Darkness and light. Tenderness and ruthlessness. It was what kept her emotions on a knife-edge where this man was concerned.

'Will you come to Bermuda with me? Please?'

She glanced at the velvet box. 'I will. But I'm not wearing that necklace.'

'Fine. We'll find you something else.'

'I don't need anything—' Her argument died on her lips when he picked up her sketchpad. She grabbed at it but he held it out of her reach. 'Theo, hand it over.' She breathed a secret sigh of relief when her panic didn't bleed through her voice.

'You're supposed to be designing me a boat.'

'I'm still working on it. I'll show it to you when it's done.'

His gaze brushed her face and settled on her mouth. The intensity of it made her insides contract. After a minute he handed the pad over and rose. 'I look forward to it. We're dining in tonight. I'm in the mood for an early night.'

He left the room just as silently as he'd entered. She realised her fingers were clamped white around her sketchpad and slowly relaxed them.

She flipped through the pages until she came to the one she'd been drawing. It was one of many featuring Theo asleep. She stared at it, seeing the vulnerability and gentleness in his face that he covered up so efficiently when he was awake. When he was asleep he was all light, no darkness. There was a boyishness about him that she only caught rare glimpses of during the day.

Darkness and light. Unfortunately, her heart refused to be picky about which it preferred because, awake or asleep, Theo had captured her emotions so efficiently she was beginning to fear she was falling in love with him.

The nightmare started the way it always did. A glow of light signalled the men's arrival. Followed by the rope ladder and the heavy descent of thick boots, tree trunk thighs and towering thugs.

Each time he'd fought back. A few times he'd landed blows of his own. But each time they'd eventually overpowered him. The tallest, toughest one, the one who favoured those smelly cigars, always laughed. It was the laughter not the pain that triggered his screams. It was a never-ending grating sound that churned through his gut and tripped his heart rate into overdrive.

He felt the scream build in his throat and readied himself for the roar.

Gentle but firm hands shook him awake.

'Theo…*querido!*'

He kept his eyes shut and reached for her, holding on tight as the images receded. The irony of it wasn't lost on him, the thought of how much he now needed the daughter of the man who was responsible for reducing him to a helpless wreck night after night for the last twelve years.

As he held on to her the thought that had plagued him for several days now took hold. He no longer wanted to pursue this vendetta. Yesterday, he'd found himself requesting that the board vote a different way to what he'd originally planned. They'd been stunned. He'd been twice as stunned.

He'd mentally shrugged and told himself there was no reason to turn his back on a healthy profit but he'd known he'd changed his mind for a different reason.

Benedicto was all but finished.

But ending it now would mean Inez would be free to walk away from him. And the very thought of that made him break out in a cold sweat.

He'd managed to buy himself a little more time by persuading her to come with him to Ari's wedding.

After that…

His insides churned as he lay in the darkness and felt her soft hands soothe him.

He pushed away thoughts he wasn't brave enough yet to truly examine.

'*Querido*, are you awake?' she breathed softly.

His heart flipped and his arms tightened convulsively around her soft, warm body. 'I'm awake, *anjo.*'

'I'm not an angel, Theo.'

'You are.'

'If I were an angel, I'd have the power to banish your nightmares,' she replied in a voice fraught with pain.

It took several seconds to realise she ached for him.

Pulling back, he stared into her face.

'You didn't do this to me, Inez.'

Her eyes clouded. 'I know. But that doesn't mean I don't wish you healed.'

His smile felt skewed. 'There's no cure for me, sweetheart,' he said, although he was beginning to doubt that. Just as he was beginning to think that the answer lay right there in his arms. If only there was a way...

'Are you sure? There's therapy—'

'Tried it. Didn't work,' he replied. When he heard the curtness in his voice he soothed an apologetic hand down her back.

She relaxed against him and he buried his face in her hair and breathed her in.

'What happened?'

'What, with the therapy?'

She nodded.

He slowly opened his eyes and stared into the middle distance. 'They spoke about triggers, breathing techniques and anxiety-detectors. There was mention of electro-shock therapy or good old-fashioned pills. I never went back for a second session.'

Her head snapped up. 'You mean all that was at your first session?'

He smiled and kissed her gaping mouth. 'I believed what was wrong with me couldn't be fixed by therapy.'

'*Believed?*'

He realised what he'd said and his breath caught. Was he grasping at straws where there were none?

'I'm beginning to think things aren't as hopeless for me, *anjo*.'

She paled a little but continued to hold his gaze. Slowly,

she nodded. Her luxuriant hair spilled over her shoulder onto his chest as she stared into his eyes. 'I really hope you find closure one day, Theo.'

Simple, frank words, said from the heart. But they froze his insides as surely and as swiftly as an arctic wind froze water.

Because he was seriously doubting that he would ever find peace without this woman in his arms.

CHAPTER TWELVE

THEY BOARDED THEO'S private jet late the next Friday. The moment they stepped on board, Inez sensed something was wrong.

Theo paced up and down, his agitation growing the closer they got to take-off.

When the pilot came through, Theo sent a piercing glance at him and the man hurried into the cockpit.

'Theo, sit down. You're making your pilot nervous.'

He barked out a short laugh and threw himself into the long sofa opposite her chair. His fingers drummed repeatedly on the armrest. 'Don't worry; he's used to it.'

'Used to what?'

'My aversion to enclosed spaces,' he answered tersely.

'Your claustrophobia.' Her heart squeezed as she watched his fingers grip the armrest and the skin around his mouth pale.

Unbuckling her seat belt, she crossed to the sofa and sat down next to him. A sheen of sweat coated his forehead and when his eyes sought hers she read the anxiety in them. Reaching around him, she secured his seat belt then took care of her own as the plane taxied onto the runway.

Taking the arm closest to hers, she pulled it over her shoulder and settled herself against him. He tugged her close immediately, his breathing harsh and uneven.

She hugged him harder, and when he tilted her face up to his she went willingly.

He kissed her with a desperation that tore through her soul. For long, anxiety-filled minutes, he took what she offered, until the need for air drove them apart.

'You get that we cannot kiss all the way to Bermuda, don't you?' she said, laughing.

'Is that a challenge? Because I bet I can,' he threw back with a heart-stopping smile.

Inez noticed that his breathing was no longer agitated and breathed a sigh of relief.

'No, it's not a challenge.' She rested her head on his shoulder and caressed his hard jaw. 'How do you normally get through flying?'

His jaw tightened for a second before he relaxed. 'Mild sleeping pills before take-off normally does the trick.'

'Why not today?'

'You're here,' he said simply. After a minute, he asked, 'Why are you helping me?'

'I cannot forget that my father did this to you. And no, I'm not offering myself as a sacrificial lamb. But I don't want to see you suffer either. I want to help any way I can.'

The reminder that her father loomed large between them grated more than he wanted to admit. 'For how long?' Theo demanded more harshly than he'd intended.

She stiffened. 'Sorry?'

'Are you counting the days until I set you free?' he pressed.

Her eyelids swooped down, concealing her expression. 'I...we have an agreement—'

'Damn the agreement. If you had a choice now, today, would you stay or would you leave?'

'Theo—'

'Answer the question, Inez.'

'I'd choose to stay...'

The bubble of joy that started to grow inside him burst when he registered her flat tone. 'But?'

'But… this could never go anywhere.'

A sense of helplessness blanketed him. 'Why not? Because I blackmailed you?'

She shook her head. 'No. Because a relationship between us would be impossible.

Theo's vision blurred at her words. He'd pushed her too far. Hung onto his vendetta for too long. His mouth soured with ashen hopelessness. 'I guess we both know where we stand.'

When she moved away, he fought not to pull her back. She stayed close—out of pity? His mouth curled. He told himself he didn't care but the voice in his head mocked him.

He cared, much more than he'd bargained for when he'd forced her to make that stupid choice. The idea of her walking away from him made his insides knot with a pain far greater than he'd ever known.

The plane hit a pocket of turbulence, throwing her against him. When she stayed close, he let her. Forcefully, he reminded himself of one thing.

He'd never meant to keep her for ever.

The Pantelides Bermuda resort was a breathtaking jewel set amid swaying palm trees and sugar-white sand. The sun beat down on them as Theo drove the open-top Jeep towards their villa.

Stunning buildings connected by dark wooden bridges under which the most spectacular water features had been constructed made for a visual masterpiece. All round them bold colour burst free in a heady mix of blues, greens and yellows that begged to be touched.

Their sprawling whitewashed villa featured high ceilings, cool tiled floors and a four-poster bed that dominated the master bedroom.

A tense Theo who hadn't said more than a dozen words

to her since they landed, instructed the porter to place their cases in the master bedroom and tipped the man before walking outside onto the large wooden deck.

'There's a barbecue later this afternoon. Perla thought we might want to rest before then. You can go ahead and rest if you want to. I'll go and catch up with Sakis and Ari.'

He walked away from her and headed out of the door.

The clear indication that she wasn't welcome stung, although why she was surprised was beyond her.

He'd held ajar the possibility of continuing this thing between them and she'd slammed the door shut.

A small part of her was proud she hadn't grasped the suggestion with both hands, while the larger part, the part that had fallen head over heels in love with Theo in spite of all the chaos surrounding them, reeled with heart-wrenching pain at what the future held.

But, as she'd told herself over and over again on the plane as he'd shut his eyes and surprisingly dozed off, she was taking the right steps now to prevent even more heartache later.

Because there was no way Theo would ever reconcile himself to having her as a constant reminder. Certainly not enough to love her.

The reality was that they'd fallen into bed as a result of some crazy chemistry. Chemistry fizzled out. Eventually, the constant reminder that a part of her was responsible for his inner demons and outer scars would grate and rip at whatever remained after the chemistry was gone.

He was better off without her.

Her heart protested loudly at that decision. Ignoring it, she went into the bedroom and lifted her case onto the bed. The cream sheath she'd bought for the wedding needed to be hung out before it creased beyond repair.

Unzipping her case, she opened it and froze. A red velvet box, similar to the black one Theo had presented her with a few days ago lay on top of her clothes.

With shaky hands she picked it up and opened it. The stunning necklace sparkling in the sunlight made her gasp.

The platinum chain had a small loop at one end, with a large teardrop diamond at the other that slipped easily through the hoop. The design was simple and elegant. And so utterly gorgeous she couldn't stop herself from caressing the flawless stone.

Swallowing a lump in her throat at the thoughtfulness behind the necklace, she jumped when a knock came at the door. Thinking it was Theo who'd forgotten to take a key, she opened the door with a smile.

Only to stop when confronted by two stunningly beautiful women, one of whom was heavily pregnant, while the other carried a small baby in her arms.

'Sorry to descend on you like this, only Theo was a bit vague about whether you were actually resting or if you were up for a visit.' The women exchanged glances. 'I've never seen him so scatty, have you?' the pregnant redhead asked the blue-eyed blonde.

'Nope, normally he's quick off the mark with those hopeless one-liners. Today, not so much. Anyway, we thought we'd come on the off-chance that you were *not* resting and say hello…oh, my God, that necklace is gorgeous!' The redhead reached out and traced a manicured forefinger over the diamond.

Then she looked up, noticed Inez's open-mouthed gaze and laughed. 'Sorry, I'm Perla soon-to-be Pantelides. This is Brianna Pantelides, Sakis's wife. And this little heartbreaker is Dimitri.'

'I'm Inez da Costa. I'm a…' she paused, for the first time holding up her relationship with Theo to the harsh light of day and coming up short on explanations '…business associate of Theo's.'

The two women exchanged another glance and she rushed to cover the awkward silence. 'Please, come in.'

Brianna paused. 'Are you sure?'

'*Sim*…yes, I'm sure. I was just unpacking…' she started and noticed Perla's frown.

'Why are you doing that yourself? We have two butlers and three villa staff attached to each residence.'

'I think Theo sent them away,' she said, then bit her lip as Perla's eyebrows shot upward.

'Did he? Ari did that once too, when we first arrived here four months ago. Then we proceeded to have an almighty row.' She smiled at the memory and placed her hand lovingly over her swollen belly.

Brianna laughed and walked to the sofa. Settling herself down, she opened her shirt and adjusted her son for a feed.

Perla sat on the sofa too and they both stared back at her. Their open curiosity made her nape tingle.

'We won't keep you long. I just wanted to run the itinerary by you because, frankly, I don't trust the men with the information. We have a casual dinner tonight, followed by a quick rehearsal. Most of the guests arrive in the morning and the wedding is at three o'clock, okay?'

'Okay.' She ventured a smile and Brianna's eyes widened.

'Gosh, you're stunning! How did you meet Theo again?'

'Brianna!' Perla admonished with a laugh.

'What?'

Inez fiddled with the clasp of the velvet box and pushed down the well of sadness that surged from nowhere. These two women were not only almost family, they were friends too. Whereas her family was in utter chaos and she had no friends to speak of.

She forced another smile. 'He had some business in Rio. I was…am helping him out with it.'

'Right. Okay.' Perla struggled upright and nudged Brianna. 'We'll leave you alone. I think the guys are rowing in about an hour. It's an experience you don't want to miss if you've never seen it before.'

Brianna gently dislodged her drowsy baby from her

breast and laid him on her shoulder, gently patting his back as she stood.

The door opened as they neared it and Theo's large frame filled the doorway.

His gaze zeroed in on her, then dropped to the box still clutched in her hand before coming back up. Her throat dried at the sight of him and the ever present tingle that struck her deep within flared heat outward.

'Um, Theo?' Perla ventured.

'What?' he snapped without taking his eyes from Inez.

'You need to move from the doorway so we can leave.'

He snorted under his breath and entered the villa. He turned with his hand on the door, causing Brianna to roll her eyes. 'We've given Inez the schedule so you have no excuse to be late.'

'I'm never late.'

'Yeah, right. You were almost two hours late for Perla's engagement party and an hour late for Dimitri's christening.'

'Which therefore means I'll only be half an hour late for this wedding. Now, please go and pester your other halves and leave me alone.'

The women grumbled as they left. He turned from the door with a smile on his face but it slowly dimmed as his gaze connected with hers.

'Did they harass you?' he asked, a touch of wary concern in his eyes.

She shook her head. 'No. They were lovely.'

'I don't know about lovely but I tolerate them.' Contrary to his words, his voice held a fondness that made her chest tighten.

Theo understood family. Enough that he'd been devastated when his had been broken. And yet he'd wanted to rip hers apart.

Despite understanding the reason behind his motives, the thought still hurt deeply.

'Inez?'

She turned sharply and headed back to the bedroom. He followed and grabbed her wrist as she reached out to set the box down.

'What's wrong?'

Her throat clogged. 'What *isn't* wrong?'

His eyes narrowed. 'If Brianna or Perla said something to upset you—'

'No, I told you they were wonderful! They were kind and funny and…and incredible.' Tears threatened and she swallowed hard.

'You only met them for twenty minutes.'

'It was enough.'

'Enough for what?'

'Enough to know that I want what they have. And that I'll probably never have it. So far my record has been beyond appalling.'

He frowned. 'You don't have a record.'

'Constantine used me to get dirt on my father and—'

'I don't want you to say his name in my presence,' he interrupted harshly.

'And what about you? You make me hope for things I have no right to hope for, Theo. What sort of fool does that make me?'

'No, you're not a fool. You're one of the bravest, most loyal people I know.' He said the words gravely. 'It is I who is the fool.'

Theo's words echoed through her mind as she watched the brothers row in perfect harmony across the almost still resort water a short while later.

He took the middle position with Sakis in front and Ari at the back. She watched, spellbound, as his shoulders rippled with smooth grace and utmost efficiency.

'Aren't they something to watch?' Perla sighed wistfully.

'*Sim*,' she agreed huskily.

'I think they do that just to get us girls all hot and both-ered,' Brianna complained but Inez noticed that she didn't take her eyes off her husband for one second.

When the men eventually returned to shore, the two women joined them and were immediately enfolded into the group.

Theo glanced her way, a touch of irritation in his eyes. Seconds later, he broke away from the group and came to-wards her.

'I didn't expect you to be down here. You should be resting.'

'I was invited. I hope I'm not intruding.'

'If you were invited then you're not intruding. Come and join us.' He grabbed her hand and led her to where Ari and Sakis were turning over the boat to dry the underside.

The two brothers gave her cursory glances but barely spoke to her. When Ari abruptly asked Theo to accompany him to the boat shed, her stomach fell.

Perla organised a Jeep to take her back to their villa and when Theo returned half an hour later, his jaw was tight and his movements jerky as he swept her off her feet and strode into the bedroom.

He made love to her with a fierce, silent passion that robbed her of speech and breath before he clamped her to his side and slid into sleep.

Her eyes filled with tears and she hurriedly brushed them away. It was no use daydreaming that things would ever magically turn rosy between her and Theo.

As much as she wanted to wish otherwise, they were on a countdown to being over for good.

The wedding was beautiful and quietly elegant in a way only an events organiser extraordinaire like Perla could achieve despite being seven months pregnant. Inez watched the bride and groom dance across the polished floor of the casino, transformed into a spectacular masterpiece that stood directly on the water, and fought the feelings rampaging through her.

Theo would never be hers. She would never have a wedding like this or have him gazing at her the way Ari was gazing at his new wife.

She would never feel the weight of his baby in her belly or have it suckle at her breast.

Despair slowly built inside her, despite knowing deep down that Theo had done her a favour by bringing her here. He didn't need her to save him from whatever nightmares plagued him. He had a family that clearly adored him, who would be there for him when he chose to let them in.

She needed to stop moping and get on with her life.

Her time in Theo's house and his bed was over. In retrospect, she was thankful she'd let him talk her into keeping her volunteer position. It was a lifeline she was grateful for in a world skidding out of control. The things she couldn't control she would learn to live without.

A tall figure danced into her view and her eyes connected with the man who occupied an astonishingly large percentage of her mind. In his arms was an elegantly dressed woman with greying brown hair and a sad expression. She said something to him and he glanced down at her. His smile was gentle but wary and Inez saw her sadness deepen.

Inez heard the soft gurgle of a baby over the music and turned to see Brianna next to her. 'That's their mother.' She nodded to Theo's dance partner. 'Their relationship has been fraught but I think they're all finding their way back to each other.' She glanced at Inez with a smile. 'I hope that you two find your way too.'

Inez shook her head. 'I'm afraid that's impossible.'

Brianna laughed. 'Believe me, I've seen the impossible happen in this family. I've learned not to rule anything out.' She smiled down at her child and danced away with him towards her husband.

Tears stung her eyes as she watched Sakis enfold his wife and son in his arms.

'What's wrong now?' Theo's deep voice sounded in her ear.

She blinked rapidly and pasted a smile on her face. 'Nothing. Weddings…they make me emotional. That's all.'

His eyes narrowed speculatively on her face before he took hold of her elbow. 'Dance with me.'

He led her to the dance floor and pulled her close.

'You have a big family,' she said, more for something to fill the silence.

'They can be a pain in the rear sometimes.'

'Regardless, you all seem to watch out for each other.'

He shrugged. 'Force of habit.'

'No, it's not. Does Ari know who I am?'

His mouth tightened. 'He suspects. I didn't enlighten or deny because it's none of his business. He's welcome to draw his own conclusions. Why do you ask?'

'Because he's been watching me like a hawk since we got here and he hasn't spoken more than two words to me. That's what I mean. What you have with your brothers isn't habit. It's love.'

His mouth twisted in a way that evidenced his dark pain.

'*Love* hasn't conquered the nightmares that have plagued me for all these years, Inez.' The raw pain in his voice made her throat clog. She forced a swallow.

'Because you haven't allowed it to. You resisted any attempt at help because you thought you had to face this demon alone, do things your way.'

The honest barb struck home. He was silent for the rest of the song. Then abruptly he spoke. 'I didn't want to appear weak. I hated myself every time I couldn't walk into a dark room or down an unlit street. I haven't been able to cope with the smell of cigars without breaking out in a cold sweat. Do you know what that feels like?' he asked in a harsh undertone.

She shook her head. 'No, but I know it will never go away if you keep it buried.'

Her warmth, her strength hit him hard and he wanted to reach for her with all he had. Suddenly, everything he'd ever craved, ever wished for seemed coalesced in the woman before him.

'It's no longer buried. A month ago I was still the messed-up boy Ari dug up from that hole twelve years ago. But you did something about that.'

'No, I'm not responsible for that.'

His hand cupped her nape and he whispered fiercely in her ear. 'You are. You've seen me, Inez. I can't sleep with the lights off. I used to panic whenever someone shut a door behind me. That's why I surrounded myself with glass. With you by my side I flew here with no need for sleeping pills.'

'Even though you refused to speak to me for hours.'

He exhaled. 'Things are upside down and inside out right now. Let's just…we'll get through this wedding and head back to Rio. And we will damn well fix this thing between us. Because I'm not prepared to let you go yet.'

CHAPTER THIRTEEN

'I TOLD YOU, you're so much better than a damn sleeping pill.'

Inez laughed as Theo tugged her dress down and lifted her out of it. Leaving it on the floor of the master cabin bedroom, he waited for her to kick her shoes off before he crossed over to the bed. The diamond pendant he'd looked incredibly pleased that she'd worn lay nestled between her breasts.

'Keep that on,' he instructed, just as the plane jerked through turbulence and they fell onto the bed together, a tangle of hard and soft limbs and hot, needy kisses.

'I'm glad I have my uses,' she said, laughing, when he let her up for air.

His face grew serious as he stared down at her. 'You've attained the ultimate purpose in my life, *querida*. Now more than ever you're my saviour: *my* angel.' He cradled her head as he kissed her.

Inez closed her eyes and imagined that she could feel his soul through his reverent kiss. She studiously ignored the voice that mocked that she was deluding herself.

When he finished undressing her with gentle hands, she tried to stem her tears as he made love to her with a greedy passion that touched her very soul.

Afterwards she held him in her arms as he fell asleep. Unable to sleep, her mind drifted back to the wedding.

Theo had introduced her to his mother and again she'd witnessed the sadness in her eyes. When he'd hugged her at the end of the evening and murmured gently into her ear, his mother had burst into tears. Inez had watched as the brothers closed around her and soothed her tears.

She was still watching them when Ari had glanced her way. His measured smile and thoughtful nod in her direction had made her swallow. It hadn't been acceptance but it hadn't been the chilly reception he'd given her either.

As they'd packed to leave, Inez had asked Theo about what had happened with his mother.

'She fell apart completely after my father was arrested. She left Athens and locked herself away at our house in Santorini,' he'd replied in an offhand manner, but Inez had seen his anguish.

Recalling his words about abandonment, she'd gasped, 'She wasn't there when you were kidnapped, was she?'

Heart-shredding pain washed over his face, but a moment later it was replaced by a look even more soul-shaking. Forgiveness. 'No. She wasn't. But I had Ari and Sakis. They were strong for me. And they were that way because of her. I told her that tonight because I think we both needed to hear it.'

His words had resonated deep inside her. But most of all it had been his statement on the dance floor that continued to flash across her mind. *I'm not prepared to let you go yet.*

Her heart lurched. He meant to keep her in his bed for a while yet. Like a trophy he wasn't prepared to relinquish. And her foolish heart performed a giddy little samba at the thought of having a few more moments with him.

She woke to kisses on her forehead and her cheek and opened her eyes to bright sunshine.

'Good, you're awake. We just landed.'

She yawned widely. 'Already? I feel as if I just fell asleep.'

He laughed. 'It's three o'clock in the afternoon. And we have much to do before tonight.'

She stared at his wide grin and her heart lifted with happiness. 'You seem in very good spirits, *querido*,' she commented.

He gathered her close in his arms and gazed down at her. 'There is a reason for that.'

'Tell me,' she murmured softly.

His face turned serious, his eyes fierce as he watched her. 'For the first time in twelve years, I slept through the night without a nightmare,' he muttered hoarsely.

Theo watched her face light up with shocked pleasure before she reached up to clasp his face. Her kiss was gentle and sweet. 'Oh, Theo. I'm so happy for you.'

'I'm happy for *us*,' he replied. With another kiss, he got up and started dressing. 'Get a move on, sweetheart, unless you wish to give the customs guy an eyeful when he boards.'

With a yelp she got up and pulled her clothes on.

Theo's phone started ringing the moment they stepped off the plane. And it wasn't until they were back home that she remembered what he'd said on the plane.

'What did you mean—"we have much to do before to-night"? We're not going out, are we?' She groaned.

He took the phone from his pocket and checked it as another text message came through. She waited impatiently for him to finish.

'No, we're not going out. But we have a guest coming.'

'A guest? Who?'

'I've invited your father to dinner.'

Inez staggered as if a bucket of ice had been poured over her.

'My father is coming here?'

'Yes.'

'And you didn't think to inform me of this? What makes you think I want to see him?'

'We have to. It's time to get this thing over and done with, once and for all.'

'And you don't care how I feel about it?'

'I thought we agreed to fix things when we return to Rio?' he asked with a frown.

'Yes, but when you said *we*, I thought you meant us, you and me. More fool me. Because there is not me without my father, is there?'

'What are you talking about? Of course there is.'

'Then why would you go behind my back to arrange this?'

A tic started in his temple. 'Because it's my fault you're in the middle of all this.' He sighed and clawed a hand through his hair. 'I got a chance to fix things with my mother in Bermuda. We may never get back what we had but I'll take that over nothing. Whatever relationship you choose to have with your own father from here on in is up to you. But this is a hardship I caused in your life and one I have a duty to fix.'

The fight fizzed out of her but the fear that something had gone seriously wrong between the airport and home wouldn't go away.

At seven on the dot, the doorbell rang. She passed her hand over her black jumpsuit and tucked a lock of hair nervously behind her ear as she stood by Theo's side.

The butler entered the living room, followed by her father.

Benedicto da Costa drew to a halt. His narrowed gaze slid from Theo to her, his face a mask of dark anger and cold malice she'd forced herself to overlook in the past.

Now she saw him for who he really was. Images of Theo's scars flashed through her mind and her hands fisted at her side.

'I won't shake your hand because this isn't a social visit,' he rasped icily to Theo. 'And I won't be dining with you, either.'

'Perfectly fine by me. Frankly, the quicker we get this over with the better. But let me remind you that you're here only because of Inez. She may be your daughter but she's under my protection now. I suggest you don't lose sight of that fact. What business you and I have will be finished by week's end.'

Her father's gaze swung back to her. 'Are you just going to stand there and let him speak to your father that way? You disappoint me.'

'That's no surprise. I've been a disappointment from the moment I was born a girl, *Pai*.'

'Your mother will be rolling in her grave at your behaviour.'

She raised her chin. 'No, actually. *Mãe* told me every day she was proud of me. She also encouraged me to follow my dreams. She wanted to be a sculptor. Did you know that?'

'What's your point?'

'She was talented, *Pai*. But she gave it up for you. It was her, not you, who taught me what loyalty and family meant. You were only focused on exploiting that loyalty for your own selfish needs.'

His face tightened and his eyes flickered to Theo, who'd been standing by her with his arms folded, a half smile on his face.

'Is this what I came here for? To be lectured by an ungrateful child?'

Theo shrugged. 'I'm finding it quite entertaining.'

Benedicto growled and shot to his feet. 'If there is a point, *son*, I suggest you get to it.'

Theo grew marble-still, his smile disappearing in the blink of an eye. Pure rage vibrated off his body and Inez watched his nostrils flare as he sucked in a control-sustaining breath.

'*I am not your son*. And you are not worthy to be a father. It's a shame you didn't learn how to be a better parent from the mother who gave birth to you in that *favela* you deny you grew up in. And don't bother denying it again. I know everything there is to know about you, da Costa.'

For the first time since he'd walked in, Benedicto grew

wary. He strolled to the drinks cabinet and took his time examining all the expensive spirits and liqueurs displayed.

Without asking, he poured a measure of single malt whisky and took a bold sip. 'So I bent the truth a little. So what? You've already discredited my campaign. What do you want? My company? Is that your end game? You want to pick up the shares for Da Costa Holdings for peanuts? Well, over my dead body.'

Theo's laugh was menacing enough to cause her skin to tingle in alarm. 'Trust me, a few weeks ago it would've been my pleasure to grant you your wish. But you're wrong on that score. Your company is of no interest to me.'

His wariness increased. 'What's changed?'

Theo's eyes flicked to her and her heart thudded. 'Your daughter.'

'Really?'

Inez shook her head in astonishment. 'Do you really not know who he is, *Pai*?' she asked.

Theo's mouth curved in a mirthless smile. 'Oh, he knows who I am. He's just hoping that *I* don't know what he did twelve years ago.'

Benedicto swallowed, his gaunt face growing pale until he looked ashen. 'I have no idea what you're talking—'

She rushed towards him, anger, pain and disappointment coiling like poisonous snakes inside her. 'Don't you dare deny it. *Don't you dare!*' Her voice cracked and a sob broke through her chest. 'You had a boy kidnapped and tortured! For money. How could you?'

Eyes she'd once thought were like her own turned black with sinister rage. 'How could I? I did it for you. The fancy clothes you strut about in and that fancy car you drive? Where do you think the money came from? I needed it to save the company. Anyway, it was my money. Why did I have to go back to farming just because Pantelides couldn't keep it in his pants or stop his bit on the side from blowing the whistle on him?'

Inez's hand flew to her mouth, her insides icing over. '*Santa Maria*, you truly are a monster.'

Her father's jaw tightened and he addressed Theo. 'Is this the point where you hand whatever file you've gathered on me over to the authorities?'

Theo's mouth twisted. 'So you can bribe your way out of jail? No.'

Benedicto frowned. 'Then what the hell do you want?'

Theo glanced over at her and a look of almost relief washed over his face, as if a weight had been lifted off his shoulders. 'That's up to Inez. And only her. I'm done with you.'

Inez raised her suddenly heavy head and looked from one man to the other.

One stood tall, proud and breathtaking. A man she'd been so determined not to let in. But whose tortured vulnerability had drawn her to him, made her see beneath his skin to the frightened child who was desperately seeking answers.

Choking tears filling her eyes, she turned to the monster who was her father. 'I have nothing else to say to you. I don't want to see you ever again. Goodbye.'

Turning sharply from both men, she rushed out of the room and fled up the stairs.

Theo wasted no time in throwing Benedicto out once Inez left the room. He'd meant what he said—he was done with seeking retribution…had been done almost from the moment he'd met Inez.

Perhaps unwisely, he'd thought the meeting with Benedicto would be swift and cathartic. Instead, he'd brought Inez even more anguish.

He slashed his fingers through his hair as he vaulted up the stairs that led to his third floor suite. Perhaps she'd been right. He'd ambushed her in his rush to get this situation sorted between them.

But he would make it right for her. They would get

through this. They had to. The feelings he'd tried hard to smother had blown up in his face when he'd woken on the plane this afternoon. With the absence of anxiety and fear, the purest reason why he wanted to wake up each morning with Inez had shone through.

The feelings had been so intense he'd almost blurted it out. But he'd decided to wait until she'd confronted her father.

Now he wished he hadn't. He was wishing he'd provided her with that additional support of knowing how much she meant to him before he'd let her father loose on her.

Pursing his mouth in determination, he pushed the bedroom door open. 'Inez, I'm sorry for—'

The sight that confronted him silenced his words and turned his feet to clay. She stared at him, eyes red-rimmed with freshly shed tears.

Because of him. But even that pulse of deep regret couldn't erase the sight before him.

'What are you doing?' he asked, although the part of his brain that hadn't frozen along with his feet could work it out.

Two suitcases were open on the bed, one filled with her clothes. *She was packing...*

The silk top in her hand trembled before she turned and threw it in her case. Then her fingers curled around the edge of the lid.

When she looked at him again, more tears filled her eyes.

'Thank you for opening my eyes to what he truly is,' she murmured huskily.

'Shelve the thanks and tell me what you're doing,' he replied tersely.

One hand swiped at her cheek. 'I'm leaving, Theo.'

'You're what?' His voice rang with disbelief. 'You're going back to your father's house?'

She shuddered from head to toe. 'No. I could never live there again.'

He frowned. 'Then where are you going?'

She gave a tiny shrug. 'I'll stay with Camila.'

He finally got his feet to work and paced to where she stood. When she grabbed her shorts, he ripped them from her hand and threw them on the bed. 'I seem to be missing a link somewhere, sweetheart. Why don't you take a beat and fill me in?'

'I can't stay here.'

A merciless vice squeezed his chest. 'Why not?'

Her face creased in fresh anguish. 'Because he is right. The food he put on our table; the clothes on my back; our fancy education. They *all* came from your suffering.'

'For God's sake—'

She carried on raggedly. 'I never stopped to think about it but I remember the day he came home twelve years ago and told my mother our troubles were over. We weren't exactly poor before then, but after he pressured my mother into selling the ranch he made some bad investments and the company suffered for it. They argued a lot and I used to go to bed every night praying for a miracle just so they'd stop arguing. Can you imagine how I felt when my prayers were answered? And now, all these years later, I find out that what I'd prayed for came at the cost of your—' She choked to a stop, then frantically threw more clothes into the case.

Theo couldn't find an answer as desperately as he tried. He was watching her torture herself and he could do nothing to stop it. '*Anjo*—'

'No. I'm *not* an angel, Theo. I'm a child of the monster, a heartless devil who tortures children and doesn't feel an ounce of regret for it. How can you even bear to look at me?'

'Because you're *not* him!' he interjected fiercely. He took her hands and forced her to face him. 'You're not responsible for his actions. Stay, Inez. We said we would talk about us once we were done with him.'

'But there is no us, is there? We...we just fell into bed because of the circumstances that brought us together. If it hadn't been for my father you'd never have set foot in Brazil.'

'So you're walking away because you think we were never meant to be?' He watched her, forced himself to think how he would feel if she walked away from him. The realisation of what was happening washed over him and ashen despair filled his chest.

'I'm walking away because you need to put everything and everyone associated with your ordeal behind you. Otherwise you will never heal properly.'

He dropped her hand and stared down at her. The ice that had started to build inside him since he'd walked into the room hardened. It crept around his heart and Theo swore he heard it crack. His eyes scoured her beautiful tearstained face, looking for a tiny chink. A tiny ray of hope that would offer deliverance from the quicksand of devastation he could feel himself sinking into.

'So that's it? That's your final decision. You're doing this for my sake but I have no say in the matter?' He couldn't stop the bitterness from lacing his voice.

Her answer was to step back and gather up the last of her clothes. With trembling fingers, she zipped up the cases and lifted them off the bed.

'Inez, answer me!'

She stilled at the door. '*Adeus*, Theo.'

'Go to hell!' he snarled back.

'Table Four need a second helping of *feijoadas*. And a bottle of Rioja.' Camila bustled into the kitchen, checked on the bubbling pot Inez was stirring and nodded in approval. '*Fantastico*. I'll be back in a minute for that order.' She sailed back out on a giddy whirlwind.

Inez wiped her sweating brow and looked over her shoulder. 'Pietro, you grab the bottle; I'll serve up the *feijoadas*.'

Her brother rolled his eyes. 'Who made you queen of the kitchen?'

'I did, when I won the coin toss earlier.'

Her grin came easier today—much easier than it had for far longer than she wanted to dwell on. She still couldn't go for more than ten seconds without thinking of Theo but if she could joke with her brother, that was a good sign that this hollow, half-dead devastation she carried inside her would eventually ease. Right?

'I still think you cheated,' Pietro grumbled.

She lifted one shoulder. 'I'll let you explain to Camila, then, why the Rioja isn't here when she returns, *sim*?'

'Tomorrow, I'm tossing the coin.' He sauntered down the stairs into the basement that served as the restaurant's larder and wine cellar. The smell of the cheese Camila kept in the small space could be overpowering and she smiled again as Pietro made gagging noises.

If there was a bright side to be seen, it was that, amid all the chaos and heartache, somehow she and her brother had grown closer than she'd ever dreamed possible.

They both were yet to decide what they wanted to do with their lives after choosing to walk away from their father and the company, but Camila had encouraged them to take their time. To heal. To reconnect.

When her mother's childhood friend had offered them a job in her restaurant they'd both jumped at it. She'd worked it around her volunteer work and, between the two jobs, it kept her plenty busy.

Keeping herself occupied stopped the tight knot of pain inside her from mushrooming into unbearable agony. In the dark of the night when she lay wide awake and aching was time enough to suffer through the hell of wondering if she was doomed to heartache for ever.

Of wondering if Theo had left Rio in the three weeks since their final bitter encounter. Of wondering if his nightmares were gone for good or if her brief presence in his life had made them worse.

Her hand trembled and she immediately curled it into a fist. Theo was strong. He would survive…

Yes, but he called you his saviour. His angel. And you walked away from him.

'No,' she breathed through the pain ripping through her. She'd done the right thing—

'No what? If you tell me I've got the wrong wine, you'll have to go and get it yourself.'

She shook her head blindly and turned gratefully to the door as Camila walked in. Her quick but assessing glance at her made Inez frown.

'We have a new booking. Table One. And an order of *feijoadas* for one.'

'Wow, you're on fire tonight, sis.'

She ignored Pietro. 'Okay, I'll serve it up and—'

'No, I didn't take a drink order. And I think they want an appetiser first too. Can you go take care of it?'

Inez's eyebrow shot up. 'Me? But I'm not dressed to serve.'

'Pfft. This isn't the Four Seasons, *meu querida*. Besides, it's time you took a break from that hot stove. Tidy your hair a bit and go and take the order.'

Inez looked down at her black skirt and grey T-shirt. It wasn't standard waitress attire but, as Camila had said, this wasn't the Four Seasons. She tucked a strand of hair behind her ear and caught the worried look in the older woman's eyes. It was an expression she'd spied a few times and she reached out and shook her head before the concern could be voiced.

'I'm fine.'

Camila's mouth pursed. 'Good. Then go and attend to Table One.'

With a weary sigh, she washed and dried her hands on her apron. Unfastening it, she hung it on the hook and avoided her image in the small mirror by the door. Her red face from manning the stove for the last three hours would depress her even more.

Plucking a pencil, notebook and menu from the kitchen stand, she nudged the swinging doors with her hip and turned towards Table One.

'You…' she choked out.

Through the drumming in her ears she heard the items in her hand clatter to the floor. A couple of diners glanced her way. Someone picked up the scattered items and placed them in her numb hands. She opened her mouth to thank them but no words emerged.

Every atom in her body was paralysed at the sight of Theo Pantelides.

She heard movement behind her. 'You can't stand here all night, *pequena*. Life will pass you by that way,' Camila said solemnly.

She exhaled shakily and forced herself to move.

Those light hazel eyes never left her as she approached his table. He looked as powerful and as magnificent as ever, even if his cheekbones seemed to stand out a little more than she remembered. His hair had grown a little longer and looked a little dishevelled.

'Sit,' he rasped.

Her heart lurched at the sound of his voice. Licking her dry lips, she shook her head. 'I can't. I'm working.'

'I've received special dispensation from Camila. Sit,' he commanded again.

She sat. He stared at her for a full minute, his eyes raking over her face as if he had been starved of her… Or he was committing her face to memory one last time?

White-hot pain ripped through her. 'Why are you here, Theo?' she blurted.

His eyes rose from her mouth to connect with hers. The breath he took was deep and long. 'I was clearing out the house and I found something you left behind.' He reached down near his feet and laid her sketchpad on the table.

She stared at it, drowning beneath the weight of her despair. 'Oh, thank you.' She paused a second before the words were torn out of her. 'So you're leaving Rio?'

He shrugged. 'There's nothing left for me here.'

Tears burned her eyes as her heart shredded into a million useless pieces. 'I…I wish you well.'

He made a rough sound under his breath. 'Do you?' he asked sarcastically. She glanced up sharply but he wasn't done. 'Problem is, I'd believe those blithe words from the woman sitting across from me. But the woman who drew these…' he flicked over the pages of the sketchpad a few times before he stopped and pointed '…this woman has guts. She was brave enough to draw what was in her heart; what cried out from her soul. Look at her.'

She kept her eyes on his face, her whole body trembling wildly as she gave a jerky shake of her head.

'Look at her, dammit!'

She sucked in a breath. And looked down. The first sketch was the one she'd made of him after they'd made love that first time on the boat. The ones that followed were variations of that first sketch. She'd captured Theo in various poses, each one progressively more lovingly detailed until the final one of him with his brothers, laughing together at the wedding. She'd drawn that from memory on their final night in Bermuda. Staring at the finished picture had cemented her feelings for him.

He turned the page and the image of Brianna and Sakis's baby stared back at her. Dimitri already bore the strong, captivating mark of the Pantelides family. It was that template that she'd used in the following sketches, when capturing her own secret yearning of what her and Theo's baby would look like on paper had been too strong to resist.

'You must think I'm some sort of crazy stalker.'

'There is no stalking involved when the subject is just as crazy about the stalker,' he rasped in a raw undertone.

Her heart flipped into her belly and her whole body trembled. 'You can't be. Theo, I'll ruin your life.'

'I thought my life was ruined before I met you. I was consumed by rage and a thirst for revenge. I let the need for revenge swallow me whole, blinding me to what was important. Family. Love. I thought there was nothing else worth fighting for. But I was wrong. There was you. My life *will* be ruined. But only if you're not in it.'

The tears she'd tried to hold back brimmed and fell down her cheeks. Theo cursed and looked around. 'What's through there?' he asked.

'It's a room, for private parties.'

'Is there a party tonight?'

Before she'd finished shaking her head he was standing and tugging her after him. He kicked the door shut and turned to her.

'Listen to me. You told me I would never see you as anything but the child of a monster. But you forget you're also the child of a loving mother who celebrated every day the special person you are. How do you think she would feel to see you buried here, punishing yourself for what your father did?'

She shut her eyes but the tears squeezed through anyway.

'Open your eyes, Inez.'

She sniffed and complied, staring up at him with blurred vision. 'Now, truly open your eyes and see the wonderful person you are. See the person I see. The brave, talented person who drew those pictures.'

'Oh, Theo,' she cried.

'You have a dream. A dream I want to be a part of.' His hands shook as they traced her face.

'I want that dream to become reality so badly.'

'Then please forgive me for blackmailing you and give us that chance.'

She pulled back. 'Forgive you? There is nothing to forgive. If anything, I should be thanking you for shaking me out of my bleak existence. Even before I truly knew you, you empowered me to fight for what I wanted.'

'So will you fight for us? Will you give me the chance to prove to you that I'm worthy of your love and let me show you how much you mean to me?'

She touched his face and inhaled shakily when he turned to kiss her palm. '*Meu querido,* I fell in love with you so ridiculously soon after meeting you, I swear I'll never confess to you when it happened.'

His stunned laugh brought a wide smile to her face. '*Anjo*…' When her smile dimmed, he shook his head. 'Don't bother to argue with me. I love you with every breath I take. You're my angel and I'll keep repeating it until you believe it.'

'We're not going to have a very smooth-sailing future, are we?'

'No,' he concurred with a laugh then kissed her until her head swam with delirious pleasure. 'But that will be part of our story. And, speaking of smooth sailing…'

'*Sim?*'

'I sent a couple of your sketches to our design guys in Greece. They're interested in talking to you about them. If you're up for it?'

Her mouth dropped open. She waited until he'd kissed it shut before she tried again. '*Really?*'

'Really. And I should bring you good news more often. That happy wriggle does incredible things to my—'

She clamped her hand over his mouth and glanced, alarmed, over his shoulder, just as two text messages beeped in quick succession. He groaned and was about to activate them when a knock sounded on the door.

'*Hell*, I knew I should've found a quieter place for this.'

The door opened and Pietro entered with a bottle of champagne and two glasses.

Theo's expression grew serious as he watched him approach.

Pietro set the bottle and glasses down and stared back at Theo. 'You took care of my sister when I was too much of a *burro* to do so. I'll be for ever in your debt.' He held out his hand.

After several seconds, Theo shook it. 'Don't mention it. Any man who's not afraid to call himself an ass is all right in my book.'

With a self-conscious laugh, Pietro turned to leave.

'Thanks for the drinks,' Theo said. 'But how did you know?'

Inez suppressed a giggle. Pietro rolled his eyes and nodded to the far wall. 'There's a partition to the kitchen. Camila's been spying on you since you came in.'

Theo glanced behind him as the partition widened and Camila beamed at them. Her gaze rested on Inez. 'Your *feijoadas* are good enough, but I always believed your destiny lies elsewhere.' She blew a kiss and shut the partition.

Pietro left and Theo stared down at her. 'Are you ready to start our adventure, *agape mou*?'

'What does that mean?'

'It means *my love*.' His smile dimmed. 'I learnt to speak Portuguese for the wrong reasons. I will teach you Greek for the right ones.'

Her grip tightened on his shirt. 'Were you really planning to leave Rio?'

'Yes. After I persuaded Benedicto to sign over the company into your and Pietro's names, I was done with that soulless vendetta. The thought that I'd lost you in the process nearly killed me.'

'I...what? You got him to sign over the company to us? Theo, we don't want it!'

'It was your grandfather's, then your mother's. It's right that it should be yours and Pietro's. If you don't really want it, I'm sure you'll find a beneficial way to dispose of it.'

She nodded. 'It would go a long way to help the inner city centre and the *favela* kids.'

'Great, we'll make it happen.'

Her heart contracted as she stared into his warm eyes. 'I love you, Theo. Thank you for coming back for me.'

'I couldn't not return, *anjo,* because without you I'm lost.'

She lifted her face to his and he slanted his mouth over hers in a deep, poignant kiss that brought fresh tears to her eyes.

'We need to talk about these tears,' he said drily, then huffed in irritation as his phone beeped again.

'Your brothers?' she guessed.

'And their wives. Ari wants to know if I'm still alive. Sakis wants to know if he can hire you to design his next oil tanker.'

She laughed. 'And their wives?'

He glanced down at the screen and back at her. 'They want to know if they can start planning our wedding.'

She took the phone, flicked the off switch and slipped it into his back pocket. Gripping his waist, she raised herself on tiptoe and leaned close to his ear.

'We will reply to each one of them in the morning. Right now, I want you to take me back to the boat and make love to me, make me yours again. Is that okay?'

'It's more than okay, my angel. It's what I plan to do for the rest of our lives.'

The look of love and adoration in his eyes as he took her hand and walked her out of the room was forever branded on her heart.

* * * * *

Keep reading for an excerpt of a new title
from the Modern series,
IN BED WITH HER BILLIONAIRE BODYGUARD
by Pippa Roscoe

PROLOGUE

LUCA CALVINO SAT trying not to stare at the man in the hospital bed attached to more monitors than Luca had seen in his entire life. That the man was Nate Harcourt, billionaire business-man and barely a few years from Luca's own age of thirty-three, was mildly disconcerting.

'It's not as bad as it looks.'

'It looks pretty bad,' Luca replied truthfully.

'It's not.'

'Okay.'

The private hospital in Switzerland was as luxurious as some of the finest hotels Luca had ever had the pleasure of staying in and the secu-rity was top-notch, as it should be. Large win-dows looked out onto a wintry forest fit for a fairy tale. Warm leather and wood accents dec-orated the room that might look like the lounge of some metropolitan apartment but hid almost half a million euros' worth of medical equip-ment to suit any emergency.

'Pegaso has a pretty impressive portfolio for such a young company,' Nathanial Harcourt said, bringing his attention back to the matter at hand.

'Is ten years that young?' Luca enquired with a hint of sarcasm, disliking that he was only slightly rising to the Englishman's bait.

'It is when you have a family business that spans four hundred.'

'Fair point,' Luca conceded. Until a year ago, Nathanial Harcourt had been the rising star of the business world. He might have come from so much family money it reeked of established nepotism, had what he'd done with it not become legendary. But then he'd disappeared off the face of the planet—reportedly to go and find himself in Goa.

This was a far cry from Goa.

'Cancer?' he asked, curious as to what Nate would choose to tell him.

There was a moment; an appraisal between two dominant men.

'Aneurism. Cerebral.'

Luca nodded, unable to stop his eyebrows rising in surprise and reassessing the man in front of him. The upper part of the hospital bed was raised, across which hung a half table on a metal arm that was doing an excellent job of supporting what looked like an office's worth of paperwork and a laptop within Nate's reach.

'Pegaso's revenue was significant last year, not such an easy thing to do in today's economic climate. You have contracts through the majority of mainland Europe with several businesses, including this,' Nate stated, his hand opened to gesture to the hospital they were in—a discreet medical facility that employed the best of the best to those who needed the utmost privacy. Luca knew this because, as Nathanial had noted, Pegaso oversaw the security of the entire facility.

'I'm familiar with my CV.'

'But you haven't managed to break into any English-speaking markets.'

'It's funny,' Luca said with a gentle shoulder shrug, 'I would have thought that as a businessman who sits on three boards, is the CEO of two more, and is *very* high up in your own family business, you'd have a little more common sense than to alienate someone you are about to ask a favour from.'

'It's not a favour, it's an offer.'

The discreet monitor trilled sharply and Luca didn't miss the wince of pain and the jerk of Nate's hand as if he'd wanted to press it against his head, but wouldn't concede to such an open display of pain. Stubborn. Luca could respect that.

'Spill, before it's time for more meds,' Luca said.

'It's not as bad as it looks.'

'Keep telling yourself that.'

Nate managed a smirk and the beeping on the monitor settled again.

'I need you to protect my sister.'

Nate pointed at a folder on the half table and Luca stood to retrieve it. He had no problem verbally sparring with the English billionaire, but he had no intention of degrading the man by making him reach for it himself. A cerebral aneurism was no joke.

Luca opened the folder: Hope Harcourt, twin sister of Nathanial Harcourt, twenty-nine years old, single, Director of Marketing for Harcourts, the world's leading luxury department store. He sat back, looking at pictures of a blonde with delicate features. Although Hope and Nathanial Harcourt were twins, there was no more than a normal sibling similarity between them. His eyes grazed over high cheekbones and fine hair, working hard not to be distracted by the bolt of attraction that struck him hard. He purposely ignored the dark, espresso rich eyes that seemed to pick at his focus and pushed aside the pictures and bio, to pick up the press articles in the back.

More Than Just a Pretty Face? Hope Announced as Harcourts' Marketing Director.

Luca scanned the next few headlines for

lesser or increasing degrees of offensive misogyny, unsurprised that the by-line bore the same name.

Harcourt Fiancé Reveals Socialite's Deep Insecurities.
Harcourts' Flawed Diamond! The Truth Behind the Breakup.

Luca rode out the familiar burn of resentment towards the tabloids who would take advantage of anything and anyone for a scoop. But he also understood that for every journalist there was someone ready and waiting to reap the rewards.

'My sister gets hit pieces like this all the time.'

'So why now?'

'Because I'm…here. I can't protect her.'

For the first time since meeting Nate Harcourt, the frustration was genuine, the anger palpable.

'You want Pegaso to protect her from the press?' She wouldn't be the first woman to court the press to advance her career, sales or reputation, Luca mused. 'What makes you think that she would even want it?'

'Because she's not like that and because something's coming. I don't know what. But the shareholders at Harcourts are being tight-lipped and they've cut me out of the loop since they believe that I'm swanning around South West India trying to find my third eye.'

'Could you have told them the truth?'

Nate stared at him long and hard.

Luca nodded, understanding without the Englishman having to explain. He knew this world too. 'They would forgive ludicrous frivolity, but not a medical complication that could see you drop dead at any minute, putting stocks and shares at risk.'

Nate nodded as if satisfied that Luca had answered his own question correctly.

'My sister and I grew up in a nest of vipers, Calvino. It may not seem like it, but she's all alone out there and I can't be there to protect her from this.'

Luca could feel himself swayed by the sibling loyalty and reached into his pocket to start recording the conversation on his phone. 'Are there any specific threats we need to know about?'

'Simon Harcourt, for sure. He's our cousin. I've never been able to pin anything on him, but he's clever enough not to get his own hands dirty. And then there's the usual hangers-on, people after her money.'

'That happen a lot?' Luca asked, taking another look at the, quite frankly, beautiful woman in the pictures.

'There was an ex. I dealt with it.'

'Name?'

'In the file. But I dealt with it.'

'Sure you did,' Luca said, knowing it would get a rise out of the man who had a no-nonsense manner and a quick, dry wit he was beginning to like.

'I'd have thought you'd have more sense than to alienate someone who's about to do you a favour.'

'You're not doing me a favour, you're making me an offer,' Luca pushed back, a smile curving the edge of his mouth. 'I'll put a team together. We can be in play in—'

'You will handle this personally.'

'That's not going to happen.'

While his company was renowned for their careful handling of high profile, very public contracts, he personally didn't. Ever.

'It is. Because if you do this—if you, just you, handle this personally, as a *favour* to me—you will have the sole security contract for Harcourts. That's not just store presence, that's internal, industrial, cyber—and all of it international. You'll have the biggest first step into the English markets by any company ever. You'll be set for life.'

Nate Harcourt was offering him everything he needed to take Pegaso to the highest heights he could imagine. Luca looked at the black and white photo of a woman exiting the world-famous front doors of Harcourts, bag perched in the crook of a bent arm and large oversized sunglasses covering half of her face. How hard could it be?

'When do I start?'

'Christmas is only a few days away. Am I taking you away from your family?'

'No,' Luca replied without even a thought of the day he'd planned to spend in the office after visiting Alma and Pietro on Christmas Eve, as he did each year.

'A girlfriend?'

'You asking me out, Harcourt?'

'And if I was?'

Luca let out a laugh. The English billionaire was a renowned womaniser. 'Very kind of you to ask, but you're not my type.'

'No. I didn't think so. And as long as my sister isn't either, then we're good.'